"He was . . . crawling up my leg! Oh, Dev!"

"It's all right, my babe," he murmured urgently, holding her close and pressing a kiss on her curls.

"It was only a very trusting small snake who forgot to go to sleep for the winter. He'd not hurt you for the world, sweetheart, I swear it. Hush, little one."

After a moment, between diminishing sobs, she said in a scratchy voice, "What . . . did you call me?"

"Little one."

"No. Be-before that."

"Er—oh. Sweetheart. In a—fatherly way, of course."

She sniffed. "And—when you . . . kissed my hair. Was that a—"

"Yes," he said hurriedly. "Of course, it was."

"Oh," said Miss Josie Storm.

Also by Patricia Veryan:

GIVE ALL TO LOVE

Patricia Veryan

FAWCETT CREST • NEW YORK

A Fawcett Crest Book
Published by Ballantine Books
Copyright © 1987 by Patricia Veryan

Library of Congress Catalog Card Number: 87-4401

ISBN 0-449-21496-6

This edition published by arrangement with St. Martin's Press, Inc.

Manufactured in the United States of America

First Ballantine Books Edition: September 1988

For Eva Ibbotson,
whose writing is so
extra-specially delicious

Give all to love;
Obey thy heart . . .

—Emerson

✑ Chapter 1 ✎

London
October, 1823.

The exquisite little shop in London's elegant new Burlington Arcade was crowded. Arms linked with those of friends or relatives, ladies wended their way among ells of velvet, silk, satin, and fine goat's wool; or admired feathers and fringes, lace and frogging and braids. The day was dark, but despite the chilly outer air the arcade was ablaze with light, the fine new gasoliers throwing out a great heat so that customers wearing heavy shawls and coats to combat the autumn chill were obliged to throw back hoods or loosen buttons, and several of the maids and footmen who followed their employers laden with packages found furs or wraps added to their burdens. The warm air rang with polite laughter and low-voiced chatter and the occasional more exuberant exclamations of friend encountering friend.

Among the throng, a slight girl wearing a long coat of dull red velvet trimmed with ermine, and a very smart matching bonnet, bent over a table to examine a card of braid fashioned in the shape of tiny red roses. "Oh, look, Pan," she cried. "How well this would be on the pink velvet for my Christmas gown, do not you think?"

Mrs. Pandora Grenfell turned a judicial gaze on the braid indicated.

Miss Josie Storm watched her anxiously, and the clerk who had come up watched the girl. She was not, he thought, a beauty. The dark curls that tumbled from beneath the stylish bonnet were luxuriant, true, but rather inclined to frizz instead of being

1

sleekly fashionable. Her chin was a little too pointed, her nose neither classically slim nor saucily retroussé, and her mouth was too wide. Yet her skin was almost translucent in its purity and there was about her an aura of happy expectancy. She put him in remind of his small daughter's new kitten—full of playfulness and fun.

At this point, the large and decidedly formidable lady said in a deep rumble of a voice, "We approve."

The girl gave a little squeal of pleasure, as though some enormous largesse had been bestowed upon her. Her eyes were dark brown, large, and brilliant, with flecks of hazel, the clerk noticed, and they seemed at this moment as if lit from within. Her lips curved to a smile; her whole face seemed to smile. He felt warmed as the smile was turned to him, and decided, firstly, that he would do his utmost to please this charming creature and, secondly, that if she were not a beauty, she was very pretty indeed.

Hugging the arm of her companion, she enquired as to the price of the braid. "Two shillings and sixpence ha'penny an ell," said the clerk. Miss Storm gave a little gasp, and again looked uncertainly to the older lady.

The clerk found himself waiting as anxiously. "It is rather dear, I allow, but it is very well made, madam," he said in his soft, persuasive voice. "You will note, I feel sure, how finely the roses are crafted."

The young lady turned a grateful beam upon him. The clerk began to cast about for ways to lower the price.

Mrs. Grenfell inhaled deeply. The clerk and the girl held their collective breaths. "Not exorbitant," quoth that great voice. The girl clapped mittened hands. The clerk grinned, measured the required yardage, and wrapped it tenderly. A footman, already weighed down with packages, stumbled closer.

"Oh, dear," said the girl. "Poor Klaus. I shall take this one."

"No, Miss Storm," mumbled the footman, his chin balanced on a large bundle. "I can manage."

"Pooh!" Miss Storm fumbled for her purse. "You never can." She counted out the required amount. The clerk handed over the small package, basked in the sunny, "Thank you," that

2

was bestowed upon him, and stood watching as the small procession proceeded towards the doors. He was so entranced that a dowager who had tried to attract his attention for a full five seconds was driven to raise her voice, and it required all the poor clerk's tact to quiet the lady's indignation.

The porter was in the act of opening the door, when Miss Storm heard her name called, and turned back. A well-groomed lady of pleasant countenance and middle years was waving at her. With a joyous exclamation, she hurried to hug and be hugged. ''Aunt Louisa! Oh, how lovely! Do you stay in Town?''

Lady Louisa Drummond led her niece into a corner somewhat out of the way of the crowd. ''Yes. Only for tonight. Yolande and Craig had brought the boys down to visit us, but are promised next to the Leiths. We accompanied them as far as Town, since I wanted to shop at all events.''

An emptiness had come into Josie Storm's brown eyes. Very well aware of it, my lady asked swiftly, ''Are you alone, my dear?''

Miss Storm denied this and called Mrs. Grenfell, who had paused to admire some lavender gauze. The two older ladies were distantly related, and entered upon a brief exchange of information regarding Colonel Alastair Tyndale and his wife, concluding which, Lady Louisa again turned to her niece. ''How is dear Alain? He is with you, I fancy?''

Again, those expressive dark eyes changed. The warmth in them was marked as the girl answered brightly that her guardian was very well, and that they stayed at the Clarendon.

''Good gracious!'' exclaimed my lady. ''We are at the Pulteney. I thought Dev usually put up there.''

''Well, he does,'' admitted Josie with a twinkle. ''But he thought his daughter might like a change.''

''Daughter!'' scoffed Lady Louisa. ''Why, the boy's not so many years older than you are. Let me see now . . .'' She wrinkled her brow. ''He must be—good heavens! He was but three and thirty in July!''

''Oh, I cannot think so, Aunt,'' said Josie demurely, ''for he insists he is approaching one hundred. I gather he has that many grey hairs, and counts a year for each one of them.''

3

My lady laughed. "Yes, and although I always thought Alain the most handsome man I ever saw, I will admit that silver streak over his right temple—"

"Left," Josie interjected automatically, and then blushed as her aunt smiled and her eyebrows arched a little.

"Left temple," my lady corrected, "makes him almost unbearably good looking. Tell me, love—I'd heard Elvira DeLange is the latest to drop the handkerchief. Will he have her, do you think? It is past time he wed, and The DeLange is a beautiful creature."

"And determined," said Josie, a grim set to her chin.

Lady Louisa giggled. "The lady who wants Dev to husband will have to be! He'll not be easily captured—not after all these years a carefree bachelor. I'd fancied Isabella Scott-Matthias had him fairly snared last year." Her eyes became sad. "I only hope Dev does not still grieve for—" She caught herself up and went on hurriedly, "Speaking of Lady Isabella, what's all this I hear about you and her brother? Naughty puss! Do you aim for a title?"

"Good gracious, no! The Viscount and I are friends, merely."

"When you danced with him at the Bolsters' ball this Spring, the look in his eyes was not that of a friend, my dear."

"Nor of an enemy, I trust?"

My lady did not at once reply, but her vaguely troubled look prompted Josie to ask, "Do you not like him? Now, how can this be? Everyone likes Elliot."

Avoiding her eyes, Lady Louisa admitted, "I've no reason not to like him only . . . He is too old for you, my love. Much older than—er, than Devenish, even."

The girl's brown eyes flashed to meet her innocent hazel ones and hold them steadily for a moment. Then, Josie smiled mischievously. "Pray do not tell Dev that. Elliot has not a single grey hair."

"And if he did, would dye it."

The sharp comment further astounded Josie, who had not in all the years she'd known this lady, heard her speak to the disparagement of another. Before she could respond, however, they were joined by Lady Louisa's younger daughter. Great friends, the two girls embraced delightedly. Rosemary Drummond was a lively creature in her mid-teens, with the auburn hair and green eyes of her handsome sire, and showing promise of the beauty that had made her sister Yolande a famous Fair some years earlier.

"I'd no notion you meant to come to Town, Josie," cried Rosemary. "Oh, *what* a dashing hat! Do you stay long? Is Dev with you? Can you come back to Park Parapine with us?"

"A capital idea," said my lady, beaming. "Do say you will, dear."

"Oh, I *wish* we could. But Dev must get home. He came only so that I could do some early Christmas shopping and because he has some sort of business to attend to. But he's in quite a pickle with one of our neighbours, and means to leave Town first thing in the morning, I know."

Rosemary looked disappointed but pressed Josie to travel back to Sussex with them. "Dev won't mind, and you can travel in our carriage. It would be such fun, Josie, and I've not seen you for an age."

Mrs. Grenfell had met an acquaintance and paused to chat with her, but now came to remind Josie that they should be leaving. Rosemary, who was almost as afraid of the ponderous lady as was Devenish, dropped her a shy curtsy and was permitted to kiss the large, florid cheek.

"Yes, and we must go, too," said Lady Louisa. "Rosemary, stop pestering Josie. We have been gone for hours and you know how Papa and your brother will fuss are we late for dinner."

"Is Arthur come home, then?" asked Josie, surprised.

"No, dear. John. He returned from Canada last week. It is one of the reasons Craig brought Yolande and the children down so early, for their new Town house is not quite ready for them, you know. Now, do ask Devenish if you may come to us. You can have a note sent round to the Pulteney, for we do not expect to leave until tomorrow. But—if you cannot, we will see you at Cloudhills for Christmas—no?"

"Lovely," said Josie, adding casually, "Shall Craig and his family stay in England until Christmas, do you think?"

"I fancy Craig would not think it worthwhile to return to

Scotland. Their house will surely be ready at any day, and certainly the Nine Knights will wish to be together, as usual.'' Josie murmuring agreement with this, my lady gathered up her daughter and her maid, and they all went into the Arcade, the commissionaire hurrying to call up my lady's carriage.

Outside, the afternoon was waning and there was a smell of rain in the air. The lamplighter had already begun his rounds, his coat flapping as he climbed his ladder. The cold wind sent the ladies' skirts flying, and whipped a gentleman's high-crowned beaver from his head, so that an enterprising street urchin was galvanized into earning a groat for retrieving it.

Josie declined an offer to be driven to the Clarendon, which would have severely taxed the capacity of the graceful brougham, and waved farewell as the vehicle edged into the stream of traffic.

Klaus, who had left some of the packages with Mrs. Grenfell while he went to the corner to hail a hackney, returned, followed by a neat coach. The hackney pulled into the kennel, the ladies were assisted inside, the fur rugs drawn over their knees, and the packages deposited on the seat opposite. As short as the delay had been, shouts of impatience were rising from the drivers of a tilbury and a carriage, and the jarvey waited only until Klaus had started to swing up beside him before cracking his whip.

Mrs. Grenfell leaned back with a sigh of relief. ''We shall be very well pleased,'' she observed, ''to return to the hotel. We hope Devenish is not become anxious.''

''I'll lay you odds,'' said Josie, her eyes full of merriment, ''he is not alone when we get back to the Clarendon. He has friends everywhere!''

''Ladies,'' Mrs. Grenfell pointed out, ''do not lay odds, Josephine.''

Her charge sighed. ''Shall I ever learn? I wonder Dev has any patience with me. Seven years since he rescued me from those dreadful gypsies, yet still I lapse so hideously at times!''

Mrs. Grenfell saw the droop to the girl's mouth and patted her hand kindly. ''You do splendidly. We are sure Devenish is proud of you.''

"I wish that I could be as sure." Josie was silent, staring into the blustery afternoon as the hackney picked its way towards the Clarendon. "Did you hear what my aunt said? The Tyndales mean to remain in Town."

"Yolande Drummond Tyndale has been happily wed for nigh seven years and has three fine children," said Mrs. Grenfell, without expression.

"And is as beautiful as ever." Inside her cosy muff, Josie's hands tightened into fists. "Oh, how I *wish* we did not have to go to Cloudhills for Christmas!"

"We are, we believe, still fond of Colonel Tristram Leith and his lady and their children. And of the Bolsters, and Sir Harry and Lord Mitchell and their wives, and—"

"Oh, I know. I know. I should not have said it. Truly, I love them all dearly. Only . . ."

"Forgive and forget, child."

"No!" A fierce and rare frown drew Josie's slim brows together. In a husky, grating little voice she said, "I shall never forgive her! *Never!*"

"You would have been happier, perhaps, to have had her for a mother?"

Josie stared at the impassive features, then gave a lilting little trill of mirth. *"Mother? My* mother? Oh, Pan, dear! Thank you for making me laugh! As if Yolande Drummond could have been my mother!"

"She is Mrs. Craig Tyndale now. But when she *was* Yolande Drummond, we are told she was most kind to you, and did, in fact, influence Devenish to make you his ward."

Josie's laughter died away again. Coldly inflexible, she said, "She tore his heart out. If you could have seen him. Even now, I remember the look in his eyes—so much worse than when his leg troubles him, or when he was ill two years ago. For months afterwards he looked dazed sometimes, like—like a child who has been terribly injured and is striving to comprehend what has happened to him."

Mrs. Grenfell looked grave, then said slowly, "Many people are so unfortunate as to suffer the pain of unrequited love. The lady had every right to—"

7

"She had *no* right! He had loved her all his life. They were betrothed! And she jilted him after she had told him to name the wedding day!"

"This was very bad, we admit. But—it was a long time ago, child, and Devenish does not seem to us a man scourged by grief. Indeed, when we all are together every year, it appears that he is fond of Yolande. If *he* does not hold the lady in abhorrence, why should you?"

Such a lengthy speech from the taciturn Mrs. Grenfell was a rarity, but Josie's silence was not occasioned by awe. The truth was that her chaperon had misunderstood the matter. Josie's concern was that Alain Devenish still felt for his cousin's wife an emotion far removed from abhorrence.

"I hope Craig may not call me out and put a bullet between my eyes!" Alain Devenish flung open the door to the parlour of his luxurious suite at the Clarendon and bowed the beautiful Mrs. Craig Tyndale inside.

Yolande laughed, stripped off gloves of soft green kid, and took off her high poked and plumed green bonnet.

"Fletcher," called Devenish, crossing to knock at the connecting door to Josie's bedchamber. There being no answer, he knocked again, then opened the door and peeped inside. "Blast! She must have gone out." He closed the door and limped back to take the cloak Yolande discarded, toss it over a chair, and grip both her hands, turning her to face him. "My lovely, lovely creature! What a delightful piece of luck to find *you* in the Strand! I can never believe you're the mother of three savage boys!" His admiring gaze took in her thick chestnut ringlets, her fine green eyes and fair complexion. She was not, perhaps, quite so slender as in the days when he had fondly expected she would become his bride, but her figure was neatly curved and, to his way of thinking, lost nothing by its more rounded lines.

For her part, Yolande was a little startled to find him unchanged since they last had met two years ago. She had been confined with her third son during the Christmas season last year, and had been unable to make the annual pilgrimage to rendezvous at one of the homes of the Nine. Now his eyes

8

seemed if anything more deeply blue and just as full of merriment as they'd been when he was her devoted swain. His slim nose was as straight as ever, his mouth as well shaped and sensitive, the chin below it as firm. But it seemed to her upon closer inspection that about the delicate nostrils and between the brows were lines she had not remembered, so that unease dimmed the happy light in her eyes. She saw curiosity come into his face, and she reached up to touch the thin band of silver that arched back through the thick, loosely curling fair hair. "Never tell me you do not dye it," she teased. " 'Faith, Dev! Can you not be content with *half* the women in England at your feet?" And she thought, 'Lord, but the man is criminally handsome!'

Any reference to his astonishing good looks irritated him, but this was one woman who could do no wrong in his eyes, and he merely said, "Fudge! I am vastly content to have *none* of them at my feet!" He led her to the sofa before the glowing fire. "Come and sit down for a moment and talk to me. Gad, but motherhood agrees with you, lovely one!"

"I am very fortunate," she said, smiling at him. "But how comes it about that you have eluded all the traps set for you, my dear?"

He chuckled. "Traps, is it? I wish I might see some." Her brows lifted in faint mockery, and he went on quickly. "No, really, Yolande, I've no wish to marry. I'm perfectly happy as I am. It's been a busy seven years, keeping an eye on my Elf, bringing Devencourt up to style—more or less, and managing the estate and the farms and so forth."

She had seized upon the one word that mattered and, leaning forward, put her white hand on his sleeve and asked with fond intensity, "Has it, Dev? *Are* you happy?"

He covered her hand with his own and replied as intensely, "Yes, love. I thank you. These have been *very* good years for me, so do not be reproaching yourself."

She had to turn away and found the room suddenly rather blurred.

"Tell me now," he said, a shade too heartily, "how's old Craig? And what of my namesake? He must be—good Gad! Is it—five? Surely not!"

9

"You know perfectly well it is, since you never miss his birthday! And Jonas Craig is three, and baby Stuart almost a year. And all healthy and strong, thank God! And now, sirrah, what is this I hear about Don Juan Devenish and the string of broken hearts he trails behind him? Let me see now . . ." She held up one hand and began to count off, "There was Brenda Smythe-Carrington—"

"Who married Owsley," he said imperturbably.

"And Deborah Grey, who they say went into a decline, and— No! Do not interrupt if you please! And Mary Lipton. And— who was that fiery, jet-haired creature . . . ?"

"Never heard of the lady."

"Isabella Scott-Matthias! Now, *she* almost had you, Dev, no use denying! And I hear whispers that she still—"

"Peccavi! Peccavi!" Laughing, he limped over to a sideboard and poured two glasses of wine. "I have only sherry, I fear, but I'd as soon not order up ratafia, if you will forgive me, Yolande. Josie will be back soon, and I'd be grateful would you keep your promise before she arrives."

"Oh, of course. I was forgetting the time." She accepted the glass he brought her, and noted that he favoured the right leg still. If the old wound was responsible for the lines in his face and the silver slash in his hair, she thought fondly that it had not soured his disposition. She raised her glass in response to his toast to their reunion, sipped her wine, and then remarked, "I can scarce wait to see your little ward. Josie must be quite grown-up by now."

"Oh, yes—or so she thinks. And a scamp, I can tell you. Leads me a pretty dance. The young fellows in Gloucestershire are mad for her."

Yolande suspected that Dev was looking at his ward through the doting eyes of fatherhood. The last she'd seen of the girl she had been no more than average in looks. Still, a year or two could work wonders at that age. "Is that why you engaged a companion for her?"

"Oh, so you heard about that, did you?"

"Mama wrote me of it. I was never more shocked! Poor

10

child—I wonder she didn't murder you. Was she *very* naughty that you must go to such lengths?''

"Lord, no. Josie's never been naughty, bless her. Only . . ." He paused, staring fixedly at her bonnet lying on the side table. "Well, as you said, she's a young lady now, so about two years ago, I persuaded Mrs. G. to come to us. She's sister-in-law to Uncle Alastair's wife, so . . ." he shrugged.

"I appreciate your feeling obliged to provide Josie a chaperon, but—*Pandora Grenfell*? Really, Dev!''

He gave her a little-boy grin. "A bit awe-inspiring, ain't she? Puts the fear of God into me, I don't mind telling you!''

"I can believe it! Whatever inspired you to hire such a dragon?''

He returned his gaze to the bonnet. "Josie's a complete innocent, you see. Impulsive as she can stare, full of joy and gaiety. The most generous, kind-hearted girl. It would never occur to her that people might—might think . . ." He reddened, coughed, and went on bashfully, "I expect I'm not a very fatherly type. And—living out there at Devencourt most of the year—''

Aghast, she interposed, "Oh, Dev—you cannot *mean* it? Surely no one, knowing you—If ever I heard anything more ridiculous! You always have been the very soul of honour!''

"Thank you, m'dear. But—tongues do wag and—'' He met her gaze squarely and said with quiet gravity, "You see, I won't have Josie touched by anything like that.''

Yolande had known this man all her life, for they had lived on adjoining estates and were distant cousins, but this was an Alain she'd never seen, and that brought her an odd sense of confusion. "I see," she said slowly. "Well done, Dev!'' And, standing, "Oh, look at the time! May we see the evidence now, if you please?''

He led her into his ward's bedchamber, opened the clothes press, and began to rummage around on the upper shelf.

Yolande ran her eye over the line of dainty gowns. Pale pink, a delicate orange, cream, white. She asked, "Is she still as dark, Dev?''

"Oh, yes. Very." He lifted down a large package and laid it on the bed.

"And—her eyes?"

"Very dark brown, with the loveliest flecks of a light hazel— almost amber when she's happy. In fact—" He checked abruptly, and opened one end of the package. "Here's the stuff she bought. I know it's for her Christmas gown. What d'you think?"

She was thinking of a lovely Spring morning in 1816, when she and Devenish had stood in the grounds at Park Parapine and she had asked him to name the colour of her eyes. And of how furious she had been when he'd said they were blue. Resentment touched her. At once ashamed of such greed, she touched the rich pink velvet thoughtfully. "Have you found anything?"

"Went over to Rundell and Bridge this morning, as a matter of fact. Here, I'll show you." He restored the pink velvet to the clothes press and closed the door, then took a jewel box from his breast pocket and handed it to her.

Yolande opened the case and gave a gasp. The pendant was splendid, the great ruby flashing fire from a chased gold setting. "Oh! It's lovely, Dev! Only . . ."

He prompted anxiously, "Only . . . ?"

"If Josie was about ten when you rescued her from those wicked men, she must be seventeen now, but—"

He sighed, taking back the case and gazing down at the ruby. "She didn't look ten to me. Eight or nine, more like. But—she insists she's older. Perhaps she is. Sometimes, she's just a babe. And sometimes—as wise as time." He smiled wryly. "She tells me she is much older than me, the minx!"

"Of course. In some ways all women are older than their men."

Devenish replaced the box in his pocket. "Well, that don't apply to us, considering I can give her fifteen years, even if she's eighteen! Now—enough philosophizing, my good girl. What's wrong with it?"

"Nothing at all. It's beautiful, but—has she any pearls, Dev?"

"Hum." He tugged at one ear thoughtfully. "She has a pearl pendant. Do you mean a rope?"

"Yes. The ruby is very striking, but—"

"I see. Rushing my fences, am I?" He grinned at her anxious face. "You're a good soul, Mrs. Craig Tyndale. I shall exchange it tomorrow."

She started to the door, then turned back. "Dev—you can do *me* a favour, if you will."

"If I will! Name it, lovely one."

She blushed and said hesitantly, "Well, Craig has been casting around for something to—er, to give me for Christmas. And—should he chance to mention it, you might—drop a hint . . ."

"Rascal! Tit for tat, eh? What am I to tell your doting slave? The Pavilion? Windsor?"

"Silly creature! No, but—that pendant might—"

He laughed delightedly, seized her in a strong hug, and swept her off her feet. "So you did like my gift after all! You shameless—"

"Oh!" gasped Yolande. "Put me down, Dev!"

He glanced around. The outer door stood open and Josie was watching them as one stunned, every vestige of colour drained from her face.

Aghast, he restored Yolande to her feet. "Josie," he gulped, his face as red as hers was pale. "I—that is, we—"

"Yes," said Josie in a rather faint but firm voice. "I—saw." She put her packages on the bed and, stripping off her gloves, walked to the two who waited in frozen silence, and held out her hand. "Good evening, Yolande," she said brightly. "How very unexpected to find you . . . here."

"More coffee, darling?" Josie held the pot poised above her guardian's cup, and yearned to pour the contents over his curly head.

Well aware that he was still in disgrace, Devenish peeped at her over *The Gazette* and declined the offer.

"As you wish." She walked with her light, springing step to the small table in this comfortable parlour, replaced the pot on its tray, and returned to perch on the arm of his chair. "Now, why," she asked mildly, "are you glowering, sir? Did that beefsteak pie we had for dinner upset your tummy?" She reached out to rest her dainty fingers on his brow and smooth away the faint lines there.

He jerked his head away. "Was I glowering? My apologies. Only—you should not address me so."

"Address you? Oh—you mean 'darling'?" Her eyes round and guileless, she asked, "Why? Is it not a word signifying affection? And what more natural than for a daughter to feel affection for her Papa?"

"Hmmmn," said Devenish, and retreated into his newspaper.

"Well, dearest ancient?" persisted Josie, folding down the top of the page and viewing him over it.

He sighed and lowered the newspaper to his knees. "In the first place, it is not a term usually employed towards a—"

"A very tottering old gentleman?" she interpolated, twining a strand of his hair into an elf lock.

"No," he answered, and watched hopefully for the dimples that usually flickered beside her mouth when he took her to task. She glanced up, met his eyes, and smiled. After a moment, Devenish recollected himself. "Moreover" he said sternly "you were not . . . Josie, *will* you stop giggling when I'm trying to talk to you?"

"My apologies, dearest." She stood, skipped across the room, and took down the mirror from above the hearth. "Only see how lovely you look."

He glanced frowningly at his reflection. Small ringlets hung down all across his forehead. "Good God!" he exclaimed, running a hand through his hair in exasperation.

Josie laughed. "Now you've made it worse. Oh, very well, if we must be grim, I'll behave." She set the mirror aside and knelt at his feet, hands folded in front of her. "I know, dear sir," she sighed, "that I am a great trial to you. 'Tis small wonder that you seek consolation in the arms of—"

"I did *not* 'seek consolation' with Yolande! I told you—"

"That she was panting with desire—"

"I said no such thing!" he gasped, horrified.

"—to see my pink velvet," she finished demurely. "That *was* what you said, was it not?"

"Yes— No! That is— Oh, dashitall, child—"

14

Wrath flared in her eyes. "Do not *call* me that! I am a woman! Why must you always—" She flung around to present her back to him.

He reached up and with one lingering finger touched the lace ruffle that edged her neckline, and after a moment, said gently, "But you *are* my child. My very loved daughter, and—"

She sprang up and leaned over him with blazing eyes and teeth that gnashed so that he drew back, blinking. "Wretched! Most odious . . . *youth*! Oh, how I would like to—to scratch you!" And her hands came up, the fingers clawed and taut with her rage.

Standing politely, Devenish sighed for the second time. "Why are we quarrelling so? If it is because you found me—er, holding Yolande, I told you how it came about."

She drew a long, hissing breath, then walked to the fireplace and stood staring into the flames. "Yes, I know. And I am not shocked because you were in the bedchamber with a married lady, if—"

Angered now, he snapped, "You go too far, miss! I have the greatest respect for my cousin's wife, and—"

"Oh, I could tell how much you respected her. Although, I would have thought you proceeded about the business . . . hind end foremost, as it were."

"Hind end—what?" he stammered.

"Foremost, Papa. Indeed, it might have proven less taxing— especially for so aged and infirm a creature—to have lifted the parcel *down*, instead of lifting *her* up. *N'est-ce pas?*"

"I wasn't lifting— Well, what I mean is—"

She turned to him. "What *do* you mean? Not that it is any of my . . . affair." She saw anger flare in his blue eyes and added rather hastily, "It is only that I worry for you—lifting such a weight."

He grinned at that. "No cause, m'dear. Yolande weighs hardly anything."

Her brows lifted. She sat on the hearth seat and said in a brittle voice that should have warned him, "Does she not? I had thought her rather—fat."

His jaw dropped. *"Fat?"* he squawked. "Yolande?" He threw

15

back his head and gave a shout of laughter, then sat down again, wiping his eyes and never dreaming how close he was to being thoroughly clawed. "Scamp! Fat, is it? Oh, Jupiter!"

She smiled, revealing an amazing expanse of white pearly teeth. All clenched. "I was only . . . funning. Truly, she is lovely as ever."

Devenish said with faint nostalgia, "Yes. Quite the most beautiful woman I ever saw."

"And so—*warm* natured."

"Indeed she is."

"How sad," she said viciously, "that she chose another gentleman."

His smile died and his hands clamped very tightly over the arms of the chair, but he said nothing.

At once, she was repentant, and with a muffled sob flew to throw herself onto his lap as she had done when she was a child, and cling to him, weeping. "Dev . . . oh, Dev! I am so sorry! Oh, *why* must I say such things? I don't . . . mean it, you know I don't! Only—I am sometimes . . . so afraid."

He recovered himself with an effort, and stroked the soft curls that tickled his chin. "Of what, my little one?"

She shook her head, speechless, and after a moment he said quietly, "Josie dear, are you unhappy because we are going back to Devencourt? It is lonely and isolated there, I know."

"Yes," she said with a sniff. "It is."

He frowned worriedly. "I should have packed you off to a seminary for young ladies, where you would have made friends."

Appropriating his handkerchief, she gave a little kitten-blow of her nose, dried her eyes, and sat up, quavering, "How could you send me to a seminary, when I was a foundling, primed for the Flash House, and must have disgraced y—"

She had felt him tense and now one hand clamped over her mouth and his eyes were a narrowed glare. "Do not *ever* say that again!" Her own eyes widened. He went on, low and furiously, "You were a sweet, unspoiled, half-starved victim of man's greed and savagery when I found you."

Josie mumbled something and he removed his hand although his eyes still blazed at her.

"And fought for me very bravely," she said humbly.

"Never mind trying to turn me up sweet. I kept you at Devencourt because—" he paused.

"Because—what, dearest?"

He settled back again and, Josie promptly cuddling under his chin once more, stroked her hair absently, his thoughts turning backward. "Selfishness, pure and simple," he said with a guilty frown. "Uncle Alastair was getting himself leg-shack—er, I mean, married. It was time for me to leave him in peace at Aspenhill and move to Devencourt. Besides which—"

"Besides which, you were lonely and miserable," she put in and, feeling him tense, went on forlornly, "Not that I could do much to cheer you, poor dar—Papa."

Devenish thought a good deal, but he said lightly, "You kept me so busy I'd no time to be lonely. What with your pranks and your creatures, and filling my poor house with oddities! I wonder my hair is not snow white."

"Brute!" She sat up at once. "You know perfectly well that you love every single one of them." Her eyes became very tender. She leaned closer. "Every . . . single . . . one."

Again, he resorted to the death grip on the arms of his chair, but managed, "If you refer to Lady Godiva—I deny it unequivocally!"

She squealed, and plunged at him, her strong fingers seeking the place in his ribs that was his weakest spot.

"No!" He dodged desperately and snatched at her flying hands. "Josie—do not! I warn . . . you . . . Ah!" And he writhed, laughing helplessly as she tickled him without mercy.

Stopping abruptly, she drew from his inner pocket the prize she'd found. "Oh! Dev—what is it?" She fumbled at the clasp of the leather case. "Is it for me? May I—"

"No!" He grabbed for the case, but already it was opened and his ward's eyes very wide as she gazed at the magnificent ruby. Furious with himself, he snatched the case away. "By the Lord Harry, a man has no privacy!"

She stood and stepped back. "I'm sorry, Dev," she said quietly. "I had no right to pry."

"Huh!" he grunted, standing and tucking the case back into

his pocket. "I'm glad you realize it. Well, my Elf, it's nigh ten o'clock. Best get to bed. We must make an early start in the morning if we're to reach Gloucester by Thursday."

She did not at once reply and he glanced at her curiously. She stood very straight and still, her face averted, and he wondered if she was terribly disappointed about the pendant. Before he could speak, however, she turned a smile on him that dazzled with its brilliance. "Oh, I am so sorry! Had I forgot to tell you? I met Aunt Louisa and Rosemary out shopping today, and Rosemary begged me to go down to Sussex for a week or so."

"The deuce! I've simply got to meet with Little's solicitor, and I fancy you'd like to go, but I don't see how I can—"

"Not you, Dev. Your wayward daughter."

"Oh."

Not looking at him, she said, "You don't mind, do you? I expect you've other things to take care of—besides Sir William, I mean."

He turned and picked up the fallen newspaper, restoring it to the table with a display of neatness that would have astounded his long-suffering valet. "Well, that's true enough," he said with a crooked grin. "And, you're likely eager to see young John Drummond again, eh?"

"Very eager," Josie confirmed, her eyes brighter than ever. "He's been abroad for two years, after all. How did you know he was come home?"

"Yolande told me. Do you—er, mean to leave early in the morning?"

"Yes."

"I'll arrange for a hackney to take you over."

"Klaus will do that. Unless you prefer he does not accompany me."

"Oh, no. I think it a jolly good notion for you to take him. He can keep all the Sussex beaux from pestering you to death."

She laughed. "I shall have to choose one soon, you know."

"Hum. Well, when must I send the carriage to bring you home?"

She shrugged and replied airily, "I—haven't decided."

"I see." His lips tightened and in an unwontedly curt voice he said, "Give them all my love, and have a nice time."

"I shall. Goodnight, Papa."

"Sleep well." He watched her walk away. 'She is behaving like a spoiled brat,' he thought, seething with indignation. 'And only because I would not let her have the pendant!'

But he was not one to hold anger and, before she reached the door, he had hastened to swing it open for her. She smiled up at him and swept past with a rustle of draperies and a drift of her fragrance.

"Josie," he said, "you forgot to kiss me goodnight."

She paused. "So I did," she said, then walked quickly into her bedchamber.

Devenish found it difficult to sleep that night. Sometimes, her behaviour so blatantly denied the sixteen he claimed. 'I shall have to choose one soon . . .' she'd said. Devencourt—without Josie. A prospect he had always known must come and to which he must become accustomed, perhaps sooner than he had anticipated . . .

Long after he had fallen into a troubled sleep, his ward lay in bed staring into the darkness. She did not see the dim outline of the clothes press, or the shadows the street lamp cast through the lacy curtains. Before her eyes was Devenish holding a lovely, laughing young woman to his heart, and saying joyously, "You did like my gift, after all! You shameless—" And a splendid ruby pendant she had not been meant to see, and that had certainly not been purchased for—a "child."

❧ *Chapter 2* ❧

Despite the fact that Sir Martin Drummond was now—as his wife fondly teased—grey as a badger, his tall, large-framed person was as trim, his eyes as alert, and his carriage as erect now that he was nearing sixty, as it had been twenty years earlier. He was a strong-minded man, firm in his opinions, proud of his house and his children, and happy in his marriage. Lady Louisa had not been a beauty when he'd married her, and there had been those who, impressed by his handsome appearance, had wondered if his parents had chosen wisely for him. Louisa had kept her looks, however, long after many accredited Toasts had lost theirs, her serene nature and happy disposition combining with the fact that she adored her husband to make her appear and feel a good ten years younger than she was.

On this unseasonably warm October afternoon, Sir Martin was irked because he had misplaced his spouse. He wandered about the house without success, ambled through the pleasure gardens, and made his way around to the vegetable gardens before he discovered her.

The impatience in his green eyes faded into amusement. He crept up behind the unsuspecting lady, and demanded, "And what are you about, ma'am?"

Lady Louisa gave a gasp and whirled around so swiftly that several of the chrysanthemums in her basket tumbled onto the path. The guilt in her hazel eyes gave her away, and her husband grinned and lowered his voice to accuse, "Infamous creature! You were spying on our guests."

"And our son, sir," she admitted, lifting her cheek for his kiss as he slipped an arm about her.

Sir Martin picked up the fallen blossoms, then directed his own gaze through the break in the hedge that allowed a clear view of the shrubbery. "I see Josie," he said haltingly. "And John. And—oh, I was not aware Fontaine had come."

"John likes him."

"Which shows I was right about your son, Louisa. I'd hoped the boy's sojourn in Canada might have given him some sense of discrimination. He'll go along better with an out and outer like Fontaine than with that set of rum touches he was used to associate with."

"To say truth, dear," his wife murmured with a smile, "I do not believe Elliot Fontaine came to see John."

Startled, he exclaimed, "Josie?"

"Now, Martin, you must have noticed at Jeremy and Amanda's ball how particular he was in his attentions."

He said nothing, but his face grew troubled and her own unease deepened.

"My love, if you think I should say something to her . . ."

He gave a small gesture of impatience. "Say what? That Fontaine is a jolly good chap but has an—er, questionable reputation with the ladies? Oh, never look at me so askance, ma'am. You don't like him, I'm aware."

"True. But—I could not say why. I just feel . . ." She paused, slipped her hand through her husband's arm, and started off with him. "I think," she mused, "it is the way he has with his eyes. Have you ever noticed? Sometimes, when he is talking and a thought strikes him, he will turn his head towards the person he's thinking of, without blinking."

Incredulous, he looked down at her. "Without *blinking*? What the plague has that to say to anything? Would you like him better, my lady, did he blink like candles in a stiff breeze?"

She said simply, "It puts me in mind of an adder."

Sir Martin frowned, but was silent.

21

"I wish," sighed Lady Louisa, "that he did not so gravitate to John. I wonder why he does."

"Why should he not?" Mildly amused, he asked, "D'ye fear his reputation for duelling? No reason for him to call John out, I fancy."

"Heaven forbid! Is he really as dangerous as they say?"

They had progressed around the hedge and were making their way down the bank. His eyes upon the slim, elegant figure of the man they discussed, Sir Martin said thoughtfully, "I've seen him take the pips out of a playing card at twenty paces. Must have eyes like a hawk. I'd not care to face him, I can tell you." Woman's intuition made him uneasy, and he added, "He likes John, as you said, m'dear."

"Yes. Only—they both admire the same lady."

His eyes widened. "Josie Storm? The devil!"

My lady halted and said with mild reproach, "She is a darling child."

"And a foundling," he observed grimly. "Lord only knows what's in her blood. Oh, do not think I dislike the chit. But I'll not have my son wed a girl of no family, no background. Lord, I'd sooner he wed some cit's daughter!"

She sighed and, walking on beside him, said, "There is likely nothing more to it than my silly imagination romancing on as usual. They have only now renewed their acquaintance." And she thought, 'And already, my poor John looks entranced.'

"We must hope that if your imagination is reliable, Fontaine will win the day. Although—whatever he has in mind will not include a wedding ring."

Irked, my lady said sharply, "And whatever her background, our Josie would settle for nothing less! And as for Dev . . . heavens!"

"My God!" he shook his head. "Fontaine would be wise to look elsewhere!"

Lady Louisa said slowly, "It is my impression that did Elliot Fontaine once decide he wanted something, he would stop at very little to possess it."

By mutual accord, they did not join the young people, but turned aside and returned to the house.

"Gentlemen! Gentlemen!" Laughing, Josie placed one hand on the chest of each of the young men who faced each other argumentatively. "No, really. I cannot be the cause of a quarrel between two good friends."

Viscount Elliot Fontaine seized her hand and bowed to kiss it.

Slightly flushed, John Drummond relaxed the tight set of his jaw. Unlike his elder brother, Arthur, he was neither dashing nor handsome. He bore a strong resemblance to his mother, for he had her kind smile, unremarkable but pleasant features, and straight, light brown hair. From his father he had inherited a fine pair of green eyes, a tall, sturdy frame, and a tendency to stubbornness. All in all, however, he was an amiable young man, and now he said coolly, "There is no cause for a quarrel, Josie. I was the first to ask if I might take you to the Tyndales' garden party at Aspenhill."

"Ah," murmured Lord Elliot in his soft, gentle voice, "but the race does not always go to the swift, my John."

"Nor to the most adroit," said Josie, smiling, but reclaiming her hand.

Fontaine's head lowered a trifle as his eyes darted to her. "Alas," he mourned. "Are we both to be cast into despair, fair lady? Only tell us with whom you *do* mean to attend the party, so that we may dispose of the wretch."

She was not a vain girl, but she could not fail to be pleased to have these eligible gentlemen in her court, especially since her birth was clouded and she knew she was not a beauty. Amused, she looked from one to the other. John, so kind and gentle and dependable. The Viscount, so full of jollity and yet so elegant and sophisticated. Her gaze lingered on him for an instant. No one could deny that he was much better looking than John Drummond. His features were finer, and framed by thick, dark red hair that was not quite auburn and inclined to curl at the ends. His light blue eyes were very clear and piercing under well-shaped brows, and his nose and chin were firm without being aggressive. She thought his mouth rather small and girlishly full-lipped, but that slight flaw often became his most winning feature, for he was aware of it and sometimes, when provoked, would pout in an exaggerated and most amusing fashion, thus winning friends to laughter or acquiescence.

"She is comparing us," he now said, digging his elbow into Drummond's ribs. "You should consider, my Fair, what a handsome couple we shall make when you choose me as your escort. Indeed, I do not see how you could do anything else. Allow me to show you my profile. I shall turn thus—against the sky. Now, only look, does it not cause your heart to flutter?"

His profile was certainly impressive as he posed, motionless, while Josie watched, giggling, and Drummond stared at him incredulously.

Fontaine's head shifted, his blue eyes, unblinking, transfixing Josie, and his rosebud mouth pursed into so ridiculous a contortion that she burst into a trill of mirth. "Besides," he said, relaxing and grinning easily, "*I* have a title, m'dear. John's only a commoner." He slid one hand onto his friend's shoulder as he spoke, his eyes twinkling at him so that Drummond could not repress a smile.

"I think you are a rascal, my lord," said Josie, her own eyes dancing.

"And you are adorable and have quite stolen my heart."

"Well, I wish to God I'd never brought you here," complained Drummond. "And had I known Miss Storm was coming, you may be sure I'd not have done so."

"You should be grateful." Fontaine offered Josie his arm as they began to stroll back towards Park Parapine.

The red-brick house was vast and imposing, with turrets in the Jacobean style, its grandeur mellowed by the rich sweep of lawn and the bright colours of the well-tended flower beds which surrounded it.

Quite impervious to the beauty of the mansion, the Viscount pointed out, "Your sojourn in the Colonies has, alas, done nothing to add polish to your manner, Drummond. You may watch me, and learn."

Josie chuckled, but slipped her free hand through Drummond's arm. He smiled down at her gratefully, and retaliated, "Learn what? How to become an insufferable coxcomb?"

"Prove me wrong, then. Convince the lady. I wait with bated breath."

"If that means you will be silent, we are reprieved," said Drummond. "Josie, *will* you give me your answer? I'll not subject you to viewing my profile, I promise you. Nor seek to sway you by puffing off my consequence."

"I did *not* puff!" inserted his lordship, indignant.

"But merely say that, although I met many charming ladies in Upper Canada, there was not one who"—Drummond's eyes became very serious all at once—"who had a jot of your charm and wit and merry good humour."

"*Charm* and *wit* and *merry good humour*?" Fontaine cast his eyes upward and uttered a groan. "You are lost, my poor John! You must tell the lady how *beautiful* she is. How *sparkling* her eyes, how *delicate* her sweetly bowed lips, how—"

Vastly amused, Josie cried, "Oh, no! Do stop! I would know it for a hum, for I am not beautiful. No, do stop protesting, gentlemen. And tell me, my lord—"

"Oh, please—never so formal, fairest. My name is Elliot."

"Lord Elliot," she corrected, dimpling prettily. "How came you to be in Canada? Has your papa properties there?"

Very briefly, she thought to see so different an expression in the Viscount's eyes that she was startled. Then, he said urbanely, "I was sent off because of a slight disagreement with my revered sire. And—you hedge, I think, Mademoiselle Josephine."

"He's right, y'know," Drummond put in earnestly.

She halted. "Since you are both so very charming," she said with a twinkle, "it would be my great pleasure to go with both of you."

The Viscount moaned, and clapped a hand despairingly to his brow. Drummond looked downcast. Josie went on mischievously, "Did I intend to go."

"You never mean to leave us?" cried Drummond. "You only just came!"

"No, no. I have been here for almost two weeks, John. And Dev—my guardian, will be sending for me very soon."

"If you go, I shall follow!" declared Fontaine dramatically. " 'Faithful in love, and dauntless in war!' "

"Sir Walter Scott!" Josie said, delighted.

Drummond parried resolutely, "Don't forget Scott also has written,

> 'The wretch, concentred all in self,
> Living, shall forfeit fair renown,
> And, doubly dying, shall go down
> To the vile dust from whence he sprung,
> Unwept, unhonoured and unsung.' "

For a second, the Viscount was utterly still. Then, he lifted his head to look levelly at Drummond, an expression in the pale eyes that caused Josie to say quickly, "Very well done, John. Tit for tat, Lord Elliot! Come now, you must be a good sportsman, and own it."

At once his droll smile dawned. "But of course. Do you truly mean to leave these tranquil pastures, dear lady?"

"I do. But I thank you for your kind invitations, gentlemen." She dropped them a little curtsy, to which the Viscount returned a flourishing bow, while Drummond inclined his head. And away she went; a blithe, slim figure, moving with light, buoyant steps across the rear terrace and into the great house, leaving behind the sunlight that seemed, to both her erstwhile companions, a little dimmer by reason of her having left it.

"But I had so hoped you would stay for the garden party at Aspenhill," said Lady Louisa. Josie had sought her out in her private parlour, and now she put aside the letter she had been writing, stood, and drew the girl she called her niece to sit with her on the cushioned bench by the unlit fire. "I trust," she went on, searching the bright, happy face, "that my son, or Elliot Fontaine have not—er . . ."

"Oh, no. For it is always lovely to hear compliments, is it not? But I must get home, for there is no saying what sort of bumble broth my poor Dev will tumble into do I leave him alone for much longer."

"He *is* a rascal, isn't he?" My lady's intent look eased. She said with a nostalgic sigh, "I miss him, you know. He was always here when he lived with Alastair, and so lighthearted and

26

full of fun. Dear Dev . . . It is as well, my dear, that he has you to—take care of him."

"So I tell him, ma'am. Much heed he pays me. I'd my work cut out to guide him in the matter of The Scott-Matthias, and *that* would never have done!"

My lady stared, then said, much amused, "So we have you to thank, do we? You minx! We quite thought he would be caught, and Isabella is such a dreadfully proud and opinionated girl. But excessively beautiful, I own."

"And likely wishes to wed him only because she thinks they will make such a striking couple. As indeed they would—her so dark and exotic, and Dev"—her eyes softened—"so fair. So very handsome."

My lady mused, "They would draw all eyes, that is certain. But—no, I cannot agree that is her reason. She is madly in love with him, Josie."

The resolute little chin tilted upward. "How unfortunate for her."

My lady laughed merrily, and they enjoyed their amusement until Josie said, "Oh, I do hate to leave you, dear Aunt Louisa. You are always so kind."

"*Must* you leave, dear? You're—quite sure John hasn't been a nuisance?"

Josie smiled and said gravely, "Do not be alarmed, ma'am. Dev insists I am too young for matrimony, and I know I am rankly ineligible and poor Sir Martin would be horrified. No—never look so dismayed. It is so. Besides, the Crichtons leave for Cheltenham tomorrow and have offered to take me home and to collect my dear Pan from Aspenhill. It is past time I left you."

Flushed and flustered, my lady protested feebly, then exclaimed, "Good gracious me! You surely do not think that wretched woman would go to Dev?"

"I'd not put it past her," said Josie smoulderingly, then added, brightening, "But—no, my ancient is probably muddling peacefully with his animals."

"If your confounded brute of a stallion was kept in his pasture," said Alain Devenish, straddling an arm of the blue bro-

27

cade sofa and regarding his irate caller without affection, "we might be spared all this fuss and bluster."

Sir William Little, his square features very red, sent a wrathful gaze scorching into the younger man's sparking blue eyes, and stamped across the great drawing room to fetch up beneath the portrait of Devenish's long-dead and lovely mother that hung above the wide hearth. "I did not ride over here," he snarled, "to come to cuffs with you, sir!"

"Did you not? I had thought you came to punch my head because you cannot keep your stallion in his paddock."

"Cannot keep him in—" roared Sir William, swinging about, his face purpling. "By God, but I can keep him in! Or could if I'd a neighbour who didn't encourage raff and scaff from all over the country to come here and open the damned gate!"

Devenish sprang up at this. "Blast it all—are you on about that again? Just because I refused to prosecute some poor devil who poached on my lands and was likely starving—"

"And thereby advertised to the whole damned country that we in Gloucestershire are easy marks, sir!" Sir William, who stood six feet three inches in his stockinged feet, and towered over Devenish, advanced and in a voice heard in the stables, declared, "There is no cause for anyone to starve in England, sir! A man may find honest work *if* he so chooses. But when there are people like you issuing invitations to every damnable ruffian for miles around to come here and live off the fat of the land at our expense, why should they seek honest work?"

His jaw thrust pugnaciously at his formidable guest, Devenish retaliated, "Honest work, my eye! Much has it cost you if an occasional poacher crosses my lands! And do you think there's honest work to be had, you're either blind or so curst pig-headed that—"

"Have a care," raged Sir William, his big hands clenching. "Have a care, or—by the Lord, you'll rue the day!"

Devenish threw back his head and enjoyed a hearty laugh.

"I came here," Sir William thundered, "with—with the best of intentions to—"

"To grass me, or try to," interposed Devenish.

"To try to reason with a young puppy! I see I might have saved myself the trouble!"

"Save, save, save! How the word haunts you, poor fellow. Do you think of nothing but your purse? I'd not guessed you are in such desperate straits, but if your stupid stallion has freshened my mare, as you claim, send me your charges and I'll pay a stud fee. Though to say truth, I do not admire the brute's lines."

All but apoplectic, Sir William snorted, huffed, and swore, and marched over to snatch up the hat and whip he had laid on a side table. "I'm not done with—with you—sir!" he panted, shaking the whip under Devenish's irrepressible grin. "If you were not—" He glanced down ragefully, closed his lips over the intended remark, then gobbled, "You will hear from my solicitor! I—I warned you, sir!"

Devenish had not missed that suggestive scan of his game leg, and the smile died from his eyes. "I wish you will stop frightening me so," he said coolly. "I vow I'll not sleep a wink tonight!"

Sir William fumed his way to the French doors, flung one open, marched onto the terrace, then swung about, to roar, "It's that damned rabble-rousing Redmond has caused you to turn against your own class! That radical friend of yours spouts the same sort of jiggery-pokery nonsense in the House of Lords as do you in Gloucestershire!"

"Thank you." Devenish limped over to bow derisively. "Mitchell Redmond is a *very* good friend of mine, and one of the finest gentlemen I know. And furthermore, Little," he went on, raising his voice as Sir William stamped down the steps to where a stableboy walked his mount up and down the rear drive-path, "if you and your kind had one jot of humanity in your collectively stony hearts, you'd show a little compassion for those less fortunate than your over-fed, pampered selves."

Inarticulate with wrath, his victim flung himself into the saddle and charged off at the gallop.

Chuckling, Devenish turned about and made his way to his study. The house seemed very quiet and the chill hall echoed emptiness. Josie should have written days ago. 'Wretched chit,' he thought. 'She is punishing me because she found me with Yolande.' But that, of course, was ridiculous. Josie would be pleased if he married again. Not that he could marry Yolande, even if he wished to. Which he didn't.

His study was cold, yesterday's ashes were still in the grate, and the wastebasket had not been emptied. He grumbled his way to the windows and threw the half-closed velvet curtains wide open to let in the pale autumn sunlight. Turning, he limped to the sullied fireplace and shook one finger at the portrait that hung above it. "You see what happens when you don't come home, Miss Josephine Storm. Only look at this mess! Your fault, ma'am. All your fault!"

The artist who had painted Josie two years earlier, when her guardian had judged her to be fourteen, had captured all her bright, eager optimism, and Devenish was silent for a moment, gazing smilingly up at that youthful face. Her features had changed so gradually, he'd not at first noticed that his waif was growing up. Growing to be beautiful. She didn't know she was beautiful, and oddly enough, some dense persons did not at first see her beauty. But in some miraculous fashion, her eyes, always bright, had become large and brilliant. Her mouth had softened and was more sweetly curved, her chin a trifle more rounded. And her dainty body— He cut off that train of thought quickly. It was as well to envision her a child, still. A gawky, perplexing, tender, loving, caring— "Hum!" he muttered, and said, scowling up at her, "If you had not surrounded me with oddities and misfits, madam, I might not now be in such sorry case. Behold my desk! Well, at least you're not here to tidy it so that I cannot find any—"

"Lordy, lordy, lor'," quoth a husky, breathless voice. "What a bloomin' mess 'tis, Mist' Dev'nish. *What* a bloomin' mess."

"Mrs. Robinson," he said uneasily, eyeing the bundled untidiness that was his housekeeper, and stepping over the ginger cat that wandered in, yawning.

"Thassme," wheezed Mrs. Robinson, beating an erratic path to the bell pull and tugging it energetically. "Get th' fireboy here, Mist' Dev'nish. Dunno what M's Josie'd say 'fshe could see this mess. Dunno, I'm sure. Shoulda rung, Mist' Dev'nish. Shoulda rung. You just sit y'sel' down, there. Just sit y'sel' down, an'—"

She advanced upon Devenish who, holding his breath, retreated to his desk chair and sat down abruptly. "Mrs. Robinson," he began firmly, "have you been at—"

His unfinished question became redundant as his housekeeper bent to pat him fondly on the shoulder and wheeze into his face that she had indeed been hard at work, but he wasn't to mind, like the good kind soul he was. She turned to busy herself at the desk, and Devenish blinked, waved away the fumes of gin, and drew a deep breath.

"Hey!" he cried belatedly. "What are you about?"

She blinked bleary, faded blue eyes at him. "Changin' y'r flowersh, sir. These be—"

"They're perfectly fine!"

"No, they're not. They're dead, sir. Been dead nigh a week. M's Josie put 'em there jus' 'fore—"

"Well, yes. But—er . . ." He watched glumly as the cherished and brittle stalks were swept into the wastepaper basket. From a bucket on the floor, Mrs. Robinson produced a glorious, fresh, vibrant bunch of chrysanthemums, which she proceeded to stuff into the vase from which the dead roses had been so ruthlessly ejected. "Cannot think how this water stays s'fresh," she muttered, knowing perfectly well why it had done so.

Devenish flushed scarlet and bent over his papers.

"Nor I can't think what's 'come o' that dratted fireboy," she went on, slanting an amused glance at her employer's fair head. She gathered her sagging shawl about her shoulders, turned, and reeled dizzily.

Devenish grabbed her arm. "Are you all right?"

She looked down at him. She was a victim of cruel circumstance: a husband who had fallen at the Battle of Vitoria, two small children who had died of measles and malnutrition, and the despair that had made her into a drunkard. Grief and starvation had aged her far beyond her forty years. Her hair was greying, her eyes rheumy, and the flush of alcohol painted her lined cheeks. But the smile that now lit her face was tenderness personified. She touched Devenish's supporting hand timidly. "I'm sorry, sir," she sighed. "I didn't mean . . . but then, I don't never mean . . ."

31

He tightened his grip. "I know. You're doing much better, Mrs. R. I shouldn't wonder, in fact, if it was *you* Squire Little came over to see this morning, you rascal!"

She giggled tremulously and moved off.

"How about some lunch for the lord of the manor?" Devenish called.

"Right 'way, sir," she croaked, and beat a wavering retreat.

Sir William's acid remarks had reminded Devenish that he'd failed to reply to Mitchell Redmond's last letter. Despite the fact that Josie had not tidied his desk, he was quite unable to find Mitchell's communiqué and gave up the search when a footman brought in the day's correspondence. Leafing quickly through it, he saw nothing inscribed in the neat copperplate hand he had hoped to find. He glanced up. The footman had not departed, and grinned at him. His wig was lopsided, and he looked fondly conspiratorial. This large chap, Devenish recalled, was the reformed pickpocket. Yearning for a stuffy, conservative footman who regarded him with bored disinterest, or even a modicum of dislike, he demanded, "Is this the lot, Cornish?"

"Ar," said the footman, and pointed out helpfully, "Ain't nothing from Miss Josie."

"So I see," said Devenish, fixing him with a hard stare.

"Never mind, guv. She'll be back in a day or three." Apparently oblivious to the frown in his employer's eyes, he added, "You got one there from Lord Bolster."

"Perhaps," Devenish remarked with icy hauteur, "you can inform me of its contents."

"Love-a-duck! Not me, mate. I mean—guv."

"Sir," said Devenish sternly.

"Cor! I thought it was lord!"

"I mean, blast your eyes, that you should call *me* 'sir'!"

"Oh. All right, cock. Keep fergettin', don't I? Anythink you says. 'Cept reading of yer letter. Can't. Read 'is lordship's writin', I mean. Bloody awful. Worse'n yours, Sir Guv."

Devenish's incensed glare was countered by a grin that spread to reveal the lack of one front tooth. Devenish tried to keep his countenance, but the ludicrous aspect of it was too much for his blithe spirit, and he laughed helplessly.

The footman laughed with him in a high-pitched scream.

Devenish wiped his eyes, and said between chuckles, "Get out of here . . . you damned . . . hedgebird."

"That's better, sir—mate," replied the footman, and took himself off to advise his colleagues in the servants' hall that "The Guvnor" was proper gut-foundered 'cause Me Lady Elf wasn't back yet.

Devenish, meanwhile, had turned his attention to the missive from Lord Jeremy Bolster. Six years ago, he and Jeremy had been members of the small and gallant band that had stood alone between England and the murderous and terrifyingly efficient plotting of Monsieur Claude Sanguinet. They were, besides, friends of long standing, and Devenish had the deepest affection for Bolster. The young peer was a brave man and a loyal friend. He had been a splendid soldier, was a devoted husband and father—and an atrocious penman, even as the footman had impertinently noted. Squinting at the convulsed and misspelled phrases, Devenish groaned and clutched his hair.

"Nothing wrong, I hope, sir?"

The aged man now reeling into the room was Simeon Wolfe, tiny, frail, uncertain as to gait, vision, and hearing, and on the far side of seventy. He should have been retired years since, but had pleaded that he had nowhere to go, no one to go to, and no idea of what to do with himself, was he turned off. Devenish had attempted to point out that he would have an adequate pension, plus a comfortable cottage on the grounds, and could putter about the garden to his heart's content if he so desired. Josie, however, had taken up the cudgels in behalf of a retainer Devenish had scarcely met until he'd removed to Devencourt. The poor old fellow, she'd argued fiercely, had given his whole life to the service of the Devenishes (a questionable statement at best) and so long as she had breath to draw, he would not be cast off like an old shoe. And so Wolfe stayed, and along with the well-intentioned, if back-sliding, housekeeper, he repaid Devenish for his continued employment with a doglike devotion that petrified his much-tried master.

Recognizing the note of pathos in the old man's cracked tones, Devenish lost no time in explaining that he was simply finding it difficult to decipher my lord Bolster's handwriting, and with one fascinated eye on the tilting luncheon tray, requested that it be set on the table before the windows.

With a knowing smile, Wolfe shook his head and set off between a hop and a stagger, the ale that had been poured with a too generous hand splashing liberally onto the floor.

Devenish shuddered and covered his eyes, waiting for the crash.

"Cheer up sir," piped the old man kindly. "Miss Josie will be home soon. Don't you worry so."

"I am *not* worrying!" snarled Devenish, standing. And then, seeing the stricken look on the wrinkled old face, said, repentant, "But—er, we all miss her, don't we?"

"That we do, sir," said Wolfe, tugging ineffectually at the chair. "Our little sunbeam goes away, and this old house is like a tomb."

A chill touched Devenish. 'Like a tomb . . .' "Nonsense," he said, starting to the relief of his struggling minion. "At all events, she'll be home before you can say—" He stepped in a puddle of ale, covered a good distance in record time, and swore blisteringly.

"No hurry, sir," said Wolfe with a kindly smile. "Easy does it."

Devenish gritted his teeth, pulled back the chair, straightened the tilting butler, and remarked that whenever someone had the time, they might be so kind as to send in the fireboy.

Wolfe nodded and lurched off. Holding his breath, Devenish eased himself into the chair.

"Hurt yourself, didn't you, sir?" observed Wolfe from the door. "Shouldn't be capering about at your funny tricks just for my sake. Not so young as you used to be, you know."

Devenish directed a seething glare at his plate and said nothing. When the door had closed behind his devoted retainer, he allowed his frustration full rein for several scalding seconds and then, shivering, picked up a stale ham sandwich.

The fireboy did not come, but another of Devenish's encumbrances put in an appearance. He was apprised of this new arrival as he again struggled with Jeremy Bolster's bewildering letter. The snuffling slurps could not be mistaken. Flinging around in his chair, he gave an irked shout.

"Damn you, Lady Godiva! Get away!"

The encumbrance raised injured eyes and quivered her ale-wet snout at him.

"You know very well what I said," he snarled. "Out!"

By way of bribery, Lady Godiva wrinkled her forty pink pounds and her curly tail jerked. She then resumed the business of cleaning up.

"You blasted pig!" quoth Devenish with perfect accuracy. He sprang from the chair, grabbed his thigh, and sat down again with considerably less verve.

Lady Godiva, who was fond of him, trotted over to peer up into his face, then sat down and rested her snout on his knee.

"Drunken . . . sot," Devenish said unevenly, pulling one of her ears.

Not one to take offence, she snorted.

"Not as young as I used to be, indeed! One might think I was ninety-three, rather than thirty-three!"

Lady Godiva wriggled in her most beguiling fashion. Absently, he gave her a piece of the musty ham sandwich, then exclaimed, "Egad, ma'am, my apologies! It might be a friend."

The pig was apparently cannibalistic and waited hopefully for the next offering.

"Let that be a lesson to you," said Devenish, having fortified himself with some of the warm ale. "Never adopt a chit. However appealing. Before you can turn around, they grow up and make you feel a dashed Methuselah!"

Edging closer, Lady Godiva voiced a coy grunt.

"Had you been what you should have been," he advised, "I'd have a dog keeping me company in my senile solitude. Since you had the poor taste to be born a pig, you'll get no more of my lunch, miss! Off with you!"

He finished his unappetizing repast, decided that Bolster's letter must wait until Josie returned to decipher it for him, and ordered up his rambunctious stallion, Santana.

❧ Chapter 3 ❧

Devenish's first encounter with the late and unlamented Sangui-net had been in the ruthless Frenchman's magnificent chateau in Dinan. It had been what Devenish described in later years as "a jolly good adventure," but for a time the outcome had been in doubt, and when he escaped he had taken with him a crossbow bolt that had transfixed his right thigh. The bolt was cast of steel and so cunningly contrived that his friends had been obliged to remove it with the aid of a hacksaw. A healthy young man, he had recovered rapidly, but he was left with a permanent limp and occasional bouts of discomfort that he shrugged off as being "a trifle annoying." The fact that he limped galled him far more than even his closest friends guessed, but on horseback he was in his element. He had always been a splendid rider, and if anything, his skill had improved with the years. The rougher the going, the more he enjoyed it, and so long as he was not in the saddle for a protracted period, he suffered no ill effects.

Santana was a big black stallion with a Roman nose, a deep barrel, straight powerful legs, and an uncertain temperament that bedevilled the grooms. With Devenish, he was docility it-self, but woe betide any stranger who attempted to ride him.

On this sunny afternoon, the air carried a chill warning of approaching winter. The clouds were shredding across the pale skies, and the tops of the trees were tossing to a strong wind.

Devenish gave Santana his head, and the big black thundered northwestward across the meadows, skirting the Home Wood, moving with his powerful, ground-covering stride that faltered not in the slightest when they came into the steeper slopes of the Cotswolds. Devenish slowed the horse, and Santana, rebelling, fought for his head again, but was subdued by the firm hand and voice that were unlike the hand and voice of any other man who had ever ridden—or had attempted to ride—him. This was the one human who must never be disobeyed or displeased. And so they came to the top of the steep rise in more sedate style. Devenish drew his mount to a halt and gazed out across the wide panorama while Santana snorted and pawed at the earth and rolled his fierce eyes, just to let the master know he had not yet begun to run.

It was very clear this afternoon. Off to the left the River Severn made its way southwest toward the Bristol Channel. Far off, Devenish could see the dark mass of the Forest of Dean. Eastward, roll upon roll, rose the green might of the Cotswolds. He was at the edge of his preserves now, and he turned Santana about, looking back to where, far below, Devencourt nestled in its valley. Even from this distance the beauty of the Elizabethan mansion was marked, and he leaned forward, one hand on the pommel, surveying his birthright.

Devencourt was built in the shape of a squared U. The central block and oldest part of the structure rose to three storeys, with half-timbered walls and latticed windows, all of which leaned a little, since the old building had settled during the long march of the years and was now markedly out of plumb. Both two-storey wings had been added at a later date, but faithfully adhered to the earlier architectural style. A great house it was, shielded by massive old oaks, set amid emerald lawns, its size and majesty softened by the graceful gardens that surrounded it. A sight to bring joy to the heart of any owner, one might suppose. Yet Devenish's eyes were bleak, his handsome features brooding. As a little boy, Devencourt had seemed to him a monstrous, living thing, reaching out to hug him to itself and keep him captive and alone amidst the tragic memories of bygone years. Even today, he feared it, dogged by a shadow of some inescapable evil.

He set his jaw, impatient with such gloomy forebodings. He'd been happy here, hadn't he? He'd had seven years of busy, full days. Seven years of laughter and contentment. The laughter of a little girl, whose endless inventiveness had been a never-failing source of wonder and delight. It was Josie who had kept at him until the new flower beds were installed. It was at her urging that he had thrown the old place open for Public Days each August, and it was because of her cheerful spreading of the word that many people had essayed the long and potholed road that wound through the hills to serve both his property and that of Sir William Little. Next, she had badgered him into taking her to Town to choose new furnishings for the main block, which had been largely neglected and unused for the past century or so. He smiled faintly as he recalled the friends she had beguiled into visiting them as she grew older. His complaints that his house fairly shook to schoolgirl squeals and chatter had been cheerfully ignored, and in some mysterious fashion he had become a part of their games. Charades and spillikins and Fish; picnics, boat parties, musicales . . . and as the merry years slipped away, charity bazaars and fetes, fund-raising activities at the church, visitations of the sick, inspections of his tenants and their properties, judging at horse shows and fairs. Activities he would never have chosen to embrace, but into which he had been swept by the enthusiasm and manoeuvrings of his vivacious little ward.

From the beginning, it had been so. Looking back over the years, he could see as if it were yesterday, their initial journey down from Scotland. A journey he had embarked upon with dark despair, for he had left behind his love, the lady to whom he had been betrothed most of his life, until she saw his Canadian cousin. All the way to London, Josie had chattered—a bright spirit beside him, combatting gloom and heartbreak. For her sake, he had been obliged to appear cheerful. And, how she had pestered him, the wretched brat. The questions! The interest! The delight over the many aspects of the great city that, having seen all his days, he had seen not at all. Despite his feeble protests, he had been inveigled into taking her to all the major sights, and had discovered that his old City was greater than he'd dreamed. He smiled, remembering how his feet had ached, and *he* had merely walked! Josie had danced and bounced and hopped through St. Paul's and Westminster Abbey. Even the mighty Tower of London had not subdued her, and several Beefeaters had been willing captives to her enthusiasm. Their visit to the Exeter Exchange had been ghastly. She had raged because she felt the wild beasts were too closely confined. Agreeing, he had tackled one of the guides and become involved in a hideous controversy that had ended with their polite ejection from the premises. And how they had laughed together. Down through the years, her laughter rang, replacing sorrow with amusement, and amusement with delight, and delight with—

'You're not so young as you used to be . . .' He scowled. He was only three and thirty, but three and thirty was too old for—some things. And he was a damaged three and thirty.

He reined Santana around and headed northwards. There was no cause to rush home. Perhaps he'd ride up to Gloucester and overnight with Guy Sanguinet. He could send word back from Stroud. Santana started down the steep slope. Devenish leaned back in the saddle. The big black slipped and slithered. Devenish swayed easily and patted the smooth flank. Coming to more level ground, he lifted the reins and, with a snort of triumph, Santana gathered his mighty muscles and all but flew.

The landscape became a green blur. The air beat at Devenish's face, snatching his breath away. He gave a cry of exultation and bent lower, and horse and rider thundered past an isolated cottage, shot down a winding lane, across open turf, and around the base of a steep rise and came nose to nose with an oncoming rider.

Santana emitted an equine scream and shied violently. Only Devenish's superb horsemanship kept him in the saddle. The other rider fought desperately to keep from being thrown, and ended with a wild leap to the ground.

"Blasted dimwit!" roared Devenish, with some difficulty since Santana was spinning like a top.

"You damned stupid cawker!" howled the other man. "If ever I saw such idiotic, reckless—" He checked, then said with a groan, "Lord! I might have known!"

"Lyon!" Grinning broadly, Devenish dismounted and ran to

seize the younger man by both arms and beam into his dark face. "By all that's holy! Be dashed if I wasn't riding over to see you and Guy!"

"Riding!" Grinning just as broadly, Lyon Cahill said with justifiable indignation, "Man, you do not ride—you fly! Lucky for me I'm still alive to tell of it!"

They laughed at each other, gathered their reins, and walked over to sit on a rocky outcropping near the foot of the hill, and when they had exchanged greetings and preliminary enquiries, Devenish asked, "Now whither are you bound, as if I needed to ask? To Devencourt. But not to see me, I'll warrant."

Lyon's dark eyes glinted. Colouring faintly, he said that he had, of course, hoped to see Devenish. "Especially," he added with a sharpening glance, "to discover how you go on."

"Oh, I'm perfectly fit, thank you. Once a doctor, always a doctor, eh?"

"Doctor, perhaps. Surgeon?" Cahill shrugged broad shoulders. "Sometimes I wonder, Dev."

"Fustian! Old lad, don't you know how proud of you we all are? What you've accomplished in these few years, considering—"

"Considering I was gallows-bred?"

Scanning the suddenly truculent expression of this powerfully built young fellow, Devenish said, "And as hot-at-hand as you can stare."

Lyon met his amused gaze; his flush deepened, and he looked away. "You may turn it off, but I fancy you'd not give us your blessing. If she'd have me, that is." He flicked his riding whip idly at a leaf that fluttered past, but, waiting, he was so tense he could scarcely breathe.

Devenish hesitated. Despite the decade and more that separated them, there was a deep affection between the two. One of the thousands of starving, unwanted children struggling to survive in London's slums, Cahill's earliest memories were of the nightmare of being a climbing boy. From that hideous slow death, he had escaped only to fall victim to a Flash House, where, between beatings, he had been trained for a pickpocket and burglar. He had improved his lot when a young aristocrat

40

caught him stealing, broke his arm, and then, becoming aware that his assailant was a child, took him to an apothecary and thence into his service. He had been known as Lion in those days, a name bestowed on him by his mentor, an unsavoury Corinthian named James Garvey. Lion had learned more of evil from his aristocrat than any simple thief or cutthroat had taught him, but when the boy had discovered Garvey was in league with the fanatical Monsieur Claude Sanguinet in a plot to murder the Regent, he had thrown in his lot with the courageous but hopelessly outnumbered gentlemen who opposed the Frenchman.

Despite the odds against them, they had won their struggle. Claude had died a victim of his own murderous scheme, but during a desperate affray had shot down his younger brother, Guy, leaving him partially paralyzed. The convalescent Frenchman had taken Lion for his personal servant. In a very short time, however, amazed by the boy's quick mind and eagerness to learn, he had engaged a tutor. That learned gentleman had lasted a year and a half, then told Guy that Lion's brilliance approached genius and required more guidance than he could provide. Intrigued, Guy had changed the boy's name to Lyon Cahill, and with the aid of several powerful friends had been able to get him into Rugby. The first months had been a nightmare for Lyon, who was shunned for his coarse way of speech and mocked for his lack of family background. Enraged, he had resorted to his fists, and within a year had become the middleweight boxing champion. Another year, and he was widely admired, the close personal friend of young men of the highest rank, and the despair of his teachers who were unable to keep pace with his voracious thirst for knowledge.

Guy, eager to provide his adopted son with every opportunity, had been blocked at every turn by the boy's lack of acceptable birth. Again, his friends had come to the rescue. Lord Belmont had taken the aspiring doctor under his wing, and in some magical fashion, Lyon had been admitted to the Royal College of Surgeons. The proudest day of Guy's life had dawned when Lyon was awarded his Licence to Practice an incredible three years later. Long years of resident study remained, however, if his lifelong dream of becoming a surgeon was to be realized, and he was overjoyed to win an appointment to the famous Guy's Hospital (which he blithely referred to as "my father's place") augmented by study with the great Lord Belmont.

Despite his brilliance, however, he had fallen victim to an ailment that had claimed many intense and impatient young men before him—the inability to recognize the limitations of the human body. Driven by ambition, Lyon had ignored warnings that he was working too hard. Early in the autumn, having for many months worked a twenty-hour day, he collapsed from exhaustion and was subsequently stricken with influenza. Lord Belmont, incensed, had read him a furious lecture and sent him back to Gloucester with strict instructions that he was to rest, regain his strength, and not so much as think of medicine for at least a month.

Now, watching the taut features covertly, Devenish thought that Guy's faith in the youth had been well founded. Cahill was a splendid young fellow. His countenance was pleasant, and he had a fine pair of dark eyes, set well apart, that met a man's gaze squarely with no sliding off or evading. His hair was thick, dark, and straight; his nose a strong swoop; his chin square and determined. The mouth concerned Devenish a little, for it was too tight-lipped for such a young man and had a tendency to sneer; but considering Lyon's early years, that was scarce to be wondered at. The right girl could—Devenish frowned inwardly. Did Josie really care for this ambitious, driven young chap?

Lyon glanced at him, anxiety in the dark eyes, and realizing he had not answered the so vital question, Devenish said ruefully, "I personally think Josie too young to be thinking of marriage for another year or two. But—perhaps I—that is, she'll have whomsoever she chooses; I fancy. Has she—er, I mean, have you offered?"

"Of course I have not! As if I would do so rag-mannered a thing! I've not asked your permission to address her!"

"Are you doing so now? Forgive me, but I cannot be sure. And it was, for some odd reason, my impression that you'd asked her many times."

Lyon grinned and said shyly, "In a way, perhaps. I—I have

asked her if she loves me. Not if she will marry me. She says she loves me. And I believe she does, but—Oh, devil take it, you know how she can be.''

It was very familiar. Devenish thought, 'Lightning strikes twice . . .' and said with ready sympathy, "You do not know if she is *in* love with you, is that it? Poor fellow. When I was just about your age, I was in the same miserable predicament. It's the devil.''

Lyon sighed and nodded. "I knew you'd understand. Though, Lord knows why any girl would have rejected *you*.'' He eyed Devenish glumly, wondering, as had so many, why the beauteous Yolande Drummond, with this dashing fellow at her feet, had chosen instead his quiet Canadian cousin, who possessed only average looks, little of Devenish's engaging charm and personality, and who had, at that time, been under the cloud of a disgraced name.

Having a fair idea of what was going on in his friend's mind, Devenish's lips quirked. He said with a sigh, "Incomprehensible, ain't it?''

"Poor old Dev,'' said Lyon kindly. "You never did get over it, did you? Well, what I mean is—you have not married.''

His eyes alight with laughter, Devenish exclaimed, "Good God! Do you fancy me to have lived a life of endless yearning for my unrequited love? To the contrary, my lad. Yolande was far wiser than I. Oh, damme! That don't sound very polite! What I'm trying to say is—'' He checked, with the sensitive man's reluctance to put his inmost feelings into words. "I care for her deeply, and always will. Only—when a fellow wants very much to—er, to have a loving wife, a home, and—God willing—children . . .'' And he had to stop again, because he did want children so very badly, and now it appeared he would never have any of his own.

Lyon said earnestly, "But—what's wrong with that? It is what every man dreams of, isn't it? To find a lady he can care for? To have a family?''

"Yes. But—sometimes people want it so much they—sort of, mistake love of the dream for—for . . . Well, there are different types of—of loving, I think. Sometimes—not often, I grant you,

43

but, sometimes people share a devotion so equal, so intense, that from the very beginning they are like . . . the two parts of one—whole.'' His eyes had become sad, his voice remote. ''Yolande and Craig have that. Truly, a gift from . . .'' He broke off, his face very red. ''Jupiter, how dashed sober we are! You have made me talk a lot of nonsense. Now, you shall tell me— do you mean to—offer for Josie when she comes home?''

Lyon groaned. ''I know how *I* feel, Dev. But—I've still some years of work before I can start my own practice. Guy has settled a generous sum on me, as you know. We'd not starve. But—I cannot tell whether *she* feels— She's so admired. So lovely and bright and—and altogether adorable. And—my fear is that . . . she may choose Fontaine.''

''Fontaine?''

Startled, Lyon saw Devenish's face transformed. The eyes were slits of rage, the fine features flushed. A voice he scarcely recognized snarled, ''Has Elliot Fontaine been slithering around Josie?''

''Why—yes. How could you not know? They met at the Bolsters' Spring ball.''

''I know that! And—since?''

''Here and there, I suppose. He's been away of late, but he is come back, and you may see him everywhere. He's very popular.''

''And very cunning, damn him! I have never once seen him hanging about her. By Gad, I'd better not!'' Devenish stood and stared southward. ''Is he friendly with the Drummonds, do you know?''

Standing also, watching the savage wrath of the man beside him, Lyon said uneasily, ''I cannot say. But I heard that he and Josie met again when you were in Town a few weeks back, and—''

''And she said nothing! The baggage! She knew damned well I'd have his liver out, if—''

''Dev!'' Lyon put one hand on the other man's sleeve, then recoiled before the murderous anger he faced. ''Lord, man! What is it? What have you against him?''

Devenish glared at him in silence, then said in a more normal

44

tone, "I know him, is all. I never dreamed he'd dare cast his filthy eyes at Josie, for she's quite beneath his touch."

"I do not see that!"

"You may not, but he does. If he wants her, it's not as his wife, of that I do assure you!"

"Why the hell not? She's been gently bred up! Her birth may not be—"

"Definitely not. He's from an ancient and proud house. He's not the kind to marry a girl with no background."

Stung, and defensive of this apparent impugning of his adored lady, Lyon snapped, "Then you should not object to *my* offer! I'll marry her tomorrow, if she'll have me, and be proud to do so. We should suit—we're both gutter-bred."

The words were no sooner out of his mouth than he was gasping as his neckcloth was seized in a grip of steel. An enraged glare scorched at his startled face; a deadly voice hissed, "Damn your eyes! Do not *dare* so name her!"

Lyon's powerful hand closed around the fine-boned wrist, but even his youthful might could not loosen that grip. The neckcloth was strangling him. "Dev!" he gasped out. "For the love— of heaven!"

With a smothered curse, Devenish relaxed his hold and turned away.

Grasping his throat, Lyon said unsteadily, "That leaves little doubt of *my* hopes . . . does it not! Good day—to you, sir!" Shaking with fury, he prepared to mount up.

An urgent hand gripped his arm. Whipping back one fist, prepared for battle, he was confronted by a remorseful smile. Devenish said humbly, "My poor fellow. Please accept my apologies. I'd no intent— It was just the thought of Fontaine, daring to— Lyon—forgive. Please! You must know that if she should choose you, I'd never stand in your way."

The dark face lit up. Lyon gave a whoop. Devenish was seized and whirled around. Laughing, he cried, "Desist, you blasted madman!"

Lyon obliged, and they walked on, side by side, leading the horses. Elated, Lyon cried, "What a day this has been! Dev—

45

when may I speak to her? I know you believe her to be sixteen, though I've often thought—"

"Yes. Many others have thought the same. It seems—that I was mistaken." With an effort, he added, "By—by two years, at least, probably."

Halting, staring at him, Lyon gasped, "Two . . . Then—then she would be *eighteen*? My God! Dev—do you mean it? You know that means—"

"That you had better choose your moment carefully, you great oaf. The fact I allow it does not mean you've won her, you—" He was interrupted for another outburst of wild exuberance, so that it was some moments before Lyon was sufficiently calm to be able to ask, "Will you tell me now what you have against Elliot Fontaine?"

Devenish's face clouded. He said grittily, "Nothing I can speak of, for I've no proof. I take it you find him unexceptionable."

"I've met him only a time or two, but he's always been pleasant. More pleasant than many."

"Oh, he's pleasant—damn him!"

Lyon eyed him askance. "This wouldn't be one of your clairvoyant starts?"

Devenish growled, fumed, but finally said irritably, "To an extent. I cannot abide the man! There's that about him makes my skin creep." He knew Lyon was staring at him, and went on impatiently, "Oh, I know it sounds mad, but there it is. As for your being shunned—I'd hoped it would be better when Guy moved here from Sussex. Has it not improved at all?"

"At first it was better. Now it's worse. I suppose the word is spreading. Lord knows how Wellington ever thought to keep the business quiet. The whispers are becoming louder, but all people seem to know for certain is that Claude plotted against the crown. They don't know how damnably close he came to murdering the Regent and wrecking the whole country. If *that* ever becomes public knowledge"—he shook his head, troubled—"they'll likely take my poor guv'nor out and lynch him!"

"They might, at that. And there'd be precious little use trying

46

to explain to a mindless mob that Guy was crippled because he opposed his brother.''

After another pause during which each man was occupied with inner forebodings, Devenish asked, ''How does Guy go on, by the way?''

''What a gudgeon I am!'' His face bright again, Lyon said, ''He can walk with only *one* crutch now, Dev! I was never so pleased!''

''I can well imagine! How splendid! Belmont told me you were trying some new treatments, but—''

''Belmont?'' Lyon halted to search his face. ''Did you see Belmont whilst you were in Town? Dammit—that leg's troubling you again! I told you last year you should—''

''It shall have to trouble me a deal more before I'll allow you to hack it off, you ruthless butcher! Do not be sharpening your scimitar on my account!''

Lyon smiled, but his eyes were worried. ''It should not distress you so after all this time. What did his lordship say?''

''That you're the best man he's ever trained, and you've the finest hands he ever saw.''

Flushed with pleasure, Lyon stammered, ''He *really* said that? By my immortal soul! I—I cannot believe it! He always makes me feel such a block! Oh, by Jove! Wait till I tell Josie!''

''She'll be proud of you, certainly—as we all are! Well, rapscallion, I think I'll head for home. Do you come with me?''

Since his beloved had not yet returned, Lyon declined this offer, eager to tell his parent Lord Belmont's opinion of him. They parted, therefore, Devenish sending word to Guy Sanguinet that he and his adopted son would be expected to arrive at Devencourt within a day or two, to stay for a week at least.

En route home, Devenish held Santana to a steady canter. The wind was growing stronger and the big black, still full of energy, chose to be alarmed when leaves fluttered past, and to shy at a rabbit that scuttled across his path. Lost in thought, Devenish paid no heed to these frivolities. Lyon's declaration had not surprised him. For a long time it had been obvious that the boy was deeply smitten. And there was no doubt that Josie was fond of him. Striving to be objective, Devenish was forced to admit

Lyon was not the mate he would have chosen for her. But to cling to the conviction that only a Prince of the blood would be worthy was to be unrealistic. If Lyon was as brilliant as Belmont claimed, and Lord knows that crusty old curmudgeon was not one to praise lightly, Lyon would become a great surgeon. Perhaps, even win himself a title someday. Josie would enjoy the good things of life. Devenish gazed unseeingly at the darkening clouds. If she chose him . . . He pulled back his sagging shoulders. She must choose someone, after all, and God knows it would be better that she choose Lyon than that bastard Fontaine! The murderous rage returned. By God, but if she'd not written by tomorrow, he'd post off to Sussex and remove her from that satyr's vicinity!

He touched his spurs to Santana's sides. The stallion's ears pricked up, he gave an eager snort, and they were away, racing along beside the curve of the river, but passed unexpectedly by a chestnut mare who shot from a grove of aspens, ears flat against her head and eyes rolling. Santana neighed indignation as Devenish reined him aside barely in time to avoid a collision. Uneasy, Devenish set the black in pursuit of the mare. She was riderless and panicked, but no match for the power of the stallion. Gradually they shortened the distance until they were level with her rump, then had passed the dainty sidesaddle and blowing mane. Devenish leaned perilously to grab at the trailing reins. On the second attempt he caught one and, adjusting Santana's stride to a nicety, began to pull the mare down, until he had brought her to a standstill.

Dismounting, he tethered the jealous stallion to a bush and approached the mare. She danced away, tossing her head up, her eyes big with fear. He spoke to her gently, stroked the foam-splashed neck, and as usual, his way with animals prevailed. In a few moments she was nuzzling against his shoulder, her shudders quite gone and her breathing normal. "You're a pretty creature," he told her. "But my large friend yonder is becoming apoplectic, and besides, we must find the lady who was riding you."

Accordingly, he mounted again and, leading the mare, turned southwards once more. When he came to the aspen grove, he rode cautiously in amongst the dappled shade of the trees. His calls won no response, but after a short while he was dismayed to discern the prone figure of a lady.

From the moment his broken engagement had become public knowledge seven years ago, he had been an object of considerable interest to the females of the south country. He was far from conceited, but would have been a fool not to know that he had the kind of male beauty that drew women of every age, style, and circumstance. He had also known for some years that fate had once again dealt him a bitter hand, and was resigned to the life of a bachelor. His *affaires de coeur* had been conducted with discretion and were for the most part of a fleeting nature, although one of his loves had proven constant. He was deeply fond of this lady, who was several years his senior, and they enjoyed a relationship of mutual affection and respect. Despite his elusive tactics with the marriageable ladies, however, and the fact that he chose to spend much of the year in the country, the lures continued to be thrown out. Unfailingly courteous, Devenish knew only scorn for the type of woman who fancied herself in love with him only because of his looks, while having not the least idea of his nature. On a few unhappy occasions he had been almost trapped by determined ladies, and had once been forced into a duel when a lovelorn creature had invaded his hotel room and been discovered there by her outraged spouse. It was, therefore, with no little apprehension that he dismounted and, tethering the horses, hastened towards the figure huddled face down amongst the ferns.

She was a statuesque female, and for a moment he was appalled by the suspicion that Isabella had once more levelled her guns in his direction. But he saw as he drew nearer that the tumbled curls were red instead of black. Much relieved, he knelt beside her. She did not move, but she was breathing. Her habit was very disordered. He could see a good deal of one shapely leg clad in a knee-length silk stocking, above which were the lacy frills of a pink chemise, and he bent instinctively to pull the rumpled habit over these embarrassments.

"What are you doing?"

He jumped guiltily. "I was—er, restoring your garments. Are you much hurt, ma'am?"

"My—dignity is, certainly." She had a low, musical voice, and striving to lift her head, said, "Oh, dear. I am so . . . dizzy."

He watched her anxiously, sure he should be doing something. Brightening, he told her that he had just parted from a doctor friend, and would ride after him.

"Oh, no!" The titian curls stirred agitatedly. "Pray do not leave me!" One gloved hand was propped against the leafy ground, and she raised her head.

Devenish reached out to aid her, but hesitated. She gave a little sound of pain, and he abandoned timidity and lifted her, turning her carefully until she lay in his arms. She was very white, and a small cut high on her forehead had sent a trickle of blood down to her right eye. He saw with relief that she was no schoolroom miss, and that she seemed more dazed than hurt. She was quite lovely in a serene way, with long grey eyes, flawless skin, and regular if not remarkable features. He was considerably aghast when she blinked at him, and then said a weak but amused, "Oh! It's . . . you!"

"My apologies. I—er, cannot seem to recall . . ."

"I am Mrs. Bliss," she provided, her voice a little steadier. "I have seen you about your—estate. I had, in fact, planned to—to call upon your daughter." She blinked again and, scanning the finely chiselled features bent above her, said with a twinkle, "Oh, dear, but—she cannot be your daughter, can she?"

He grinned, warming to this forthright lady. "She is my ward, ma'am. And—alas, I am still bewildered. Which is of no importance. Pray tell me if you are hurt anywhere."

She moved tentatively, said that everything seemed workable, then added, "Oh, you have found my horse! She is very well mannered, but a quite big branch came down and knocked me from the saddle, and she ran off, I suppose."

"I wonder you were not killed! Where did it strike you?"

"Luckily, the main branch did not, but the smaller limbs and all the leaves caught me. I think I can stand now, if you would be so kind as to help, Mr. Devenish."

He did so, handling her with such care that she leaned on him without the least shyness. He supported her briefly until she could regain her sense of balance and, with her head against his neckcloth, she murmured, "You are very good, sir. I should tell you that I am—newly come into Gloucestershire. My husband was Major Percy Bliss, and fell at Waterloo."

A widow! He tensed and murmured polite regrets.

A low ripple of laughter sounded. Lifting her head, she looked him straight in the eye and said whimsically, "Have I alarmed you? Pray be easy. I have no designs on you. Oh, dear! Now I have shocked you. But you see, I have heard how you are—er, hunted." He flushed, but she saw the smile creep back into those incredibly blue eyes, and said candidly, "And you are too young for me. Besides which—I really did fall."

He could not restrain a chuckle, but made her sit on a convenient fallen treetrunk while he dabbed his handkerchief gently at her brow. "One is always supposed to have water available at such a moment," he said ruefully. "What a clodpole I am to have no least idea where there is any, closer than the river. May I ask where you are staying, Mrs. Bliss?"

"Not far out of your way," she replied. "I stay with my eldest brother, Sir William Little."

"Oh—begad!" gasped Devenish.

Chapter 4

"Welcome home, miss," quavered the butler, beaming at Josie's radiance.

"Thank you, Wolfe." Starry-eyed, she looked around the vast chamber of the old wing that was again the Great Hall. "How lovely everything is, is it not, Pan?"

"We are weary," uttered Mrs. Grenfell austerely, and ascended the stairs, supported by the ever-attentive Klaus.

"Lady Godiva!" exclaimed Josie, bending to stroke the pig who had trotted through the assorted humans gathered around this pleasant girl, and was emitting piercing squeals as she butted her head against Josie's skirts.

"She's missed you," said Mrs. Robinson, her faded eyes bright.

"We all have," agreed Wolfe. "The master, especially."

Josie straightened. "Where is he?"

"Out, miss," put in Cornish, carrying in her dressing case and valise.

"I wanted to surprise him. Oh, never say he's gone to fetch me?"

"Just out riding, miss," said Wolfe, fixing the footman with a fierce eye.

"Santana," said the footman. "Shouldn't of."

"You may take Miss Storm's things upstairs, Cornish," said Wolfe awfully.

"Right, mate." Cornish made for the stairs.

Watching him, amused, Josie asked, "Is Santana not in good condition?"

"Fresh as a daisy," said Wolfe.

" 'E's a 'orrid 'ack," supplied Cornish from the stairs. "And the guv's been a bit chin sunk."

"That—will—do!" decreed Wolfe, so emphatically that he rocked himself off balance and teetered back and forth.

Frightened, Josie said, "Mr. Devenish is not ill?"

"No, no, miss," soothed the housekeeper, walking to the stairs with her.

"Just a trifle out of temper," contributed Wolfe, more or less keeping pace on Josie's other side.

Cornish stuck his head around the corner of the first floor landing. "And 'e 'ad a bloomin' great row wiv Sir Willyum!"

"Oh, no! About the road, Wolfe?"

"I couldn't say, miss," piped the butler, his murderous gaze on the landing.

"I think it was on account of the master wouldn't have that poacher transported," said Mrs. Robinson. "Awful hard man is the Squire. Went out of here with his face so red as any lobster. Roaring, he was. And the master laughing at him."

"Oh dear, oh dear! I knew I should have come home sooner." Josie hurried up the stairs, but paused to call, "Do we set out extra covers tonight, Wolfe?"

"I think not, miss. Though the master said Colonel Leith might be coming to us very shortly."

"Oh, lovely." Josie hummed as she hurried on to the front suite two flights above the Great Hall which Devenish had caused to be remodelled for her birthday last year; a date she had fixed as May 20th, that having been the date in 1816 on which she had first entered his life, and when—to her way of thinking—her own life had begun.

It was a delightful suite, decorated in shades of pink with white and fuchsia accents. The parlour was spacious, there was a well-equipped dressing room, an adjoining bedchamber for her abigail, and a large and luxurious bedchamber. Josie proceeded to the latter room, which was dominated by a graceful canopied bed, its pink and white brocade curtains tied back with fuchsia

53

satin ropes. It was a room of thick rugs, fine satinwood furniture, highly polished random-width plank floors, and tastefully hung small oils and watercolours. Above the marble mantelpiece was an exceptionally fine print of a badger, and the air carried the faint fragrance of Josie's favourite scent, *Essence de Printemps*. She closed her eyes for a second and breathed it in happily, then ran to her bedside table and took up the miniature she had so longed to have with her in Sussex.

Devenish had loathed every moment that he had sat for Coleridge Bryce to paint his portrait. The young peer was in great demand, the Top Ten Thousand having discovered to their delight that the talented artist was one of their own. He was also a wizard of the canvas and, looking down at her guardian's pictured face and the lurking smile Colley had captured so cleverly, Josie's eyes blurred. "Dev . . ." she whispered.

"Brought yer hot water, miss," said Fletcher, hurrying into the room with a large copper jug. The gaunt, middle-aged woman looked as though she would be more at home in a Billingsgate fish market than wearing the neat uniform of an abigail. Her husband had been killed in the Peterloo riots; her child had died of influenza and, driven to desperation, she had turned to prostitution until she had lost one eye in a tavern brawl. That disaster had ended her unhappy career and she had been arrested for stealing bread when Josie, one of the customers in the bakery, had interceded for her. Devenish had come nigh to fainting when he discovered that his ward intended to make the battered wreck of a woman her abigail, and had, in a rare display of anger, put his foot down and said a flat No! Josie had looked up at him, her schoolgirl face unwontedly grave. "But do you see, dearest Dev," she had said, "she is what I might have become, but for you." He had been appalled, but even so it had been one of their longer tussles before he had thrown up his hands and agreed to Maisie Fletcher being added to what he privately referred to as his *ménage bizarre*.

Fletcher, who would cheerfully have done bloody murder for her young mistress, was quite aware of the reservations of the head of the house and kept well out of his way until the time that Josie had been stricken with diphtheria. Fletcher's devotion had won the terror-stricken man's heart, and when he had attempted to thank her, the weary voice whispering, "I'm dirt under her pretty feet, but—I do so love her, Mr. Devenish," had compelled him to say, "It is the best thing any of us can give her, m'dear. She had precious little of it in her childhood, Lord knows," and there had been no more suggestions that Fletcher obtain employment elsewhere.

The following half-hour was devoted to ensuring that Mr. Devenish would be pleased by his daughter's appearance when he returned. When their efforts were completed, Josie surveyed her reflection in the standing mirror. She had chosen a gown of light blue taffeta, the bell-shaped skirts scalloped at the hem that was in the daring new ankle length. White embroidery lent elegance to the skirt and was repeated around the low neckline. Fletcher had pulled the corset laces very tight, with the result that Josie's waist was tiny, enhancing the rich curve of her ample bosom. Her gaze lifted to include her features. Care and love and good food had changed her immeasurably from the half-starved waif Devenish had rescued, but she knew she would never be a beauty, no matter what kind gentlemen like Lyon and Guy and John Drummond and Fontaine said to the contrary. Still—Dev had no cause to be ashamed of presenting her as his ward.

Fletcher added a small spray of white silken flowers to her curls, and draped a crocheted wool shawl about her shoulders. "It's a sight late in the season to wear such a light frock, miss," she scolded.

"I know, but I do so want to look my best tonight."

Josie hurried downstairs, her heart singing because she was home. When he came, she would make him laugh by telling him of the wrangling that had gone on between John and Lord Elliot, and he would tell her about all that had happened at Devencourt, and they would have such a lovely evening. She must go to the kitchen and see— She checked, hearing horses outside.

A lackey hastened across the Great Hall, his elegant self reflecting in the polished parquet floors that had been laid over the original flags. He swung the door open, the resultant inrush of cold air causing Josie to gather her shawl closer. Perhaps it was Dev. She ran lightly down two more steps, then stopped.

It was indeed her guardian. And, once again, he held a lovely woman in his arms, the lady protesting in a rich, amused voice that she was perfectly able to walk.

"Nonsense," said Devenish, smiling down at her. "You shall be sent home in a carriage, ma'am, and—" The grey eyes of the lady he carried shifted past him, their expression such that he turned to follow her gaze. "Josie!" he gasped, and set Mrs. Bliss on her feet, but kept his arm about her.

Having taken in the shocked disbelief of the girl who watched them, Mrs. Bliss glanced at her escort. Almost at once, his face reflected no more than a deep affection, but she had seen a brief, transforming glow, and her fine brows arched a trifle higher. She disengaged herself gently.

Scarcely noticing she had done so, Devenish strode to reach up and take his ward's outstretched hands. "You're home!" he said delightedly. "And—let me look at you—how lovely you are!"

Josie said nothing, but launched herself into his arms. He laughed and whirled her around, and she laughed up at him. Seething.

"You little rascal," said Devenish, eyes alight as he drank her in. "You should have let me know you were coming."

"So I see," she said, with a glance to the quiet bystander.

"Oh! Good Lord!" He turned about. "My deepest apologies, ma'am." He led Josie forward. "Mrs. Bliss, may I present my ward—Josephine Storm. Josie, this lady had an accident, so I—"

"Brought her home," Josie interpolated sweetly, as she dropped a small curtsy. "But of course. As usual."

An appreciative twinkle lit the stranger's quite horridly lovely eyes. Josie looked to Don Juan Devenish. His lips were compressed, his eyes empty, his brows slightly raised in the austere hauteur that meant she would hear about this later.

He said with cool aplomb, "Yes. For she is Sir William's sister. Perhaps you will be so good as to help her. She was hurt."

Horrified, Josie noted the cut over the white brow, and the creased and torn condition of the expensive riding habit. She felt her face flame, and ran to put her arm about their unexpected guest. "How dreadful for you, poor soul! You shall come up to my bedchamber and rest while we prepare the carriage. Dev— please have hot water sent up, and some lint and basillicum powder and—oh, Mrs. Robinson will know. Can you walk, ma'am?"

Assuring her that she could walk, Mrs. Bliss was nonetheless glad of the strong young arm about her. Nor did she demur when she was led into the pretty bedchamber and required to lie down. Later, when Josie had sent her abigail running for some hot tea and a little brandy, and the housekeeper had brought the required medical supplies and been sent off, Mrs. Bliss expressed her apologies for "being such a great nuisance."

"As if you are," said Josie, carefully bathing the small cut.

Faith Bliss watched the rapt young face, and smiled because of the tip of the tongue that hovered upon her nurse's upper lip.

"To think you are sister to Sir William," murmured Josie, concentrating. "Have you been for very long at the Manor?"

"You are thinking I should have called on you. Well—I did start to do so. Only . . ." Her words trailed off.

Josie glanced at her, curious. "Only I was away?"

"Your—er, guardian has a certain . . . reputation," Mrs. Bliss evaded.

At once Josie stiffened. "Indeed, ma'am?"

"For being pursued," went on Mrs. Bliss demurely. "I can readily see why. And—I am a widow." She saw the fierce jut of the little chin, and the flash in the dark eyes, and could appreciate why her brother had told her that Miss Storm was a most taking little lass. She sighed, and appended with a mournful air, "Were I but ten years younger . . ."

Both relieved and obliquely ruffled, Josie said, "My guardian is older than he looks, ma'am!" And, realizing what she had implied, dropped the cloth, her hands flying to her mouth in a way her guest thought most endearing. "Oh! I am so sorry! I— I only meant—Dev is three and thirty, not—"

"Is he so?" said Mrs. Bliss with a giggle. "I'd not have set

57

him a day over twenty-seven, despite that fascinating grey band in his hair. But—my dear, you waste your embarrassment. I am four and thirty, and have pinned my hopes on finding a gentleman at least five years my senior, as was my dear late husband."

A wistful sadness had touched her eyes. Responding to it with all her tender nature, Josie touched her hand consolingly. "How awful it must be to suddenly be widowed."

"It is very bad. But Percy's death was not really sudden. I had, in fact, expected it for some time." She realized that the great brown eyes were very wide, and went on in a lighter fashion, "I have—occasionally—an unfortunate gift of prescience. My husband was a born soldier and I felt . . . almost from the start, that we had very little time. But, he died as he would have wished, and with great valour, leading his men in a charge against impossible odds to cover the retreat of a gun carriage."

Josie felt chilled, and shivered. "Leaving you alone." She completed her first aid, and said, "I was rude when you arrived. I do apologize. I have a wretched tongue."

"Do you? How lovely. So do I."

They exchanged smiles, then Fletcher hurried back in with the tea and put the tray on a nearby table. Watching Josie measure a small amount of brandy into a teacup, Mrs. Bliss asked, "Will you be my friend? In spite of my ferocious brother?"

"Oh, yes, if you please! Is Sir William ferocious with *you*, ma'am?"

"You must call me Faith. And William is seldom really cross with me. And if he is, I can manage him. But—he is difficult. All men are, do not you think?"

"Yes, indeed. Dev is hopeless. If you *knew* the trouble I am put to only to keep him from making a disastrous match."

"I quite understand. I heard he had only barely eluded Bella Scott-Matthias."

They looked at each other, then laughed.

"Are you acquainted, Faith? She is lovely, but—"

"But horrid," said Mrs. Bliss, entering willingly into this character assassination. "Just a little milk and two spoons of sugar, if you please."

"She always manages to make me feel a child of the gutter,"

said Josie, complying, and handing over the cup. "I am, you know. I was stolen by gypsies when I was still in leading strings. Dev thinks, though he is quite mistaken, that I was about eight when he found me in 1816. He rescued me from them." Her eyes became dreamily remote. Stirring her tea, she murmured absently, "And brought me here, although he really didn't want to. At first. But he has been so good to me. So generous and kind."

"Oh—you poor girl," cried Mrs. Bliss, genuinely horrified. "Have you no idea who your parents were? Your family?"

"Dev is my family. And—I have many adopted aunts and uncles and cousins, who spoil me dreadfully."

"Well, that's good. You must be very grateful to him. Even if he is—difficult."

"He's not—really. Just hopeless about . . . some things."

"Such as—finding the right lady. Have you—er, anyone in mind?"

Josie glanced at her sharply. Mrs. Bliss had lowered her tea-cup, and the wise grey eyes were very grave. She felt her cheeks burn, took a rather reckless gulp of her tea, and coughed. "Well—no. Not yet. But she will have to be gentle and—and understand his moods, and turn his temper when he flies into the boughs over some trifling thing. It is really very easy, you know; you just have to make him laugh. And to take care of him, for he will never admit he is ill or has done too much. Just—make him happy." She stared rather fixedly at the tray and was silent.

Mrs. Bliss watched her, then murmured, "And—is he happy now? At Devencourt?"

Paling, Josie's gaze flew to her face. "It is—his home. His birthright. Only—he fears it. He always has. Years ago, when I was just a little girl, I heard him talking with Tris Leith—they've been bosom bows forever. He said, "Desolation, despair, Devencourt!" I'll never forget the way he said it. He sounded so bitter, and that's not Dev's way. But his uncle, his mama's twin, was like that, they say. In touch with forces other people do not know about. Oh, ma'am! What is it? Can you also sense something here? Tell me, I beg you!"

Faith Bliss found that her hands had become icy cold. She set aside her cup, remembering her first sight of this fine old house, and the dreadful premonition that had overtaken her. She'd felt the power of it, and she had run away, returning home to lie to her unimaginative brother that she had decided to respect his wishes and not leave a card at Devencourt. She had managed to frighten the girl; those great eyes were searching her face. Somehow, she managed a smile. "I do sense something, I'll not deny. But I could not tell you what it is. Perhaps it will come to me if I visit you again. I am allowed to do so, I hope?"

"Of course, oh, of course! I am so glad you have come, for most of my friends live some distance off. Dare I come and see you? Oh dear, I suppose not. They quarrelled again today. Did you know it?"

"Yes. That was why I rid out without a groom. I was so angry with my brother. But now I really must go, for the silly man will be quite frantic. You'd not guess it, but he dotes on me."

With a naiveté that caused Faith to chuckle, Josie said, "Does he? Then he cannot be all bad! Now, if you do not feel well enough to walk, you shall be carried. But you must meet Lady Godiva, and the cats—we have several, for a friend of ours has a dear cat named Little Patches, and we were given one of her kittens. And now, since she was a girl kitten, we have several more. But they are all nice—not at all catty like—" She twinkled conspiratorially as Fletcher came back in and held the door for them. "Like a certain femme fatale. Would you please help Mrs. Bliss on that side, Fletcher? Is it not the strangest thing, Faith, that brothers and sisters can be so different? I mean—Lady Isabella so unpleasant, and her brother such a jolly and dear person?"

Faith tensed, slightly frowning, but did not interrupt the ingenuous discourse.

Having said her goodbyes to her new friend, Josie repaired to the kitchens, where she had a discussion with Signor della Casa regarding desserts for dinner, Devenish being almost as partial to sweets as was Jeremy Bolster. Returning to the Great Hall, she wandered down the east wing, looking into the bookroom and two saloons without success. Her heart sank. He had either gone out, up to his bedchamber, or into his study. Of the three, she most feared the study, for that was, he often asserted, male territory and inviolate, and it was, besides, where he always retreated when he meant to scold. She eased the door open and peeped inside. He was there, sure enough, one elbow resting on the desk, chin in fist, as he stared at a vase of flowers put there by Mrs. Robinson, since there were far too many blooms for the vase.

She crept inside, closed the door very softly, and flew to put her hands over his eyes. He started up, but she kept her hands tight, saying, "Now it is of no use for you to take me to task, Papa, for I had no idea she was a guest."

He removed her hands, and turned to fix her with his stern look.

"I thought," she went on hurriedly, "she was one of your light—"

"Jo-*sie!*" He removed the white cat from the top drawer.

"Well, I did. And how am I to know? There are so many."

Her glinting eyes teased him. His lips quivered responsively, but he sprang up, foiling her attempt to sit on his lap. She scowled, but then occupied his big chair, and curled up in it, beaming at him like a triumphant imp, as he told her.

"Well, it is no use your pretending not to be pleased because I am come home," she said, as he perched on the desk beside her, "for I know you are. The servants told me you were—er, 'chin-sunk.' "

He groaned. "Cornish! Josie—how ever did we acquire such a—er—"

"Prigging cove?" she supplied innocently.

Irked, he said, "I have asked you not to use cant."

"And I have asked you not to be forever flinging your gloves into the faces of other gentlemen!"

His angry eyes fell away. He muttered, "I have not done such a thing. Now, tell me of your visit. How are the Drummonds? Did you see my Uncle Alastair?"

"No, for he was in Paris on some business. Pandora went to Aspenhill to stay with Constance. The Drummonds are all well, and send their love. And why did *you* not escort Mrs. Bliss to Oak Manor?''

"Because it would have been to rub salt into the wound." He chuckled. "Poor Little is going to be fairly slobbering with rage, for he left here vowing all kinds of terrible consequences, and will now fancy himself indebted to me. Besides, Mrs. G. is well able to handle the old Friday face if he cuts up rough. He'll do well to watch his tongue with that lady! Indeed, Yolande said—" He checked, wishing he'd not mentioned the visit that had ended so awkwardly, and went over to let the white cat out.

"Yes, Papa? What did the beauteous Mrs. Tyndale have to say?"

"She said she wondered you did not strangle me for having chose Mrs. Grenfell as your—duenna." He grinned unrepentantly and returned to her side.

"What nonsense. I love Pan—she's a darling."

"My God! A darling dragon! But never mind all that. Tell me about your visit."

So she did, making him laugh with her tales until she said, "And Lord Fontaine came, and you should—"

Devenish leapt to his feet. "The devil he did! I might have known! How often have you met that"—his lip curled—"that noble gentleman?"

Astonished, she stammered, "Why—I have known him since—since I left the schoolroom, Dev."

"A whole two years," he sneered.

"Only because you would insist I was *fourteen* when all the world knew I was eighteen!"

"Including our nobleman, evidently! Continue, if you please. What is your—relationship?"

She stared at him. *"Relationship?* My heavens! What would you think?"

"I would think you should know better than to associate with such a rake! And I shall ask your darling dragon if she is wits to let for allowing you—"

Really annoyed now, she flared, "To do—what? Converse at the home of mutual friends or relations with a gentleman of the first stare, who may be seen anywhere?"

His eyes savage, Devenish growled, "He'd best not be seen *here*, or I'll—"

"Run him through, I suppose?" But in spite of her irritation, she knew his hot temper and she knew Elliot Fontaine's reputation, and her heart beat faster. "What stuff! Duels are out of fashion today, my Gaffer, and—"

"With swords, perhaps. But there are always pistols, thank God!"

"How can you use the Lord's name in connection with such savagery? And why should you be so savage? Dev . . . ?" She stood, and reached up to take his averted face between her hands and turn it back to her. For a moment, angry blue eyes met anxious brown ones, while the clock ticked softly, and the deepening chill in the room went quite unnoticed. Then Devenish moved her hands away and said in a rasp of a voice, "I'll not have him putting his slimy eyes on you! I warn you, Josie. Do not lead him on, or—"

"Lead him . . . on?" She walked a step or two away, saying with her back to him, "When have you seen me lead a gentleman on?"

"A hundred times," he said with harsh inaccuracy. Furiously indignant, she spun to face him. "Oh, I grant you don't know you do it. You're so dashed innocent, you've no notion—But—a man like Fontaine! I'd think you had more sense!"

"What a disappointment I must be, dear sir! Elliot Fontaine is well born, well liked, very rich—"

"There's where you're out! *He* is not. His father is!"

"Besides which," she swept on angrily, "*I* have heard not one word against the gentleman!"

"That's no surprise! He presents two faces to the world!"

"And—you have seen the other face?"

How straight she stood. How regally she faced him. He coloured and looked away. "Not—exactly. But—but I can sense the kind of man he is. And I suspect—" And again, helplessly, he was silent.

Her chin lifted even higher. She said—disdainfully, "You *sense* and you *suspect*—and for these nebulous notions I am to abandon my friendship with a most charming—"

He fairly sprang to grip her wrist and jerk her close to him. "Do you think I say such things lightly? Pay heed to me, little elf. If I catch him trying to fix his interest with you—"

"Fix . . . his interest? But—but you have said I am too young to be thinking of such things."

He released her, took up his quill pen, and stared down at it. "I—er, had supposed you to be—so. But, I have come to think I was—mistaken."

Unutterably shocked, she studied his averted profile. "Do you say—my arguments have at last won you over, dear sir?"

For possibly the first time in his life, Devenish began to tidy his desk. "That," he mumbled, "and—and other things."

Instinctively, her hand went to her bosom.

"No, no!" he said. Then, scarlet, added, "Well—I meant, what *others* said of it—I mean—of your probable age."

"I see. Then—you think I am of an age to—to receive offers?" She waited for a denial, but none came. Her heart sinking, she went on, "In which case you should perhaps give me a list of—of acceptable gentlemen, so that I may not—disgrace you further."

The paper he held was crushed convulsively. "For Lord's sake! As if you have done so!"

"But—you just said . . ."

"Oh. Fontaine. Yes—well, *his* pretensions you must certainly depress." His jaw set. "Or I will! As for the rest—"

She returned to stand very closely before him and prompt meekly, "Yes, Papa?"

Reluctantly, he looked down into her upturned, trusting little face. His own softened. He said, "You roast me, you vixen. You know very well."

"I am confused," she said with a sigh. "To have been sixteen this morning, and one and twenty this afternoon is—unsettling. As always, I need your guidance dearest—ancient."

He wrenched away again and said disjointedly, "How may I know who you will—like. There are many fine young fellas your own age. That nice Van Lindsay boy; or Freddie Hilby. Or—what about young Drummond? Or—Lyon? Now, there's a—"

Josie had retreated to the window during this summation, and now interrupted, "So you have heard of John's attentions to me."

A pause. Then he said coolly, "No. He—likes you, does he?"

"He says he does. And I like him. Very much."

"Oh." He leaned back against the desk, watching his ward's slender but shapely figure outlined against the window. Josie and John Drummond . . . "Well then," he said heartily, "that should do very nicely, I'd think."

She whirled and flew to stand before him, crouching a little, her eyes blazing.

Startled, he drew back.

"Horrid! Evil man!" she hissed.

"N-Now—Josie—you have plagued me to—to admit you are older. And you said you liked the boy, and—"

"And of a sudden you can scarce wait to push me to the altar, can you! You cannot *wait* to be rid of your—your encumbrance!"

"Encumbrance, is it!" But her lip trembled; he saw the glitter of tears and, groaning, pulled her into his arms and, stroking her hair, murmured, "My little elf—how can you even *think* such stuff?"

"B-because," she sobbed, "I know what—what a trial I've been to you."

"Never!" He put her from him, smiling into her tear-wet eyes. "You were never naughty, or sulked, or went into tantrums. Or very seldom. How I shall go on without . . ." He frowned, and stopped, wondering why he was saying such things when he had determined to behave quite differently.

"I am so glad, Dev," she said, hugging him tight. "Then we may go on comfortably. Just as we are."

"We-ell, yes. Until I—er, become a benedick, at all events."

She all but leapt back. *"What?"* She searched his face. "Have you—fixed on a lady? Who? I have been hearing whispers of the infamous Isabella."

"There is nothing in the least smoky about the lady," he said loftily. "Even if her brother is unspeakable. Bella is"—he turned to his untidy desk once more—"very lovely, and does, I feel sure, return my regard, so—" His words were cut off as a cush-

65

ion bounced from his head. "Wretched brat!" Grinning, he turned on her and snatched away the cushion. She was at him in a flash, her darting hands tugging at his neckcloth, tearing the handkerchief from his pocket, seizing a handful of flowers and jamming them into his thick hair, eluding his desperate attempts to restrain her, until he caught her at last and, weak with laughter, they clung to each other.

"Colonel the Honourable Tristram Leith," announced Wolfe imperturbably.

∽ Chapter 5 ∾

"Tris!" Rather red in the face, Devenish greeted their guest, both hands outstretched. "Welcome! Welcome!"

Returning his strong clasp, Tristram Leith's fine eyes, alight with amusement, flashed to Josie's blushes. Badly wounded at the Battle of Waterloo, Leith's face was still streaked on one side with scars that failed to render him less than a fine-looking man. Before the battle, his looks had been such as to reduce London's ladies to sighful yearnings. The scars had faded now; his thick hair was near-black, his dark eyes keen, his tall frame as lean and supple as it had been when Devenish first had met him several weeks after the battle. He wore a well-cut riding coat and tight-fitting moleskins, and his topboots gleamed. He had no need to apologize for his appearance, but said, "Had I known you intended to array yourself for my benefit, I'd have worn something more formal."

Devenish scanned him uncertainly.

Leith removed a blossom from the untidy fair hair. "A fine way to behave," he scolded, *sotto voce*, then turned to bow over Josie's hand and drop a kiss onto her uplifted cheek. "Lovelier each time I see you, Milady Elf," he said with a fond smile. "You'd best take care, Dev, else you'll have some lucky fellow taking your ward off your hands."

"Just as I've been telling her," said Devenish blandly.

"He has, in fact, been instructing me on whom I am to choose," Josie explained.

"Oh, has he?" Leith chuckled. "So that was the cause for the uproar. Lucky I came when I did."

"Lucky for us," Devenish said heartily. "You can stay a week at least, I hope?"

"Have you brought Rachel and the children?" asked Josie eagerly.

"My four ladies are still at Cloudhills," he answered with a smile. "And I regret that I can stay no longer than tonight. I've a message for Guy, and then must dash home. Craig and his family are joining us for a week, and I've the deuce of a lot to attend to now that my father and Dora are in Brazil."

Disappointed, Devenish said, "No, but they'll not miss you for a day or so."

"Perhaps. But I miss them. Dashed if I can see how you stand the life of a bachelor!"

On her way to give instructions to the servants, Josie said, "He will not be one for much longer, Tris." She directed a mocking glance over her shoulder. "My aged soul is to be wed—very soon."

"Devil he is!" Taken aback, Leith asked, "To whom, slyboots?"

Devenish tightened his lips, irritated.

Josie called sweetly, "Tell him, dearest . . ." and closed the door.

"Baggage!" muttered Devenish, and waved the Colonel to a chair.

Watching as he limped over to the credenza whereon rested decanter and glasses, Leith grinned. "Yes, but what a charming one."

"Isn't she?" Returning to hand his friend a glass of Madeira, then sit on the edge of his desk, Devenish said proudly, "Who'd have dreamed that tragic waif would become such a beautiful lady?"

Leith glanced at him, but his response was tardy. He was at once the recipient of a blazing glare. Devenish snarled, "I suppose you think she is *not* beautiful?"

Leith's deep chuckle sounded. "Swords, or pistols? No—truly, I think her delightful, and if I judge her pretty rather than beautiful, I am likely prejudiced because to me there is but one beautiful lady in the world, and I have her.''

Devenish threw a frustrated glance at the ceiling. ''Once a Staff Officer, always a Staff Officer!''

''No—really, your little elf is a delight, and has grown up, Dev. Which is more than I can say for you. What's this I hear about a feud with Little? I vow you're the same fire-eater manoeuvred me into that damnable fight with Shotten, the very first minute we met!''

''*Manoeuvred* you! Like blazes, Tris! The truth is, you stole my quarrel!'' He grinned, his anger vanished. ''At the Cat and Dragon, wasn't it? And do you remember the time that rascally farmer was trying to sell a ten-year-old nag to some poor moonling—''

''Whereupon you had to intervene and tell the moonling the hack was *ten* rather than six, and the farmer called you—let me see—ah, a dang rude little shrimp of a dandy!''

''Whereupon I punched his fatuous head for him!''

''Yes—and he and his damned great hulking sons beat you to a pulp, and I'd my work cut out to bring you off still breathing!''

They both laughed. Devenish said, ''Those were good times! It seems such a little while ago. Only yesterday, in fact, since I found my Elf.''

There was a wistful quality to his slow smile, and Leith, his lazy dark eyes seeing so much more than they appeared to, asked quietly, ''Nothing wrong, is there, old fellow?''

''What? Oh, no. Nothing. Save that—I wish the years had not flown quite so fast.'' He shrugged. ''The cry of all fond parents, I fancy.''

Leith gazed thoughtfully at the fire, then murmured, ''You could not expect to keep her safe hidden for—''

''*Safe hidden?* Now, just what the hell do you mean by that?''

''Saints preserve us! *Must* you take me up so? Dev—you have, in a manner of speaking!''

''Then I take a dim view of your manner of speaking! Besides—I've not hidden her well enough, apparently. Fontaine's spotted her.''

"Of course. He spots every pretty girl. He was captivated by her at Jerry's ball last—"

"Blast it! Everyone seems to have seen that, save me! Why didn't you warn me, Tris?"

"Why the deuce should I warn you?" said Leith, mildly amused by his volatile friend. "You have, I presume, eyes in your head. And at all events, what's so wrong about Fontaine's interest? Good catch, I'd think."

"Had he marriage in mind."

Leith stared and, considerably shocked, said, "He's a gentleman, Dev."

"He's a *nobleman*! The two ain't necessarily synonymous!"

There was a moment of complete, taut silence.

All his amusement flown, Leith, knowing this man almost as well as he knew himself, said quietly, "Can you tell me?"

"Dammit—I have no proof." He hesitated. "But—just in case," he said reluctantly, "and on the understanding it cannot be repeated . . . you remember that beastly Morrissey business?"

"Good God!" Leith leaned forward. "You—think the man was Fontaine?"

"I happened to see him with her very late one night. I'm dashed certain her family didn't know she was out. She stopped after she got out of the carriage, and looked back. I saw her face . . ." He was silent briefly, then said, "And his sire banished him to America. The Earl's been in a black rage ever since. Won't hear his name spoken."

Leith said, "Not much to go on, Dev. You could be wrong, old fellow."

"I could be." But Devenish's face was grim, and Leith, dismayed, knew that there was no doubt in his friend's mind.

"Well, enough of that ugly business," said Devenish. "You said you've a message for Guy. I think you meant for me, as well."

Leith shook his head, smiling faintly. "Yes. Right, as usual. I saw Mitch in Town before I went down to Sussex."

"How is he? Has he set fire to the House of Lords yet?" But, something in Leith's expression warning him, he asked sharply,

"He's all right? He's so blasted outspoken in his efforts for the working classes! I'm afraid he—"

"No, no. Nothing like that. Mitch is very well, and sends you his affectionate regards. It's—Guy."

"Oh, Lord! Lyon said people were getting stirred up again."

"They are. Mitch thinks some hotheads are entertaining thoughts of—well, an impromptu trial. Or worse."

They exchanged grim glances.

"Deuce take it! What does he mean to do?"

"Said he'd talk with Canning and Wellington. The thing is—" Leith frowned worriedly. "I wish poor Castlereagh were alive still. Canning's a rather chilly sort. And the Duke's not too well, I think, and badgered to death, as usual."

They were quiet then, the shadows lengthening in the room, and both men mentally reliving their desperate and hard-won struggle against the might of Guy Sanguinet's ruthless brother.

Devenish said, "It's as well I've asked Guy to come down here for a few days. I'll try to keep him longer. He has Lyon, of course. Which reminds me, that young rascal means to offer for Josie. They'd make a good match, don't you think?"

Leith took a swallow of his Madeira, leaned back his head, and regarded his friend without answering.

Devenish reddened, squirmed, sampled his wine, and said explosively, "All right, blast it all! What?"

"You know what."

"Don't be ridiculous. She's a young and lovely girl, and shall marry someone of her own age. If not Lyon—well, you say I've kept her hidden, but—dash it, I cannot have her presented, Tris. And she'd never be given a voucher for Almacks. If I gave her a Season in Town and—well, if those fools snubbed her because of her lack of birth, I think I'd—"

He looked ready to do murder just at the thought of it. Leith hid a smile and suggested, "You could give her a come-out ball."

Devenish thought that over. "I could, I suppose," he muttered. "But it must be soon."

A faint frown tugged at Leith's heavy brows. "Dev," he said, "you may tell me to go to Jericho, but—a few months ago you were insisting your Elf was a mere child. Now you've encouraged her to consider offers of marriage and are planning a ball to launch her. What the deuce are you about?''

Devenish took their glasses over to be refilled. ''Josie told you. I'm planning on a wedding of my own.'' He turned back, met Leith's stunned expression, and said quickly, ''But I'm not ready to make an announcement, so be a good fellow and do not tease me. Where do you propose we hold this ball? In Town?''

Struggling to regain his composure, Leith said, ''What? Oh—well, with Christmas so near I fancy most parties are already planned. Why not here? You'd have to accommodate a crowd overnight, at least, but you've room enough, Lord knows. There's the Crown in the village, and you're not impossibly far from Stroud and Gloucester. You know all our lot would come, and rope in whomever we can in addition. Between the lot of us, we might even snare a Duchess or two. Lucinda Carden will help; she's fond of Josie.''

''By Jupiter!'' said Devenish. ''Be dashed if I won't do it!''

The air was cold in the early morning, and a fine mist wound about the stableyard, eddied to the movements of the impatient horses, and left a wet gloss on the cobblestones. Devenish cupped his hands and bent to receive Josie's foot and throw her up into the saddle. She smiled down at him as he adjusted her stirrups, then touched his cheek with her whip. ''Well, poor old soul,'' she said, twinkling at him. ''I have been away for almost three weeks and this is our first ride together. Are you not going to tell me how well I look?''

She wore a riding habit of blue wool, with collar and cuffs of silver fox, and a jaunty cap of the same fur was perched on her dark curls. She looked very well indeed, and he said, ''Of course you look well. I'm sure your mirror has already told you so.''

''How ungracious.''

''Very well,'' he capitulated, grinning. ''You are the loveliest sight to gladden my aged eyes these past three weeks.''

''Not *too* gracious, Dev,'' she cautioned. ''Lady Isabella will be jealous.''

Climbing into his curricle, Leith checked for a startled second, his dark eyes becoming very wide, but he said nothing as he settled himself.

Devenish mounted up and restrained Santana, who showed an inclination to jump over Leith and the curricle. "Lady Isabella thinks my daughter is exceeding pretty," he said lightly, "if ageing rapidly."

Josie flung at him, "I hope Santana sits on you!"

Laughing, the Colonel took up his whip. "Peace, my children. Or I shall be off without you."

Devenish on one side of the curricle, Josie on the other, they clattered out of the yard and followed the drivepath through the estate until they reached the lane that wound through the hills to connect with the Stroud road. Along the way, Josie chattered happily with Leith about the proposed ball, Devenish listening and inserting an amiable comment from time to time, until at last he remonstrated, "Give over, little one! You will drive poor Tris to distraction. Since he was so clever as to suggest a ball for you, you must not now submerge him in it."

Leith at once disclaimed, but Josie cried anxiously, "No, am I doing so? Oh, I am sorry, Tris! Dev's right—it was so good of you to think of it. I know I'm being a prattlebox, but—oh, I am *so* excited!" From the corner of her eye she saw the twitch to her guardian's lips and laughed. "Very well. I shall say no more about it. Leith, you will give my love to your dear wife and children, and— Rachel will come to the ball, no? Oh, and we must not forget, dearest, to invite Tristram's General—what's his name? I always forget, and— Oh, dear, now I've done it again!"

She looked comically dismayed, and the two men laughed heartily. And so they went on through the misty morning, three good friends, too warmed by their pleasure in one another's company to be chilled by the dank air that swirled about them.

They said their farewells at the crossroad, and the two riders sat their fidgeting horses looking after the curricle until Leith turned at the last bend to wave back at them, then disappeared from sight.

"Dear Tris," said Josie nostalgically, as they turned about. "How well he looks."

"Yes. He's the best of good fellows. And greatly blessed to have such a gentle lady to take care of him."

"Does that suggest, I wonder, that I do not take care of you, sir?"

"You do very well, Milady Elf, considering you're not a young matron, but the merest snip of a rascally brat."

"Oh!" she exclaimed joyously. "A challenge, is it?" And then, dismay coming into her eyes, "You did not wear a scarf! If that is not just like—"

With a whoop he was away, crouched low in the saddle, the big black stretching out eagerly as he spurned the earth beneath his flying hooves.

Josie gave a cry of indignation, touched her heels to her mare's sleek sides, and was after him like the wind.

With very little effort, Devenish could have been entering the house with his ward half a mile behind, but he held the affronted stallion back just sufficiently to allow her to come up with him. The cold wind rushed past, the mists whirled madly, and the thunder of hooves and creak of leather increased as the mare drew level. Turning an exhilarated face, he saw Josie's eyes bright and her cheeks glowing with colour. Neck and neck, they galloped down the last sloping hill. Neck and neck, they raced to the hedge and cleared it side by side, and a hare chose that of all moments to shoot out from under the mare's hooves. A squeal of fright, a wild scramble, and for one of few times in her life, Josie was unseated. She landed so hard that the breath was driven from her lungs and, winded and humiliated, she lay for a moment, collecting herself.

There came a rush of running steps; a frantic gasping of her name. Devenish was on his knees beside her, holding her hand, gazing down at her, his face chalk-white, his voice shaking. "Josie! Little one . . . how badly are you hurt? Dear God! Can't you speak? Josie, Josie—talk to me!"

She blinked up at him. He looked so anguished! She said, "I am dead."

Speechless, he bowed his cheek against her hand. Then, blinking rapidly, he slipped one arm around her. She could feel him trembling.

"I am—quite all right," she said breathlessly. "Dearest—do not be so afraid."

"Oh, I am not," he managed with a stiff, twitching smile.

"Only that I—I feared I might be obliged to carry another lady back to Devencourt. Dreadfully hard on an old gentleman's back."

He helped her up, and she said, "I am much lighter than Mrs. Bliss," but was glad enough to lean on his arm as he led her over to the mare.

"Yes. And much more precious to me," he said quietly.

He assisted her into the saddle as though she were made of spun glass, and watched anxiously as he handed her the reins. "You *can* ride? I'll hold you in my saddle if you are unsteady, Elf."

She assured him she was much better, but he walked the horses back to Devencourt. When they arrived, he lifted her from the saddle, then gave her into Mrs. Robinson's care with strict instructions that she was to be laid down upon her bed and if she felt at all unwell was not to come down for dinner that evening.

Devenish watched her being tenderly escorted upstairs between the solicitous housekeeper and Klaus, who had come running when he saw the disheveled condition of his beloved young lady. The steward was waiting, as requested, but Devenish was in no frame of mind to engage in a discussion of the worsening condition of the access road, and sent the man off.

He made his way to his study, poured himself a strong measure of brandy, and took up Bolster's letter, but his hand trembled, and he put it down again, and sat frowning at the vase of chrysanthemums until roused by a shove against his knee. Lady Godiva grinned at him. He patted her thoughtfully and told her he had nothing for her to eat. She had entered through the unlatched French door to the terrace, with the result that a chill stream of air was now blowing into the room. Devenish closed the door, and Lady Godiva sat down beside the hearth. She looked despondently at the empty grate and, amused, he enquired if she would wish that he order a fire laid. The pig turned a tragic gaze on him, and curled up, but he saw that she was shivering. He limped over to cover her with a brown fur rug that

Josie had set before the fireplace to conceal the hole burned in the carpet last winter by a falling log. "I wish," he grumbled good-naturedly, "that someone would tell me what earthly use you are."

The pig regarded him with such obvious gratitude that he could only chuckle and tuck the rug closer about her. She burrowed under it happily and Devenish crossed to tug on the bell pull before he seated himself at the desk.

In about ten minutes, a shuffling step in the hall apprised him of the fact that Wolfe had negotiated the not inconsiderable distance from the butler's pantry to the study, and was now leaning against the wall outside, recovering himself. After an appropriate pause, the door opened. Somewhat out of breath still, Wolfe reeled in, and waited respectfully to be advised of his employer's wishes.

"Wolfe," said Devenish, "we are going to give a ball."

"Haaa . . . wheee . . ." wheezed the old gentleman, swaying. "In—Town, sir?"

"Here. And it must be soon, before everyone is completely immersed in preparations for Christmas entertainments."

Wolfe regarded him with glazed eyes.

Devenish went on, "We shall have to hire more servants, naturally, but I leave all that to you and your staff."

"Of . . . c-course, sir. May I ask how—how many we are to—invite?"

"Lord knows. But—oh, at least a hundred couples, I'd think. So we must ready the ballroom." He frowned. "Jove—is the floor safe?"

"I could not say, sir. No one's been in there for several years. Save to dust."

"Hmmmn. I'd best go and have a look. Meanwhile, please tell Mrs. Robinson and Signor della Casa so they may begin to mull on the matter."

He ignored the old man's dismayed look and, aware of his chef's nasty temper, wandered nonchalantly from the room, feeling a most heartless cad.

The Great Hall looked much more livable and welcoming these last years since Josie had badgered him into having the whole central block redecorated and refurnished. He crossed its handsome new floor, his limping steps echoing through the vastness, and made his way to the west hall and the newer part of the great house, passing the main dining room, the morning room, three saloons, and the music room, before he came at last to the ballroom.

A footman who had followed unobtrusively now sprang to fling open the doors, then step aside, maintaining a cool and disinterested attitude that was a relief to his bedevilled employer.

Devenish murmured his thanks, strolled into the ballroom, and recoiled. He had quite forgotten how enormous was this formal chamber. It stretched before him in chill and daunting grandeur, its furnishings shrouded in Holland covers, its four chandeliers looking like so many huge laundry bags hanging from the ornately plastered ceiling. Devenish, who had vaguely remembered two chandeliers, was stunned, and hoped fervently that not all the lustres would need washing, which would surely constitute a tremendous task.

The floor was dusty, but its parquetry still retained an element of shine and it looked solid enough. The pale cream walls were sadly cracked and a touch mildewed here and there, but a coat of paint would fix that, and when the tapestries that once had hung here and were now packed away somewhere for safe keeping were restored, the place might not look too dreadful. Wandering about, Devenish felt like an interloper in his own house, and the eerie sensation that sad and long-dead eyes watched him took possession of his mind as it sometimes did when he was alone in some part of the mansion. He had known the same feeling in his cousin's Scottish castle. He remembered Craig saying comfortingly that some men were more in touch with the occult than were others . . .

A sudden gust of wind slammed against the west wall, making him start. The room seemed to sway. Staring, aghast, Devenish realized that it was not the walls that swayed. He investigated and found that the "cracks" were cobwebs, blown about by intrusive draughts. "Good God!" he muttered, but he did not keep an enormous staff of servants as was the custom on many great estates, and could scarcely blame his retainers for failing to keep up a room that had not been used for several decades.

The floor creaked as he crossed the room, but all wood floors creaked, surely? He stamped a few times. The creaks were louder, as though the floor were shocked by this unaccustomed usage, and he stamped about in several areas, finding nothing ominous. After all, although some dancers would be considerably more weighty than himself, they would scarcely stand in one spot and jump up and down. He grinned to himself. Josie might. Most, however, would be dancing quite circumspectly. At least, one would hope so. He began to twirl about the floor, defying the sensation of being intimidated by the size of it. Solid enough, but just to be on the safe side, he gave a couple of strong leaps, taking care to land on his left foot.

"By . . . Jehosophat!"

With a gasp, he spun around. Sir William Little peered at him uneasily from the distant doorway. He gave an inward groan of embarrassment and wished his maligned ballroom floor might open and allow him to sink through. Of all people to discover him leaping about like a looby! "Just—er, testing the floor," he gulped, knowing his face was scarlet, and advancing to extend a courteous hand to his unexpected guest.

"Oh," said Sir William, looking relieved. "You give me a nasty turn, Devenish, damme if you didn't! Your butler said you'd come here, and I told him I'd announce m'self. Knew it would've taken him a month of Sundays to bring me! Then, when I saw you hopping about like a curst kangaroo, I don't mind admitting, I thought—"

"Yes. I do not doubt it, Squire. Let's adjourn to a warmer part of the house, shall we?"

When they reached the study, Devenish offered his guest a comfortable chair and a glass of Madeira. "Thinking about giving a come-out ball, you see," he explained. "For my ward."

"Delightful little gel," said Sir William, nodding in his ponderous way. He sipped his wine, acknowledged that it was "damned good," and added, "Don't imagine you expected to see me again, Devenish. Didn't expect to be here, I don't mind telling you."

"I'll admit you seemed annoyed when you left, sir," said Devenish.

"Annoyed, is it?" Little scanned him suspiciously, met an amused twinkle, scowled, grinned reluctantly, and repeated, "Annoyed? Man—I was *enraged*! Went out of here fully intending to write to my solicitor and have the access road closed to you!"

Devenish's good humor evaporated. "You can't do that," he declared, bristling. "It's a deeded right-of-way."

"Yes, but it ain't irrevocable! You cross my preserves at two points on that road, and— But, no matter. I did not come to select fleas. M'sister tells me you were very kind when she took her spill yesterday."

"What did you expect? Lord sakes, any fellow would have been! I'm very sure you would do the same for Miss Storm."

Gratified, Sir William relaxed his stiff manner. "Aye, I would." He took another pull at his wine, and settled himself more comfortably in his chair, saying expansively, "Don't usually care much for the fair sex, but m'sister's a *rara avis*, if I say so m'self. Dashed fine woman."

"She's certainly a handsome creature. I wonder she hasn't married again."

"Well, it ain't from want of offers, let me tell you, sir!"

"I didn't say it was! Lord, but you're hot at hand!"

"*I* am?" shouted Little, slamming down his glass. "I come here out of the goodness of my heart, and be damned if y'don't turn around and insult m'sister!"

"I did nothing of the kind," said Devenish angrily, slamming down his own glass. "Devil take you, Little, you've the disposition of a—" He checked. "What's the matter now?"

Staring at the hearth, the Squire asked in a voice of mystification, "What the deuce *is* that?"

Following his gaze, Devenish gave a gasp. Lady Godiva was stirring. If the Squire knew a pig ran tame at Devencourt, he'd be laughing forever! Happily, she dozed off again, whereupon he said airily, "You mean the dog?"

"Dog . . . ?" Sir William stepped closer. "Don't look like no dog I ever—Where's its face?"

"He's a—er, rare type," said Devenish, adding hurriedly, "I'd not get too close, were I you. If I'd known you were coming, I'd have put—ah, Hercules out."

"Vicious, is he?" said the Squire, halting. "I'm quite a dog man m'self, y'know. What breed did you say?"

"Eh? Oh—a . . . Tasmanian Devil."

"Never heard of it." The Squire, fascinated, took another step, his gaze fixed on the furry brown shape by the hearth. "Where's it hail from?"

"Van Diemen's Land," said Devenish promptly, blessing the erring Cornish who, having once been transported, had contrived to bribe his way back to England, and had once or twice engaged in converse with his employer regarding the great Australian continent.

Lady Godiva shifted and emitted a drowsy grunt.

" 'Pon my soul!" the Squire exclaimed, and again stole forward.

The rug shifted agitatedly. Devenish cried, "I say, I wish you wouldn't venture so close," adding a desperate, "He's er, a tiger when roused!"

"Is he, by God! I wonder you allow him in the house at all! Jupiter, but he's an odd-looking chap. Can't wonder at it if he's a bit grumpy, eh?"

Devenish laughed hollowly.

"Tasmanian Devil, y'say . . . I'll have to tell m'sister. She's quite an authority on—" He checked as the "Tasmanian Devil" contorted, reared up, and stood there, the picture of the grotesque. "Lord—what an ugly brute! Which end is— By Beelzebub! He's got a curly tail!"

Devenish stifled a groan. "Sir—I do apologize, but it really ain't safe! You'd best—"

The "Tasmanian Devil," hearing a friendly voice, trotted in the direction of it, squealing indignation at being unable to see. With a little yelp of alarm, the Squire hopped onto his chair. Lady Godiva, eager to come at the source of the friendly sound, gave a great shake. Even as Devenish, fighting hilarity, made a dart for her, the rug flew off.

"It's a triple-damned *pig*!" howled Sir William, springing

down and turning a purpling face on Devenish's mirth. "Playing a curst May game with me, was you? *Tasmanian Devil*?" He brandished his fist. "I'll Tasmanian Devil you!"

Laughing helplessly, Devenish gasped, "No, but—sir, I—I really—"

"Think it's damned funny to make me hop up on chairs, eh? Having a good joke? Damn and blast your eyes and limbs, we'll see who laughs longest!" Livid with fury, Sir William stamped towards the doors, bellowing about the goodness of his heart and the gibbering damned idiots hereabouts. He wrenched the doors open and strode onto the terrace. "Pigs running loose in the damned house! I'll Tasmanian the damned—" At this point, recalling his hat, he turned about.

It was an unfortunate move. Clinging to the desk, sobbing and wiping his eyes, Devenish looked up in time to see Lady Godiva trotting after the Squire, doubtless having mistaken him for her owner. Sir William's sudden about-face took her—and him—by surprise. He uttered a shocked yell. Equally shocked, she darted for safety. Between his legs. A crash, a howl, and Devenish was sprinting for the terrace. For the third time in two days, he bent above the prone victim of a bad fall. Between roars, Sir William glared at him and waved his arms about.

"I say, sir," said Devenish, genuinely repentant. "I'm most devilish sorry. Here—let me help—"

"Do not *touch* me!" bellowed the Squire apoplectically. "Don't put *one* . . . damned *finger* . . . on me!"

"Come now, sir. You know I did not mean it. Oh, very well. Can you stand alone, then?"

"*Stand*? Damn your ears! I cannot *move*! My *back*! Oh, hell and damnation! My back's *broke*!"

✆ *Chapter 6* ✆

"*Je vous assure,* this was the case most special," said Guy Sanguinet, leaning heavily on his crutch as he accompanied Devenish along the east corridor.

"I can believe that," said Devenish with a smile. "From what he told me, Lyon is fairly beside himself with eagerness to offer for Josie. I know he would be here if it was at all possible. When old Belmont decides the boy has had time to recover, it is on the instant, isn't it!"

"*Oui.* My Lord Belmont, his communiqué it say that this is a case *très bien* for Lyon. It seem this unfortunate former Naval officer have carry the musket ball in his leg since the war. It is high above the knee, and when they try to remove it, the success it not come, and he say—never again!"

"Don't blame him a bit," said Devenish, slowing his pace to accommodate his struggling friend, but knowing Sanguinet too well to offer his arm. "Lots of poor fellows died under the knife. Still do. The shock, I'm told." He shuddered. "Once was enough for me, I don't mind telling you!"

"Ah, but you had no choice, *mon cher* Alain. You could not for all of your life walk about transfixed by the crossbow bolt my brother tell Gerard to put in you."

Devenish grinned. "Dashed hard on my tailor, I grant you. Am I to deduce, then, that our brilliant lad has been summoned to town to watch Belmont remove the musket ball after all this time?"

"No." Guy paused. "Pardon, Alain. This new way of progressing—I have not yet quite master it. And your house—it go on everlasting, no? Our situation now is this—my son does not go to watch. Nor is the bullet to be removed. The leg it must come off, and Lyon, *mon ami*, have what Belmont call 'the hands,' so—"

"Jupiter! D'you mean that Lyon is to *perform* the surgery?"

Guy nodded, his hazel eyes alight with pride. "Almost this it is so. He goes to assist Lord Belmont. As you would say—famous!"

"By Jove, but it is! We must have a celebration!" Devenish ushered his friend to a chair and asked a hovering footman to request that Miss Storm join them as soon as she came downstairs. The afternoon was cold, with leaden skies and a hint of rain in the air. A fire had been lit on the oversized hearth and roared merrily up the chimney, brightening the enormous drawing room. It was necessary, however, that one sit quite close to the hearth if any benefit was to be gained from the blazing logs, and Guy held his frail hands to the warmth.

There had been three Sanguinet brothers. Claude, the elder, had been obsessed with power and had commanded the wealth to augment his dreams with a plot to seize control of the throne of England. His person had not been impressive, for his height was not remarkable and, although he had always been elegant, his looks were nothing out of the way, save for a pair of light brown eyes that had seemed when he was angered to take on a red glow. His colouring had been sallow, and his hair the same jet black as that of his favourite brother, Parnell. The second born, Parnell had early earned the sobriquet Monsieur Diabolique. His looks had been as striking as Claude's were ordinary, his thick hair slightly curling, the clear skin seeming almost stretched over finely chiselled features, the mouth full-lipped and sensual, and the strange, pale eyes excessively brilliant. His preference to wear black tended to impart a Satanic look that accorded well with a disposition of such unrestrained lust and cruelty that several times Claude had been obliged to intervene lest he be clapped up in Bedlam.

Guy, the youngest, bore little resemblance to his brothers,

save that he, too, was not above average height. More sturdily built and fair complected than either Claude or Parnell, his hair was a rich brown, his eyes a friendly hazel, and his features regular. The product of his father's second marriage, he had soon been informed by Claude that the wedding ceremony had been a fraud, and that he was permitted to exist as one of the mighty Sanguinets only out of his sire's charity. His young life had been a nightmare, but he had endured it until Claude had launched his ruthless thrust for power. Mitchell Redmond and Charity Strand had been trapped in his brother's Hebridean fortress, and Guy had risked his own life to get them away. All three had managed to escape, but later, when Claude had been about to shoot down Tristram Leith, Guy had leapt between them. Claude, enraged, had not diverted his shot, and for months Guy had been paralyzed. Gradually, he had regained the use of one arm and, almost a year later, the other. He never complained and no one knew how much it cost him, but he had doggedly persisted in having his useless limbs exercised until, two years after he was wounded, he had at last managed to stand. He had begun to drag himself about on crutches, and if his friends saw the exhaustion in the shadowed eyes and ached with sympathy for his wasted life, Guy was elated and would urge them to mark his progress. "Keep you on at your sparring and riding and the foils," he would say gaily. "For very soon now, this wicked Frenchman he will challenge you all!"

At thirty-nine, he was far less the invalid than he had been, although he was still too thin, but he was the only survivor of the brothers. Parnell had been shot by an unknown assailant while attempting a brutal murder, and Claude had succumbed to the poison he had intended for the Prince Regent. Had it not been for Guy, his brother's ruthless schemes might very well have succeeded—a prospect Devenish did not care to even think about, but because it had been judged necessary to suppress the story of Claude's plotting, Guy's valour had never been made public. Despite all efforts, rumours had spread, and his name now brought him contempt and loathing. 'And the Lord only knows,' thought Devenish apprehensively, 'what the end will be.'

Guy glanced at him curiously. "You are very quiet, *mon cher*. Where is our ray of sunshine? She have not again go away, I trust?"

"Josie's upstairs. Lord, but I wish Lyon *had* come with you."

"*Tiens!* She is not ill?"

"Heaven forbid! But we've a sick man in the house. The Squire."

"Little? Here? This indeed is a strange thing!"

"Yes, a most wretched train of events. I chanced to be of some small service to his sister, a charming widow lady, and Little came charging over here to thank me."

Perplexed, Guy murmured, "I do not see how . . . ?"

"He fell over Lady Godiva. Thought he'd broke his back. It turned out he hadn't, but he gave it a severe sprain and we've been told he mustn't be moved for a week or two. The old grimphiz is beside himself with rage, which ain't helping him recover."

"If he decide to fall over Josie's pet pig, I fail to understand that for this he can hold you to blame."

Devenish stood and went over to kick at the logs. "To tell the truth," he admitted with a guilty grin, "I'd been rather baiting the old cawker. Well—not baiting, exactly. I'd thrown a rug over Lady Godiva because she was cold. Completely forgot about her, and when Little spotted her, I was so dashed embarrassed, I said she was a dog. I'd convinced him she was a Tasmanian Devil, and he was standing on a chair when—"

"Guy!" cried Josie, her joyful greeting cutting through the Frenchman's laughter.

Guy slipped his crutch under one arm, struggled to his feet, and swept her into a hug. "Let me look at you," he said fondly, scanning her bright face and all the glowing vibrant youth of her. She pirouetted for him, the wide skirts of her peach silk gown swirling. The low neckline was trimmed with tiny rosettes of cream satin, a peach velvet ribbon held back her glossy curls, and about her throat was the pearl pendant Devenish had presented to her when she'd completed her studies. "*Délicieuse*," he said admiringly. "Truth it is that you are lovelier each time I see you, *mon petit chou*."

She kissed his cheek and danced across to Devenish.

"Hello, little one," he said, his eyes holding the tender light that shone only for her. "Glad you could join the old crocks."

It was the term by which he and Guy styled themselves, but it had never won favour in her eyes. She said pertly, "*You* may be an old crock, my poor Dev, but only look at our Guy! Isn't he splendid?"

Guy threw her an elaborate bow, lost his equilibrium, and had to grab for the chair. He lowered himself into it, laughing up at them.

"Never mind about turning his head," said Devenish, his heart easing down from his throat as Guy leaned back in the chair. "We've a celebration, Josie m'dear. You tell her, Guy. He's your son."

"And would like to be yours, also," said Guy, with a mischievous glance at the blushing girl. "But of this I must not speak. Well, *Mademoiselle*, what do you think? Our Lyon has go to London. To *perform* the surgery *trés difficile!*"

"Old Belmont asked for him especially," put in Devenish.

Josie gave a squeal of excitement and jumped up and down, clapping her hands. "I knew it! I always knew it! He is so clever, and has done so *well*! Oh, Guy—how *proud* you must be!"

Devenish poured two glasses of wine and one of ratafia, and they toasted the absent Lyon, and then sat together around the blazing fire while Guy told Josie all over again how it had come about. "He has the *hands*, Belmont say," he finished. "Is a God-given gift."

"It is, indeed," she agreed. "Such a talented pair of hands to serve those in need!" And after a brief, comfortable pause, she said dreamily, "Do you remember when I used to tell Dev he had the Rat Paws, because he has such an amazing power with animals?"

They all chuckled, recalling that childish designation. Devenish said, "And it was you, Guy, who finally realized she was speaking French, and that the expression she had not perfectly recollected was not Rat Paws, but *rapport!*"

"As well as if it were yesterday," said Guy. "Indeed this, it sometime seem like yesterday. And is long ago. Yet we are no closer to discovering who really is our *très belle jeune fille*.''

The door opened abruptly. Cornish entered, looking glum and dishevelled. "You best come, guv," he said baldly.

Devenish stood, frowning. "Little?"

"And loud," said his unorthodox footman with a wry nod. "Miss Fletcher was feeding 'is nibs 'is soup too 'ot like, and 'e yowled at 'er like wot 'e does and scared 'er so she knocked over the bowl. All over 'is stummick. Lor'—to 'ear 'im yell, you'd think 'e was bein' boiled!"

"Oh dear!" Josie jumped up. "I must go. I am sorry, but I'll come back as soon as I can—no, please don't get up, Guy."

She went out with the footman, Devenish watching them worriedly.

Guy said gently, "You should perhaps go also, Alain. This Sir William he is not the most *pacifique* of men."

"By God, but he's not. I wish his sister would come, but apparently she went off to visit an aunt for a day or so. Guy, you'll think us very shabby mannered, but—I don't want Little screaming at the Elf, so if you'll forgive me . . ."

Guy said with mock indignation that he hoped he was sufficient of a friend to be "at home, *parfaitment*," and Devenish hurried out. For a moment Guy gazed after him, pondering the chat he'd had with Leith concerning their unpredictable friend, then he retrieved his crutch and hobbled across the room. It was a pleasant chamber, the furnishings gracefully unostentatious, the rug an excellent example of Persian craftsmanship, and the colour scheme of warm beiges and browns, with splashes of orange here and there, brightening a cold autumn afternoon. At the rear, three pairs of French doors opened onto the broad terrace, matching those of the ballroom in the west wing. Outside, the rain was now coming down steadily, and he wandered over to look out at the gardens. He was intrigued, a moment later, to see a grey horse dash up the drivepath and a woman dismount, toss the reins to a running stableboy, and hasten towards the steps.

It was ridiculous, of course, but he was seized by the longing just once to meet someone without appearing a cripple. He retreated with reckless haste to the long table that backed the sofa, perched against it, and whipped the crutch underneath and out of sight. Luckily, a book lay open on the table, and he snatched it up a second before the door burst open.

As though taken by surprise, he glanced to the young woman who trod quickly into the room.

"Pray excuse my informal arrival, sir." Obviously much agitated, she came to hold out her hand. "I am Mrs. Bliss. I believe my brother is here?"

Her habit was soaked and her red hair straggled damply, but he thought her quite lovely with her intelligent grey eyes, her beautiful English skin, and her lack of affectation. Clasping her cold hand, he said, "How do you do, *Madame*? I am a guest, which is of *peu d'importance*. Your brother lies up the stairs and is, I assure you, the best of care receiving."

She was as intrigued by his thin, sensitive face and French accent as she was affronted by the fact that he had not stood up when she offered her hand. She was long past her schooldays, of course, and must look a fright, but one would think he could at least observe the simple courtesies. She thought with a flood of impatience, 'And what nonsense to be worrying about so stupid a thing!' She was the youngest of six children, and fifteen years Sir William's junior, but he was her only surviving brother, and despite his rather irascible disposition, she was deeply attached to him. All she had been told upon returning to Oak Manor was that he had suffered a bad accident and she was urgently needed at Devencourt. Now, hesitating, she asked, "Do you know what happened? How badly is he hurt?"

Unable to escort her, and miserably caught in this trap of his own making, Guy was aware that she must judge his manners execrable. Embarrassed, he blundered, "Devenish said they thought his back it was broken—"

Before he could finish the sentence Mrs. Bliss whitened and with a little shocked cry started for the door. He grasped her arm. "Wait, *s'il vous plaît*! This, it is—"

But, frantic, she tore free and ran towards the door.

Guy, having leaned too far, was thrown off balance and fell heavily.

Mrs. Bliss heard the crash. Glancing over her shoulder, she checked, amazed to see the Frenchman sprawled on the floor. She started to stammer apologies, while waiting for him to get up, a process that appeared to cause him a surprising degree of difficulty. Bewildered, she saw him twist around and reach under the table. He kept his face turned away, but as he retrieved the crutch, he slanted a glance at her. His face was crimson and he looked utterly humiliated. Her heart fluttered oddly. She flew back to kneel beside him, and said with her warm smile, "I am so glad this is why you did not stand when I came in. I thought you fancied me so horrid a sight I did not warrant your courtesy."

It was the last thing he had expected her to say. And she was neither making frantic efforts to help him stand, nor babbling her remorse for having caused him to fall. His agony of embarrassment faded. He said, indicating his crutch, "I am a little the disabled one, you see."

"Yes. Was it from birth? Or the war?"

Amused by her frankness, he hesitated, picturing her horror was he equally frank. "It was," he replied, "a—sort of war. And the thing important, Madame Bliss, is that your brother has not the broken back. A bad sprain, merely. Devenish and Miss Storm, they are with him now."

"Oh, thank heaven!" She gave a deep sigh of relief. "Sir William can be tiresome, you know, but I am rather short of brothers, and should purely hate to lose him." She stood, smoothing her habit. "I fancy," she added with a twinkle, "that poor Devenish and Miss Storm will be not at all reluctant to lose him, however! I must go up." Hesitating, she ventured tentatively, "I expect you would prefer I not offer to help. People who have to endure such a nuisance are usually so very proud."

He grinned, and suddenly did not feel at all proud. "If you could be so kind as to the little stool bring, I can get onto that, and then, together, we may restore my equilibrium."

She went gladly to fetch the stool, and by the time she returned, Guy had managed to struggle to his knees. He was able to perch on the stool, and then, with the crutch on one side and

Mrs. Bliss's helping hand on the other, he regained his feet. *"Voilà!"* he said breathlessly.

"Fata viam invenient," she cried.

He regarded her uncertainly, "Alas, my Latin she is not just excellent. Fate will—er . . . ?"

" 'The Fates will find a way.' *My* Latin, you see, is better than my French! And if you will forgive me, I must go to my brother now, *Monsieur*— Oh dear, here we are, chatting away, and I do not even know your name."

A wary light came into the fine eyes. He said gravely, "It is Sanguinet, *Madame*. Guy Sanguinet."

Her expression did not change, yet he could feel her withdrawal as she responded politely and left him.

Josie had donned her new evening gown, a pale blue velvet with a deep frill at the hem, a low, heart-shaped neckline, and long, fitted sleeves that tapered onto her hands in extended peaks. An opal pendant sent its subtle gleams from above her white breasts, and opals were also in her ears. She knew she looked very well, and this happy knowledge was confirmed when the two gentlemen stood to face her as she entered the drawing room.

"Ma foi!" said Guy admiringly. "You have entertain the princess, I see, Alain."

"For seven superlative years." Devenish crossed to take his ward's hand. "It was well worth the wait, m'dear."

She blinked archly at him. "Oh no, have I kept you waiting? Very well, we can go in to dinner now, if you wish. Pan is having a tray sent up, for she has the headache. I restrained Cornish from thrashing the gong in the nick of time."

Devenish grinned, offering his arm. "Thank the Lord for that! Poor old Little would likely have fallen right out of bed."

They commenced the long journey to the dining room, and Guy asked, "How does he go on, this victim of your fiendish pet?"

"I am sure his sister will manage to calm him," said Josie, thinking that Dev's limp seemed more pronounced of late. "I understand you were the one to receive her, Guy."

"And on the instant cast myself at her feet." His smile went a little awry. "Is a most charming lady, that. We had the—ah, what is it you say? The cosy chat. Upon the floor."

They halted, Josie with a ripple of laughter, Devenish staring his astonishment. Guy chuckled and, as they resumed their stroll, told them what had transpired. "She is, so I understand, the widow," he finished idly.

"Aha!" Devenish clasped the slender hand that rested on his arm. "Methinks I detect a note of interest. What say you, milady?"

Josie leaned to him, replying exuberantly, "I think it would be perfect! Guy—she is just the one for—"

"Par grâce!" Guy threw up a hand, laughing. "We just now have meet and you have us already wed! You must harbour against the *pauvre dame* the big grudge do you choose for her husband such a one as myself!"

She frowned at him, wondering if he could really be unaware that despite his affliction he was an extremely attractive man. "One judges a person by the soul—not the ability to waltz," she advised severely.

Guy murmured, "You are sure your ward has only seventeen of the years, *mon ami*?"

"Changed my mind," said Devenish. "Fifty, if she's a day!"

"Evil old man!" Josie exclaimed.

"In either event, you speak with much kindness, *ma belle*. But—one must be honest. I am far from a—a fit mate for the desirable young lady."

"He means," said Devenish, laughing, "that you are surrounded by crocks!"

Josie wrenched her hand from his arm and, as they both turned to her, flared, "I am surrounded by idiots! I could scratch both of you! And I would—if only—" Guy was watching her with dismay, and Devenish, clasping both hands behind him, stood with his fair head bowed like a chastened small boy, an attitude that never failed to make her laugh. She snatched Guy's hand and slipped her arm about Devenish. "Only—I love you both so very much," she said merrily. "And I refuse to let your silly denigrations spoil my happiness. Guy—did you know I am to have a come-out ball? It is to be the very *grandest* affair! You *will* come? In fact— Oh! You had just as well *stay*, hadn't he, Dev? We have set the date for three weeks from tomorrow! Oh, do say you will stay, Guy! Lyon can come straight here when he returns from Town, and it will be so much fun for us to make the lists. You can help write the cards. Do say you will!''

For a long moment, Guy was silent. He had no need to glance at Devenish, who would, he knew, repeat the invitation. He wanted very much to accept—not only for the pleasure of being in this merry madhouse with these dear friends, but for another reason as foolish as it was unwise. He said slowly, ''*Merci bien*, Milady Elf. I will stay.''

''Bedlamites, I tell you!'' declared Sir William vehemently, restoring his fork to a well-cleaned plate. ''With the possible exception of poor little Miss Storm! How she has managed to retain her sanity in a house full of pigs and servants who either cannot see or cannot walk about properly, or have not the remotest notion of proper conduct, is beyond me!'' He shook an admonitory finger at his sister's amused face and added, ''I'll tell you what I think, Faith—I'll be lucky do I get out of here alive!''

''Oh, come now, dear,'' said Mrs. Bliss, taking the tray and setting it on the chest of drawers. ''It's not that bad, surely? Mr. Devenish was perfectly charming to me when—''

''Charming, is it? I wish I may have had you with me when I found him hopping all over his ballroom like a dashed rabbit!'' Sir William cast a quick glance to the door and, lowering his voice, hissed, ''I swear it! And when he wasn't hopping—he was dancing!''

''Dancing? With whom?''

''A home question! With *himself* my lass! All—*alone*! Mad, I tell you! And then there was all that gammon about the pig being a Turkish Dervish or some such balderdash! Aye—smile! I wonder you don't laugh out loud because I'm lying here with my back almost broke!''

Whereupon, of course, she fussed over and cherished him and assured him she meant to do everything in her power to make him comfortable.

"Well, so you can," he said. "Get me gone from this madhouse!"

"Yes, dear. In a few days, perhaps—"

"Few days, my black hen! At once! Today!"

"Now, William, be reasonable. The doctor says you must not be moved for at least a week."

"The doctor's an ass, to give him the benefit of the doubt!"

"Very likely. But I do not mean to argue the point with him and perhaps cause you to suffer irreparable damage. Mrs. Robinson is preparing a room for me, and—"

"And she may cease wasting her time! You will not overnight in this den! Have you lost your wits, ma'am? This is a bachelor establishment!"

Her patience beginning to wear thin, she said, "William, how can you be so Gothic? Mr. Devenish's daughter is here, and—"

"Daughter my eyebrow! The chit ain't but a few years younger than he!"

"Her companion is a most *formidable* dowager, and there is the housekeeper, who—"

"Who tipples."

"No—does she? How very odd that— Oh, what matter? The point is that I am a respectable, middle-aged widow, and you must be aware that Devenish would scarce seek to compromise me in front of his family and friends."

"What friends?" he demanded, fixing her with a suspicious stare. "I heard a coach drive up. Who arrived? Three blind mice, I suppose!"

She laughed. "No, no. The gentleman seems quite sane, and besides, is an—er, invalid. Scarce a menace, you see."

"Perhaps not." Shifting painfully, he grunted, and moaned, "What's the fella's name?"

"Oh—I paid no heed," lied Mrs. Bliss, straightening his pillows. "A Frenchman, I believe, but most mannerly."

"If that ain't just like Devenish! Well, that settles it, m'dear! I'll not have you sleeping under the same roof with a Frog! Never met one yet who could leave the women alone! Ring that blasted bell, and we'll have one of the loobies in here. No—it ain't no manner of use arguing, Faith. You can come back in the morning. And bring Wright with you. Should've sent for him before this. I'll give you a list of what he's to pack . . .''

Nothing would move him. Sighing resignedly, Mrs. Bliss crossed to the bell pull, wondering what her fiery brother would say when he discovered the identity of the Frenchman.

Three days later, Faith Bliss settled herself against the squabs of the luxurious chaise and turned to her radiant companion. ''How very kind of Mrs. Grenfell to have volunteered to play chess with my poor brother so that I might accompany you to Cirencester today. William is quite an enthusiast, but will never admit that he cheats. I dare swear he has told me fifty times how the game is played, but whenever he makes a move I do not understand, he tells me it is a rule he'd forgot to explain.''

The two young women laughed merrily. ''It is the very same with Dev,'' said Josie, her face framed by the sable of her hood. ''He tries and tries to tell me about some facet of the law that Mitchell Redmond is fighting to change, and I declare each time he tells me, it becomes more ridiculous. Either I am very wooden-headed about politics, or our laws are completely stupid. What with the Corn Laws and the Enclosure Acts, one might think we were governed by a set of ogres!''

Mrs. Bliss arched her brows. ''Mitchell Redmond . . . ? Good heavens! You never mean *Lord* Redmond? Why, I am not even allowed to speak his name at the Manor. The very thought of him is anathema to my brother!''

''And to many others, I'm afraid. Mitch will fight to the last drop of his blood for the rights of the poor, which makes him exceeding unpopular—especially among the mine and factory owners. But he is the dearest man you could wish to meet. And''—she put a hand on Faith's arm, adding with a twinkle— ''extreme handsome!''

''He is? I'd fancied him to be old and shrivelled up, and so evil he had four horns on his head and cloven hoofs!''

Josie laughed delightedly. ''But, no! Mitch is—now, let me see—I fancy he is no older than Dev, and married to the very dearest lady. They have two sturdy little boys, and a darling baby girl.''

"Bless my soul! And you say he is handsome. As handsome as your guardian?"

"Oh, no. But then, who is?" Josie sighed, her eyes becoming troubled. "We worry about Mitch, for he takes such dreadful chances. There are those, Dev believes, who would stop at nothing to silence him."

"Surely not! In England?"

"I pray not. But only look at poor Mr. Perceval. Murdered by a madman in the House of Commons, in front of everyone!"

"Yes. Dreadful! But that was eleven years ago. I cannot think such things would chance today."

"They do, though. Only last week, Mitchell was attacked. Dev had a letter from Jeremy Bolster telling him of it. He could not read it—very few people can read Jeremy's hand. But when I deciphered it, we learned that Mitchell was confined to his bed by reason of a brick heaved at his head by some rabid hooligan."

"How awful! I expect it must have been in the newspapers, but what with my driving to and fro each day, I've been remiss in my reading of late. Is—er, that where Monsieur Sanguinet went driving off to in such a hurry the other day?"

The sparkle was reborn in Josie's dark eyes. Suppressing a smile, she replied, "Yes. They are the very best of friends. I fancy Jeremy and Harry will be en route to Sussex also, and should it transpire that Mitch is badly hurt—which Jeremy thought was not the case—why, then they all will go. All the Nine Knights, as the King calls them." Her eyes dreaming, she murmured, "There were really twelve, you know, only one was a lady and Prinny does not include poor Diccon, because they said it was his duty since he was an Intelligence Officer, and Craig refuses to be included, because he said he did nothing save join in the battle for a few minutes and get himself shot. But—" She broke off with a gasp. "Oh! I am not supposed to speak of it!"

Mrs. Bliss, who had listened to this incomprehensible rambling with breathless interest, said, "Well, I didn't understand any of it, so you need not worry, my dear. Only—one thing I admit, puzzles me." She paused, then went on hesitantly, "I am sure you will have heard the rumours that are abroad. It is probably nonsense, but my brother believes it all.''

"About Guy Sanguinet?"

"Yes. And—and some sort of plot that nearly succeeded. The—er, one you referred to, I think?''

"Oh. What do they say of it?"

"That it was an attempt to murder the King—when he was Regent, of course. And the Prime Minister, Wellington, and most of the Cabinet.''

Josie frowned. "How? Do they say?"

"William says he was told that Claude Sanguinet invited them all to his estate in Chatham, and there fed them veal and mushroom pie. Only they were not mushrooms but toadstools. And that they all were stricken, but . . . but—'' Mrs. Bliss checked. "Josie! How can you laugh at so dreadful a thing?"

"My apologies,'' moaned Josie, drying her eyes. "But—pray do go on. How . . . how did they survive this unkind menu?''

"I do not know, but 'tis said that Claude Sanguinet made the mistake of eating some of the pie himself, and that his brother was shot when the guards ran in and—''

"And found the Regent and all his ministers prostrate!'' gasped Josie. "Oh, dear me! I should not laugh, but—how wicked a thing is rumour, to take something, and—''

"Then—there *was* something?'' asked Mrs. Biss shrewdly. "But—if it is truth, how can Mr. Devenish allow Guy Sanguinet to visit you? And how is it that Monsieur Sanguinet is not in the Tower—or long dead? Oh dear, I do not understand at all. And—he does seem such a nice gentleman.''

Josie dabbed her handkerchief at her eyes and said, "I cannot tell you all that really happened, Faith.'' Her expression was very serious all at once. "And I must have your word of honour that you will not repeat any of our conversation to a soul.''

Awed, Mrs. Bliss gave her word. "Were you involved in it, then? You must have been only a child! Are you sworn to secrecy?''

"Not really. Nor was I involved. But over the years I have often crept downstairs to listen to the gentlemen chatting in the evenings, long after they fancied me asleep. And gradually, I was able to piece it all together. Most of what you have heard is untrue. There was"—she dimpled irrepressibly—"no veal and mushroom pie. Neither the Regent nor any of his cabinet was poisoned."

Her smooth forehead puckering, Faith muttered, "Then—the rumours lie?"

Josie shook her head. "Not entirely. It was a terrible plot, engineered by Claude to break the financial structure of the nation and to murder the Regent. That it did not succeed is due only to the Nine, for no one would believe them and they were forced to fight Claude and his followers alone, until each one of them was hurt or made ill. At the finish only a handful were able to go on, and they struggled so gallantly that they were able to prevent tragedy. Even so, had it not been for Guy's help, the end may have been very different. He is one of the bravest gentlemen I ever met, and took his wound most valiantly, in saving Tristram Leith's life."

Gripping her hands tightly, the widow said, "Then—Monsieur Guy Sanguinet was not, in any way, involved in his brother's schemes?"

"No," replied Josie simply. "Guy is one of the Nine, do you see?"

❧ Chapter 7 ❧

The grey morning had become a greyer afternoon, the leaden skies donating a steady drizzle to the sodden West of England, and a chill wind sending red and brown leaves scattering like flocks of tiny sparrows.

James Neblett drew the scarf tighter around his throat and pulled up the collar of his frieze riding coat. Noting the gesture, Devenish, seldom affected by cold weather, said, "Sorry to drag you all this way on such a day, James, but I couldn't get away sooner."

The steward nodded his head. "Your hands is full, sir. And now, with Squire and all—cripes! I'd not be in your shoes, I'm thinking. I'd not reckoned you'd be able to get out today at all."

"Well, the ladies are off to shop for their ball finery, and Monsieur Sanguinet"— Devenish paused, frowning,—"went into Sussex for a day or so."

"How long do you reckon Squire will stay at Devencourt, sir?"

"Another week, likely. But since Mrs. Bliss brought his man, he has seemed less irritated by us."

Neblett, who had spent many more years on the estate than had his young employer, grinned, and said with the privilege of the long-time retainer, "Pinching at you, is he? Well, Squire's a hard man, Mr. Devenish. A hard man."

"But an honest one," said Devenish good-humouredly. "Even so, as things stand, I rather doubt he'd agree to repairing the

98

road, and with Miss Storm's ball less than three weeks away, something must be done. I cannot have our guests axle-deep in mud and unable to get to the house."

Neblett ducked as a sudden gust blew icy drops into his face. Devenish pulled his collar higher and, glancing up, gave a startled exclamation. "Jove! Looks as though I'm slow and sorry! Somebody's already mired down!"

An elegant barouche leaned at a precarious angle on the slope of the hill ahead. The vehicle was considerably low on the right side, and the guard and a footman were wandering about, gathering shrubs to stick under the wheel that was deeply mired in a large pothole.

Devenish touched his spurs to Miss Farthing's sides and cantered forward. "Hello there!" He left Neblett talking with the groom and rode up to the window of the coach. "Good day, ma'am," he began, lifting his hat as the window slid down. "You seem to have come to . . . grief!"

"Alain! Dearest boy, you have rid to my rescue! I might have known!" A lady appeared at the window, a lady whose ermine-trimmed hood framed a face of dark, exotic beauty. Her ringlets were glossy and almost black, her slumbrous heavy-lidded eyes of a dusky brown, yet her complexion fair and at the moment daintily flushed. Full red lips curved to a tender smile, and one white hand stretched out to him.

Bowing over it automatically, Devenish stammered, "Isabella! How—ah, delightful." And he thought, 'Oh, my God!'

Fate had an even less welcome shock in store for him. From the deeper shadows, another occupant of the carriage leaned forward. Lord Elliot Fontaine drawled, "Devenish! Hail fellow . . . and all that sort of drivel. We come to see the fallen Caesar. Understand our cousin is recuperating at your place."

The perfunctory smile Devenish had dragged up for Lady Isabella now vanished, leaving his blue eyes as chill as the wind that buffeted the group. "I had quite forgot you are distantly related to Sir William," he said coolly. "I am happy to tell you that he goes along very well, but you will wish to see for yourself. Neblett—a couple of branches from the fallen elm down by the stream will serve better than those shrubs, I fancy."

Watching him ride off with his steward in search of the branches, Isabella Scott-Matthias leaned back against the pink cushions, smiling.

"Lord help the poor fella," murmured her brother, hurriedly closing the window. "I know that Giaconda grin."

"Wretch!" She clasped his hand as he sat down again. "Lord, but he's in my blood! The very sight of him sets my heart beating like a kettle drum!"

"A call to arms—as it were," he sneered. "I vow the fellow must consign his looks to perdition, the way you women swoon at his feet."

"It is more than looks," she argued dreamily. "He is fearless and kind, and gentle. And yet there is a flame in him, and he—"

"Goes with a most unattractive limp!"

"Which does but make him the more intriguing. And see how he sits his horse—he rides like a centaur."

His lordship yawned. "Desist, desist! Such drooling adulation bores me."

She turned to look at him squarely. "I want him, Taine."

"It seems doubtful that your desire is returned. No, seriously, Bella—would you not become soon bored watching him hobble about? Gad—'twould revolt me!"

Her eyes sparked with anger. "Any affliction revolts you! Devenish was wounded by a crossbow bolt, I heard. If that can be called an affliction, it is a noble one." She leaned to grip his arm and shake it. "Taine—I *want* him! *Only* him! Help me."

He turned his head, to watch her from under his drooping eyelids. "Or is it that you want him *only* because he don't adore you like the rest of London and Paris? How typically contrary you women are. Even so, I'd help if I could, m'dear. Perhaps," he amended, with a slow and not quite pleasant smile, "I should say—I *will* if I *can*. One must try to be positive. However, I fancy it a forlorn hope. For some inexplicable reason, your beau ideal does not seem to—er, admire me."

"Then *make* him like you! For my sake!"

Fontaine had a suspicion of the reason behind Devenish's obvious dislike, and doubted the emotion could be reversed. He had interests of his own at Devencourt, however, and thus said musingly, "How odd, that we should both be drawn to the same household. Very well, Bella. I shall try."

With a squeak of gratitude she swooped to kiss him. He chuckled, for in his way he was fond of his beautiful sister. "For a—consideration," he amended. She drew back, eyeing him guardedly. "If I succeed," he went on, his light eyes glinting at her, "you must repay in kind, my love."

Isabella's lovely mouth tightened. "The Storm chit?"

He nodded. "She intrigues me. She is so fresh and—unspoiled. Now never frown, Bellissima—it makes you look hard." He laughed as her eyes narrowed. "Now you look positively fiendish! Come now—you desire Devenish, I desire the chit. Fair exchange."

"Devenish has looks, charm, poise, a fine old name, a beautiful estate, and a fortune. What has his waif? No background, no fortune, and certainly she is not beautiful. I'd not even call her pretty."

"We differ. She has an inner light. A warmth and interest in others glows from her like a beacon. In her way, she is as sought-after as her . . . guardian."

She scanned him suspiciously. "Why do you say it like that?"

"If you did but use those glorious eyes of yours, m'dear, you would see that do I take Mistress Storm away, I do you a large favour."

"Nonsense! He is fond of her as a parent is of a child. Nothing more. And besides, do you mean to serve her as you did the Morrissey girl—"

Fontaine's long fingers darted to close around her wrist. "You will oblige me," he said, his voice very soft but ineffably threatening, "by not again mentioning that matter."

"Taine! You're hurting me! Oh, all right, all right! But—you know what I mean. Devenish would kill you if—"

"Extremely doubtful, m'dear." He settled back in his corner again, watching his sister massage her wrist. "Besides—how do you know I don't mean to make it legal this time?"

Isabella laughed scornfully. "*You*—and a *foundling*? Never!"

"You know me too well, alas. Ah, here comes your Adonis,

101

and I fancy we must venture into the cold. Have we an understanding, Bella? Quickly now."

"Only if you promise not to do anything horrid."

"Whatever I do," he said, speaking with low urgency as the horsemen cantered up, dragging clumps of branches, "will not harm your plans. I promise."

Still, she hesitated, biting her lip and eyeing him with apprehension.

"I'd not say much for your chances without my—assistance," he warned.

She tossed her lovely head. "Very well. If you help me, I'll help you."

The Viscount blew her a kiss.

When placed beneath the trapped wheel, the branches achieved the desired result and the barouche was soon freed and rolling across the meadows towards Devencourt. Having waved the coach on, Devenish rode behind it. Neblett, after one look at his employer's expression, maintained a discreet silence, and as soon as they rattled into the stableyard, slipped unobtrusively away.

Devenish dismounted and walked to the carriage. The footman had already opened the door and let down the steps. Devenish handed Isabella out. Her hood was up against the drizzling rain, but a few drops sparkled on her smooth cheeks when she lifted her face to bestow a dazzling smile on him. Climbing out nimbly, the Viscount threw a swift glance around at well-kept stables and coachhouse and the great loom of the old house. "What a fine place," he said admiringly. "And I can see you keep it in the prime of condition, old fellow."

Devenish smiled, but a thoughtful look came into his eyes as he ushered his guests to the side door.

When they reached the Great Hall, Cornish hurried towards them.

"Allow me, ma'am," said Devenish, assisting Isabella with her cloak.

"Now, this is charming," said Fontaine, turning to Devenish with a warm smile. "Jove, but I was half froze. Lucky for us you came along, Dev."

Only close friends addressed Devenish by the abbreviation of his name, and his back stiffened. An almost imperceptible reaction, but Cornish had seen it. Devenish handed him my lady's cloak, and the footman winked outrageously and dug an elbow in his ribs, jerking his head approvingly at the beauty.

Fontaine, chancing to intercept this little byplay, lifted his quizzing glass and, astounded, surveyed the footman through it.

"I'll take yer coat, mate," said Cornish, fastening a firm hand on the back of the Viscount's collar.

For once in his life, Fontaine was so stunned as to be speechless as his coat was wrenched from his back and borne off by a man he was later to describe as an aspiring fishmonger.

Greatly amused, Devenish observed his guests.

Lady Isabella whispered a barely audible, "Heavens . . !"

Simeon Wolfe was crossing the Great Hall at a teetering trot, peering at the visitors with an anxious smile.

Fascinated, the Viscount once more had recourse to his quizzing glass.

His eyes alight, Devenish said, "Oh, there you are, Wolfe. Lady Scott-Matthias and Lord Fontaine are concerned for the welfare of their cousin. How does Sir William go on?"

"Wheee—heee," wheezed the butler, staggering to a halt.

Devenish said innocently, "Is that so? And is Mrs. Grenfell with him?"

"Doooh . . . think . . . sooo, sir," panted Wolfe.

"Good God!" said Fontaine under his breath.

"I fancy you will like to freshen up," said Devenish. "Wolfe, show our guests to suitable rooms, if you please, and have refreshments sent to the drawing room."

Wolfe bowed. In the nick of time, Devenish grabbed him and straightened him up. Fontaine exchanged an incredulous glance with his sister. Wolfe beckoned a footman and gave him some breathless instructions, and the awed visitors were conducted up the stairs.

Devenish took himself to his own bedchamber and indulged in a hearty laugh.

* * *

"How delightful to be able to have this *tête-à-tête* with you," trilled Lady Isabella, snuggling closer to Devenish on the drawing room sofa.

It had been a mistake to occupy the sofa. He'd fancied himself safe when she selected the chair, but her strategy had been superior, for once he was settled, she had arisen on the pretext of carrying him another cup of tea, which she could quite easily have passed to him, and then had sunk down so close she had all but sat on his lap.

Beginning to sweat, he said lightly, "Now, Isabella, what would your brother think did he find us cuddled up and alone like this? Surely you should have stayed with him to cheer your ailing kinsman."

She leaned closer, pouting a little, and trailing one finger down the firm line of his jaw. "William has Mrs. Grenfell and Taine. Why should I leave poor you, all alone?" And, remembering her promise, she enquired idly, "Where is your little girl? At school?"

Her perfume was dizzying and she was very beautiful. He said, shaken, "Oh, no. Josie is quite the debutante. She makes her come-out next month, in fact."

"She does? Oh, Dev, shall you give her a party? Do say I may come."

"I—er . . . That is, I do not believe the—ah, cards are sent out as yet," he lied, trying vainly to draw away from her twining arm. "Now—tell me of—of yourself, Isabella. I heard you have been captivating Brockton. He's a good man."

"Yes, he is. But dull. And—oh, my dearest Dev"—she turned his face towards her, running her soft fingers through the crisp hair at his temple and saying huskily—"do you recall the Bolsters' ball last Spring, when we walked in the gardens, and"—she leaned closer, her hand holding his head captive until they were almost lip to lip—"and you were so naughty as to—"

But this time, hers was the tactical error. It was at the Bolsters' ball that Fontaine had apparently become fascinated by Josie. Irked by the reminder, Devenish seized the opportunity offered as a log rolled from the grate, and sprang to his feet.

Even so, Fontaine was very prompt. "What are you two about—all alone in here," he drawled, sauntering into the room.

His sister threw him a frustrated look, but Devenish, retrieving the log and replacing it on the fire, said easily, "Oh, we were speaking of old times. How do you find your cousin, Fontaine?"

"Raving," said the Viscount, directing an apologetic shrug at Isabella as Devenish replaced the tongs. He went over to occupy a wing chair. "Miss Storm's duenna beat him at chess, and he regaled me with tales of Transylvanian Demons and pigs and—lud, but I fear the poor fellow's taken leave of his senses, for such bizarre things could not chance in your gracious home."

Devenish returned the gentle smile. "Bizarre things—even very ugly things—may chance in the most gracious of homes, no? At all events, your kinsman is making excellent progress, so Dr. Rayburn tells us, and may soon be safely returned to his own home. Tea, Fontaine?"

Isabella poured dutifully, and Devenish took the cup and carried it to the Viscount, then perched on the cushioned hearth seat. "I fancy Sir William told you that his sister has visited him every day. A most charming lady."

"Yes, a dear creature," agreed Lady Isabella, with commendable if false enthusiasm. "I adore Fanny. I expected to find her here, in fact."

"She is gone shopping, so I'm told," said Fontaine. "With Miss Storm. And her name is Faith, m'dear."

Her silvery laugh tinkled out, but the meaningful gleam in her brother's eyes had not escaped her. She chattered on, praising Devenish for his generosity in seeing to it that their damaged relation was so kindly cared for, and going into ecstasies over the great house until at length her reluctant host had no alternative but to conduct his guests on a tour of the building. The afternoon was drawing to a close, when a door opened somewhere, and in a few seconds Josie came into the drawing room.

The cold air had painted roses in her cheeks, her eyes sparkled over the packages she held, and her fur hood slipped back to reveal her curls in a pretty untidiness. "Lord Elliot!" she cried gaily, dumping her parcels into Devenish's arms, and running to hold out her hands to the Viscount. "Oh, how lovely!"

Charmed by such unaffected spontaneity, Fontaine bowed to

kiss each little hand. "Lovely, indeed," he said, smiling down at her. "You know my sister, I believe?"

Josie crossed to shake hands with the beauty, and Devenish deposited his burdens on the sofa and went to take his ward's cloak. "Had you a nice time, Josie?"

She spun to him, dimples flashing as she kissed his cheek. "Delightful, I thank you. And I need not have worried that we were so long, since you have such nice company." Unseen by the "nice company," her eyes quizzed him, but he managed to preserve his countenance and enquired as to the whereabouts of Mrs. Bliss.

"She went straight up to see Sir William."

Devenish said rather pointedly, "You will like to go up and see her before you leave," and was gratified when Isabella took the hint and stood, saying that they really must get back to the Manor. He went swiftly to open the door, and ushered the beauty along the hall.

It was a long hall, and she contrived to walk very close beside him, clinging to his arm and murmuring scandalous gossip that he alone could hear, and that made him laugh. He was not so amused, however, that he did not keep an eye on his ward. There was little doubt but that she liked Fontaine very much, and the Viscount was as obviously attracted by her. 'She is so trusting, so guileless herself,' thought Devenish, irritated, 'that she does not look for duplicity in others.'

Their carriage had not yet reached the front steps. Josie, striving to be cordial to the woman she detested, chattered to Isabella, and Fontaine turned to shake hands with his host. "Awfully good of you to put up with Sir William. He's a crusty old curmudgeon at times."

"Not at all. I am only sorry he was injured in my house."

"Unfortunate, I grant you. But," the pale eyes gleamed, "one man's meat, as they say . . ."

Devenish succeeded in looking puzzled.

His lordship grinned and said, man-to-man fashion, "Gives us a chance to visit you, my dear fellow."

"Thank you," said Devenish frigidly. "I'd not realized you was so fond of my company."

"Had you not?" The graceful brows rose in amusement. "But how could I fail to seek your company when you have such enchanting—relations?"

"Ah—so it is my ward that attracts. I must warn you, my lord, that Josie has many admirers."

"What? Even though you've kept her so carefully isolated? You surprise me."

Quivering with rage, Devenish responded, "I am sure you would be the first to appreciate that it is sometimes necessary to keep lovely things—guarded."

Fontaine's gaze had returned to Josie, but at this he moved in the way that was so peculiarly his own, the pale eyes, unblinking, slanting to Devenish before the burnished auburn head swung slowly to him. "From . . . what?" he enquired.

Devenish shrugged. "There are, sad to tell, monsters even among the noblest of our families, who do not shrink from blasting innocence." His eyes very steady as they met Fontaine's narrowed stare, he went on. "Only consider the case of poor little Miss Morrissey."

For a long, still moment, the Viscount did not respond, but stood there, seeming scarcely to breathe. Then he murmured, "I had interest in that direction at one time, but cannot, alas, take your charitable view. Since the lady refuses to name the man who fathered her bastard, one can only suppose it to have been a case of unbridled passion, repented at leisure."

"Or of rejected lust, followed by a merciless rape?" His level stare holding unmistakable disgust, Devenish said, "She was beaten, did you know?"

"Likely by her papa." The Viscount shook his head in amused chiding. "No, really, Dev, it is too deliciously dramatic. Besides, were it as you say, the girl would only have to name the man, surely?"

"True. Unless, perhaps, she has been threatened. Certainly, her father or her brother would call him out, once she accused the swine."

"Ah . . . yes. And you imply that if they are inept shots, and her lover an experienced duellist, it would bring more tragedy into her life, eh? Gad, but it's a grisly villain you paint." Fontaine eased on his gloves. "Too far-fetched, my dear chap."

"Oh, no," argued Devenish with a grim smile. "The implications are, I think, sufficiently obvious that I am not the only one to have noted them."

Fontaine jerked his glove so viciously that the fabric tore. "Now see what I have done," he said mournfully. "You have quite overset my nerves with your dastardly scenario. Ah—here comes the carriage, at last." He turned to regard Devenish with fond admiration. "Farewell, my clever friend. And do pray have a care. You have no proof of your melodrama, and if your noble—ah, monster should learn of your beliefs, he just might—er, turn on you."

"Never fear," said Devenish. "I, you see, am *not* inept with either sword or pistol." His eyes became hard and hostile, "As our monster will discover does he hunt my ward."

They smiled at each other.

"And they say women chatter!" My lady swooped down upon them, extending one hand for Devenish to kiss. "Taine, we shall not reach Oak Manor before dark do we not leave now. And poor dear Dev has enough on his hands without having to accommodate us for the night."

"It has been lovely to see you," said Josie, beaming upon Fontaine. "You will visit your cousin again, I hope."

"*Assurément*, dear lady." The Viscount bowed over her hand. "No one could keep me away."

"There," Josie crossed the drawing room to hand Devenish a glass of brandy, and seat herself in the wing chair by the fire. "Now we may be comfortable, at last."

Mildly astonished by such propriety, for she usually curled up as close to him as was possible, Devenish raised his glass to her.

"Faith will be down in a moment," she explained with a twinkle.

He grinned. "Just so. Now, Elf, tell me about your day. I'm very sure you had to stop in at the church."

"Dear old St. John the Baptist. As lovely as ever, Dev. Faith had never been inside, and thought it splendid. She is such fun to shop with. There was a wonderful tang of winter in the air, and the shops were all so bright, and everyone bustling and cheerful.'' The enthusiasm in her vivid little face vanished. She said severely, "I collected something that I *meant* to give you for Christmas.''

His lips quirked. He said, "But will not do so because I am in deep disgrace.''

"You may smile, dearest, but you know very well she will not do for you.''

"Considering you find the lady's presence so offensive, you lost no time in hurling yourself into the arms of the—gentleman.''

Josie noted both the hesitation and the sudden bleak look in her guardian's eyes. She giggled. "I wish I might have made a sketch of your face when I came into the room. You looked fairly desperate. Had they been here long?''

"Most of the afternoon, deuce take it. I had to show 'em all through the house.''

"Which my lady gushed over and 'adored,' I do not doubt. Poor Dev.''

He said thoughtfully, "Oh, it is not the lady to whom I object.''

"Huh! The way she throws herself at you is fairly disgusting.''

"How odd. I do not find it so.''

She scowled at him in the way he found particularly delicious. "In that case, why did you look so thunderous when you were talking with Lord Elliot just before they left? I vow you quite frightened me. For a moment I fancied you were really quarrelling.''

Devenish said nothing, but tilted his head, listening.

"Oh, no!'' Josie wailed. "Not *more* company!''

"Anti-social baggage . . . Oh, it's Guy, I think.''

They both stood as the Frenchman made his difficult way into the room.

"Welcome back,'' cried Josie, running to greet him with a hug and draw him closer to the fire.

"You travel fast, *mon ami*," said Devenish, shaking his hand. "What news of Mitch?"

"Oh, never worry for that one," answered Guy, making preparations to occupy his favourite Chippendale chair. "He have feel a little less well than he say, I think, but he have the head of rock, just the same." He smiled his thanks for the cognac Devenish brought him. "Which is a good thing when one is struck by the brick."

"Exactly where did it hit him?"

Guy put a hand on the back of his head. "Here. He will not—like our splendid Tristram, have the scar on the face."

"Thank heavens it was not serious!" Josie, reassured, proceeded to ply him with questions concerning Lord Redmond, his wife, and his children. He replied politely, but she noticed that he looked tired, and soon broke off her interrogation.

Devenish met her eye and suggested it was probably time for them all to go upstairs and change for dinner.

Stairs were implacable foes for Guy, making it necessary that he humble his pride and accept assistance. This was not a painful matter at Devencourt, however. Maintaining breezily that he had his own problems in climbing to the upper floors, Devenish required Josie to lend her aged parent a hand, and summoned the nearest manservant, who chanced to be Cornish, to aid his companion in infirmity. The journey took a little longer than was needful, being accomplished with a good deal of raillery and laughter. Josie detained Devenish at the landing, asking anxiously about refreshments for the ball, these questions leading inevitably to others, so that he at last warned her they would be late, and they repaired to their separate chambers, hers being in front of the house in the central block, and his towards the rear of the west wing.

Guy was first to leave his room. Cornish, having arranged his tasks with an eye to this moment, was waiting, and rendered assistance downstairs again, tactfully taking himself off as soon as the Great Hall was reached.

In earlier times, when Josie had been a schoolgirl and safely in bed by seven o'clock, Devenish and his friends had been used to gather in the red saloon, which chamber was situated in the west wing between the morning and music rooms. His thoughts elsewhere, Guy instinctively wandered in that direction, and not until he was halfway across the hall did a piping voice halt his erring steps.

He manoeuvred himself about. Wolfe was weaving more or less towards him, waving his arms. "Not that . . . room, sir," he puffed. He had worked up to quite a good speed and, unable to stop, came perilously close, took three steps backwards, pitched forward, and grasped Guy's free arm. "Le' me . . . help," he wheezed, clinging desperately to the swaying Frenchman. Exerting all his strength, Guy managed to remain erect. "Thank you, Wolfe," he said, convinced they both must go down at any second, but having not the least intention of humiliating the old man by rejecting his "aid." The ensuing struggle was really exhausting, and he was much relieved when they reached the drawing room door and he was able to insist that he could manage by himself now. The butler conveyed that he had been only too glad to be of assistance, and went off at a pace somewhere between a stagger and a reel.

Guy heard the cracked old voice raised in greeting, and turned about to see Mrs. Bliss coming gracefully into the room. She had undoubtedly seen the fiasco in the hall. His nerves tightened, and his face grew hot, but he bowed as well as he could, thinking how very lovely she looked in the gown of dusty-green tulle, a fine lace shawl of white, trimmed with palest green rosettes, draped around her shoulders. He had been very conscious of her avoidance of him in the two days prior to his departure and, having seen to it that she was comfortably seated, he made his way towards a distant chair, not wishing to embarrass her with unwanted conversation.

"That was very kind, Monsieur Sanguinet," she said in her musical voice.

He glanced at her in surprise, and hesitated.

"The poor old fellow would have been mortified had you made it clear that you were holding him up rather than t'other way round," she said, her green eyes twinkling at him in the friendly way they had done on that first afternoon.

Heartened, he said, "He have mean so well, you know, *Ma-*

111

dame," and took a tentative step back towards her. "Would you permit that I bring you the glass of wine?"

The light of the flames was echoed in her bright curls as she nodded her head. "Ratafia would be nice, if you please."

So she thought him capable of carrying the liqueur to her. Further, she had apparently forgiven him for being the scion of such an infamous house. Guy turned eagerly to the sideboard.

Josie had determined to ride out with her guardian next morning, to inspect the progress, if any, that had been made on the repairs to the access road. Before they left, however, she wanted to look over the ancient and allegedly valuable tapestries that had been packed away for decades, but that Devenish had now ordered restored to the ballroom walls.

She ate breakfast with Mrs. Grenfell in the breakfast parlour. Devenish was off somewhere, and Guy did not put in an appearance. As soon as the light meal was finished, the two ladies repaired to the vast, cold ballroom in which the tapestries were being assembled. Several large rolls already had been deposited on folding tables that were usually employed for al fresco picnics. Two footmen were carrying in another roll, Simeon Wolfe supervising the process. Josie asked, "Is this all of them, Wolfe?"

"All we could find, miss. They hang between each pair of windows."

Dubious, Josie touched a long, dusty roll with the tip of one finger. "What do you think, Pan? They look awfully dreary."

"We cannot tell," rumbled the chaperon. "They are inside out."

Josie requesting without much enthusiasm that this condition be reversed, the footmen untied the wide strips of cloth that had been used to bind one of the rolls, and the tapestry was spread. It was quite creased. The two men held it up and shook it out helpfully as Josie stepped nearer, and she was at once enveloped in a cloud of dust.

"Oh . . . dear!" she gasped, and retreated, sneezing.

Clapping a handkerchief over her nostrils, Mrs. Grenfell declared resonantly, "We cannot like dust!" and fled the room.

112

Josie persisted, however, wiping her eyes, and drawing near again. The workmanship was superb, but the colours were rather faded, as well they might be after several centuries. "What on earth is it supposed to represent?" she murmured, peering.

"Good gracious!" cried Wolfe, and launched his erratic way between Josie and the tapestry. "Do not look, miss!" he implored, spreading wide his arms.

"What's to do?" enquired Devenish, coming briskly into the room and eyeing his butler with amusement. "Charades, Wolfe?"

"It is—not fitting for the young lady," declared the butler, agitated.

"I think Wolfe finds your tapestry improper, dear sir," Josie said with a dimple.

"Is it, begad! Step aside, my Elf, and let me see." His ward dutifully retreating a few paces, Devenish in turn inspected the tapestry, guided by Wolfe's whispered comments. Chuckling, he spun about and clapped a hand over Josie's eyes. "Disgraceful! If that's the way they behaved in those days, one would think they'd have tried to keep still about it, rather than raise great embroidered monuments to their depravity!"

"Depravity?" she said, trying to remove his hand. "I did not see—"

"Nor shall you, my girl!" He jerked his head, and the footmen, grinning, laid the offending tapestry to one side.

"Let's see the next," said Devenish. "Josie, perhaps you'd best go and knit, or something."

Released, she replied indignantly that she would do no such thing, and they both bent their interest upon the next *objet d'art* to be held up for inspection. This one, in tones of muted greens, faded blues, and dejected pinks, depicted some extraordinarily well-endowed maidens cavorting in a most abandoned way around a maypole. A bullock of heroic proportions was being roasted over some pallid flames, and various rather distorted cottages wavered beside the village green. "May Day," read Josie, squinting at the lower edge.

"What d'you suppose these shepherds are up to over here?" muttered Devenish.

Josie joined him, gave a gasp, and put her hand over his eyes.

"The deuce!" he exclaimed, taking her hand away. "Jove, but they were a warm lot! I don't know about our ancestors, m'dear!"

"Your ancestors," she corrected him primly. "I'm sure mine, being poor, were figures of propriety"

"Probably," he agreed absently, frowning at another scene. "Whoever bent her needle on this lot didn't know her business! Only look at all these legless birds. They're not flying, and whoever heard of birds just hanging in the air like that? I'll tell you what, Josie, let's forget about these mons—"

"Foolish creature! They are ducks," she said.

"They are? Where's the pond?"

They both leaned nearer. "I think this must be it," said Josie, gesturing. "Perhaps, if we stood farther back . . ."

"Now, this is rather well done," he said, interested. "See how the wolf is killing that sheep." He pointed, and Josie gave a shriek as "the wolf" scampered off, leaving the placid sheep untouched.

"It's only a spider, silly chit," said Devenish, laughing as she threw her arms around him.

"I don't l-like spiders," she said, shivering.

"Then I shall murder it for you." He raised his boot.

"No!" she shrieked, clinging to him and pulling him back.

She caught him off balance, and his game leg gave out. Trying to restore him, Josie fell also. They both toppled into the tapestry, the footmen staggered, the ancient fabric split, and Devenish and his ward fell through the middle, the tapestry, wrenched from the footmen's hands, folding in upon them.

Hilarious, Devenish pulled the equally amused Josie to him, and the footmen, chuckling, lifted the tapestry.

"What . . . a tragedy," spluttered Devenish, waving away dust, and, turning Josie's laughing face, asked fondly, "All right, my Elf?"

Her eyes very tender suddenly, she said, "Yes. Are you?"

"This is the jolly hide-and-seek game, *oui*?"

Guy stood watching, balanced on his crutch. He was smiling,

but there was a gravity in his eyes that brought a deep flush to Devenish's face.

"A fine pair of wits-to-let you must think us," he said, scrambling up and assisting Josie to her feet.

"Speak for yourself, my Gaffer." She danced over to the Frenchman. "Wait till you see these prize possessions, dear Guy. They are the very naughtiest things!"

"But so sly that I doubt anyone will notice," added Devenish.

She glanced quickly at him, wondering at the vexation on the handsome features. "Dev—you never mean to hang them?"

"But—these, they are splendid," said Guy, coming closer and viewing the maligned works of art with an experienced eye.

"*Splendid?*" exclaimed Josie. "They're dusty and faded, and all droopily out of shape! They would look awful! Surely, we can use something else?"

Guy pursed his lips. "Do you know," he said thoughtfully, "if they were with care cleaned and repaired, and the fine frame put around them, they might do much better."

"You do not *frame* a tapestry," said Devenish, aghast. "Ain't done!"

"But we cannot hang them as they are, dearest," Josie argued.

He shook his head, then said a breezy, "Oh, all right. You are in charge of tapestry restoration, Monsieur Guy!"

"But—can it be done in time?" Josie threw an appealing glance at Devenish. "I do so want everything to be perfect."

He smiled at her. "Of course you do. And it shall be, I promise."

"We shall help," called Mrs. Grenfell from the doorway, "if they first remove the dust."

Sanguinet had hoped to enlist the aid of another seamstress, but he said without a hint of inner disappointment that he was sure between the two of them, they would complete the task in time for the ball.

Thanking him, Devenish invited that both he and Mrs. Grenfell accompany them on the road inspection, but the new partners declined, Guy saying he meant to inspect the rest of the tapestries, after which it would be necessary to take measure-

115

ments so that frames might be constructed. They left him busily occupied, with the footmen helping, Mrs. Grenfell calling advice, and Wolfe watching anxiously lest he might be obliged to support the Frenchman again.

through the morning. And then, from below, he could faintly hear her laughter, and Wilby, answering eagerly, and he thought he might be happy, for a moment, in spite of everything.

❦ Chapter 8 ❧

"You are very quiet this morning, Dev," said Josie, as they rode through the cold, grey morning.

He brightened at once. "I was just thinking about—er, those dashed tapestries. Do you suppose Guy's idea will help the stupid things?"

"It might. It was most kind in him to offer to help. Although, you rather foisted the task upon him, now that I come to think of it."

"Give him something to do. He's likely been bored to death since he came, poor fellow."

"Oh, no."

"Well, at all events, with your dragon's assistance, it shouldn't take too much of his time. And, they seem to get along well enough."

"True. I doubt she will help him, though." He stared at her, and she went on with a mischievous smile. "Did you not notice Faith's carriage driving up as we left?"

"Well, of course I did. Waved to the lady, didn't we? What has that to do with Mrs. G. not helping?"

"It has everything to do with it, blind one."

He gave a shocked gasp. "You cannot— My Lord! You never mean—Pandora Grenfell and—and Sir James . . . ?"

Her mirth over that remark resulted in her having to request his handkerchief, to dry her tears. Handing over the article, he said rather wistfully, "Gad, but I love to hear you laugh, Josie."

117

She turned her merry face to him. Her habit of rich brown wool fitted snugly about her shapely figure, and the matching fur-trimmed cap framed her glowing cheeks, the big dark eyes seeming illumined by her laughter.

After a lost interval, Devenish wrenched his eyes away. "What did you mean, then?" he asked hurriedly.

"Foolish one, Faith Bliss has been coming to visit her brother every day for over a week, and you've not noticed?"

He frowned. "Mrs. Bliss? Oh, come now, Elf. Not *Guy*?"

At once her amusement vanished. "Why not? I believe she was drawn to him from the moment they met."

"And purely fascinated when he fell at her feet," he said scornfully.

"What a perfectly miserable thing to say!"

"And what a true one! Romancing is all well and good to a point, my girl, but you must face reality. Guy is scarcely a desirable *parti*."

"For shame, Dev! He is a gentle, gallant, wonderful—"

"Cripple."

She levelled a pale-faced, furious glare at him, lifted her reins, and kicked home her heels. The mare was off in a flash, but Devenish was after her like the wind. He came up fast, leaned to seize Josie's reins, and drew the mare to a halt.

His ward made no attempt to resist, but sat with her face turned away and her little chin high.

"My apologies if I upset you," he said firmly. "But—truth is truth, however unpleasant."

"The only unpleasant thing is you," she said.

"Josie—look at me."

"No!" And then, perversely, she jerked her head around, revealing eyes ablaze with anger. "I hate you when you are like this. I *hate* you!"

His gaze fell for an instant. He said quietly, "As well, perhaps. All children hate their parents at one time or another."

"I am *not* your child," she said through her teeth. "And you are *not* my parent!"

"I'll own I've not been a proper one. The point is, Mrs. Bliss is a lovely, healthy young woman. I cannot feature Guy being so selfish as—"

"*Selfish!*"

"As to saddle her with—"

Very white now, she said, "Dev—stop. I vow I'll hit you if you do not! Stop, or let me go."

He met her gaze levelly. Infuriated, she swung her whip high. Devenish lifted his head slightly, but did not slacken his grip on her reins.

"Good gracious me," cried a mocking voice. " 'The quarrel is a very pretty quarrel as it stands; we should only spoil it by trying to explain it.' "

Devenish swore softly, intensely, and audibly.

Josie's face lit up. "Lord Elliot!" She lowered her arm. "A quotation, I think. Byron?"

"Sheridan." Fontaine removed his hat and bowed gracefully in the saddle. "I hope we do not—er, interrupt anything?"

"I would say we arrived at a most opportune moment," said his sister, her magnificent eyes flashing wrath as they rested upon Josie.

"I would have to agree, ma'am," Devenish said, ruefully.

"Bella," said the Viscount with amused magnanimity, "it is clear that 'our task is not to negotiate, but to deflect.' Come then, do you divert poor Dev, and I shall endeavor to lighten the mood of the fair Josephine."

Devenish's grim look at Fontaine was countered by a guileless grin. The Viscount waved an expansive invitation, Lady Isabella guided her dainty white mare to join Devenish, and off they went, two and two.

And who could have been more carefree than Mistress Storm, her little peal of laughter so frequently enchanting her adoring escort? Who could have been more cheerful and witty and entertaining than Alain Jonas Devenish, his full attention focused on the beautiful woman at his side, his own deep laugh occasionally countering the musical ripple that drifted from his vivacious ward? Isabella glowed that grey morning, for however barbed her criticism of some member of the *ton*, however thinly veiled the double entendres that dropped from her ruby lips, not once did the man of her dreams contradict her, or evade the subject. And as for my lord Fontaine, surely the girl was not born who could fail to be flattered by his admiration, or remain glum in the face of his whimsy.

The men labouring on the road looked enviously at the riding group. The foreman hurried over to knuckle his brow and report that despite the weather, the work was well begun and with luck would be completed in time for Miss Storm's party.

Devenish saw the pit yawning at his feet, and was powerless.

"Party?" murmured the Viscount, as they turned back towards the house. "Have you a birthday approaching, lovely one? And I remiss in observing it? Now, woe is me! I cannot but lose stature in your eyes."

" 'Tis no use your dropping hints, Taine," his sister called over her shoulder. "I already tried that and was cleverly turned aside." She gazed soulfully at Devenish. "I believe we are not wanted at the party."

With a brief and savage mental disposition of Elliot Fontaine, Devenish replied that he was perfectly sure all their friends would be invited.

Josie's heart seemed to stop. Breaking an instant of taut silence, she trilled, "We are still writing our cards, I'm afraid, but certainly it would be my very great pleasure if you could come, my lord. And your sister, of course."

Isabella called, "Prettily said, Miss Storm. Can you respond as charmingly, Taine?"

"Assurément," he declared, flourishing his beaver. *"Merci beaucoup,* Mademoiselle Josephine. We are *enchantés,* and shall be most pleased to attend." He added in a stage whisper, "I should include Devenish, perhaps?" He grimaced in his grotesque parody of a pout. "Although, I do not think he quite approves of me."

Leaning closer to Devenish, Isabella said a provocative "I can but pray he approves of *me.*"

Devenish gave her a warm smile and said he would like to meet the man who would *not* approve of so delightful a lady. But he glanced at Fontaine and thought, 'By God, but I must get William Little out of my house!'

The opportunity arose much sooner than he had anticipated, and in a way he was to regret.

The air had become colder by the time they reached Devencourt, and, trapped by the dictates of common civility, Devenish offered his callers some hot coffee before they went up to see their kinsman. They repaired to the drawing room, where they found Guy Sanguinet and Mrs. Bliss, the dark head very close to the red curls as they leaned over the harpsichord on which was laid one of the tapestries.

Mrs. Bliss was saying triumphantly, ". . . and it is a fox, just as I said—see, here is his tail!"

"Bested again, *hélas*!" mourned Guy in exaggerated anguish. "There is not the way out—I must do away with this Frenchman!"

They both laughed, and Mrs. Bliss cried, "Oh, no. Pray do not!" resting one hand on his arm as she spoke, her green eyes full of merriment.

Fontaine's breath hissed through his teeth, and he stood very still.

"Good heavens!" said his sister. "It is that dreadful Sanguinet creature!"

Devenish, who had paused for a moment to talk to Wolfe, came up just in time to hear the latter remark. Mrs. Bliss and Sanguinet glanced around guiltily. Guy groped for his crutch and Mrs. Bliss straightened, her face a little flushed and resentment replacing the laughter in her eyes.

"My dear Guy," said Devenish deliberately, "I fancy you are acquainted with Lady Scott-Matthias and Lord Fontaine."

My lord gave Sanguinet the briefest of nods and bowed elaborately to his distant cousin. Isabella allowed her dark eyes to flicker disdainfully over Guy before advancing to hold out her hand to Mrs. Bliss.

"My poor Faith—how loyal to deny yourself the pleasure of a ride, only so as to stay close to William. It must have been dreadfully dull for you."

Guy moved back a little.

Her colour heightening, Faith replied, "To the contrary. I have passed a most pleasant morning, I thank you. But I—"

Fontaine intervened, "But now I think we should go at once to see William." He turned to Devenish, his eyes chill. "You will excuse us do we not wait for coffee." His gaze slanting pointedly to Guy, he said, "Come, Faith—Isabella."

Mrs. Bliss became as pale as she had been flushed. Her eyes fairly darting rage, she turned on her cousin. The look she met appalled her. It was very obvious that if she objected, they would be treated to a fine scene. Fuming, she walked swiftly from the room, her relations following. Not a word was spoken as they ascended the stairs, for servants were all about, but once the door was closed in her brother's bedchamber, Faith whirled to Lord Elliot and said in a voice that shook with wrath, "How *dare* you put me in such a position?"

"Eh?" grunted Sir James, startled from a nap. "Oh, hello, Elliot, Bella."

Ignoring him, Fontaine said acidly, "I extricated you from the untenable position in which you had placed yourself. And I think you forget, ma'am, that I am the head of your house."

"I think *you* forget, Elliot, that your papa is not yet deceased!"

His eyes narrowed. He said in a soft, deadly voice, "My papa would have heartily endorsed what I was just obliged to do."

"What's all this?" demanded Sir William, blinking.

"You cut him dead," raged Mrs. Bliss. "And he has done nothing except to behave as a perfect gentleman!"

"Is that why you were hanging on his arm?" said Isabella mockingly. "La, but you pay little heed to the proprieties, my dear coz."

"Hanging on *whose* arm?" rasped Sir William testily.

"I am no longer a little girl," snapped Faith.

Fontaine said contemptuously, "Which being the case, one would suppose you to know better than to be in the same room with the fellow. Much less—alone! He's a veritable pariah! Why they let him roost here is past understanding. Everyone knows he and his brother plotted to destroy England."

"Destroy England?" Sir William shouted. "The devil you say!"

"Then everyone is wrong," flashed Mrs. Bliss. "Guy Sanguinet is—"

"*Sanguinet?*" Sir William's bellow rattled the windows. "*Sanguinet* d'ye say? Where's the dirty bounder?"

Fontaine glanced at him. "Here. It seems he and Devenish are regular bosom bows."

"*What?* By God, if that don't do it!" His face crimson, Sir William rang for his valet and read his sister a searing lecture that left her shaken and close to tears. Fontaine was dispatched to send a groom for his cousin's coach, and Devenish was summoned, to be informed in no uncertain terms just what Sir William thought of him, his damnable house, his demented servants, sundry assorted pigs, and filthy Frogs. My lord Fontaine, realizing too late that his abhorrence of Sanguinet had destroyed his excuse for frequent visits here, looked with real dismay at his equally dismayed sister. Not in the least dismayed, Devenish bowed and assured Sir William that every effort would be made to ensure his rapid departure.

Within a hour, they were gone.

Josie was seldom able to hold angry feelings, and when Devenish found at dinner time that he was still being treated with polite indifference, he realized he had sunk into deep disgrace. Josie chattered brightly with Guy, but since Mrs. Grenfell's conversation consisted almost entirely of unanswerable positive statements, Devenish felt marooned, and was glad when the meal came to an end. The ladies adjourned to the drawing room, and the two men relaxed over their port, Guy lighting up a cheroot, and Devenish hauling out his favourite pipe.

"Well," said Guy with a furtive smile, "you are rid of one of your—encumbrances, Alain. Yet—am I under the misapprehension dwelling, or are you less than *aux anges*?"

Devenish sighed and turned the pipe over in his hands without lighting it. " 'Fraid I've displeased Josie. I'd fancied she would have forgiven me by now. She don't usually despise me for such a long interval."

"It is not my wish to pry, but—is she angry because you do

not like Fontaine? Or because his sister have *beaucoup* admiration for you?''

''Both, I think. But—'' Devenish's gaze flickered and fell away. He said slowly, ''But—that's not the main reason. It was —because of you.''

''Mon Dieu! I am remiss in my tapestry duties?'' But Guy sobered as his friend lifted an unusually grave countenance. ''Ah—so this it is the matter *sérieux. Expliquez, s'il vous plaît, mon ami.''*

Devenish, uncomfortable, said slowly. ''We'd no right to discuss it, save that we all are friends, you know. Josie seems to think—It's none of my affair—Oh, the devil! She fancies that you and—and Faith . . .''

''I see.'' Guy watched the spiral of smoke from his cheroot. ''And you have tell her this it is not likely—eh?''

''Yes.'' Devenish began to ram tobacco into his hapless pipe. ''I told her that—under the circumstances, you would not—er . . .''

''These 'circumstances' being my—infirmity.''

The curly fair head jerked up. His eyes remorseful, Devenish admitted, ''Dammitall, Guy, I'm sorrier than hell. But—yes, that's what I said.''

''But of course.'' Guy nodded. ''And there is not the need for you to scourge of yourself for this truth. Save that you—how is it said?—you have evade the real truth.''

Devenish sat very still, his eyes quite blank. ''I do not take your meaning.''

''Mais oui, mon cher Alain. Whatever you have say to our little sunbeam, and I think it must have been clumsily said to make her so angry, you say it to mean yourself. Not me. And our Josie, she know this.''

Paling, but with two spots of colour high on his cheekbones, Devenish said haughtily, ''What the devil are you jabbering at? I've not the remotest interest in Mrs. Bliss—save that she's a most pleasant lady.''

With a faintly chiding smile, Guy waved the cheroot at him. ''And once again, you evade and dissemble. No, no! Do not send me the sparks from your eyes, for you cannot call me out. You have spoken your thrust, you must allow me my *riposte*—no?''

A stranger stared at him. A stranger with a bleak, closed face, his head proudly up-tilted, his voice glacial as he replied, "As you wish."

Devenish was closer to Sanguinet than any blood relation he had known, and he quailed to the dread that he might lose that friendship, but he said gently, "You are both very right, you see. When first I meet Mrs. Bliss, I think her the most beautiful lady. Next, I find she is kind and so very—comfortable to be with. With her, I am not made to know the embarrassment when I—lurch and stumble about. Soon, I am feeling a good deal more than these things. And she also, I think, have—perhaps, like me a little. But—" He shrugged and said sadly, "*En effet*, it is as you say—I cannot make the generous offer that she share the life of a man who can almost, but not quite, stand up without help."

His warm heart touched, Devenish forgot his wrath. He leaned to grip Guy's arm and say in his gentlest voice, "My poor fellow. I am so sorry."

"*Merci*. I shall, I expect, survive. But you, *mon cher* Alain. You must not think yourself like me only because you limp the little piece."

Devenish tensed and stared down at his still unlit pipe.

"Oh, my foolish one," said Guy softly. "Can you think I have watch you all these seven years and see nothing?"

Devenish neither moved nor spoke, but the flush died from his cheeks to leave him very pale.

"She loves you," said Guy. "Do not be the proud fool, Alain. Seize with both hands your happiness and thank *le bon Dieu* for it."

His voice barely audible, Devenish muttered, "She's grateful, is all."

"This, there is, of course. But more. So very much more."

"No," said Devenish, still in the low, repressed voice. "She's a child, Guy. She thinks she knows what she wants. How can she know, when she has seen so little of life and the world?"

"She has seen more than you think, *mon ami*. And she is widely admired, much courted. Me, I shall be surprised if she have not receive offers more than she may have tell you."

"I am much too old for her. Near twice her—"

"Never! I would say—"

Recovering his poise, Devenish looked up and interposed with the faintest hint of boredom, "Yes, I am sure you would. But you mistake the matter in one sense, Guy. Josie has a special place in my heart. As my loved daughter. But when I marry, it will be a lady of sophistication and elegance, and—some awareness of the world."

"Ah. Such as the lady who just have leave? The beautiful Isabella?"

Devenish's chin lifted. "Why not?" He stood. "Shall we join the ladies?"

Sighing, Guy commenced the struggle to stand. "I have not mean to put my nose into your business," he said rather diffidently.

"Let's say you gave me back my own, rather," said Devenish with his usual carefree grin, and waited until his friend hobbled around the table to come up with him.

At the door, Guy gripped his arm. "Alain—*mon cher ami*—you *cannot* over my eyes drag the wool!"

"Why should you think I would do such a thing?" said Devenish, amused.

"Because—ah, how can you not know it? You kiss each other—with your eyes—each time you meet. It is very clear to see."

Stunned, Devenish opened the door, and said not a word.

The three-quarter moon was often hidden by racing clouds, and the wind was chill, but long after the great house was quiet, Devenish wandered slowly across the pleasure gardens, both hands thrust deep into the pockets of his driving coat, the many capes fluttering in the wind. Coming to the terrace, he sat against the low balustrade, shoulders hunched, staring blindly across the wide park to the distant darker loom of the hills. After a few minutes he fished out his pipe and filled it, then took out his tinder box and struck vainly at the flint.

A faint whiff of *Essence de Printemps*; slender white fingers that took the tinder box from his hand. Devenish glanced quickly at the half-seen little face and looked away again.

"Here," said Josie, handing him the lighted flint.

"Thank you." He lit his pipe and puffed at it. Blowing a cloud of smoke skyward, he risked another glance at her. "You may go to bed now you have performed your good deed, little one."

She said nothing, continuing to lean against the wall beside him.

"It is too cold for you," he observed.

"Then why are you outside?"

"For peace and quiet."

"Which I disturb?"

"Very much."

She laughed softly and leaned nearer. "Do I so disturb you, oldest of the old?"

He did not answer, and she shrugged and informed the moon, "When the gentleman says nothing, it is because he dare not speak his thoughts."

"You would not like it if I did so, and I will not risk your anger twice in one day."

"You do not, sir, for I have not yet abandoned my first anger."

"Hmmmn."

"How much," she said to the moon, "is meant by that grunt. I believe it must be one of those elusive 'cryptic remarks' one hears about. There is the 'hum!' when he is thoughtful, the 'huh!' when he is irked, the 'hah!' when he is ready to fight, the 'hmmmn' when he is troubled or does not agree with what is said, and that becomes 'hmmmnnnn' when his admired future bride wiggles past."

He laughed. "What a summation!" And, humbly, "Am I forgiven, then?"

"You were horrid," she said in a stern voice.

"Yes. I told Guy."

"Oh!" She sprang up, whirling on him in a flame. "You never did!"

"But, of course. Did you think I would say something like that behind his back and *not* tell him?"

"I suppose you think that honourable!" She threw an exasperated glance at the heavens, so that her hood fell back and all her curls bounced. "Do you not know how cruel it is to be truthful?"

"That'll teach me. Now I'm in the suds again." He sighed heavily.

Fuming, she sat down again and asked after a pause, "What did he say?"

"He said . . ."

"What?"

"Nothing."

She gave a superior little snort. "So much for truth!"

"But you just said it is cru—"

"Oh, never mind!" She was still for a moment, while he smoked in silence. Then she burst out, "I suppose now that you have broken poor Guy's heart and made me utterly miserable, you are in a very ecstasy of joy!"

"I did nothing of the kind," he protested, indignant. "Had you not done your level best to ensnare that—to ensnare my lord the Viscount, he'd not have gone slithering up to tell Little that Guy was our guest also."

"Good heavens!" Aghast, she took his arm, looking up at him, all great eyes and anxiety. "Is that why they left in such a rage? You said Sir William was upset because Pan caught him cheating at cards."

He pulled her cloak closer around her. "Did you expect me to say, 'They have all run off, Guy old chap, because they refused to stay under the same roof with a pariah and anarchist such as yourself'?"

"Wretched man! They never said such things."

"Oho, did they not? I wonder you did not hear Little, he was so explosive." He drew her hood up over her curls, having first straightened a very frizzy one that had become left out when the others settled down. "You're shivering. Come along, my girl. Into the house with you!"

"No." She nestled closer against him. "I like it out here. Please, Dev."

He gazed down indecisively at the bundled little shape.

"If you could spare an arm, Gaffer," she said demurely. "I need not be so chilled."

He hesitated, then slipped an arm around her. "One might suppose us a case of—Spring moon," he said gruffly.

"Instead of which, we are an old gentleman and a young lady who are very cross with each other."

Devenish made no response, and in a moment she murmured. "Ah, that's better. My brain is thinking again."

He chuckled. "Had it stopped?"

"Yes. It does when I freeze. I remember when I was with the gypsies—"

At once, his hand was across her lips. "No," he said flatly.

"Very well." And, worrying, "Dev . . ."

"Yes, my Elf?"

"Do many patriots hate poor Guy, as Elliot Fontaine does?"

"Huh! Fontaine is no patriot, do not delude yourself!"

"Then why did he look at Guy in such a horrid way?"

"Heigh-ho! My head goes onto the block again! He hates Guy for the same reason, or perhaps one of the reasons, he hates me. Guy is a—flawed being. A cripple."

She wrenched away, and stood to stamp her foot at him. "Beast! You *limp* slightly. You are not—Oh! *Now* see what you almost made me say!"

"Even so," he argued, standing also, "many people feel that way, m'dear. Were I like Guy, not one of the ladies you claim have dropped their handkerchiefs would waste one second on me. Nor should I blame them."

She said huskily, "I would love you just as much. More."

For a moment he could not speak, then he said unevenly, "Because you are my—very loved daughter, and would be willing to sacrifice your youth and beauty to minister to my feeble uselessness."

Josie caught her breath audibly, then stepped a few paces distant and stood with her back turned.

"Egad," he said with rather forced lightness. "I only meant—"

"You only trample, poor old man. Very much the bull in the proverbial shop, carelessly destroying that which is pure and beautiful."

Mute, Devenish gazed at the proud tilt of her head, at the gleam the moonlight awoke on that one rebellious curl that had again escaped her hood. And then she gave a sudden thin little scream.

With an involuntary leap, he was beside her. "Dear God! What is it?"

Paper-white, she said threadily, "Something is . . . crawling around my ankle. Oh, Dev! Oh . . . *Dev* . . . *!*"

He dropped to his knees and groped under her skirts. "Please—*please* do not faint. It is likely only one of the kittens, or— What the . . . Oh, it's all right, love. It's only a garden snake. See—"

"Aaah!" she screeched.

"Hush, dear, please hush," he implored, glancing apprehensively at the dark sprawl of the house. "Look here," he held up a long, narrow shape that coiled itself around his arm. "It won't hurt you. Only think how friendly it was to have—" He detached the snake quickly, dropped it among the shrubs, and leapt to support Josie's swaying figure.

"It's all right, my babe," he murmured urgently, holding her close and pressing a kiss on her curls as she clung to him. "It's all right now. He's gone home. You are quite safe."

Shuddering, she gasped, "He was . . . crawling up my leg! Oh, *Dev!*" She began to weep hysterically.

"Now, now—where is my brave girl? It was only a very trusting small snake who forgot to go to sleep for the winter. He'd not hurt you for the world, sweetheart, I swear it. There, there, never weep so. Hush, little one."

After a moment, between diminishing sobs, she said in a scratchy voice, "What . . . did you call me?"

"Little one."

"No. Be-before that."

"Er—oh. Sweetheart. In a—fatherly way, of course."

She sniffed. "And—when you . . . kissed my hair. Was that a—"

"Yes," he said hurriedly. "Of course it was."

"Oh," said Miss Josie Storm.

130

✑ *Chapter 9* ✑

Preparations for the ball went ahead at full speed. Guy spent many hours in the company of Mrs. Grenfell, inspecting, selecting, and supervising the repair and cleaning of the usable tapestries. He was driven into Cirencester to arrange for frames to be constructed and, upon his return, remarked with proper nonchalance that he had chanced to encounter Mrs. Bliss and that she sent her compliments to Josie and Devenish together with thanks for all their help and the information that Sir William was much improved and now able to sit up and occasionally to take a few steps.

Josie was often busied with Mrs. Robinson, allocating rooms to the various guests who would overnight at Devencourt, and inspecting these apartments, many of whose furnishings had been under Holland covers for years.

Devenish conferred with his head groom and his steward regarding the clearing of unused parts of the stables, coach house and barns, and ensuring there would be space for the carriages and feed for the mounts that would soon descend upon them.

Due to the late notification of a major entertainment at a time when holiday parties were already under way, plus the rather remote location of the estate, most of the popular caterers had declined the commission. The one establishment willing to take on the catering for Miss Storm's ball sent out an extremely supercilious young exquisite, who chanced to encounter the party working on the road. The wagon carrying supplies to the workers had fallen afoul of one of the potholes and lost a wheel. Devenish, arriving a few minutes earlier, had dismounted to lend a hand. The catering company representative, deducing from his dress and his educated accent that Devenish was a step or two above the other workmen, supposed him to be the foreman and indulged himself with a few snide remarks anent woodenheads who decided to hold a ball three weeks before the event. He discovered his mistake when Devenish's hot temper flared, and much to the amusement of the workers, he was—as the foreman later related—"cut down, chopped up, and sent packing in jig time!"

As a result, Wolfe became much courted by local merchants, a steady stream of grocers, bakers, butchers, dairymen, fishmongers, greengrocers, and florists beating a daily path to his door from as far away as Cheltenham and Bristol. Exultant because the house was to have a great party again and himself entrusted with most of the details, the old gentleman reeled about, snapping out conflicting orders to his underlings, playing the overworked martyr to Mrs. Robinson, assuring Devenish that everything would run so smooth as any top, and thoroughly enjoying himself.

A Gloucester registry office had undertaken to provide temporary servants, and these individuals, uniformly complaining of the remote location, began to arrive to be interviewed. Devenish came into the Great Hall one afternoon and found it occupied by a small group of menials being conducted on a familiarization tour by Cornish. He retreated, only to collide with a flying seamstress, her arms full of pink velvet and having several pins in her mouth. She became shrilly convinced that she had swallowed one of the latter, and although this was found to have lodged in her ruff, Devenish was unnerved and fled the house.

Acceptances were coming in, and one foggy afternoon a week before the date of the ball, Josie was seated at her small desk in the bookroom, going through her lists, when large hands swooped from behind to cover her eyes.

"Oh!" she squealed, always excited by a game. "Let me

guess! Uncle Alastair?'' The hands were not removed. She went on eagerly, "Tristram? Oh, I know—Jeremy! No? John . . . ?''

"John who?'' growled an irate voice.

"Lyon!'' She spun around and jumped up to hug and be hugged. "Our famous surgeon!'' she exclaimed, as he released her, then kissed each hand in turn. "Oh, Lyon, *do* tell me—was it a success? Were you pleased? What did Lord Belmont say?''

Lyon Cahill smiled, his brown eyes drinking her in eagerly. "One at a time, me proud beauty. Jove, but you look nice in that red—er, thing.''

"I hope you know more about your surgical procedures than you do about ladies' apparel,'' she scolded, sitting down again. "It is a Spencer, foolish boy. And I wear it over my gown because the weather has turned so cold.''

He perched against the edge of her desk, folding his arms across his broad chest and regarding her with such patent joy that she blushed a little. "Well, it's very fine on you,'' he declared. "As for the operation''—his face clouded—"it went so well. We did it last week. Belmont said it was superb, but . . . the patient died next day, poor fellow.''

"Oh, Lyon! I am so sorry!''

He sighed. "Shock, mostly. And it was so high, you know. Had it been at the knee, perhaps . . .''

Josie shuddered. "How frightful it must be. I cannot bear to think of such an ordeal.''

"I was talking to Belmont about it. He worked on the streets of Brussels during Waterloo. He arrived after the battle started, and was kept so busy with returning wounded, he never had the chance to get out to the field. He told me he will not soon forget the bravery of the men whose limbs he had to amputate without so much as a drop of laudanum. Most of them uttered not a sound.''

"And soon died,'' she said dismally.

"Not all, m'dear. He had quite an impressive rate of survivals. We can do much better in his lordship's private hospital, of course. And would do better yet could we but find some way to alleviate the pain.'' He frowned. "That is our biggest hurdle, and irremediable, alas.'' He saw the distress in her expressive

133

face and added heartily. "Well, enough of me and my burgeoning career. Where's the guv'nor?"

She smiled up at him. "Yours, or mine?"

"Mine. Does he go along all right?"

"Excellently well. I believe he is becoming more accustomed to his crutch."

"He stuck to just the one, then? Famous! I never thought he would! It's so miserable for the poor man. Does he seem very wretched?"

"No! Never look so anxious. Guy is happier than I've seen him in an age. Indeed, he is out driving at this very minute—all alone."

Lyon's jaw dropped. "But—but he never goes out alone! For one thing, he is not strong enough, and for another, he knows how people feel about him. Was some group of blockheaded yobboes to come upon him, Lord knows what might happen!"

Alarmed, she cried, "Oh, my! I'd not thought of that! And he has been driving out every afternoon this past week and more. I thought only that he needed a change, for the dear creature has been working so hard."

"Working?" Mystified, Lyon asked, "At what, dare I ask?"

"You may, but I shall not answer." She dimpled at him mischievously. "It is a secret. None of us is allowed to see until he presents his task, *le fait accompli*."

"I see you've been up to your tricks again! What else have you been about?"

"Very much. Oh, Lyon, I never dreamed there was so much involved in giving a simple little ball."

"Little!" Devenish, who had come in a moment after Lyon, but had stood quietly unobserved until now, crossed to welcome the new arrival. Lyon was startled to note that Devenish was using a walking cane, but he did not comment.

"Never allow yourself to be coerced into hosting a ball," warned Devenish. "You'll be badgered to death from morn till night, and driven from under your own roof by the pandemonium. The ladies, God bless 'em, are gone quite berserk!" He went to the sideboard and poured two glasses of sherry, one of

134

which he handed to Lyon. "Sit down, my dear fellow, and tell us all your news. I fancy you've some bragging to do."

Lyon sat as close to Josie as he dared, and apprised Devenish of the sad results of his initial venture into surgery.

"One takes one's chances when you butchers sharpen up your little knives and saws," said Devenish, rather unmoved. "I feel sorry for his lady wife, but—" He paused, watching the young man curiously. "Cheer up, nipperkin! I'm quite sure you did your very best."

Lyon, who had been frowning into the fire, started. "Oh— my apologies. You know, our old London is strange at times. When I left the surgery that day, a man was waiting for me. The nurse said he'd been there for an hour. He was a well-set-up old fellow. Thin, neatly dressed, with snow white hair and a pair of the most snapping black eyes I ever saw."

"Wanted you to amputate that white thatch, I'll warrant," said Devenish with a wink at Josie.

"You're out there, Dev. He wanted me to look at his—dog."

"Dog?" echoed Josie, incredulous. "Whatever did you say?"

"Be dashed if I see anything remarkable about that," said Devenish, at once indignant. "Animals need doctors just as badly as do human beings."

Josie pointed out smilingly, "We have a very good farrier in the village."

"Farrier, my eye! What we need are veterinary surgeons. I doubt there are a hundred the length and breadth of England!"

"Well, we've some fine veterinary schools now, at least," said Lyon. "Will someone pray tell me how we came to discuss this deficiency?"

"You started it," Josie accused, but with her fond gaze on Devenish. "You dared to say the fatal word—dog. You might have known 'twould set old Rat Paws off!"

They all laughed, and Devenish said, "*Mea culpa*, as usual! Do go on, Lyon. What about the aged gent's animal?"

"Well, I looked at it, of course. Poor creature had a small twig that had somehow worked down into its ear. I was able to get it out. Much thanks I got!" He held out one badly bruised hand.

"You'd likely bite someone had you a twig in your ear," said Devenish. "Were you reimbursed for this work of mercy?"

"Not a sou. But—do you know—" Lyon's gaze returned to the fire—"before I left, the old fellow suddenly asked if my name had always been Cahill."

"Did he, by God!" Devenish sat up straighter.

Josie said intently, "Then he knew you, Lyon?"

"So I thought. And I'd a feeling I'd seen him somewhere before. But Belmont called for me, and when I went back, the old gentleman was gone. He'd left me a note, though." He took a slip of paper from his waistcoat pocket and handed it to Devenish. "Oddest thing."

Unfolding it, Devenish read aloud the message that had been inscibed in a neat, rather spidery hand. " 'You think not to have been paid. You have eased the suffering of the one being on this earth that I ever have loved. Payment will be in keeping with the value of your help. Lavisse.' Hum . . ."

"Quite correct, dear Gaffer," said Josie. "The thoughtful grunt."

He grinned at her absently. "Lavisse . . . Is it familiar to you, bothersome child?"

She shook her head.

"Lyon!" Guy hobbled to join them, his cheeks aglow from the cold. *"Bienvenu, mon fils!"*

Lyon jumped up and they shook hands, the brown eyes and the hazel ones warm with the affection they shared.

"How well you look, sir!" Lyon said gladly. "This Devencourt air must agree with you. And you are walking so much easier!"

"All thanks to my so clever investment in yourself. Do you know, Lyon, I really think that very soon I shall be able to manage with just the cane."

Josie murmured. "You would seem to progress as rapidly as Dev retrogresses."

Guy looked embarrassed, Devenish was apparently absorbed by his wineglass, and Lyon directed a shocked glance at his beloved, amazed that such an unkind remark could have issued from the lips of so kindly natured a girl.

There was little time for reflection. Guy was full of questions about his stay in Town, and then Lady Godiva came trotting in and took up residence at Devenish's feet, this prompting a joint recital of the fall of Sir William and the subsequent events. Josie, Devenish, and Guy all collaborated in the telling, and the tale became so amusing that the air rang with laughter and the time flew.

At five o'clock, Devenish and Guy excused themselves and went upstairs to change their clothes. Lyon was alone with his love, but his attempt to declare himself was foiled, Josie saying that she also must change. The best he could do was to obtain her promise to meet him in the bookroom in an hour's time and to accompany him on a short walk before dinner.

Josie was not one to keep a gentleman waiting interminably while she decided which bracelet to wear, and he had been in the bookroom for only ten minutes when she entered, wearing a rich grey velvet cloak over her full-skirted evening gown of blue silk, and with sapphires sparkling in her ears. Lyon shrugged into his redingote and led her out through the French doors.

The early evening was chill, with vapours swirling listlessly about, but the air was fresh and clean, and Josie, who had been in the house most of the day, was only too pleased to take Lyon's arm and walk along the drivepath towards the distant lodge gates.

"At last, I have you all to myself!" he said triumphantly. "I've waited and waited, for I have so much to say to you."

She said, "It is nice, isn't it? We all are so proud of you, Lyon. Can you stay for the ball, or must you go home first?"

" 'Fraid I must. I shall have to pack, and I've a few patients to look in on before I come. However, I've already had a few words with Dev, and—" He checked. "Josie, how long has he been using that cane?"

Her chin set and for a moment she did not reply. Then she said, "A few days. If he remembers." She frowned darkly. "It is all fudge, Lyon, and done purely to convince me of his age and decrepitude."

Much shocked, he asked, "Why should he wish to do so? To

137

keep you with him? I cannot credit that he would be that self-ish!''

"It is only amazing how much less infirm he is when Isabella Scott-Matthias is about! You'd scarce believe the transformation.''

"Is she about, then? I fancy her ladyship stirs up the neighbourhood! She's certainly a glorious sight.''

"She is interested in stirring only one gentleman. She and her brother were invited to my party, but I doubt they'll come after the contretemps with Sir William. My, but they left in a flame.''

"I fancy Dev was glad enough to see *him* leave.'' He frowned suddenly, a suspicion striking him. "He thinks Fontaine has a *tendre* for you.''

She smiled faintly and, noting his expression, enquired, "Don't you like Lord Elliot either?''

"I think him a well enough fellow, but—perhaps Dev's dislike is justified. He's not one to take people in aversion in the usual way.''

"Well, he has this time. As a matter of fact, they were so mutually enraged at one point that I really fancied they would come to cuffs.''

Lyon whistled softly. "I'd not like to see Dev go out with a man of Fontaine's reputation. You must try if you cannot calm him, Josie.''

She said nothing, her brow furrowed.

Cahill clapped a hand to his head. "What a pudding head to so waste my opportunities!'' He halted, faced her, and, nerving himself, said in an unsteady voice, "Josie, I am going along quite well in my profession. I'll never have the fortune of a Fontaine, or of John Drummond, for that matter, but in a year or so I could give you a comfortable life, and— Well, Dev has come to think you are old enough to wed, so will you make me a very happy fellow please, and—and say you will marry me?''

It was done! He pulled out his handkerchief and mopped his sweating brow.

"Poor Lyon,'' she said, both touched and troubled by this clumsy proposal. "What an ordeal for you. And how very dear to be asked such a question by one of whom I am so fond, and who is, I suspect, fond of me . . ."

"Oh, Lord!" he groaned, clutching at his hair. "How could I be such a blockhead? I knew I'd spoil it! But, surely you know—" He took her by both arms. "Of course you know. I've been in love with you for years and years."

She detached her arms and took his hands instead, saying gently, "I think perhaps I did know, my dear friend. And I am indeed most deeply honoured, but—"

He paled and jerked away, interrupting harshly, "But you do not want me." His eyes were bright with anger and there was a bitter twist to his mouth.

Josie knew that look and said, distressed, "I want you and always shall, for my loved friend, but—"

"There is not the need to sugar-coat it, I thank you. I'm gallows-bred, I know."

"What a horrid expression! As if you are, Lyon. And if it were a matter of birth, my own is no better than yours."

Standing half-turned from her, he growled, "I doubt that. Whoever your parents, they were likely of better quality than mine. Besides, you've the chance to raise yourself far above my station. I was a fool to hope—"

"No, no!" She caught at his arm, and said tearfully, "Lyon, *please* do not be so unhappy. I care for you deeply, for you are one of my dearest friends. It is just—I have no plans to marry yet. But—but when I do, it will not be for wealth or rank or social position, but because I love with all my heart and soul. And am as loved in return."

He was not greatly surprised, for he had sensed she did not return his devotion, but he had clung to hope, and it was very obvious that for him there was none. All his pride in his really splendid achievements crumbled to dust. For the first time he wished that Guy Sanguinet had never taken him up; that he had been left in the gutter, where at least he would have been with his own kind, and not inspired to aim for the impossible in life. A life that now loomed ahead in cold emptiness.

Some of his bitter despair showed in his face, and Josie was shattered. "Lyon," she pleaded brokenly, "do not hate me. You'll find the right—"

"Oh, spare me! Shall we go back to the house?"

Head down, half blinded by tears, she started to walk beside him.

Hating himself because he had made her cry, he yet could not curb his disappointment, and muttered, "I suppose if I were an aristocrat, I'd take it with a smile and tell you not to be distressed and that I'd try again. Well, I won't!"

"N-no. I would not blame you at—at all if you . . . never spoke to me again."

He halted, and with a muffled groan swept her to him. She wept openly and he fought to control his own grief, and even in that painful moment was exultant to hold her in his arms. Somehow, he regained his control, took out his handkerchief, and dabbed clumsily at her tears. "Let's pretend," he said huskily, "that it never happened. Let's pretend I never asked you."

"All . . . right," she gulped. And they went on, and did not speak again.

Devenish was crossing the Great Hall when they walked in. He paused, his shrewd gaze flashing from Josie's averted countenance to Lyon's pale, stony face. He could guess what had transpired and, because he had experienced that agony of loss, he ached for the boy.

Josie mumbled something and fled to her bedchamber and Fletcher's consoling arms.

Lyon went silently past Devenish and down the hall to the drawing room, where Guy sat chatting with Pandora Grenfell. The Frenchman took one look at his adopted son's face, and was still.

"I must get home, sir," said Lyon, with the vestige of a smile.

Guy said with grave courtesy, "I am sure you know best what it is for you to do. Ride safely, my Lyon."

Cahill smiled again with that bleak curving of the lips that lent no warmth to his empty eyes and, bowing to Mrs. Grenfell, he stalked away.

Guy sighed and glanced to the large lady. They had come to

140

understand each other during their work on the tapestries, and a deep friendship had sprung up between them.

"We sympathize," she rumbled.

"*Merci, Madame.* Though—it was not altogether the result unexpected."

"Naturally not," she said.

To go down to dinner that evening was one of the most difficult things Josie had ever done. She could not know how wan she looked, nor how that look wrought upon her guardian, but she was grateful that Lyon had gone home, and more grateful that not by word or glance did Devenish, Guy, or Pandora betray their awareness of what had happened. Devenish was in high form, winning a laugh from Mrs. Grenfell by describing an encounter he and Josie and Craig Tyndale had once had with a performing bear, and teasing Guy about his solitary rides. The Frenchman's thin face became quite pink and, forgetting her own sorrow, Josie cried eagerly, "Guy, you have been seeing Mrs. Bliss!"

Sanguinet's colour deepened. He stammered and evaded, but at last admitted that he had "chance to meet the lady *quelquefois, de temps en temps,*" this, of course, leading to more teasing until poor Guy begged for mercy. It was all very light and frothy and, as each of them knew, designed purely to bring the light of laughter back into a certain pair of haunted brown eyes.

By the time Devenish handed her her candle at the foot of the stairs, Josie was much restored. Mrs. Grenfell had already made her majestic way to her bedchamber, and they were alone in the Great Hall. Standing on the second step, Josie hesitated and, looking down at her guardian, began hesitantly, "Dev . . . I . . . ."

He said in a very gentle voice, "Do you want to talk about it, dear?"

She shook her head.

"Then go to bed with a good book and read until you drop it. Then go to sleep."

She blew him a kiss. "Goodnight, then." But halfway up the first flight she again turned back. He was still standing there, watching her, and with a flurrying whisper of silks she was beside him again. "Dev—I *did* not mean to hurt him so!"

"If you cannot bear to give your suitors an honest answer, my sprat, you will end up with fifty husbands."

Her laugh was rather shaken. "I have not near that many suitors."

"You cannot know how that relieves my mind. Even so, I am preparing to be besieged. You must let me know which you favour and which I am to frigidly repulse. Give me your candle and I'll light it again. There. Now, do pray contrive to move less precipitately, Milady Elf!"

Promising to draw up some Frigid Repulsion Lists, she went upstairs.

Devenish limped across the hall smiling to himself. The white and the ginger cats stalked him and a black and white kitten bounced along ahead.

Two days later John Drummond arrived from Park Parapine, escorting his sister Rosemary to the ball. Josie and Mrs. Grenfell were visiting an ailing pensioner in Devendale Village when the Drummonds arrived. Devenish, who had been engaged in a rather bewildering discussion with Wolfe regarding the numbers of cases of champagne that had been ordered, hurried to greet these, the first of the guests to arrive. Rosemary, always struck dumb when she was near Devenish, blushed and stammered and amused him with her obvious hero worship. John, who had never seen his sister behave so, was as amazed as she was overawed, and told her audibly to stop being such a figure of comedy. Devenish gave the embarrassed girl into the hands of Mrs. Robinson and took John into the bookroom. The young man lost no time in enquiring when Josie would return.

Devenish looked at him thoughtfully. "Within the hour, I fancy."

"Oh, good," said Drummond with a sigh of relief. And then, in new anxiety, "Does Fontaine stay here, Dev?"

Lifting the white cat from his chair, Devenish snapped, "Certainly not!"

Drummond saw the flare light up those incredibly blue eyes.

"My apologies. I only meant—Well, I suppose I should approach you first, Cousin."

'My God!' thought Devenish. 'It's a deluge!' "Regarding my ward's friendship with Lord Fontaine? I'd not thought your acquaintanceship with Josie of such duration that you would seek to influence her friendships."

Reddening, Drummond said, "No! Of course not, only— Well, I did see her often when you brought her to Sussex before I went abroad, and—I've a great admiration for her. In fact—er, it is my hope you will allow me to address her with—ah, regard to . . . to her becoming my wife."

His voice positively squeaked on the last rush of words, and Devenish took pity on him. "I would have not the least objection to your doing so—" He heard the breath of relief, and added, "At some future date." The green eyes, so reminiscent of Yolande's, scanned him anxiously. He went on, "Josie has been most upset of late by the—the sad experience of a friend to whom she is very attached. I think it would be in your best interests, as well as hers, if you did not speak of this until—at least after the ball."

A beaming smile lit the rather sober young face. "Whatever you wish, sir. I'd not dream of adding to her distress. I'm only glad you do not object, after my sister—" He broke off, biting his lip in an agony of mortification at having blundered into such a morass.

Devenish, who had been thinking that every time one of these young bucks called him "sir" he felt a hundred years old, laughed. "No, no, do not be embarrassed. Yolande is dear to my heart, and always will be, as are all your family. Speaking of which, John—have you discussed this matter with Sir Martin?"

Drummond's lips tightened and the smile left his eyes. He said slowly, "Yes. I expect you may guess that he does not approve."

"I expect you may guess that fact infuriates me."

From what Drummond remembered of this fire-eater, it took very little to infuriate him, but he nodded. "I can, indeed. Papa is a very good man, but—well, old-fashioned."

"And you mean to go ahead, over his objections?"

The earnest eyes met his steadily. "I do. I—my regard for Josie is such that I cannot be swayed by what I consider to be unwarranted prejudices."

Although they had grown up on neighbouring estates and were distantly related, Devenish had seen little of John Drummond. His own activities since leaving University had kept him so occupied as to preclude anything but an occasional encounter at family holiday gatherings, and the eight years that separated them inevitably resulted in a minimum of shared interests. He found now that he liked this young man very well. There was an indefinable air about Drummond that met Devenish's ideal of the true gentleman: strength, coupled with good sportsmanship; an impeccable sense of honour; an obligatory gentleness towards all creatures weaker than himself. But . . .

Watching him, Drummond said apprehensively, "You have reservations?"

"I wish I could say I did not. Certainly, I approve of you as a candidate for my ward's hand. Only—I know her, perhaps better than anyone knows her. And I doubt she would wed against the wishes of her prospective parents-in-law. Especially if they are people of whom she is very fond."

"I know. I've worried about that also." Drummond said with a sigh, "In which case I can only hope that, if Josie will have me, we can win my father over. I know he likes her. It's just her lack of background he—er, objects to. Even so . . . I do not see how he can resist the sweet soul."

Tight-lipped, Devenish said, "No more do I."

With each day the great house became more a beehive of activity. New servants were arriving, and Wolfe took on the manner of a stern major domo, issuing strict orders that he as often amended; assigning supervisory tasks to long-time staff, and then interfering with them. Carts rumbled up the drivepath delivering cleaned draperies, eiderdowns, and new bedding that would replace items taken from storage and in many cases found so moth-eaten as to be unusable. Storage cabinets in the basements were unlocked and treasures rediscovered that had long since been forgotten. Hunting for suitable vases and urns for flowers to be placed in guest suites, Mrs. Grenfell unearthed a magnificent silver epergne and four cruets, all black with tarnish. These, she declared, must be used, and the kitchenmaids began to polish frenziedly, eventually producing a dazzling, if somewhat startling, design of scantily attired Grecian maidens and their completely unclad admirers. Devenish, amused when he discovered Josie and Rosemary giggling over the epergne, protested its placement on the dinner table, and pronounced it more shocking than their naughty tapestries.

By this time it was no secret that Guy and Mrs. Bliss were fast friends, and the Frenchman had several times ushered the lady into the house upon his return from his afternoon drives. Faith was among the select group summoned to the ballroom on the Wednesday afternoon before the party, to view the now hung tapestries. Guy had made quite a ceremony of it. A table had been set up in the adjoining music room, with tea and cakes and tiny sandwiches. The guests were to assemble there at four o'clock, by which time Lyon was expected to return from Gloucester. Mrs. Grenfell, Rosemary and John Drummond, Josie, and Devenish, arrived as instructed. Mrs. Bliss, flushed and happy, poured tea, and Josie nudged her guardian and winked at him when she saw the smile the widow bestowed on Guy. Lyon arrived as they were chattering over the refreshments, and if he seemed less talkative than usual, he was courteous to all and apparently much taken with Rosemary.

They were preparing to go into the closed ballroom, when Cornish strutted in, to bellow, "Major and Mrs. Craig Tyndale!"

Josie put down her cup with a hand that trembled, and turned, smiling brightly to join Devenish in greeting his cousins.

Major Tyndale was tall and fair complected, his hair a few shades darker than that of Devenish, and his features sufficiently good that he was termed a very attractive man. His parents had migrated to Upper Canada when he was three years old, and he had lived in the Crown Colony until he had returned to Europe in 1813. He had fought gallantly against the French, been twice wounded, and arrived in England, after a long convalescence, in an attempt to find his relations. He and his cousin Alain had disliked each other on sight, but fate had thrown them together, and a deep friendship had resulted. That friendship had been sorely tested when Tyndale fell in love with and eventually won the girl to whom Devenish had been betrothed since childhood. Time, and Tyndale's persistent efforts at reconciliation, had eventually bridged the gap between the cousins, and Devenish had by now quite forgiven the Canadian for stealing away his lady.

Josie liked the quiet, rather reserved Tyndale, and welcomed him warmly. To his lovely wife she was properly courteous. Yolande, perfectly aware of the fact that Devenish's ward disliked her, exerted every ounce of her considerable charm to extend Josie's smile from her lips to her cold dark eyes, and failing, wondered sadly if the girl she so longed to befriend would ever unbend towards her.

The Tyndales, who had left their three little boys with the Leith children in Berkshire, were soon drawn into the merry company, and the tapestry viewing was delayed until they had shared the refreshments. Lyon made no attempt to engage Josie in private conversation, as she had dreaded he might do, and since Yolande and Mrs. Bliss had struck up an immediate friendship, she was able to relax and enjoy herself.

At half past five, Guy rang a little bell and announced, "The exhibit, she is now open!" and they all went along the hall to the ballroom.

Cornish and one of the new lackeys stood rigidly at attention before the closed doors. At a nod from Guy, those doors were flung open and the little party trooped inside.

Devenish's earlier misgivings about the chandeliers had been well justified; each individual lustre had been removed, washed in hot soapy water, and replaced. As a result, the chandeliers, now ablaze with light, glittered like four enormous diamonds. The walls had been thoroughly cleaned and all the woodwork washed down. The floors shone, and between each soaring pair of windows hung the tapestries, majestic now in their narrow, carven frames, the colours much restored. The whole was an impressive sight and, after a moment's admiring silence, everyone broke into applause. Guy and Mrs. Grenfell, who had stood side by side waiting anxiously, beamed at each other.

Josie thanked "the restorers" with real delight, and Devenish exclaimed, "My little Elf, your ball must be a great success! How could it fail, now that it is to be set in such sumptuous surroundings?"

"And launched with such an impressive alliteration!" teased Craig Tyndale.

They all laughed, but, glancing at Mrs. Bliss, Devenish wondered if it was just his imagination, or if for a moment her eyes had reflected the same foreboding that had inexplicably taken possession of his own mind. He detached the black and white kitten from his shoe, and stroked it absently.

ও Chapter 10 ও

The last of the new servants had reached Devencourt on Tuesday, and by Thursday many of those guests who had travelled long distances to attend the ball were arriving. Notable among these were most of the men the King had dubbed his Nine Knights, these being Lord Mitchell Redmond, as controversial as he was admired; his brother, Sir Harry Redmond, who had earned such a splendid reputation with his Regiment during the Peninsular Wars; the Reverend Mordecai Langridge, uncle to the brothers Redmond, who looked very mild and middle-aged in his clerical garb and not at all like the fine fighting man he was; golden-haired Lord Jeremy Bolster, unfailingly amiable and good-natured—until aroused; and Justin Strand, fair-haired, wiry, and intense, his blue eyes as alert, his manner as brisk as ever. These gentlemen and their wives soon gathered together with those of their number already present, and there was much back-thumping and hand-shaking among the gentlemen, and hugs, kisses, and merry chatter among the ladies. All were concerned for Lord Mitchell, whose handsome head had made such violent contact with the brick, and who, although rather pale still, assured his friends that he was "perfectly fit" and had in fact been readying his next blast to be delivered before the House of Lords. The laughter that followed this blithe remark was struck to dead silence by a piercing whistle.

All heads turned. A tall, untidy footman stood at the open doors.

"What the devil . . . ?" demanded Devenish angrily.

"Sorry, guv," said Cornish with his leering grin. "Couldn't get through and you've got another lot toddlin' up the drive-path."

Mitchell Redmond exchanged grins with his brother, and several ladies hid amusement behind their fans.

Cornish, however, saw the look in his master's sparking eyes. "Cor, lumme!" he muttered, and beat a hasty retreat.

Josie went out with her guardian and, slipping her hand into his, heard Devenish's muttered oaths. She said cheerfully, "Isn't it lovely, dearest, to have our good friends here with us?"

"It'd be a dashed sight lovelier," he grumbled, limping rapidly along the hall, "if we'd one or two halfway human servants to receive 'em. I tell you, Josie, I dread to think what may happen! Do you apprehend that we've the Duke of Vaille and his Duchess invited, to say nothing of—"

"Yes, but Vaille's not a *royal* Duke, dear," she interpolated soothingly.

"To say nothing," he went on, slanting a stern look at her, "of a Marquis—"

"Who—Camille Damon? Why, he's the very dearest thing and not at all stiff-rumped."

"Good God! Don't let anyone hear you make such a remark!" he gasped, his scold losing some of its effect as he went on. "Cam can be deuced stiff-rumped when he chooses, I'll have you know! At least four Earls, a brace of Generals, three Countesses, and a couple of lowly Viscounts! And if your assortment of bizarreries—"

"But only think of all the starched-up new servants we've brought in, Dev. I met a footman this morning who was so icy, he scared me to death!"

He chuckled, squeezed her hand, and then was welcoming the elegant Philip, Duke of Vaille, and his lovely Duchess, Charlotte. Scarcely had these august aristocrats been ushered to their rooms than Josie, with a little squeak of joy, had thrown herself into the arms of one of her favourites, Vaille's only son, the darkly handsome Camille, Marquis of Damon, his Marchioness,

149

Lady Sophia, laughing merrily as she, too, was hugged and exclaimed over.

"Dev," said Camille, shaking hands with his host, "I see you haven't beaten all the spontaneity out of your Elf as yet."

Gingerly separating his whitened fingers, Devenish groaned, "Which is more than I can say for my poor hand! You might remember I'm a frail human being, Cam, and no match for your solid steel grip!"

Damon, a notable musician renowned for his brilliance at the harpsichord, apologized and inspected the remains with such exaggerated concern that Devenish was moved to cuff him, drawing forth his deep laugh.

Lady Sophia, holding Josie back a little as the men walked across the Great Hall together, whispered, "Josie dear, forgive me, but—is it true that you number one of the Sanguinets among your guests?"

Fond of this beautiful lady, Josie caught her breath and admitted it was truth.

"Oh, dear," murmured Sophia, looking troubled.

"Do you know Guy?" asked Josie, at once irked.

"No. And Camille and I are persuaded you would never have invited him unless he was a fine gentleman. The thing is—well, my papa-in-law is—er, rather set against him. And if Geoffrey Harland should come—good heavens!"

"The Earl has accepted the invitation, as has Lucian." Josie paused, and turned to scan her guest's violet eyes. "You do not think they would leave us because of Guy's presence?" she asked anxiously.

Sophia hesitated. "I fear they will cut him—at the very least. Cam said he knows his father would not have come had he dreamed Sanguinet would be here. Vaille is the dearest man imaginable, Josie, but when he is angered, oh my!"

Josie's heart sank.

The guests came thick and fast after that; the great house rang with cheerful talk and laughter, for most of these distinguished people moved in the same circles and were well acquainted, if not close personal friends. Josie was beside Devenish to welcome her guests, and warned him of her conversation with Lady Sophia.

Immediately furious, Devenish was also dismayed. He realized belatedly that Guy's presence might cast a cloud over the ball that was the most important event of his ward's young life. Nothing must hurt Josie, yet Guy was much too good a friend to be shamed or driven to leaving the festivities. Worried, Devenish managed a word with Jeremy Bolster, as a result of which the two young men cornered Philip, Duke of Vaille, and had a private conversation with him. Nothing was said in violation of their given word, but sufficient was implied as to leave his Grace considerably astonished and promising to do whatever he might to prevent trouble.

That the trouble did not materialize that day was largely due to Guy himself. He slipped away on his usual afternoon drive and, returning rather later than was expected, was drenched to the skin so that Lyon insisted he go at once to his bed. A tray was carried up to his room. Josie, full of concern for her beloved Guy, worried that he was keeping himself out of sight so as to spare her any possible embarrassment, but since it really had been raining hard and Guy had been very wet, she palliated her conscience by sending a lackey to the head gardener with the request that a large bouquet of whatever flowers were still available in the gardens or greenhouses be brought to her. The footman she had found so chilling once before brought the message that the flowers had arrived. He conducted her with grand condescension up the stairs to her sewing room, where lay the blooms and a basket of assorted fern. Several vases, a large pitcher of water, and a pair of shears had been provided. When Josie asked why the flowers had not been left in the scullery, the footman replied that the scullery and potting room were "very full of persons, and the chef full of vexation."

"Oh, of course." She smiled at him sunnily. "These are lovely. Please convey my thanks to Addicott."

He bowed and took himself off, not once having looked directly at her.

"Brrr!" she exclaimed softly, and applied herself to the flowers. The house was bright with the bouquets provided by the

151

florists, but these were for Guy and must be their own blooms. She chose a broad-mouthed vase of Chinese porcelain and was completing her arrangement, when the door opened and her guardian stuck in his fair head. "What's to do?" he enquired.

"I should be with our guests, I know, but this won't take long. They're for Guy." She stood back, surveying her creation with head on one side.

Devenish came over to slip an arm about her. "Jolly nice. And a kind thought, m'dear." He smiled down at her. Then, putting one slim finger under her chin, tilted her head up and said, "You can do something for another of our guests, if you will."

She was fairly sure of what the request would be and at once irritated, returned her attention to the vase, adding a spray of fern to the blooms.

"It's about Yolande," Devenish began, eyeing her warily.

"What a surprise," she said with rare sarcasm.

He frowned and turned to the door.

Whirling about, she said, "No, do not go off in a huff. What is it?"

He leaned back against the door, watching her. "Craig and I are perhaps closer than most cousins, since his sire was twin to my mama. Besides which, I owe him my life. I cannot like to see his wife treated unkindly in my home, Josie."

"I have not been unkind! I avoid her if I can, but I doubt she notices."

"You are your usual delightful self to every lady *except* Yolande. She would need to be dense indeed *not* to notice. And I do assure you the lady is not in the least dense."

"That is a matter of opinion," she muttered rebelliously.

He said icily, "It is my opinion. Twice I have seen her go out of her way to be friendly, and you were so polite and so distant, I could scarce believe it of you. You are her hostess. It will not do, Josie."

Perhaps twice in her life had he addressed her in such a tone and with such a look. She felt as if she had been spanked. Tears flooded her eyes and her heart twisted. Somehow, she managed to say in a strangled voice, "I am very sorry, Dev. I—will try to be . . . better.'' She waited for him to come and hold her tight, as he always did when she wept, but with her head bowed through a brief pause, she heard him say a clipped, "Thank you,'' and then the door opened and closed.

With a gasp she flung up her head. He had gone. She took up a chrysanthemum and stared at it blankly. He must be very angry indeed. 'It is that wretched woman,' she thought. 'She has come to my ball to spoil everything! Well, I won't let her!' She blinked away tears, added the chrysanthemum to the vase, and, realizing it was too much, took it out only to have half the flowers become disarranged in the process. Replacing them rather savagely, she wondered if the Flash House would have been so very dreadful, after all . . .

Fletcher found her young mistress unexpectedly subdued while she was being dressed for dinner. Longing to restore the happiness to the wan little face, she was relieved when a scratch sounded at the door.

Josie's heart began to beat very fast. Dev had come to apologize and be friends again. She looked up with a shy smile as Fletcher ushered the visitor into the room, and the smile was replaced by dismay. Dismissing her almost equally disappointed abigail, she stood to greet this very unwanted caller.

Yolande Tyndale said quietly, "I have come to ask if you would prefer that Craig and I slip away before your ball tomorrow.''

"Oh, no!'' cried Josie, aghast. "Have I been *that* rude?''

Yolande smiled and, occupying a chair, replied, "You have not been rude at all. You never are. Only—a woman can sense when another woman dislikes her, do you not think?''

So it was to be the moment of truth between them. Accepting that, Josie sat on the end of her big bed. She seemed very small and vulnerable, framed by the lofty brocade bedcurtains, her pale orange taffeta with its dainty white embroidery and scalloped flounces giving her an ethereal look. She was, thought Yolande, rather endearingly pretty, and she added, "I wish you did not, you know.''

"I wish I did not, either. But I just cannot help myself. When I try to like you for Dev's sake, I keep remembering how it was,

153

at first. How terribly you hurt him.'' Josie put a hand to her lips, knowing she was being outrageous, but then she blurted out, ''And you didn't care! You sent him off, breaking his dear heart for you. And you—you didn't give a snap!''

With a rustle of draperies, Yolande ran to sit beside her and take one cold, unwilling little hand. ''Oh, my dear! Never think that! I cared—very much. And so did Craig.''

''Dev loved you,'' Josie said accusingly.

''And I loved him. Very much. That was what made it so hard. I always had loved him, and I would have married him, probably, had I not met Craig.''

''His own cousin,'' said Josie with a curl of the lip. ''Poor Dev always says in his loyal way that Craig saved his life. He thinks the world of him. In spite of his . . . treachery.''

Yolande's back stiffened and she frowned a little.

Noting the change of mood, Josie said, ''I'm sorry,'' and added forlornly, ''There I go again. Dev will be so cross with me.''

For a moment Yolande was quiet. Then she tried again. ''Josie—Craig *did* save Dev's life.''

''I know. And Dev saved *his*! I saw it.''

''That is true. There is such a deep bond between them. I used to pray it would be so.'' She bent her head, her thick curls of that lovely shade between auburn and brown glowing in the candlelight. And then, looking up from under her arching brows, she said softly, ''The problem was, you see—Dev never was in love with me.''

Josie's mouth fell open a little with shock.

Yolande smiled into her stunned eyes. ''We had grown up together, as you know, and it always had been understood we would marry. Dev just . . . took me for granted.'' Her smile was wistful. ''You will think it silly perhaps, but—I wanted to be courted.''

''No. No, I quite understand. Oh, I *do* understand, but—'' Her face crumpled. ''But—I *don't* understand.''

And somehow, they were both laughing and holding hands.

''How could he not court you?'' asked Josie. ''Didn't he bring you gifts?''

"Indeed he did. I remember one of his last offerings. It was a fox kit he had found. It was full of fleas, bit one of the maids, and wrecked the kitchen. But—it wasn't only that, of course. Not the unromantical gifts. It was just—everything." She sighed nostalgically. "He loved me as—as something he owned. Not as a sister, I mean. But as though I were a requisite part of a picture he had painted. He was in love with the *picture*, do you see? He was in love with—with love. Not with me."

Josie sat very still, her eyes wide.

Yolande said gravely, "I asked him once what he most wanted from life. He said he wanted to prove himself. He never fought on the Peninsula, nor felt he had served his country. Then, he said, he wanted to make his uncle proud of him. And, of course, he wanted a complete life: a home, children, and—me." She smiled wryly. "I came in a rather poor last. And the worst thing was—he didn't even realize what he had said because loving me—fitting me into his picture—had become a habit. His battles with that dreadful Claude Sanguinet satisfied his first two wishes. When the time is right, he will find the rest of his happiness, and it will be a much deeper joy than ever he could have found with me. He knows that now."

Josie whispered, "He—knows?"

"He admitted to me quite some years ago that I had been perfectly right." Yolande gripped the hand she held. "And so— if *he* has forgiven, do you think—you might . . . ?"

Josie threw herself into the arms of this woman she always had despised. "Oh, yes! Yolande, thank you! Thank you!"

They sat down forty-two to dinner that evening and, looking down the long line of distinguished gentlemen and lovely ladies, Josie thought with a surge of pride that all these noble aristocrats were come to do her honour. Certainly, they knew of her lack of background; assuredly, they all had received other invitations they might well have accepted for this weekend, most being closer to home than an isolated estate in Gloucestershire. Yet— here they were. And even if they were really here out of respect and affection for Dev, they were pleased with her, or seemed so. Surely, he must be just a little proud of her?

155

At the far end of the table, she saw his fair head tilt a little, the better to see her around the enormous glitter of the epergne. Even at that distance she could see a trace of anxiety in his face. He lifted his wineglass and inclined his head very slightly. She smiled at him, and a slow smile answered her, and she knew she was forgiven.

The musicians, who had played softly during the meal, later moved into the ballroom, and a small dance party ensued. It was Josie's weekend, and she was the undisputed centre of attention. Her more youthful swains were cast into the shade by the magnificence of the Duke of Vaille, the fame of Lord Mitchell Redmond, the charm of his dashing brother, Sir Harry, the shy gentleness of Lord Jeremy Bolster, all in good-humoured competition for her hand in the dance.

It was very late when she stood at the foot of the stairs with her guardian to bid goodnight to their guests, and she saw his surprised expression after she hugged Yolande and wished her sweet dreams.

"Thank you, Elf," he murmured.

"Do not take the credit, sir," she said airily. "Yolande and I have sorted out our differences. She is the one you should thank, and—Oh, Dev! She is the dearest creature! No wonder you love her!"

There was no time for more, the Duke of Vaille leading up his beautiful Charlotte and telling Devenish he must get a good night's sleep was he to do full honour to Mistress Storm on the morrow.

Devenish and many of the younger gentlemen stayed up, but Josie soon went to bed in a daze of happiness, knowing that her success tonight was only a prelude to the splendour that was to come.

She was more tired than she knew, and almost fell asleep while Fletcher was brushing out her curls. The night was very cold, and a strong wind had come up that set the shutters to rattling, and sent occasional puffs of smoke down the chimneys. Fletcher had placed a warming pan between the sheets at eleven o'clock, and by midnight Josie's bed was snugly warm. She curled up under the blankets, but would not allow Fletcher to draw the bedcurtains in spite of the draughts, saying she wanted to awaken with the first ray of light.

She was asleep almost at once, but during the night the wind grew louder, disturbing her slumbers, and the eiderdown slipped so that she shivered and tried, half-waking, to get warmer . . .

A powerful hand gripped her arm bruisingly. She could smell gin and dirt and sweat. A crude voice snarled, "Thought ye'd get away, did yer, Tabby? By goles, but I'll whip some sense inter yer!" Evil, narrow eyes glinted. A cruel face, stubbled by whiskers, thrust at her. A muscular hand holding a sapling branch whizzed down. She screamed shrilly and fought to get away. "A nice little shape yer gettin'—all ready fer the Flash House. A good price ye'll bring, dang yer claws!" She screamed again, frenzied, fighting, but the iron grasp tightened inexorably . . .

"Josie! Little one! It's all right! It's all right!"

Gasping, terrified, her heart thudding madly, she opened her eyes. The door to her bedchamber stood wide. By the light from the hall lamp she saw that Devenish, a dark blue dressing gown over his nightshirt, sat on the edge of the bed, holding her, trying to calm her. Sobbing and incoherent with fear, she threw herself into his arms. "Dev . . . it—it was—"

"I know," he said soothingly. "Akim and Benjo. You dreamed they had you again. But they do not, dearest. You're safe. You're quite safe."

She clung to him, shuddering, sobbingly telling him how ghastly it had been, how real it had seemed that this time, for sure, she'd be sold into—

"Hush, my babe. It's all gone. Easy now. It was just a dream. Too much excitement for my little girl."

Her head was comfortably on his shoulder; his strong arms held her safe and close; his deep voice murmured reassurances until her sobs eased to spasmodic little gulps.

Fletcher, who had come running when she woke to that terrible screaming, stepped forward, and Devenish laid his ward back upon her pillows, dried her tears very gently, and bent, smiling, to kiss her forehead.

157

"Dev . . ." she pleaded, clinging to his hand as she'd done so often down the years, "you won't—go away?"

"My room is not so far distant," he said. "And Maisie will stay with you."

She smiled a grateful smile, and he patted her hand, then left her.

And closing the door, turned to come face to face with Lyon, his dark eyes holding a fierce accusation, his mouth a down-swooping line of fury.

Sitting up in bed, his hair tousled, his eyes grave, Guy Sanguinet watched the youth who paced like a caged beast at the foot of the bed. "Truly, it is that I am growing old," he muttered. "My room she is as far as Dev's, yet I heard not the sound."

"No," snorted Lyon. "And I should not have disturbed you, for you were tired out. I'm a thoughtless dolt."

"Mais non. You were upset and should come to—"

"Upset!" Lyon ran a hand through his hair. "I was *revolted*! I still am! Of all the disgusting—" He closed his lips and resumed his pacing.

Guy thought, 'Me, I knew that this sooner or later it must come.' And he asked, "What did he say to you?"

"Some nonsensical bilge about Josie having a nightmare. I pushed him aside and got away from there. By God, but I think I would have struck him had I not done so! If you'd *seen* it, Guy! The way he *looked* at her! And her so sweet, so trusting! Never dreaming—*Damn* his nasty soul! He *wants* her!"

"She is his daughter, and he loves her as—"

Lyon whirled about to hold the end bedposts, one in each powerful fist, and lean over the foot of the bed, saying through his teeth, "As a *father*?" He threw back his head and laughed bitterly. "That's rich! The affection in his eyes was not *parental*, I can tell you!" He turned away and, Guy remaining silent, muttered, "All these years I've admired him as one of the bravest men I ever knew! I looked up to him! And all these years he's been posing as that dear girl's father—while he kept her shut away in this lonely place. Gloating over her!" He rammed one fist into his palm and swore savagely, the crude gutter oaths of the slums he was born in.

Guy intervened angrily, "He is the very soul of honour! I am sure—"

"And so am I! When I offered for her, something she said made me suspect that he did not mean her to marry—ever! I have never been more shocked! I fancied he intended to keep her here to wait on him, so he would not be left alone in his old age. But I was wrong!"

"Of course you were. His is too generous the nature for such—"

Eyes blazing, Lyon snarled, "But not too generous to *desire* that fresh-souled, glowing young girl. At *his* age!"

"One moment, Lyon! Alain is but three and thirty, and—"

"And has claimed that she is—what? Seventeen, perhaps? *Half* his age!" He began to pace again, fanning his rage to white heat. "Damn his dirty slyness! How *dare* he? He warned John Drummond off, I know, for John told me! *John* is not too old for her! Neither is he crippled! I wonder he does not—" The rush of angry words died in his throat. He swung to stare in horror at his benefactor, and with a groan bowed his face into his hands. "Oh, God! Sir . . . I am so sorry!"

"There is not the need," said Guy, but his voice trembled and he was without colour. "It is the reaction *naturellement* from anyone young and—and undamaged, for someone who is not—"

"No, no! Do not say it! I never meant—I only—"

"You only saw, *mon fils*, what I have seen—what others have seen these many years." Lyon's abased head jerked up. Guy smiled faintly and moved his hand in the way that only the French can do effectively, and that said, "It is useless to fight it; it was inevitable; there is nothing to be done," all in the one comprehensive gesture. "It was," he said, "the case of the act charitable, that became, I think, a delight; a child growing up, filling his lonely days with laughter and busy-ness. Stealing away his heart before ever he knew it."

"He knows it now," said Lyon in a sibilant hiss that appalled Guy. "If *you* knew, why did you not warn me?"

"For several of the very fine reasons, *mon cher*. First—it is not my right to interfere. Second—you mistake emotion for resolution." Lyon continued to glare at him. He sighed, and went on, "The fact that my dear friend have love his little ward, does not mean he intend to claim her for his own. Indeed, I think this is just what he means *not* to do."

"Why?"

"Because, my fierce young gallant, it is in my mind that all of the so-bad things you have say about him have been already said by Alain to his own self. He thinks himself too old for her. That he is not—the whole man. That she is too young her mind to know." He sighed. "Is sad, this."

Lyon took a turn about the room. Returning to gaze down at the man who had given him his chance in life, he asked soberly, "And you? What do you think?"

Guy hesitated, then replied slowly, "I think, my Lyon, that no matter what I think, or you think, or Devenish thinks—our Josephine she have the strong little chin. And she will do—exactly as she please."

The wind had blown away the weather, or so Cornish cheerfully advised Josie when she went downstairs at half past ten o'clock the next morning. By that hour every servant in the house knew that Miss Storm had suffered a violent nightmare the previous evening, that her guardian had rushed to calm her, and that Dr. Cahill had glared bloody murder when he found Mr. Devenish sitting on Miss Josie's bed in his night rail, holding her in his arms. The regular servants, knowing the principals in the case, had little to remark, and what they thought was kept among themselves. The new servants sniggered, and one temporary footman was so unwise as to make a coarse jest, in consequence of which he lay on his back in the servants' hall, with his legs kicking in the air, and the aged butler cackling with glee as he complimented Klaus on a "flush hit!" The new servants ceased to snigger and no further reference was made to the incident. At least, not between the two factions.

"It's a bit nippy outside, miss," Cornish added, thinking that the young lady looked a trifle heavy-eyed. "Be nice and clear though, fer Oliver."

"Oliver . . . ?"

He jerked a thumb upwards. "The moon, miss. Be 'andy ternight!"

Despite the chilly weather, Devenish led those of his guests who fancied a ride on a tour of the estate, leaving Josie to welcome any early arrivals, although most of those coming on the day of the ball were not expected to appear until dusk. Even so, the number in attendance had swelled considerably by the time luncheon was served. This was an informal meal, with people arriving and leaving as the fancy took them, and servants bustling about, bringing in new platters and bowls as supplies diminished. Signor della Casa, the culinary craftsman below stairs, had arranged a selection of cold fowl, ham, and roast beef, platters of sliced cheeses, bowls of fresh fruit from the succession houses, fragrant hot breads and scones, muffins, nutmeats, cakes and jellies, and delicate pastry baskets filled with lemon curd, strawberry preserves, or caramel creme.

The large dining room, which was very large indeed, had been rearranged to hold five long tables, and rang with merry chatter and laughter. Only in one corner was the atmosphere less convivial. Guy had braved the throng at last, and made his awkward way to the end of an empty section of the last table. It remained empty until Lyon joined him, muttering furiously that he emphasized his guilt by sitting away from everyone else.

"But, you see I have not the wish to embarrass Josie," said Guy simply. At this point, Tristram Leith arrived with his lovely Rachel on his arm. They were an immediate centre of attraction, the Colonel's good nature having won over many of those who had censured him for his unorthodox departure from the military, followed by his even more unorthodox marriage to a lady who had become the subject of much unsavoury gossip.

The instant Rachel saw Guy, she tugged at her husband's arm. Leith glanced over, but astonished Rachel by refusing her suggestion that they at once join the two lonely gentlemen. If ever there was a man who had every reason to champion Guy, it was Leith, but he pointed out softly that since they were known to

161

have had some connection with Claude Sanguinet, it might be better if a gentleman not associated with that notorious individual should first join Guy. Spotting a familiar fair head towering almost as high as his own above the throng, Leith took himself over to greet the gentleman.

"The very person I need," he said, clapping Viscount Lucian St. Clair on the back. "You've not met Guy Sanguinet, I think?"

"Nor have I the least wish to do so," responded Lord Lucian, who had just glimpsed his wife seated where there was no vacant chair available. "If all I hear of that lot is—"

"It isn't," said Leith firmly. "Come on, there's a good chap." He seized the reluctant Viscount and shepherded him toward the distant empty table.

"The devil!" expostulated St. Clair indignantly. "See here, Leith—"

"*Colonel* Leith."

St. Clair's smoky grey eyes, so admired by the ladies, narrowed as he eyed this man he had served with in Spain. "The war's over, Tris. It's not a bit of use your throwing your rank at me."

"No," Leith admitted whimsically. "I was going to ask it of you as a friend, but it seemed less finagling to order you to help me."

"You are really serious about this? Never say you are bosom bows with a Sanguinet, for I'll not believe—"

"I fancy you can see me standing here."

A grin crept into St. Clair's eyes as they travelled the broad-shouldered giant beside him. "A great deal of you. Sir."

"Well, I wouldn't be had it not been for that particular Sanguinet. Nor would he have been paralyzed for two years and still unable to stand without crutches."

St. Clair gripped Leith's arm briefly, then moved over to the corner where Lord Jeremy Bolster was already greeting Guy and Lyon. It would have been difficult to find two more popular men than Bolster and St. Clair, and the gap in the table very soon ceased to exist. Nonetheless, the conversation included Guy only when the Viscount or Bolster so contrived it; the other guests, while chatting easily among themselves, neither addressed a sin-

162

gle word to the Frenchman nor appeared to hear his occasional quiet remarks.

Lyon, talking later that afternoon with Mitchell Redmond, told the fiery young baron that it would be better for all concerned if he and his mentor left Devencourt. "I've already seen Guy cut dead more times than I can stand," he growled angrily, "and the ball ain't even begun!"

"That's easily remedied," said Redmond, with the determined set to his jaw that his friends knew well. From that moment on, Guy was never without several of the Nine beside him. Their unobtrusive championship of the pariah was remarked, and puzzled many, but despite their efforts the guests split and eddied around them, and although laughing comments were called to the rest of the tight little group, well-bred eyes drifted past, over, or through Guy, but never rested squarely upon him.

Standing beside Devenish in the Great Hall, wearing a gown of primrose yellow silk, and with primrose ribbons containing her ringlets, Josie thought it impossible that she could be any happier. Her hand ached from being wrung by the second wave of guests, and her cheeks were even more radiant for all the saucy kisses pressed upon them by arriving gentlemen. And how gay was the banter, how warm the good wishes, how kindly she was exclaimed over, and how many times Devenish, obviously delighted, was told he might well be proud of his charming ward.

General Sir Andrew Drummond, who had journeyed from Ayrshire to Sussex, arrived with the rest of the Drummond contingent. The General had at one time been eager to adopt Josie, and she was a great favourite with him. He presented her with a beautiful shawl in the Drummond tartan, and a great silver and ruby pin to fasten it. "Just tae show ye what ye missed, ma bonnie," he said, grinning broadly at her joy. Not one to restrain her impulses, she gave him a hug and a smacking kiss, and his ruddy cheeks became bright scarlet, his fine whiskers vibrating with mingled delight and shyness.

Drifting past the receiving line, the General made his way to the bookroom, where he found an old enemy, General Sir Nevin

Smollet, engaged in quiet converse with Leith. Entering and closing the door behind him, Drummond was greeted by both gentlemen, and came right to the point. "Is't truth they've a Sanguinet here?" he asked. "If 'tis, there'll be hell to pay. I'd no' thought Devenish tae be sic a muckle fool—though he's never been very sonsy, y'ken—as tae spoil the wee lassie's party!"

Leith, who had been discussing this same sticky problem with the Intelligence Officer, exchanged a glance with that rugged little man, and drawled, "He's one of us, sir. And you know I owe him my life. I don't see what—"

"Well, I see what, blast it all! Fella should have changed his name. Lord knows we all begged him to do so!" Drummond, whose Scots accent came and went with his moods, swept on. "I fancy you know Geoffrey Harland is expected, *and* Westhaven, neither of whom could abide Claude, and who know nothing of the real state of affairs. Why in the devil *some* explanation couldn't have been given out by the authorities is beyond me." He glared at Smollet, who met his gaze with equal ferocity, and silence.

"It is—unfortunate," Leith agreed carefully, feeling like a man trapped between two barrels of dynamite.

"*Unfortunate*, is it? Whisht, mon! T'will be a sight more than unfortunate, d'ye find ye've a full-scale exodus on y'r hands, and if ye dinna ken the likelihood, ye're a pair of muckle fools!"

"One presumes you have the solution, Andy," said Smollet acidly.

"Well, I dinna," returned Drummond, and reverting to his punctilious English, "Speaking of Sanguinet—why did he choose the name Cahill for that foundling of his?"

Leith frowned. "It seems Guy said something of it years ago, when we all were suggesting possible names for the lad. I believe there was a Cahill in some way related to his mama—Guy's I mean."

Smollet gave a short bark of laughter. "Not related, Leith. Her lover."

"Good God! Are you sure, sir? From what I've heard of Sanguinet Père, he was the fiend incarnate and not the type a woman would have dared make into a cuckold."

"It's true," said Smollet. "How did you learn of it, Drummond?"

"Fella named Monteil told me. Swiss chap—munitions. Hand in glove with Claude, I discovered later. We were staying at the same chalet near Domstadt. Got snowed in, and spent a few days huddling around the fire, trying to keep warm. He was friendly as a barracuda till we found some bottles of a pretty fair brandy. Monteil was a proper sot, and when the subject of Claude came up somehow, he starting laughing like a treacle-wit and told me about the old man and his second wife. She was a most beautiful lady from what he said, poor creature."

"She died," Smollet said baldly.

"Aye. Of grief, Monteil said, though if his tale of the lover was correct, I'd not have given much for her chances of living."

Intrigued, Leith asked, "What became of the lover?"

"Just what you'd expect," Smollet muttered. "Found floating in the sea with a knife in his back."

"Aye," said Drummond. "Monteil said the old man taunted his wife with the details of it. She was still weak from her confinement, and she collapsed and was dead within a week. Broken heart, he said. Awful thing."

Leith nodded. "I wonder if Guy knows all this."

"Likely not," said Smollet. "Would you wish to tell him, Leith?"

"Lord—no! Thanks just the same, sir. He's got enough disasters!"

Devenish was also encountering disasters. Small ones at first, such as Lady Godiva who, misliking the cold wind, strove with zeal and determination to slip into the house each time a door was opened. Several guests were understandably startled to find a pig among them, and the Dowager Duchess of Banbury, who had once suffered an embarrassment with a rat at the country seat of the Earl of Harland, emitted a shriek of fright when she bent to stroke what she presumed to be a household pet who had burrowed under her train, and found herself nose to snout with a pig. Devenish was obliged to tell Cornish to put the little animal in the stables, and Lady Godiva was borne off, complaining raucously.

The next disaster was of greater proportions. The temperamental genius below stairs sent a minion for his vat of cream, only to discover that this indispensable commodity was soured. His wrath knew no bounds. Signor Devenish seldom gave the lavish entertainments, but tonight was the opportunity grand! Tonight Dukes and Duchesses would taste della Casa's creations! But how may he concoct his famous Creme à la Casa without the fine cream? What of his fabulous Della Snow Trifle? Or the Mocha Della Surprise? Pronouncing himself ruined, his reputation 'tramped ina the duster,' he flung his apron from him and deserted the kitchens, weeping, leaving behind a crowd of witless cravens, and poor Wolfe considering the merits of a nervous breakdown.

The recipient of a desperate summons, Devenish quickly stepped into the breach and sent grooms galloping to Cirencester, the Home Farm, and the villages to procure every last teaspoonful of available cream. Returning to the kitchens, he was faced by a demoralized chef who had, he sobbed, been betrayed by envious assistants. He himself had tested the cream when it arrived, and it had been fresh and of an excellence. "It isa the vicious plot, Signor," he wailed, tearing at his already sparse hair. "I ama the finest of chefs. I ama of the great ones. So I makea the bad friends. Mya nerves, they are defrayed! I ama all in the fragrants!"

" 'E means 'fragments' guv," Cornish translated helpfully.

Devenish set his jaw, banished the other members of the staff, and closed the door. What he said to his devastated employee no one was ever to know. The door remained closed for several minutes. When it opened, della Casa's brown eyes were very round, his demeanour all but cringing as he bowed to his patron. Wolfe, aware of Devenish's hot temper, was later to remark in an awed voice that never had he seen so deadly a glint in the master's eyes, nor so grim a line to his mouth.

Turning to the anxious group waiting in the hall, the chef announced with a grand gesture that he would save the day by returning to his tasks. "For," said he, "I shall be devoured by dormouses before I willa cause Missa Josie one small grieve!"

The staff returned with much relief to the kitchens. Devenish took himself off, pausing at the foot of the stairs to wipe his brow and thank providence that he was finished with the kitchens.

His gratitude was premature. Half an hour later he was again obliged to descend the stairs when three lackeys became very drunk in the wine cellar. They had found their way to the rear of the stores and, well hidden, had indulged themselves to the point that they were singing uproariously and discordantly, despite all attempts to quiet them. Devenish ordered the celebrants hauled to the stables and tossed into the frigid horse troughs. While in the cellar, however, he was astounded by the quantities of fine champagne that he now possessed. Quite enough, he later informed Leith, to have kept the Light Division happy for a year!

He demanded an accounting from his butler, and poor Wolfe, staggering in his remorse, admitted he must have made a mistake and ordered the wine twice. Viewing rank upon rank of stacked wine cases with a glassy eye, Devenish gasped, "Whatever do you mean to do with it all?"

"I hope to persuade the merchant to take it away after the ball, sir. I was unable to get it through the heads of the drivers and, rather than cause a—a uproar, had it stored down here. Temporarily. I—I suppose"—he wrung his frail hands—"I must be getting old! I cannot blame you if you turn me off!"

Steadying him, Devenish told him not to be a nitwit and that there was no real harm done. Twenty minutes later, however, it appeared that more harm had been done than they had suspected. Slipping quietly away from the party in response to a footman's whispered message, Devenish, groaning, retraced his now familiar path, and found a worried Mrs. Robinson ministering to the drunken lackeys in the servants' hall.

"There's something very wrong here, sir," she told him. "Only see how they shake, and their innards is paining 'em cruel!"

That the miscreants were in a bad way was all too obvious. Dr. Cahill was summoned, and Devenish, Wolfe, and Cornish returned to the wine cellar. Devenish sampled a few drops from one of the bottles that had been illicitly opened. It tasted a little flat and seemed to him to have an odd odour. He asked Wolfe to open another bottle, and again the same slightly musty odour could be detected, although the butler could not distinguish any variation.

Cornish said, "Let me sniff it up me nose 'oles, mate." He sniffed the bottle Devenish handed him, and pulled a wry face. "Gone orf, guv. A few swallers of this 'ere and you're sick as a sloth in a skiff."

Wolfe gasped, "Oh, my! And we've a house full of guests!"

"Lord!" exclaimed Devenish, appalled. "Have we served any of this stuff today?"

The butler peered at labels. "I—I don't think we have, sir, though it's difficult to say. I fancy this is all from the first order, because when the second lot arrived, we just piled it in front. Those miserable lackeys crept to the back so they wouldn't be seen."

Devenish muttered, "They may have saved us a real nightmare! Let's check the newer batch."

Wolfe led them to the second consignment and Devenish sampled a few random bottles, none of which showed any sign of spoilage. He then put Cornish in charge of personally sniffing each bottle as it was opened. "Your nostrils are going to be considerably overworked by Sunday, poor fellow," he said with a grin. "But no sampling, understand! We cannot have you out of commission until the last guest has left us!"

Cornish was not in the least dismayed, and said he'd be glad to be of service to Sir Guv. Devenish promised to repay him. And went upstairs again, brows knit, plagued by a deepening premonition that his troubles had only begun, and trying to recall if he'd ever heard of champagne having "gone off."

❧ Chapter 11 ❧

At seven o'clock there was to be a light buffet supper, and by five most of the ladies were either changing their clothes or resting. Josie was able to slip away and change into the new pink velvet gown she had intended to wear on Christmas Eve. It was a charming style, the rich material falling in graceful folds over her many petticoats, the décolleté neckline not so plunging as to offend her guardian, who could become very prim over such matters where she was concerned, and the soft pink colour enhancing her faultless skin and complemented nicely by the pretty braid she had found in the Burlington Arcade, and that edged the deep flounce at the hem.

She was just applying a light dusting of powder to her straight nose, when a scratch at the door announced a lackey delivering a box tied with pink ribbon. Inside was a dainty corsage of small dark pink roses, charmingly arranged, and the holder set inside a bracelet of gold filigree sprinkled with pearls. The note was from Guy, and written in French: To the pure child who has too quickly grown into the beautiful young lady. Josie was still exclaiming over the gift, when another arrived, this being an exquisite fan of hand-painted silk with ivory sticks delicately carven, and a card reading: To our favourite debutante with love and admiration. This signed Tristram, Mitch, and an undecipherable jumble that was Jeremy Bolster's erratic hand. Her heart full, Josie laid the fan beside the corsage, and waited hopefully as Fletcher pinned a pink velvet flower among her curls. Another knock at the door. This gift was a flat box wrapped in silver paper, secured with a silver ribbon. The message on the card was brief and gave little indication of the hours Devenish had spent worrying at it. *God bless you, Milady Elf. Dev.* The box contained a single rope of perfectly matched pearls, their lustre rivalling the happy tears that shone in Josie's eyes as Fletcher fastened them about her throat. Jumping up, Josie ran to the standing mirror and gazed at a vision: The lady she had dreamed of becoming when she'd been a terrified, half-starved little girl, unloved, and without hope.

Two more boxes were delivered just before she went downstairs. Both were corsages, one—of blue cornflowers and white daisies—was from John Drummond; the second was of tiny pinks and lily-of-the-valley and containing the calling card of Lord Fontaine.

"Oh, dear," sighed Josie. "I fear I must disappoint poor John, but really I cannot wear the blue with this gown."

"And if you was to choose between Lord Fontaine and Monsieur Guy, it'd be no race," grunted Fletcher, who did not admire his lordship.

Josie smiled and selected Guy's flowers.

Fletcher carefully affixed the corsage, watched her radiant charge trip lightly along the hall, and closed the door. Returning to the dressing table, she took up the pinks Fontaine had sent. "Now—I wonder how you knew," she murmured, touching one bloom thoughtfully. "I fancy you don't leave much to chance, me noble lord . . ."

Josie, meanwhile, had come to the head of the staircase. Several gentlemen were waiting in the Great Hall, and she ran her eyes over them fondly. Guy was sitting on a bench against the wall, Lyon beside him, surprisingly elegant in his evening dress. Leith, Harry Redmond, and Jeremy Bolster had acceded to her request and wore their full dress regimentals. They presented an impressive sight; Leith, straight and splendidly built, his dark head towering over the others; Bolster, rather astonishingly poised and his yellow hair very neat for once; Sir Harry, slim, dark, and dashing, the epitome of Wellington's dauntless Captains, one hand lightly resting on Bolster's sturdy shoulder as he laughed at some remark Leith had made.

As Josie watched, Devenish and John Drummond came from the east hall to join them. Her eyes held on the slighter figure, his carriage erect despite the limp—and thank goodness he had forgotten that silly cane tonight! The lamplight gleamed on his fair hair, the black long-tailed coat was as though moulded to his shoulders, the white brocade waistcoat impeccable, the black stockinet pantaloons, now accepted for evening wear, subtly emphasizing his well-shaped legs. As though he sensed her presence, he glanced up at her. His handsome features registered a stunned expression that made her heart turn over. She saw his lips form her name. The other men turned to look up. For a moment she basked in their admiration, then sped down the stairs, quite forgetting all Fletcher's stern instructions to move with leisurely grace.

The buffet supper was as excellent as it was elegant. Small tables had been set up in the morning room, two ante rooms and the music room in the east wing; a trio wandered about playing light and pleasant airs to charm the diners, and there could be little doubt but that they were charmed. By half past eight, more guests were driving up along the access road that was fortunately flooded with moonlight, and also lit by the torches held by grooms and farmhands who were stationed all along to the main road.

An hour later the ballroom was crowded, most of those expected had arrived, and Devenish and Josie were able to leave their positions inside the front doors and join their guests. Devenish had claimed only one of her dances, and when the music rang out in the lilting refrain of a country dance, he led her onto the floor. The dancers whirled and paced; the ladies' ringlets shone, their great skirts swung wide with a flutter of petticoats and lace; the gentlemen, manoeuvring with grace and sureness through the complicated measures, were variously jolly, grave, or flirtatious; and very elegant. Watching his ward's radiant little face, Devenish knew it had all been worthwhile. When the dance brought them together and he was able to hold her gloved hand,

171

he murmured, "Happy, my Elf?" and her glowing smile was all the answer he needed.

At the edges of the floor, the more mature guests gossiped happily, a few hopeful young ladies flirted with the unattached males, and in one corner the Duke of Vaille murmured, "I fancy Geoff Harland won't come now, Camille."

His son nodded. "Just as well, perhaps, sir."

The dance had barely ended, however, before Devenish was summoned with the word that more carriages were coming up the drive. He could not locate Josie, and made his way alone to the wide-open front doors.

Geoffrey, Earl of Harland, accompanied by another gentleman, and preceded by Lord and Lady Westhaven, came gratefully into the warm hall.

"How very good of you to venture all this way after dark," said Devenish, bowing over Lady Westhaven's plump fingers and shaking hands with his lordship.

"We would not miss your ward's come-out for the world," declared the pleasant woman, and turned to smile at Josie who came hurrying along the hall to greet them.

Harland, his aristocratic features always putting Devenish in mind of his son, Lucian St. Clair, apologized for his late arrival. "To say truth," he admitted, "I've a friend newly come from Paris—I knew you'd not object did I bring him along." He put a hand on the arm of the scholarly-looking grey-haired but oddly youthful gentleman at his side. "May I present the Chevalier Émile de Galin—Mr. Alain Devenish."

"Couldn't be more pleased than to have you here, sir," said Devenish, taking the Frenchman's rather frail hand. And he thought, 'What a marvelous face—like the brass of a sainted martyr.'

Josie came eagerly to greet Harland and be presented to the newcomer. The Earl had no sooner introduced his friend, however, than Devenish, who had been watching the Frenchman uneasily, sprang forward. White as death, the Chevalier sank limply into his arms. With a cry of shock, the Earl assisted Devenish to lower his friend to the floor. The two lackeys at the doors came running, and Josie sent one racing for brandy, and the other in search of Dr. Cahill.

"How beautiful he is," she said, watching Devenish feel for the heartbeat. "Poor soul! He is not dead, surely?"

"No, praise God! My lord, is the Chevalier subject to fainting fits?"

Harland was aghast that his uninvited friend should be so stricken, and replied that he had never known the Chevalier to collapse. "He fought at Salamanca, was beside the Marshal when Marmont was hit, and was himself levelled a few seconds later. I think he has never quite regained his health, but he's truly a splendid chap."

Josie, who had knelt and was chafing the Chevalier's limp hand, gave a sigh of relief as the long lashes fluttered and a pair of bewildered dark eyes blinked up at her. She said in French, "Do not be alarmed, dear sir. We have sent for a doctor."

Even as she spoke, Lyon sprinted across the Hall. Extremely agitated, the Chevalier protested that he was perfectly well. He must, he stammered in excellent English, merely have become chilled on the drive. Lyon took charge. He brushed aside the Frenchman's quite understandable distress at being the cause of such a scene, and required the lackeys to assist him to the nearest saloon, where he might rest while Lyon examined him. Flushed with mortification, the Chevalier was borne off, Harland walking alongside and attempting to calm him.

"Poor fellow," said Devenish. "The stuff of which nightmares are made."

"Yes. But you were so quick, dearest. Did you think him ill?"

"No. But I chanced to notice that he lost all his colour suddenly. Lucky I was able to catch him, he went down so fast."

"Thank heaven you did. He should stay here tonight, do you not think?"

"I'll have a word with Harland. Did you ever see such a magnificent— By Jove—more hardy travellers!"

They took up their positions as the doors were thrown open for the newcomers. Josie was astonished to see a lady alight from the carriage with no gentleman following. "Good gracious!" she exclaimed. "It's Faith!"

"Did Guy know she meant to come?"

"I'm sure he did not, but— Faith! How lovely that you can come to us!"

A charming sight in a dark blue taffeta gown, Mrs. Bliss proclaimed with a mischievous smile that she did not share her brother's prejudices. Devenish laughed, said that it was their good fortune, and excused himself, limping off to the east wing to check on the condition of the unfortunate Chevalier.

Walking arm in arm with Faith, Josie asked, "Does Sir William know you have come?"

"No. And straitly forbade me to do so. Such nonsense! I'm well past coming of age, as I told him. Still"—she smiled rather ruefully—"I was not sorry when some cronies came calling and he went off to Gloucester with them."

"I believe Dev would call that getting over heavy ground as lightly as possible."

A waltz was in progress in the ballroom. Tristram Leith, whirling his lovely wife about the floor, grinned at Mrs. Bliss and jerked his dark head toward the terrace. John Drummond came up, eagerly claiming what was left of the dance he'd signed for. Josie hesitated, but Faith excused herself and made her way to the rear of the crowded floor, so she allowed Drummond his waltz. He danced quite well. 'Better than Dev,' she thought, but lacking the skill of Leith, who was the best dancer among her friends. In a few minutes, Leith brought his Rachel alongside. "Who else arrived?" he called easily.

"Harland and the Westhavens," she replied. She thought he looked disturbed, but then he had whirled away again, and Drummond was remarking admiringly upon what a fine fellow he was, and how very well he waltzed.

"Oh, yes. Leith is splendid. And he would naturally be a good dancer, having been on Wellington's staff."

"And at Waterloo. How I envy him!"

"Envy him! My heavens! From what I have read, I'd think it to have been a nightmare! All those lives sacrificed. Forty thousand men—forty thousand grieving families; wives and children left destitute and starving! Ghastly!"

174

He said quietly, "Very true. But sometimes a man has no choice but to fight tyranny, ma'am."

Looking up at his clean-cut pleasant face, she thought that he was just the type to go off willingly to fight for his country and his ideals. And just the type never to come home. She felt a pang, for she was very fond of him, and she smiled at him with such warmth that his hopes soared.

At that same moment Devenish was leaving the quiet saloon in the east wing. "Cahill is young, I know," he said, closing the door. "But he's a good man for all that, sir. If he says your friend is recovered, I'm sure he is right."

"Damned fortunate he was here. I'm sorrier than I can say that this has spoiled your ward's come-out party," said the Earl, repentant.

"No such thing, my lord! Josie's not the type to be flung into despair over such a circumstance. Did Cahill say what brought on your friend's attack?"

"He agreed with de Galin, that it was likely fatigue, but he told me in an aside that he suspected some kind of agitation of the nerves. Perhaps something he saw that brought an unhappy memory of the war."

"Gad, I hope not! I've several reserve officers here tonight, sir, wearing regimentals."

"Do you, by God! I must have a word with the Westhavens, and then I'll come back to Émile. Your doctor friend kindly offered to stay with him for a short while." They started off along the hall, Harland continuing to apologize for the commotion. "Poor Émile has had a rotten life, one way and another, though Lord knows, he deserves the best. You will like him, I am very sure. Matter of fact, he has an Arab mare you'll not be able to resist."

This, of course, awoke Devenish's immediate interest, and they were still chatting amiably when they entered the ballroom.

A waltz had just ended, and the guests were standing about in little groups. Harland was at once hailed by several friends. He started across the room towards Lord Westhaven, and by pure mischance, at that very moment Guy, with Mrs. Bliss beside him, made his difficult way from the terrace. The Earl came face to face with him, and froze, an expression of abhorrence on his lean features. Halting also, Guy stood as straight as he could, very pale, but with his head well up.

Geoffrey Harland had loathed Parnell Sanguinet, and had once told his friend, Vaille, that the only apparel fit for the noxious clan was tar and feathers followed by a hempen rope. Now, his back ramrod stiff, the Earl's icy gaze moved to Faith. "May I be of assistance, ma'am?" he said with a slight bow, and offered his arm.

The inference was so obvious that the hush deepened. Several standing near Guy drew back, their politely concealed hostility surfacing at this public dénouement.

Bravely, Faith laid her hand upon Guy's arm. "Thank you, my lord, but I am Monsieur Sanguinet's partner this evening."

A look of contempt was slanted at her. His mouth tight, the Earl bowed again. For a searing moment he contemplated leaving, but he had Émile's well-being to consider, and, glancing to Devenish, who had hurried to his side, he saw the man's mute pleading, and relented. He had been the cause of sufficient of an uproar, he decided, and without another word crossed to join the Westhavens.

Devenish gestured sharply to the musicians. A quadrille was called, the squares began to form, and the music struck up. Devenish went over to Guy. "My dear fellow," he murmured. "I am so sorry. What a damnable coil this is!"

Guy said quietly, "We should have anticipate it, *mon cher.* My sorrow is that this lady has been trapped in the er, coil, also." He looked regretfully at Faith. "You should have been wiser, *Madame*, to have go with the Earl."

She smiled at him. "I choose my own friends, *Monsieur.*"

"Is something the matter?" Coming to join them, Josie asked anxiously, "Dev—the poor Chevalier is not worse?"

"No, no. And how does it come about you are not dancing?"

"I will be delighted to remedy that defect."

The smooth voice brought Devenish's brows twitching angrily together.

Josie cried, "Lord Elliot! And Lady Isabella—welcome!"

Devenish bowed over Isabella's hand. She caught a brief

glimpse of rage in his eyes, then they were veiled and he was apologizing for not having greeted them at the door. He had little opportunity to say more. Those who knew my lady well knew of her waspish disposition, but she was a very beautiful woman, her rich figure clad tonight in a striking gown of blue-green brocade, cut so low as to attract every male eye. Within seconds, she was surrounded. She was a little vexed, because her passion for Devenish was genuine, but she was as vain as she was lovely, and to be blatantly adored by these distinguished gentlemen could not fail to please.

Keeping an eye on Fontaine and Josie, Devenish was button-holed by the Duchess of Banbury, and by the time he escaped that garrulous lady, he was unable to discern his ward. A hand gripped his shoulder and he found Mitchell Redmond beside him.

"Dashed fine party, Dev." The grey eyes scrutinized him keenly. "Nothing amiss, is there?"

"No, my Tulip. I was looking for Josie."

"She was here a minute ago. Saw her with Fontaine, over—What the deuce? There *is* something wrong!"

Devenish forced a grin. "Stop being a nanny, damn you. How's that wooden head of yours?"

"Not so wooden as you think, my lad. Don't much care for our Viscount, do you?"

Through gritted teeth, Devenish replied, "No."

"If you look at him like that, he'll be charred around the edges before the night is over. Best come with me. There's a gentleman wants a word with you."

❧ *Chapter 12* ❧

Monsieur le Chevalier Émile de Galin was seated on a love seat in the east hall, talking with Lord Coleridge Bryce. The artist's fair young face wore an entranced expression and, amused, Devenish thought that he might have guessed Colley would soon be drawn to this man's side. Dropping a hand onto his lordship's shoulder, he asked with a smile "Well, *Monsieur*, has he yet bullied you into sitting for him?"

De Galin gestured deprecatingly. "I can but be flattered to have won the interest of an artist so notable. Lord Bryce is most kind."

"And if you will kindly go away, Dev," grumbled the "most kind" peer, "I may yet convince the Chevalier to allow me to paint him."

"No, Colley, I cannot have you bullying my guests, you know. Are you aware that Lady Scott-Matthias has arrived?"

Bryce rose at once, for he was an ardent admirer of the beauty. "I am bribed into leaving you, sir. But do not be imagining yourself safe. I shall not be so easily vanquished." With a dramatic bow and a grin, he went away.

Devenish took his place. "I believe you wished to see me, sir? I trust you are feeling yourself?"

The grave dark eyes fastened upon his face with an odd intensity. "It is my desire, *Monsieur*, to be with you very—how is it?—above the board. Since arriving at your house I have sustained a great shock. You will, I pray, forgive my inexcusable

178

behaviour, and allow that I may call upon you within the few days.''

"It would be my pleasure, but we can have a talk tomorrow if you will consent to overnight with us.''

"*Merci beaucoup*, but that is, I regret, not possible. Would Thursday next be *convenable*?''

They agreed upon a time and then the Chevalier was captured by the Countess of Carden, and Devenish returned to the ballroom in search of his ward.

Josie, however, had been taken in to supper by John Drummond, who had noted the way both Cahill and Fontaine looked at her, and had decided to allow no grass to grow under his feet. Having shepherded his lady to a small corner table of the noisy dining room, he saw that she was comfortably seated, and hurried to gather two plates of delicacies. Returning with his spoils, he told her that this was far and away the jolliest ball he ever had attended.

Josie thanked him. "I hope Dev shares your opinion, John. I had thought he appeared a trifle harried a little while ago, had you?''

"I cannot say I'd noticed, but that was probably because I was looking at you, not at your father.''

She laughed. "Dev is not my father. You know very well we are not at all related.''

"Well, he has been like a father to you, and I must be eternally grateful to him for rescuing you and allowing you to bloom into the exquisite lady you— Heavens! Have I offended?''

She nibbled at a cheese puff, and lied, "No. Only you sound like Lord Elliot. Has he been instructing you as to how to captivate the ladies?''

"I am interested in only one lady,'' he declared ardently. "Josie, I must—'' Here his ardour got the better of him; the pastry he held shattered and shot over the table. Aghast, he gazed at a large piece that had taken up residence in his lady's champagne glass. Josie sternly suppressed a dimple and began to chat about the beauteous Lady Isabella.

"Yes. Very lovely, but—I want to talk about *you*. No—do not try to turn me aside, I beg of you. Devenish said you were upset and I should not speak, but—"

"Then I think you should heed him, Cousin John."

"I dare not. You are beset on every side." He reached across the table to grasp her hand and said desperately, "You must know how I feel. I love you, my dearest girl. Dev said I may pay you my addresses, and—"

She stiffened. "But I understood you to say he cautioned you against—"

"Only because he thought you were upset. You do not seem to be upset, so—"

"But I am," she alleged, grasping at straws. "John dear, I am so grateful for your affection. Indeed, I could not wish to be held in such regard by a nicer boy, but—"

Frowning, he intervened, "I am almost five and twenty, and—"

"And kind and gentle and courteous. And will therefore exercise all three qualities, and not persist with—with—"

"With a declaration that would be unwelcome. Is that it?"

His face was a little flushed now, his eyes glinting with hurt and resentment. Josie saw several people glance their way, and she murmured, "Hush—you will be heard. And, John—you know very well that your papa would not approve your offering for someone of no family."

"I admire and respect my father, and would do all in my power not to hurt him, but in this I must retain the right to decide for myself. Josie, if that is your only objection. . . ?"

He looked so eager now, and he was such a very nice young man. She pointed out gently, "It is a powerful objection, John. Your parents have been very good to me for all these years since Dev took me under his wing. I have been accepted by them as though I truly were one of the family. Do not now ask me to bring them distress."

His attempt to remonstrate was interrupted as Jeremy Bolster, having noted the intensity of their conversation and guessed at its cause, wandered up and warned Drummond he was not going to have the belle of the ball all to himself. "I was obliged to l-leave Mandy at home," he said dejectedly, "so I cl-claim the

180

right of a lone and l-l- l-l- abandoned guest, Josie, and shall join you.''

Perfectly aware that Drummond could cheerfully have strangled him, he saw relief in Josie's dark eyes, and with a covert wink at her, drew up a chair.

''I simply never heard of such a thing, Wolfe,'' said Devenish. ''You've likely had far more experience than I. *Is* it possible for champagne to become tainted?''

The old man had a few ideas of his own, including a suspicion that some of the bottles he had opened had already been opened and cunningly re-sealed. However, to voice his thoughts would only bring more worry down on the head of a man he often wished to be visited by some dire peril so that he might charge to the rescue. Therefore, he said he believed this circumstance was fairly common and, blithely uttering falsehoods that would have curled the hair of any self-respecting vintner, asserted that if the bottles had been improperly cleansed or an error made in the ageing process, customers could be made ill upon imbibing the brew. Devenish left him, somewhat cheered, and went to look in on Cornish. The footman was looking rather owly-eyed and said he'd fair sniffed hisself boozy, but was not going to abandon his task. Devenish thanked him, assured him that his devotion to duty would not go unrewarded, and turned to find Mrs. Robinson at his elbow. The housekeeper warned that they had now run out of room, and if more unexpected guests arrived with the need to remain overnight, it would be necessary that some people share accommodations.

''Good Lord! Cannot do that,'' he cried, appalled. ''What about the servants' quarters?''

''Full as a squirrel's cheeks, sir. And I've had to put some of our people in the outside servants' quarters, at that.''

He shook his head worriedly, but told her it was unlikely that any more guests would arrive since it was already half-past eleven o'clock.

On that optimistic note, he repaired to the ballroom. He was unable to locate Josie, nor could he see Fontaine's glowing curls. Anxiety seizing him, he wandered along the hall. There was no sign of either of his quarries. He crossed the Great Hall rapidly and turned down the east wing. This corridor was quiet, most guests keeping to the other side of the house. From a small ante room he heard a sudden shriek, however, and a moment later the door flew open and Hortense Barrington, the pretty but rather foolish daughter of a widowed diplomat, made a decidedly precipitous exit. She was pale and agitated, and tugging at the strap of her gown. She blushed scarlet when she saw Devenish, gulped something in a tearful way, and all but ran off.

Lips tight, Devenish strode inside. He immediately located one of those he had sought, wherefore his concern for the other could be abandoned, but that a guest in his home should be embarrassed was galling. Swinging the door shut behind him, he said a clipped, "Miss Barrington seemed distressed."

Elliot Fontaine chuckled and smoothed his rumpled curls. "She's a silly widgeon, but a pretty one. If her papa don't keep a tight rein on her, why, all's fair, eh?"

"Not," said Devenish, "in my house."

That strangely reptilian movement of the head brought Fontaine's eyes around to him. "Come on, Dev. Never be so stuffy. I'll warrant you've had your share of slaps and tickles. Josie certainly—"

"We will not discuss my ward, if you please. Save that I'll tell you to keep away from her. She's not for you, Fontaine."

The Viscount was taller than Devenish but, oddly, he felt as though the other man regarded him from an immense height. It was an unfamiliar sensation and he was too proud to accept it with equanimity. "Perhaps you will be so good as to tell me for whom you are saving the chit." His quizzing glass swung gently from one well-manicured hand. His lips curving into a sardonic smile, he added softly, "You are—er, *saving* her?"

Devenish caught his breath with a faint hiss. "You'll explain that, damn you!"

The Viscount struggled with his own soaring temper. That this man, who had no title at all, should presume to criticize him had galled him for some time, and it was with an effort that he said easily, "Why now, what should I mean? Certainly, I intended no offence. What's a little dalliance, so long as it's— er, all in the family?"

White to the lips, Devenish all but sprang at him. "Do not judge others by yourself, you dirty-mouthed lecher! I have never laid a hand on my ward!"

His wrath escalating, Fontaine snapped, "You're very free with your accusations! From what I hear, you're the one should be more careful where you and Miss Storm conduct your—*réservé* flirtations." He clicked his tongue mockingly. "A *veneer* of propriety at the least, my dear fellow."

Quivering with fury, Devenish rasped, "You . . . lie!"

Fontaine tensed. It was the ultimate insult and he said with a small titter, "No really, my dear fellow. I did not see it, of course, but I am told it was quite amusing to watch you crawling around on the terrace after dark, with your hand up your ward's dainty skirts. If that—"

Devenish wasted no more time on words.

Tristram Leith marched swiftly across the Great Hall, his dark brows drawn into a frown. Dev's rickety old butler had assured him the master had come into the east wing, but— "Oh, there you are," he said, relieved. "You should— Good God! Whom have you murdered?"

His face pale and twitching, Devenish managed a tight smile. "Be a good old lad and find Isabella Scott-Matthias for me, will you?"

"Why?"

"Her brother—er, wants her. In the gold ante room."

Unconsciously, Devenish was gripping his hand. Moving very fast, Leith grabbed his wrist and removed the left hand from the bloodied knuckles it covered. He said with an exhalation of breath, "Fontaine?"

Devenish nodded.

"You triple-damned clod. Have you no social graces? One don't strike a guest! A fine way to cap Josie's ball!"

"I know it. But—blast it all—had it been you, I fancy you'd have broke his greasy neck!"

Leith's narrowed eyes scanned the flushed features. The provocation must have been considerable, for Dev was well bred and a good deal less hot at hand these past few years. He sighed. "I'll second you, of course. When do you meet?"

"We—er, did not discuss it."

"Asleep, is he?" Leith's grim mouth twitched. "By Gad, but he's not the only one. That's why I came seeking you. Don't ask me how, but your musicians must have dipped into your wine cellar. They're considerably *hors de combat*, my deprived host!"

"Oh, my God! *All* of 'em?"

" 'Fraid so. I suppose we could have party games the rest of the night."

Devenish groaned. "Where are they?"

"At the *lieu du crime*."

Devenish started away, then checked. "Tris—about Fontaine."

"I'll be your aide-de-camp, old boy."

Devenish smiled his thanks and hurried off, wrapping a handkerchief around his broken knuckles. As he turned into the hall leading to the lower stairs, a lackey sprinted from the west wing. Apprehensive, Devenish slowed.

The lackey panted. "Trouble, sir! Come quickly!"

"What a novelty," muttered Devenish, and followed.

Josie noted when she returned to the ballroom that the musicians had left the dais and that those guests who had not already gone in to supper were milling about, renewing acquaintanceships or conversing amiably. The room was comfortably warm, not unbearably hot, as was often the case at such gatherings, and despite the temporary lull, everyone seemed happy and well pleased. Moving among these friends, chatting with this one, being teased by the other, grateful for the variously fond, admiring, or complimentary remarks that came her way, she looked ever for a certain curly head and did not find it. Lady Louisa Drummond, with a rather searching glance, told her that she was quite devastatingly pretty tonight.

"Thank you, dear Aunt," said Josie, taking her hand. "And you need not look so worried." She lowered her voice. "John did offer, and I was able to refuse without making him too dreadfully unhappy, I believe."

184

"Oh, my dear child! You know that it is not— I mean, we do not— That is . . . well, Dev said he had warned John off."

"I believe he did, but—"

She was interrupted by a sudden disturbance at the rear of the large room. Her heart sank as she recognized a stentorian voice, and she excused herself and hurried towards it.

Sir William Little boomed, "You will do as you're told, my girl! And at once!"

Faith Bliss said, low and angry, "I am of legal age, William!"

Trembling, Josie felt a hand on her elbow. Devenish, his eyes fixed on the far scene, was beside her.

"Stay here," he said firmly, and made his way through the curious crowd as Sir William bellowed that he fancied he was still the head of his house.

Breaking through, Devenish saw that his neighbour, wearing evening clothes under a caped coat, had entered by the simple expedient of walking in through the terrace doors. Mrs. Bliss, very pale, stood facing her incensed brother, and Guy, a little flushed and his eyes bright, was close beside her.

". . . quite aware that people are staring," roared Sir William. "Likely they feel just as I do!"

"What a fellow you are, Little," drawled Devenish, "to cause a scene at my ward's ball. If you have something to discuss with your sister, allow me to show you to a room where you may be private."

"Aye, you'd like that I do not doubt," snarled the Squire, turning on him. "A fine thing that you've encouraged this damned traitor to lure m'sister away against my wishes, and—"

"Pardon, *Monsieur*," Guy's voice cut icily through that accusation. "You have neither the right to name me traitor, nor to remark that Mrs. Bliss I have lured. Neither of these things I have done!"

His face dark with passion, Sir William boomed. "I make my apologies to you, Miss Storm. As for you, Devenish, by God, but you number some dirty dishes amongst your friends, sir!"

A ripple of excitement was followed by an expectant hush. All interest in the dance had faded, but an odd shift was taking place among the guests. Jeremy Bolster and Harry Redmond, conspicuous in their military scarlet, quietly ranged themselves near Guy and Faith. As if taking up the gauntlet, Lord Ridgley, the Earl of Harland, Lord Westhaven, Sir Ivor St. Alaban, and Lord Owsley drifted closer to Little. From the corner of his eye, Devenish saw Justin Strand and Mitchell Redmond striving to come through the throng. He thought, 'All we need is a pitched battle at my little one's party!' And he said with spurious calm, "What you think of my friends can scarcely be of interest to the rest of us, sir, and—"

"By Jove, but it can!" cried someone in the crowd. "We want no treacherous assassins numbered among our acquaintances!"

"We have no proof Guy Sanguinet has done anything treacherous," cried the Duke of Vaille, his clear voice cutting through a rising growl of endorsement.

"All England knows him for a rogue and a villain," argued Little. "All England knows he and his damnable brother nigh succeeded in murdering the King when he was Regent! And nothing done about it!"

"No time like the present!"

"Throw the dirty swine out!"

The Nine were all about Guy now. Mrs. Bliss, eluding her brother's outstretched hand, stepped closer to the slight figure of the Frenchman. The hostile crowd surged closer, ladies retreating hurriedly, as the room became Bedlam, everyone seeming to shout at once.

Stepping between Guy and Little, Devenish threw caution aside. "If anyone's to be thrown out, Little—"

"I'd damned well like to see you try it, sir," raged the Squire, lifting the heavy horsewhip he carried.

Camille Damon, who had struggled vainly to make himself heard above the uproar, fought his way to the musicians' dais, and a stirring and familiar melody rang out, a melody so unexpected that the din ceased as if by magic, every head turning in astonishment to the pianoforte Damon played with thunderous pomp.

Her fear turning to bewilderment, Josie thought, ' "God Save the King" . . . ?' Turning, she saw Camille standing as he

186

played, and jerking his dark head in desperate warning in the general direction of the hall.

And then, those closest to the doors were moving back respectfully. Astounded, Josie saw gentlemen bowing low; ladies sinking into curtsies the depth of which could mean only one thing.

As in a dream, she heard Devenish gasp, "Good . . . God . . . !"

❧ *Chapter 13* ❧

King George IV now filled the open doorway, on the arm of the gentleman-in-waiting at his side. Devenish, who had not seen the King in some time, was as aghast as he was astonished. He'd heard that George had become enormously fat, but the man he remembered seemed to have doubled in bulk. Recovering his wits, he hurried to bow low before the monarch.

The King extended one chubby hand. "Devenish, m'dear chap," he said breathlessly, as Devenish bowed over that hand. "You'll think us a pretty lot to invade your party."

"We are very much honoured, sir. That you would come all this way—I am overwhelmed!"

"Pish! We do not forget those who serve us as nobly as have you. Ah, there is Redmond! Come here, Mitchell! You wicked rascal, I never dreamed when you saved my life you'd become such a thorn in my flesh." He ignored the little buzz of excited comment, and went on, "How is that fine head of yours? We heard it lately attracted a rather dense admirer."

The royal retinue tittered at this witticism. Mitchell, who had hastened to make his bow, thanked His Majesty for his concern and assured him he was fully recovered.

George patted him on the shoulder and waddled on, remarking to a friend, "Jolly fine fellow that, Knighton. Saved my life back in 'seventeen, did you know?" He nodded absently. "Brother's a good boy, too. Served under me in Spain."

Those near enough to overhear this entirely fallacious comment exchanged uneasy glances, but if the King's mind was wandering, it soon recovered itself, and he made his way through the throng, pausing now and then to chat briefly with some distinguished guest or lovely lady. Despite his bulk and the fact that he was obviously tired, he was graciousness itself and, watching him, Josie was reminded of the most recent disagreement between Dev, who had always defended "Prinny," and Mitchell, who found him exasperating. "His faults are legion, I'll own it," Devenish had said. "But he has many good points, which have been deliberately ignored by that flock of vicious satirists who so delight in defaming him." Lucinda, Countess of Carden, knew the King well, and had once told Josie, "He is like a small boy who is often very silly, but he can be kind and generous and, when he is in a good mood is the best of hosts and great fun to be with. He yearns to be loved by his subjects but, alas, usually sets about it in quite the wrong way." George was not loved, and he knew it. It seemed to Josie that there was a suggestion of wistfulness in those flabby, sweat-beaded features and, although there was much about him that she deplored, she could only feel sorry for the lonely man before whom the crowd parted and dipped like meadow grasses swaying in the wind.

Devenish led the way to a sturdy sofa and prayed it might accommodate the royal bulk. With an audible groan of relief, King George lowered himself to the cushions. The sofa groaned also, but held firm. Praying again, Devenish expressed the insincere hope that Devencourt was to be honoured by His Majesty choosing to overnight here.

George beamed. "Dashed good of you m'dear fellow. We stay at Berkeley, but took the waters at Cheltenham. Heard of the ball for your young lady, and could not resist stopping to renew old acquaintance."

Devenish, his smile fixed, his eyes glassy, wondered how they were possibly to find space for the King and his retinue, which appeared to number at least thirty ladies and gentlemen, to say nothing of carriages, horses, grooms, and servants.

Peering about, the King asked, "Which is your gel?"

Bolster took Josie's hand and led her to Devenish. She was more than a little frightened, but Devenish smiled at her, gave her fingers an encouraging squeeze, and ushered her to the royal presence. "Your Majesty, may I present Miss Josephine Storm?"

She sank into a deep curtsy.

"Stand up, you pretty creature," said the King, managing to lean sufficiently far as to chuck her under the chin. The protuberant eyes surveyed her fresh young face and generous little figure. "Ah, but you've grown into a comely lass," he said, winking at her. "Were I but a few years younger now . . ."

Well aware that he preferred the company of more mature ladies, Josie responded audaciously, "Or I a year or two older, sir."

"A year or two, is it?" A delighted grin overspread George's face. "You saucy puss! Did you hear that, Francis? A year or two, she says!" He went into a guffaw that set every layer of him jiggling, and brought cautious laughter rippling from his entourage and the crowd. "You must come and see Windsor, you little rascal. Bring her down, Devenish. You'll not recognize the old place. We've not finished, of course, for it was gone to rack and ruin, but we have brought much of it up to style and filled it with treasures." His lower lip sagged into a pout. "They're saying we've been extravagant, you know. They always do. Perhaps we have, but—by God, when we're gone, England will have something nice to remember us by." He sighed dismally.

Josie said, "We have some quite fine tapestries, Your Majesty."

He brightened. "Where, my pretty? Ah—I see. We shall have a closer look, but they appear splendid. Where'd you find them, Devenish? We'd likely have outbid you, had we known."

"They were in the basement, sir." And with a flash of inspiration, he added, "Sanguinet helped us restore them."

The King stiffened. "Sanguinet?"

Sir William Little said, "Never fear, Your Majesty. We're watching him."

"Then we thank you for it. Come here, if you please, *Monsieur.*"

A few grim chuckles were heard. Guy struggled forward. The

Earl of Harland, his face stern, accompanied him each step of the way, ignoring his son's frantic attempts to catch his eye.

Guy's bow was not very successful and he lost his balance for a second. Someone sniggered. The King, his face suddenly bleak, scanned the crowd. Silence fell. Returning his attention to the man who waited before him, George said in a very kind voice, "My dear fellow, how pleased we are to see you up and about again."

The silence was absolute. Guy, who had not dreamed of being publicly addressed by the monarch, was overcome and powerless to respond. For once in his life taken completely by surprise, Geoffrey Harland's aristocratic jaw dropped ludicrously. Sir William Little, coming forward and staring as if he could not believe his eyes, quite forgot protocol and stammered, "But—but he's a traitor, sir. A scheming Frenchy who plotted against your life!"

The King frowned and, turning to Devenish, said testily, "Who is that silly fellow? We do not at all care for his manners!"

Sir William turned red as fire and backed away.

"He is my neighbour, sir," said Devenish with a grin.

"And he is also the staunch patriot," Guy put in shyly. "It is natural he should suspect me, Your Majesty. With my name . . ." He shrugged.

"Nonsense! We have heard something of the ugliness to which you've been subjected. Time it was stopped. We shall give you a new name. Should've done so long since. Remind me, Francis. Now, listen, all you people—this man is a Sanguinet, which is to be regretted. He is also, however, a very fine gentleman, and owes his disability to a gallant attempt to protect us. We'll thank you to treat him with kindness." Here, the royal eye alighting upon a hovering footman with a well-laden tray, he said cheerily, "By Jove, but that looks pleasant! Run along, you people, and enjoy your dance. I say, this is frightfully good of you, Devenish."

Devenish's response was lost in the sudden buzz of chatter. Wolfe appeared and led the royal retinue to the dining room. Guy started away, but Harland stepped up to him and bowed.

"*Monsieur—en effet*, I have been under a misapprehension. I am sorry for it, and humbly beg your pardon."

It was just the beginning. The emotions of the guests had come full circle. From a heady desire to lynch the Frenchman came the need to make amends for their treatment of him. It appeared that everyone present asked nothing more than to speak to him, to shake him by the hand, to tell him they were "jolly glad" to make his acquaintance.

Josie, overjoyed, rushed to hug the tearful Faith, and Sir William, looking miserable, hung back until at last, catching Guy's eye, he muttered, "It was very sporting of you to—to defend me, Sanguinet."

His throat choked by emotion, his hazel eyes suspiciously bright, Guy put out his bruising hand. Sir William took it gratefully.

Lyon came up, beaming. "Congratulations, sir! You're cleared, at last! You're also looking rather tired and no wonder."

"No," Guy managed gruffly. "*Merci*, but I am very fine."

"And will be the better for a short rest," said Faith with an undeniably proprietary air.

Guy flushed, said happily that doubtless *Madame* was right, and went with her towards the hall.

The King waved a chicken wing and said merrily, "Come along now! On with the dance!"

His heart thudding into his shoes, Devenish smiled, bowed, and hurried off. His faint hopes proved unfounded. The musicians had salted away several bottles of the tainted champagne and, to a man, were prostrated. Tearing his hair with frustration, Devenish sought out Mrs. Robinson and threw that poor lady into a near-fainting condition by telling her all the accommodations must be changed so as to make room for the royal guests. He left her, white and shaking, and went back upstairs.

Crossing the Great Hall, he met Leith, who informed him that Viscount Fontaine had been loaded into his chaise and with his sister in attendance was being driven home. "You've made a dangerous enemy, Dev," the tall man said gravely. "I wish to God you'd not hit the fellow."

"Oh, pox on the wretched hound! Tris, the damned musicians

are all sick as a sea lion! And there sits Prinny, waiting for music!''

"Lord save us all! He'll go off in a huff!''

"Yes. And I cannot have that . . .''

Devenish made his way through the crowd, waiting a little impatiently now for the dance to resume. He clambered onto the dais and pounded discordantly on the keys of the pianoforte. The chatter faded. He held up his hands and begged for quiet, and gradually it was achieved. From the corner of his eye he saw Josie watching him anxiously and, off to the side, his monarch, busily applying himself to the contents of the tray, but with his eyes fixed upon the dais.

"My friends,'' Devenish called clearly. "I have a disaster to announce! My musicians found their way into my wine cellar . . .'' There was a roar of laughter. The king grinned around a cheese tart. "They are quite unable to play,'' he added. At once the grin faded from the fat countenance. The tart was lowered and so was the royal lower lip. Devenish raised his voice to be heard over the clamour of disappointment. "I know we have many fine musicians amongst us. It is unforgivably rude of me to ask it, but''—his brilliant grin swept the sea of upturned faces—"will you help me?''

The response was immediate. Viscount Stephen Whitthurst and several friends picked up Camille Damon bodily and carried him to the pianoforte. "Here's a volunteer!'' yelled Whitthurst. Lady Carlotta Bryce, mother of the famous artist and an excellent harpist, needed little urging to take her place by that beautiful instrument. Lord Edward Ridgley, who played the violin well, said good-naturedly that he'd "give it a try,'' and in no time an orchestra was assembled.

With the help of two of his gentlemen, King George regained his feet. "And I shall lead you, ladies and gentlemen,'' he proclaimed, beaming. "By Jupiter, but this is a jolly party!''

A sturdy bench was carried forward, His Majesty was lowered onto it and, after a short consultation and some small disagreements among the musicians, Damon called something to the King, and George bellowed, "Take your partners for the waltz!''

Another guest chose that moment to put in an appearance. Lady Godiva trotted through the welter of skirts and pantaloons. Whether she supposed that the one individual seated alone must be her god, it would be difficult to guess. Suffice it to say that she made her way to the bench and sat beside it, facing the dais.

Comparison was inevitable. Scores of dainty fans fluttered up to hide convulsed faces; countless linen handkerchiefs smothered chortles of mirth. Cold with horror as Mitchell Redmond led her to the floor, Josie darted a frenzied glance at Devenish, who was preparing to return to the lower areas and assist his unfortunate housekeeper. He returned her look with some puzzlement, turned in the direction of her nod, and gave a gasp. The royal temperament was uncertain at best. If George decided he was being mocked, he could be merciless—as he'd been in the case of poor Brummell. Devenish started to run. Even as he reached for the pig, King George raised his arms to start the volunteer orchestra, saw Lady Bryce's horrified expression, and glanced down. He gave a startled yelp, and the baton Damon had passed him fell from his hand.

"S-sir," stammered Devenish, seeking frantically for a logical explanation, "I cannot tell wh-why, but this animal is a pest and, whenever we have company, seems to delight in seeking out the most distinguished of our guests and attaching herself to him. I pray you will forgive this—er, intrusion."

Through the following absolute hush, not a soul moved, and Devenish held his breath, waiting for the wrathful explosion.

Lady Godiva wriggled and uttered a tentative snort.

The King's staring eyes blinked. He looked narrowly at Devenish's pale, tense face. Suddenly, he chuckled. "No, no. Let her stay," he said, reaching down to pat the pig's head. "What's her name?"

"Lady Godiva, Your Majesty."

George laughed. The gentlemen-in-waiting laughed. The guests laughed. And Devenish could breathe again.

"You little varmint," said the King, as Lady Godiva smiled up at him, "damme if you ain't fatter than I am!"

* * *

194

Peering at her brother's face, dimly illumined by the carriage lamps, Lady Isabella asked, "Is it stopped bleeding, love?"

"Yes," replied the Viscount thickly. "But—by God, if that bastard has broke my nose . . . !"

"Never say so! Taine, you—you mean to call him out, of course?"

For a long moment there was no answer, the only sounds the plodding of the horses' hoofs and the rattle and squeak of the chaise as it followed the narrow, moonlit ribbon of the road.

Fontaine said in a thoughtful drawl, "No. It would interfere with my plans."

Isabella closed her eyes briefly. Emboldened by this unhoped-for decision, she next asked, "Whatever did you do to cause him to knock you down?"

"I accused him of compromising his ward." Fontaine chuckled faintly. "To say the least of it."

She gave a despairing wail. "Then I am quite undone! He'll never come near me again!"

Unmoved, he continued to dab cautiously at his nose and pronounced it unbroken. Isabella began to weep and he snapped impatiently, "Oh, be still! Why you should *want* the block is past understanding! Aside from his looks, the fella's scarce a great matrimonial prize. He's as hot at hand as he can stare, and will likely be tumbling into disasters for as long as he draws breath. He cannot walk straight, which is enough to turn one's stomach. His fortune is not large. And as for that disgusting old pile of his— Egad, Bella! It would drive you distracted inside a month! Certainly, you'd have to turn off every single freak he calls a servant! A fine beau you've chosen! Take your noble lamebrain and be thankful!"

"My 'noble lamebrain,' " she retaliated, wiping fiercely at her tearful eyes, "is six and sixty, has no hair, and Waterloo teeth!"

"Ah, but you would be a duchess, m'dear! And such a rich one! *Certainement,* you could find *l'amour* elsewhere."

"Oh, but you are hateful!" she cried fiercely. "I *love* Dev! Can you not understand? I love him, and I want him!" And in response to his derisive snort, she said in a flame, "Laugh then!

195

But consider, dear brother, *you've* a lust for his wretched found-ling, and you may be sure she never will glance your way now. He is sure to tell her what you said."

Amused, he murmured, "No, do you think so? I doubt it. Whatever his faults, the fool *is* a gentleman. Besides . . ." He paused, and in a little while went on with a slow smile, "There is, my beautiful, more than one way to skin a cat."

❧ *Chapter 14* ❧

On Monday morning the east wind was keen, and Josie went shiveringly downstairs to find Lady Godiva huddling by the bottom step, trying to keep warm.

"Poor little thing," she said, bending to caress the pig. "We shall have to make you a coat, my dear, to keep out the cold."

She glanced up as the door opened and an icy gust swept across the Great Hall. Devenish came in, the collar of his long riding coat turned high, and his cheeks aglow. He snatched off his high-crowned hat and flourished it at her, two cats and a kitten rushing past him and racing for the kitchens.

"Slugabed! I suppose now the last of your guests is gone, you mean to rest on your laurels while the rest of the world labours."

"But of course," she said, dimpling a smile as she tripped over to take his hat and coat and hand them to the lackey who was perfectly capable of performing that small task, and knew better than to attempt it. "Where have you been? And have you eaten breakfast?"

"I've been out with Little. We had a look at the access road and I think are agreed on a just sharing of more permanent repairs."

"Oh, splendid!" She clung to his arm and accompanied him to the breakfast parlour, where a bright fire sent flames licking up the chimney and the air was fragrant with the smells of coffee and toast. The table was set, a footman sprang forward to assist with chairs, Wolfe lurched in, followed by a maid bearing a laden tray, and Josie busied herself with coffee and cups. When the servants left them alone, Devenish said with a sigh, "Jove, but it's nice to have the old place to ourselves again."

"Yes, I know. But—oh, it was a *wonderful* ball, wasn't it, Dev? Everything went so well, and—" She saw his stupefied expression and laughed merrily. "Well—all things considered . . . No, really, the King was so kind, and—"

"Kind! Do you realize, my girl," he said, waving a crumpet at her, "what we went through, getting everyone's belongings moved, and rooms cleaned and ready for the royal crew, only to have Prinny say airily at the last moment that they 'must be getting back to Berkeley now'? Good Gad!"

"Yes, dear, but the poor soul thoroughly enjoyed himself, and the musicians seemed fairly well recovered by the time they left. And only think how Guy was vindicated!"

Slicing some tender ham, Devenish grinned. "True. Our Guy became quite a *cause célèbre*, and well past due!"

"And Faith as proud as though they were already wed."

He paused, slanting a quick glance at her, then went on carving.

She held out her plate and he deposited some fine slices upon it, then served himself, adding two eggs from the covered tureen.

"Well?" he said mildly. "Why scowl at me? I said not a word."

"You looked a whole chapter! Dev, he is exonerated! Surely you can see he cares for her. Sir William can no longer object."

"Can he not? Guy would object. And it is no use for you to try and trick me into quarrelling with you, because I don't intend to do so. You're much too pretty this morning."

She tried, but could not restrain a smile. "How wicked of you to so efficiently spike my guns, sir."

"Isn't it. But I've done it and will now turn the conversation in another direction." He laid down his knife and leaned to put his hand over hers. "Happy, little one?"

"Yes. Oh, Dev—so very happy. Thank you, thank you! I felt—like a princess!"

He smiled. "You looked like a princess. Winning every man's heart, and—"

She leaned to him, her eyes like stars. "Did I, Dev? *Every* man's?"

He took up another crumpet and began to butter it. "Well, not Prinny's perhaps, but he is so besotted by Lady Conyngham, that—"

"Wretch," she scolded. "I did not mean the King. Can you guess who—I did mean . . . ? Before you take a third crumpet, that is."

Startled, he looked at his plate and the crumpet still remaining. He felt his face become hot, and Josie said with a sigh, "I suppose it is asking a lot of you. At your advanced age."

"To remember my manners and not be a glutton?" he asked, flustered.

"No. To guess whose heart I have won."

"Oh," he said, concentrating upon his abundant crumpets.

"Never mind, dear," said Josie, watching him from under her lashes. "I will give you a hint. I received another offer at the ball."

He began to butter his recent addition again. "Jeremy said he thought you might have. Young Drummond, eh? He's a—er, jolly fine lad."

"Lucinda Carden says that 'lad' is a word belonging in the stable."

"Yes. Absolutely right. Well, then. I'd think John is—er, just what any girl would—ah, wish for."

"But then," she murmured, obligingly moving the rack of crumpets closer to his hand, "you know so pitifully little about my wishes, don't you, Papa?"

"No. I mean—yes. That is to say—don't you fancy him?"

She was silent. "He is, as you say, everything any girl would wish for."

"Oh, absolutely." He bit rather savagely into his first and neglected crumpet. "Salt of the earth."

"And," she mused, "he says he—cannot live without me. A girl likes to hear that. I tell you, so you'll know."

"Hum," he said, eyeing her uncertainly. "I can understand

199

that she might.'' He sighed, saw her swift, bright glance, and blurted out, ''Poor—Lyon. The boy adores you.''

''Yes. But—so does the man I have chosen.''

The man she had chosen. ''He does,'' he said. ''I mean—he does? Well, he would, of course. Have you—er, told him? Of your decision?''

''You dropped a piece.'' She pointed to a scrap of ham. ''Thank you.'' And having waited through an interval while she smiled so dreamily he could have strangled her, he said, ''Well? Have you?''

''Have I what, dearest dodderer?''

''Told young Drummond.''

''Good gracious, of course not! A girl does not accept an offer the first time she's asked.''

''No. I suppose not.'' He smiled cheerily. ''You pretty creatures love to keep a fellow dangling.''

''It is more than that, Dev. John must consider carefully. His papa will likely be difficult because I am such an—an unknown quantity.''

Rage blazed in his eyes, and the hand on the napkin he had just neatly deposited beside his plate clenched itself.

''Besides,'' Josie said demurely, ''I have to think of . . . you.''

He started. ''Me?''

''Well, of course, you great silly. Who's to look after you when I am off somewhere being a young matron?''

Staring at her, he thought, 'My little Elf . . . a young matron . . .' And he said in an automatic response, ''Isabella.''

Her mischief routed, she said irritably, ''Oh, for heaven's sake! Do be serious!''

''I am perfectly serious. The fact that you do not admire the lady has kept me from—ah, declaring myself, but since you are in a way to being comfortably settled, I can now be frank.''

She snarled, ''What a pity you cannot also be truthful!'' His only response being a sigh, she enquired with malice afore-thought, ''Are you feeling not quite the thing? You look sick. Or sickening. I cannot be sure which.''

''Do you know,'' he said with a dreamy look, ''Isabella says my hair drives her to distraction?''

She glared at the fair, rather windblown curls. "I can see why it might. Perhaps did you have the grey streak dyed it would not so offend."

"And that my eyes," he went on, keeping them lowered so as not to reveal his mirth at her excellent riposte, "are blue as the Spanish skies." He blinked at her soulfully.

"Does she so? Well, of course, I would not know, never having been to Spain. Is she Spanish, then? I'd fancied she might have gypsy blood. La, but with a scarf around her head and big gold earrings—"

Here, Devenish succumbing to shouts of laughter, she sprang up and ran around the table to tug at his hair until he begged for mercy.

She sank to her knees beside his chair and, laughing with him, said, "Wretched, most *evil* of men! You were teasing me. It was all a fudge, after all." She took up his hand and held it to her cheek. "Own it, you villain. You have not the least interest in that predatory creature."

His expression changed. Despite all his stern self-lectures, his hand seemed to turn of its own volition to caress her velvety skin. With a real effort, he said, "Bella cares for me, my Elf. She is beautiful and much admired, and is, besides, a sophisticated lady. I think we will deal very well together. And now that I—"

She jumped up and hissed, "Now that you are free! Is that it? You are rid of me at last!"

"No—never that." He pushed back his chair and stood, reaching for her hands, but she jerked them behind her and faced him, breathing tempestuously.

He said, "I'm not getting any younger, Josie. It is past time I was setting up my nursery. And Isabella is—very much of a woman."

She was breathlessly still for a moment. Then, "Only think," she said with a bright smile, "we shall be starting married life at the same time—you and I. Whoever would have . . . dreamed it." And she turned and walked quickly from the room, leaving him to sit down again and stare blankly at the coffee pot.

After some while, there came a new arrival. Cornish stood

beside the table, his face wooden, and a silver salver in one muscular hand which he thrust out while gazing at the top of the curtain rod.

Devenish reached rather wearily for the card, then turned about, glancing up also. "What're you looking at?"

"A 'igh point, guv."

"What the deuce are you talking about? What high point?"

Cornish lowered his gaze. "Crikey! If it wasn't giving me a crick in me perishin' neck! But that's what 'e says you gotta do. 'Stare at a 'igh point,' 'e says. Somethink to do with a cove called Dicky Rorum."

A quirk disturbed the stern set of Devenish's lips. "And who is your instructor in decorum?"

"That there lump o' ice—Finlayson. 'Im what Mr. Wolfe brung in."

Casting his mind back, Devenish recollected that Josie had said something about a very frigid footman. "Oh—is that the pale fellow with the light eyes?"

"Ar. Sticks out, they does. Like a perishin' flounder."

"Hum. Well, he's gone, so forget him and do not be staring at my ceilings. It unnerves me." He glanced down at the card in his hand, which contained the name of the vintners who had provided their vast quantities of champagne.

"No, 'e ain't gone, Sir Guv. Young Mackey took ill with the grippe, so Wolfe kept 'im on. Finlayson treats the old duck like 'e was a bitta dirt, so Wolfe's proper took with 'im. Cor!"

Frowning at the card, Devenish said, "Why am I given this?"

"Cos Wolfe's proper doddipolled, poor old cock. Arst if you could see the cove."

Devenish groaned. "Very well, Sir Elegance. Ask Wolfe and Mr.—er, Short to step into my study."

Mr. Short, who was indeed short, was outraged. He could, and did, supply copies of the original orders and waybills in support of Mr. Wolfe's orders. He was quite willing to take back any unused crates—or at least, he *had* been willing to do so, until Mr. Wolfe had "cast such a haspersion on the fair name of Messrs. Short and Brinkley!" The champagne, he averred, his square face becoming mottled with indignation, had been in

202

perfect condition when it had left their warehouse, and furthermore, it was clear to see that the tainted bottles in Mr. Devenish's cellars were not tainted at all, but had been deliberately tampered with *after* they had been delivered. "Hi do not know why, sir," he said huffily. "Hi can only say has our company his one has serves the *noblest* of England's families!"

This declaration reinforced the unease that had gripped Devenish since the apparent "spoilage" had first been detected. It was very likely, he thought grimly, that whoever had poisoned the champagne had also soured the cream. A nasty little plot to turn Josie's party into a disaster. The tainted wine bottles had been put at the back of the cellar so that whoever was responsible could serve the ugly brew at the most effective moment, and to the most distinguished guests. The thought that the King would quite logically have been chosen to be made ill brought sweat starting onto his brow. He controlled his dismay, however, and set himself to placate the offended tradesman. Mr. Short, bristling, encountered the full force of an engaging grin, and was scuppered. The interview proceeded on a far more agreeable plane. By the time Mr. Short departed, having been plied with his own champagne and convinced a disgruntled servant must have been the culprit, he was in an extremely mellow mood, expressed his disgust at so heinous a crime, said he hoped Mr. Devenish would "go very 'ard on the villin," and promised to take back as many crates as had not been tampered with and were not needed.

Wolfe returned, having handed the vintner over to Mrs. Robinson, to find the master leaning back in his chair, his riding boots irreverently propped on the littered desk top. Wringing his hands, the butler was near tears as he said he had feared just such a scheme, but had no least notion as to which of the servants would have done such a dreadful thing.

Devenish commanded that Josie was not to learn of it, and said he very much doubted it had been one of their own people. "Likely, one of the temporary servants," he said grimly, "and I doubt we'll ever know who it was."

"But . . . but—*why*, sir? I can think of no one we have turned

203

off these past years who might harbour a grudge. Should we have the constable in?''

He was so distraught that it became necessary for Devenish to invent a suspicion of a friend of Claude Sanguinet who had chosen this method of revenge, and sent the old man off, bristling with wrath that such evil schemes had been brought against his beloved master.

Left alone, Devenish stared frowningly at his boots. It was very possible that the little fantasy he had invented for Wolfe was the true answer. He was not without enemies, but he knew of few men who would resort to such dastardly means of exacting vengeance. Claude's adherents would. His frown deepened as Elliot Fontaine's face came to mind, but he had not *really* quarrelled with Fontaine until the ball itself, and the business of implanting an agent in the house and poisoning the champagne must have been planned in advance. Little certainly disliked him, but the very thought of someone as straightforward as the Squire resorting to such underhanded methods was laughable. Old Wolfe's absentmindedness had saved the day, certainly, for without the extra order they would very likely have run short of usable bottles. And had the lackeys not crept back there to have their own party—! It did not bear thinking of! Josie's ball might well have gone down as the disaster of the season. He could imagine how devastated the dear little soul would—

''Villain!'' accused the ''dear little soul,'' sweeping into the study with a swish of taffeta and a whiff of *Essence de Printemps*.

With a guilty squawk, Devenish swung his legs from the desk top, thereby depositing a good half of the contents on the floor. He rubbed nervously at a scratch his spur had left on the mahogany, and jumped up. ''I didn't—'' he began, but was quelled by one small hand tossed imperiously into the air.

''Didn't me no didn'ts,'' decreed Josie, with what he was wont to term her ''Empress of Elves'' air. ''You most certainly *did*!''

''Did what, your Imperial Majesty?''

She fixed him with what she supposed to be a basilisk stare. ''I heard a carriage.''

''Did you now?'' he said admiringly.

She stamped closer, her brows drawn down, her eyes shooting sparks. Devenish retreated until he fell into the chair once more.

"Who?" she demanded, standing over him.

"You mean—whose."

Her jaw set and her small hands lifted, fingers crooked.

"Now—Josie . . . !"

"Was it Elliot Fontaine?"

The laughter left his eyes and he stood again. "It was not. Won't you sit down?"

"Are you and Elliot going to"—her great eyes searched his face—"to meet?"

"I sincerely hope not. Josie, if you will sit—"

She clasped her hands together. "Then, you did *not* call him out?"

"No such thing."

"Thank heaven," she breathed, and stretched out one hand. He took it and on the instant her grip had tightened and she was inspecting the skinned knuckles. "You told me you scraped this."

"Ow!" Trying unsuccessfully to free himself from her clinging fingers, he mumbled, "I did."

"On what, you wicked, deceitful creature?"

"Oh, I don't know—some sort of thing. What matter? Now, if you—"

"*Tell* me! You attacked him, didn't you?"

"I—er, wouldn't say I—attacked him, exactly. One doesn't attack a slug. One merely—"

Tears glistened in her eyes. "Dev—for heaven's *sake*!"

"Now, don't cloud up, for Lord's sake. I sort of—ah, levelled him." She threw her hands to her mouth, gazing at him with such tragedy that he added a feeble, "Just a little bit."

She sank into his chair and, relieved, he sat against the edge of the desk, but almost immediately she sprang up again so that he had, perforce, to come to his feet once more.

"*Why* must you be forever rushing from one end of England to the other," she demanded rather unjustly, "fighting and brawling and—"

"The deuce, Josie! I've scarce left these hallowed halls this past—"

"You couldn't *wait* to ride off with Tris and Jeremy and the rest, to help Mitchell when—"

"Good Gad! Did you expect me to stay home and twiddle my thumbs while Claude slaughtered poor Mitch?"

"You could have let the others go, but—no!" With a wild gesture, she cried, "You know you are not as—as able to—"

His face bleak, he interjected a stiff "I am still—I hope—a man."

Josie was extremely afraid, wherefore she ignored the danger signals and rushed on. "You are a child! A naughty, headstrong, undisciplined little boy who cannot be left an instant but what he is—"

He said quietly, "I think that will be about enough, please."

"Well, *I* do not think it nearly enough! Only look at that awful business with Valentine Montclair! There was no cause for you to—"

"Val is my friend, and they came damn near snuffing the blockhead. For heaven's sake, Josie, you know very well a man don't stand by and—"

"One might suppose you the *only* man in all England, sir! Merely because you limp a little, you seem to think you must prove yourself with every shift of the wind!"

"Now, by the Lord Harry! I—"

"You deliberately provoke Sir William on every possible issue! It is a miracle *that* business has not ended in one of your ridiculous duels!"

"Well, it has not! And if all this harangue is out of spleen because I knocked down your precious roué Elliot Fontaine, I can only say your judgement is fair and far off, my good girl!"

"I think it not so far off if I judge you to have a Sir Galahad fixation, my good Gaffer!" And seeing the tightness to his jaw and the thin line of his mouth, she continued hastily, "Do you ever give *one thought* to what your quick temper and recklessness do to—to my peace of mind?"

"I have been very patient with Little. But, by God, I'll not have a guest in my house— Well, never mind. But if you crave a title, you would do well to set your cap for—''

"Set . . . my *cap*?'' She said furiously, "Dev, you deserve to be scratched! And if truth be told, I believe your quarrel with Elliot came about purely because of his devotion to me!''

"Oh, do you? In other words, you say I am lying in my teeth! Well, be comforted, ma'am. Slippery Elliot ain't about to call me out.''

She said, worried still, "He might not, were I to ask it, for I know he—''

Devenish caught her wrist and jerked her closer. Through clenched teeth he said, "You will not—go *near* the carrion! Do you hear me?''

Stunned by a rage she had never before witnessed, she stared at him, then, suddenly drained of emotion, she wrenched free and half-turning from him, said, "He has never laid a hand on me, Dev.''

"God help him if he does! Besides, there is not the need for you to cast yourself at his feet in a lovely bit of melodrama to save me.''

She gave him a reproachful look, but she had wounded him more deeply than she guessed, and he went on acidly, "You are flattered by the notion that Fontaine admires you. It so happens that his sister is—er, fond of me. Now, if Elliot wants you, and Bella wants—er, likes me, what a flat he would be to call me out. And the lascivious lord ain't a flat, whatever else!''

The coldness in his voice was making her knees shake. She said tremulously, "Oh. Well, Dev, if you think him not the proper husband for me, I—''

"Husband!'' He laughed mirthlessly. "Open your eyes, child! If he wants you, it's not as his wife!''

He had intended to imply a criticism of my lord's character. To the overwrought girl, however, his words pointed up her own ineligibility. As hurt now as was he, she said, all prideful disdain, "How fortunate I am, to have a more sincere admirer. John Drummond has no such base motives.''

"True,'' Devenish muttered, immediately deflated. "John's a good boy.''

"A good *catch* for me, I think you mean."

He hesitated. "Why—yes. I would give him my blessing."

"You are too kind, sir. I suppose it would please you to think I care for him."

Looking as pleased as a man treading up the steps of the gallows, he said, "Every father wishes that for—for his daughter."

"Indeed? Then your wish is granted, Papa. I told John that I love him!" And with a toss of her chin and a swish of her skirts, she crossed to the door.

All day Tuesday, Josie kept herself so busy that the hours flew past. On Wednesday, wanting only to avoid Devenish's cool courtesy, she told Klaus to have the bays put to her new phaeton, and drove out alone. Her desire for solitude was thwarted when John Drummond rode from the Nailsworth road, waved joyfully, and galloped up, pleading to be allowed to join her. He tied his well-mannered chestnut on behind and took the reins as he climbed into the vehicle beside her.

"I am rather surprised that Dev allows you to drive out unescorted, Josie."

"Oh, Dev is very forward-thinking, you know. I do not drive very far, of course. Only to the villages and once or twice to Cirencester, but then he goes with me, and takes the reins before we reach town."

"So I should hope!" He tucked the rug tighter around her, and thus missed the irked glance she shot at him. "Are you sure you are warm enough? The wind is from the east, I think."

Her irritation fled in the face of his solicitude. She said teasingly, "Well, you may be glad of it, sir, for had it not been, your Aunt Pandora would have been with me, and there would not be room for you, for I could scarce ask her to get down and ride your horse."

He chuckled at the thought of such a scene, and dropped his hands so that the team came to a trot. "I send the elements my thanks. Certainly, I had not thought to be so lucky as to find you alone." He slanted a glance at her but, unable to read her

208

expression, went on, "I had no chance to finish what I was trying to say to you at the ball."

She lowered her lashes. "And—have you come all the way back to Devencourt for only that reason, John?"

He said fervently, "I would journey to the other side of the world for that reason."

"I see. You have—perhaps, spoken with your papa?"

He nodded, looking crestfallen. "It is the most infamous thing, but—confound it, I'll *not* be bound by such antiquated notions!" He drew up the horses again, secured the reins around the ring, and turned to take her hand. "Dev said he approves of me. I think you are not averse to me, and I am deep in love with you, Josie. Will you be my wife?"

There would be no home for her here, once Dev had married his glorious Isabella . . . She thought wretchedly that this was a very unkind reaction to his heartfelt declaration, and said, "My dear friend, I am indeed very fond of you, but—John, you must see it is impossible. Even were I willing to marry against your father's wishes, how would we manage? Do you mean we should go to Gretna Green? I think Dev would not like that."

"No, of course not," he exclaimed, horrified. "As if I would suggest such a thing! We would be fairly disgraced. But—I could get a special licence, I think."

She looked at him doubtfully. "Do you know how?"

"No." He bit his lip. "I've never done so before, and— Oh, Lord! What a stupid thing to say! As if it were something one does every quarter day!"

"I'm sure you could manage it," she said kindly. "Only—I simply could not enter married life in a clandestine way. I would feel ashamed."

"Yes, of course you would." He raised her hand and kissed it tenderly. "You are everything that is good and I respect you the more for your principles. Oh, curse it all! Here is Mrs. Bliss coming up! Josie—I adore you!" He untied the reins. "Never fear, I'll find a way for us."

"But, John—I have not—"

"Hello!" called Faith, waving gaily. "What a lucky chance! Do you go to the village? May I ride with you?"

"Indeed you may, ma'am," said Drummond with unfailing courtesy. "The more the merrier."

It was rather disconcerting, thought Devenish, going through the great pile of bills on his desk, that a simple ball could cost so very much! Not that the old coffers would collapse, of course, but he'd have to tighten the girths a trifle for the next few months. Although Josie must have a fine wedding, of course . . . His hands stilled, and he stared numbly at the statement he held upside down. Had anyone asked him if his day could get any more dismal, he would at that point have answered an unequivocal No. But, glancing up, he saw that he was mistaken.

Lyon stood in the doorway, watching him coldly.

"Welcome." Devenish stood, but the younger man made no attempt to shake hands, walking a few steps closer and halting again.

"I've come to say my goodbyes. I am returning to Town and will likely remain there on a permanent basis."

His voice was flat and hostility glared from the dark eyes.

Devenish replied, "I rather fancied you would. Belmont thinks you've a brilliant career ahead of you, and it's natural enough you'd wish to be in London. I expect you want to see Josie. 'Fraid she's out just at present. Will you take a glass of wine while you wait?"

Lyon refused politely, but he occupied the chair indicated, and Devenish sat at his desk, very conscious of the tension in the room. "Guy will miss you," he said, longing to restore their friendship.

"Yes. And he will be lonely. I'm sorry for that."

"Perhaps he won't be too lonely. It would not surprise me if we were to have an interesting announcement very soon."

His smile was not returned. Looking squarely into his eyes, Lyon said, "It would surprise *me*. Guy is too decent a man to offer for so lovely a lady in his condition."

The contempt in his voice was unmistakable. Devenish felt his face grow hot and suddenly, although he fully shared those sentiments, he was both embarrassed and enraged. He said sharply, "Mrs. Bliss is no child. If she cares for him—"

"If she does, it may well be an affection based on pity." And wanting only to hurt this man, Lyon went on ruthlessly, "The best type of woman is so often willing to sacrifice herself. And a clever man can trade on his infirmity." He saw shock come into the blue eyes and, with pleasure that was also a pain, knew his barb had gone home.

For a moment Devenish sat very still, staring at him. Then he said coolly, "Let's have our cards on the table. You mean me—no?"

Lyon sprang up, his rage and disappointment boiling over. "All these years," he snarled, "I've honoured you for your care of a homeless child." He gave a wild laugh. "What a joke! When all the time, you—"

"Have a care," interposed Devenish very softly. "You appear to find three and thirty a great age, but I assure you I am not too infirm to knock you down, my nasty-minded cub."

"Nasty-minded? Blind, more like! When I think of how cleverly you managed to convince everyone she was 'too young' to marry! How cunningly you contrive to run off any man interested in her!"

By this time Devenish had also stood, and faced him, his fists clenched at his sides, his head a little lowered. Lyon knew that stance of old, and didn't care. If Devenish struck him, he could drive his own far more powerful fist into that disgustingly handsome face, which would afford him tremendous gratification. He swept on passionately. "When she told me how you moaned about your age and your feebleness, I was shocked, for I thought it was your selfish way of keeping her tied here all her days— waiting on you hand and foot as you've trained her to do."

"Now—by God!" gritted Devenish, pushing his chair aside.

"Which only shows you," Lyon went on, "how stupid I was! How incredibly gullible! You brought that innocent child here 'to protect her' you said. 'To give her a chance in life.' Pah! A chance for *what*? To do what she always thought you wished? She's not sufficiently well-born to be your wife, but you *desire* the sweet innocent! So you groomed her to be the perfect mistress, while you brayed to the world of your nobility, and—"

With a muffled growl, Devenish sprang. Lyon's fist shot up,

but Devenish was very fast and struck first. Lyon staggered back, vaguely astonished by the power the slighter man could muster. Devenish was after him like a wild man, his face suffused, his eyes narrow slits of wrath. Lyon steadied himself against the bookcase, then leapt to meet that headlong charge.

A faint scream sounded from the hall.

Devenish's poised fist checked and, dreading lest Josie should be witnessing this ugly brawl, his head jerked towards the sound.

For Lyon, there was only rage and hurt and the need for vengeance. All sense of fair play lost, he threw a right jab with all his strength behind it. From the corner of his eye, Devenish saw the knotted fist whizzing at him. He leapt aside, but swift as he was, he could only partially deflect that mighty blow. His upflung arm was slammed aside, and Lyon's fist caught him glancingly along the jaw. Hurled back, he crashed into the end of the desk. Pain jabbed a vicious spear through his leg, and he sagged helplessly.

Before Lyon could press his attack, however, someone was between them: a crouching ferocity, her face twisted with hatred, a dagger gleaming in one upraised hand.

"Vicious, thankless murderer," hissed Mrs. Robinson as she confronted the halted Lyon. "After all he's done for you! It was *him* got Lord Belmont to take you—did you know that? Mr. Guy wanted it and paid for it, but it was the master went to his lordship to plead for you! When Lord Mitchell was in Paris three years ago and the master found out how your governor was being hounded, it was *him* found your new house, and got the other gentlemen to help persuade Mr. Guy to move here. Couldn't do enough, he couldn't. Small thanks that you think such evil of him in your nasty, filthy mind! That you'd raise your wicked hand against him!"

Very pale and stiff, Lyon said, "Madam, I think—"

Devenish, who had watched this exchange with dulled incredulity, now intervened breathlessly. "Thank you, dear lady, but—I can only hope . . . Dr. Cahill will think better of . . . what he said."

Lyon flashed a seething glance at him.

From the doorway, Cornish grated, "Yer nag's saddled up an' ready, Doc."

Without a word, Lyon stamped from the room. He was escorted every step of the way by Cornish, two frigid lackeys, and the bootblack.

By the time Devenish had been fussed over and ministered to by his valet, urged to rest by various and sundry footmen, and eyed with tender concern by sighing maids, his need to escape was desperate. Defying Hutchinson, he donned a riding coat, hat, and gloves, took up his whip, and went downstairs. En route to the stables, he detoured into the kitchen hall.

Mrs. Robinson, starting out with some keys in her hand, saw him, halted, and blushed furiously.

"Come here, you fighting fury," he said huskily.

Timidly, she came to stand before him. He pulled her into his arms and gave her a hearty buss on the cheek. When he drew back, her face was averted. He turned it gently and smiled into her misted eyes. "You are a friend worth the having, I think," he said.

She moved so quickly that before he could prevent it, she had pressed a kiss on his hand. "Ain't nothing I wouldn't do for you, sir," she gulped. "Nothing!" and fled.

Deeply moved, he took himself into the cold outer air, and began to walk, heedless of direction. He did not walk alone, however, a development that was viewed from the windows by many amused eyes. As he made his way along the path below the terrace, he acquired a retinue. First, a fluffy white tail, high-held, came into view above the low hedges that lined the walk. Next to put in an appearance was a striped ginger tail, thinner, but equally high-held and politely keeping its place as third in line. After a space came another tail, curly and pink, and finally, a very small black spear that bounced along in Lady Godiva's wake and could not be identified by the uninitiated until the master struck off across the grass, at which time it was seen to belong to the diminutive black and white kitten known as Bits and Pieces.

Having come at last to the bridge over the trout stream, and being safely out of sight of the house, Devenish perched against the wall and massaged his right thigh. He was not surprised to perceive his fellow travellers, and rescued Bits and Pieces, who was looking decidedly wilted after the long stroll. Stroking the tiny creature and listening to her gravelly gratings, he told her that the trouble was, he kept forgetting. Unimpressed, Bits and Pieces chewed ferociously on the heavy brass button of his coat. Lady Godiva smiled up at him, then sat on his left foot and prepared to go to sleep. The ginger cat threw itself down and became fanatically obsessed with cleaning a front paw, and the white cat brushed his whiskers on a weed.

"I tell myself," explained Devenish, "that I'm going to be staid and grandpapa-ish. But somehow, when she looks at me with one of her—special looks, I lose track of what I mean to do and . . . and then people begin to have wrong thoughts. Like Lyon, for instance. Just because she had a bad dream and I comforted her, he said I . . . desire her." He leaned down to pull up a weed and stare at it. "And that I've trained her to . . . to be . . ." He swore furiously and flung the weed from him, "Filthy-minded young bastard!"

The whiskers having evidently been groomed to satisfaction, the white cat jumped on the wall and picked his way fastidiously to butt his head against Devenish. "The fact remains," Devenish continued, stroking him absently, "that if Lyon, who used to think highly of me, has come to that conclusion, others might." The white cat gave a trill and turned upside down on the wall. "Guy said that we—kissed . . . with our eyes . . ." He groaned and drew a hand across his brow. His companions were alarmed. The ginger cat got up, jumped onto the wall on the other side of him, and made a determined attempt to climb into his lap. The white cat jumped onto his shoulder, and Lady Godiva clambered to her feet and peered up at him anxiously. Even Bits and Pieces stirred and uttered a drowsy mew.

Devenish sighed heavily. "You are all very kind. But—we know what must be done, don't we?"

He restored both cats to the ground and repaired to the stables, carrying the sleeping Bits and Pieces, and with the remainder of his escort trailing rather grumpily along behind. He startled one of the grooms by giving the kitten into his care and asking that Miss Farthing be saddled. This beloved old friend greeted him with delight, an emotion he shared, and within a very short time he was riding out at a canter, behaviour that caused the groom to stare after him in so troubled a way that a colleague abandoned his currying of a promising filly to join him. "What's up, Alf?"

"You see that bruise?" asked Alf, plucking the straw from between his stained teeth.

"That there Cahill's got a good right."

"And the master's got his hellbender look."

"Couldn't of. He rid Miss Farthing."

"Ar," said Alf. "At a canter."

They looked at each other.

The object of their concern soon slowed Miss Farthing to a pace that would have caused Alf's honest eyes to become very round indeed. Grappling with his problems, Devenish was halfway to Cirencester before he realized he was very cold. Shivering, he turned Miss Farthing for home.

His mood did not improve when he saw the gentleman who approached mounted on a splendid grey stallion. Devenish groaned, and reined up, sneezing.

"Good afternoon Dev-enish" said Lord Fontaine amiably. "Jove, but that's a nasty bruise."

"Matches your own," replied Devenish less amiably.

Fontaine smiled upon him.

His temper worsening, as it always did when he was thrown into close proximity with this elegant individual, Devenish blew his nose and demanded, "Well? You've something to say, I presume?"

"Eh? By thunder, but you're right! I was a—er, clod, Dev. You were absolutely right to mill me down."

"Good . . . God!" gasped Devenish, staring at him.

The mettlesome grey danced, and whirled around. Reining him in, the Viscount's face was grave when he resumed. "I was well over the oar, old fellow. I'd already taken Bella to a rather jolly dinner party, y'see. The dear girl was fairly furious with me, and insisted I seek you out and"—he looked down, his grip on the reins very tight—"and make you my most humble apologies."

Devenish had been almost looking forward to a savage quarrel, probably climaxed by a challenge, and he was so astonished as to be momentarily rendered speechless. He knew a great deal more about the Viscount than he had told Leith, knowledge that encompassed cruelty, wildness, and an often uncontrollable temper, besides several duels, one of which had left Fontaine's opponent, a young man on the brink of a brilliant diplomatic career, bedridden for life. That the Viscount was a rake was public knowledge. That he was a ruthless libertine was not, but Devenish knew. And Fontaine now knew he knew.

His lordship leaned forward in the saddle and held out one gloved hand. "Will you forgive?" he asked, his fine eyes pleading.

"Er—" said Devenish, and was enormously relieved when the grey took violent exception to a clump of branches tossed by the wind, and spun skittishly.

"Must get home," shouted Devenish. "In a hurry."

Fontaine glanced up, and frowned. "Jove! Surely it's not coming from—"

Jerking his head around, Devenish was suddenly bereft of breath. To the southwest a great black column of smoke boiled upward before it was whipped ragged by the gusts. He thought a numbed, 'Josie!' and was away at a headlong gallop.

His expression very different now, his lordship followed.

It had been many years since Miss Farthing had felt spurs, but as they tore up the last hill, she was shocked by the sharp bite of steel. She had tried hard, but if her god needed more, she would run until she died, and she laid back her ears, gathered her powerful muscles, and fairly flew.

✺ Chapter 15 ✺

There could be no doubt now. That black and terrible smoke column came from Devencourt. The smell of it drifted to them on the wind, and as they came over the hill, the full and ominous sight of it struck Devenish like a physical blow. Smoke poured from every window of the old wing, the top floor windows showing, horrifyingly, the pulsing red tongues of flame. Devenish shrank, flinching, in the saddle. To see the old house, the home of his ancestors, in such agony, wrought upon him in a way he would not have dreamed possible. He knew in that first rending instant that he had long sensed this was coming and that he had refused to acknowledge that awareness, even to himself.

Only for a very brief instant did that knowledge fill his mind, then it was gone, for above all else lurked the deeper dread; the fear so paralyzing that his brain reeled with terror of it.

A bucket brigade had already been set up, men and women toiling frantically, passing buckets in and out of the breakfast parlour windows and a smoke-blackened Cornish wrenching with incredible energy at the pump on the west end of the house beyond the large dining room. Two ladders were placed to the first floor level of the newer wings, the buckets being handed up to the men inside.

Even as they thundered across the lawns, ignoring the loop of the drivepath, Devenish saw Mrs. Robinson stagger, coughing, from the wide open front doors, carrying Josie's jewel box. A grimy footman ran to aid her. Above the crackle and roar of the flames rose a confused uproar of shouts and cries, while men and maids ran in and out of the doors, or climbed from the lower windows, bearing some treasured painting or object.

A new shout went up as Devenish flung himself from the saddle and went in an awkward limping run towards the house.

Hutchinson, his usually immaculate coat torn, his neckcloth awry, his face dirty, reeled to him. "Sir," he croaked, "I—don't know where it started! We'd no—no warning!"

Devenish gripped his arm steadyingly. "Is everybody out?"

The man swayed, his face the colour of putty beneath the grime of smoke. "I—doubt it! No . . . no warning . . ."

Fontaine ran up. Devenish shouted, "Take him!" The Viscount pulled the valet's arm across his shoulders as a muffled roar came from within the house, and the lurid glare of flame began to lick at several second floor windows.

Two heavily laden footmen stumbled from the doors. It seemed to Devenish that he glimpsed a staggering figure behind them, and he sprinted madly for the steps.

"No, sir!" gasped a man he vaguely recognized as Finlayson. "Stay out! Hopeless!"

His eyes smarting as smoke billowed around them, Devenish shouted, "Where is Miss Storm? Did she come home?"

"I don't know, sir. Klaus is here, and I think I saw the phaeton, but—" He jerked around as someone shouted. "Oh, my God!" he groaned.

"What did he say?" Devenish demanded frantically.

"He must be mistaken, sir. He said Miss Storm is upstairs, but—"

Devenish had already plunged inside.

At once, he could feel the heat. Smoke choked him and stung his eyes. Two floors above raged an inferno, and somewhere in that inferno—Josie! Spluttering, he threw an arm across his eyes. Someone stumbled into him and sagged downwards. He gripped the frail figure. "Wolfe! Dammit, man—get out!"

The old man mumbled something and peered blearily at him. He was clutching something, and Devenish saw it to be the portrait of his father that hung in the Great Hall. He relieved the butler of the heavy painting, tightened his grip on Wolfe's arm, and hauled him outside, then paused, gulping in the cold, damp air.

A gust of wind sent sparks and flame whipping. A groom ran up to take Wolfe. Devenish thrust the portrait at a black-faced maid and shouted, "The stables! Let the horses out, just in case!"

Two men reeled from the house carrying a limp female form. Devenish ran over, frantic. The eyepatch identified Maisie Fletcher. He roared, "Where was she?"

"Crawling to . . . the stairs."

"Kept trying to tell us summat 'bout . . . Miss Josie."

Behind them, a man who had evidently ridden in to help gave an hysterical shout and pointed stabbingly upward. "Up there! Look! Look! A lady!"

Devenish was inside again. He had seen the flames at those windows, and he thought in frenzied anguish, 'God keep you, little one! I'm coming!'

The smoke now was like a solid wall. All about him was heat and sound—the hideous grinding roar that told of the voracious appetite of the flames. Dimly, he remembered someone—Tris, he thought—telling him that in a fire the air closest to the floor stays fresh longest. He was coughing rackingly, and he dropped to his knees and crawled upwards. Someone collided with him. He croaked, "Who's there?" A pink snout shoved at his face. A terrified squeal rang out above the hubbub. He gripped Lady Godiva's head and wrenched her around. "That way . . . !" he said. "Go!" He dealt her a hard slap on her round rump, and she scuttled down the stairs. He heard someone choking, and legs tottered through the chaos. Someone was tearing at him. He blinked up. Alf, he thought, the groom. "Ain't no use . . . sir! Can't—can't get up there. C'mon, 'fore it's too—"

"Go! Let me be!"

Another great thunder of sound. The stairs shook. "Sir!" screamed Alf. "Go—damn you!" croaked Devenish. Alf went.

Somehow, he was at the landing. But Josie's room was on the second floor. He must—somehow he *must* get up another flight! Oh, Lord, but it was hot . . . and the noise! 'The fires of hell,' he thought, in an odd, detached way. Josie had done nothing to

219

warrant the fires of hell. He must find her. If she was to die, he would die with her . . .

Head down, choking, fighting for breath, he dragged himself upwards. The heat hit his face searingly, but he was on his feet, handkerchief clasped over his mouth. 'Sorry, Tris. Too slow your way, old lad.'

"Dev!"

A familiar voice behind him. Clutching the rail, he peered back. A rumpled dark head hove into view. Two long grey eyes, rimmed with red, blinked up at him.

"Mitch! Damned ass—get out!"

"Don't be . . . fool" wheezed Mitchell Redmond, swaying drunkenly. "Too blasted . . . hot . . ."

Devenish tried to tell him he shouldn't have come. That he must find Josie. But he couldn't speak, there wasn't enough breath. His lungs were smothering. He turned and fought his way upwards.

A deafening crash, and the landing exploded into a pulsing red glare. A fierce blast of heat sent Devenish staggering. He heard a muffled cry. Burning wood began to rain down and dimly he realized he could no longer see Mitchell. Why the devil had the damned idiot come? Why could he not have stayed safely outside? He thought despairingly, 'Josie! Josie!' and tears were flooding some of the soot from his eyes, but he groped his way down, his hands seeking through the smoke. A crumpled form. A weak voice that urged him to "trot . . . along . . ." Hating Redmond, aching with grief and loss, and the wretched knowledge that this way would have been so much simpler, he wheezed between oaths, "Come on . . . Mitch! Damned . . . sluggard!"

Together, they fought and strove and at last fell downwards. Tumbling helplessly and agonizingly, Devenish thought that he had tried. And it really didn't matter anymore. From a great distance, he could hear a woman screaming. He prayed, fadingly, that it was not Josie . . .

Clinging to Josie as John Drummond sent the phaeton racing up the hill, Faith saw the girl's face pale and frozen with dread,

220

the eyes wide and dark, fixed unblinkingly on that ghastly, writhing column of smoke.

They plunged over the brow of the hill and Faith's blood seemed to congeal in her veins. It was just as she'd envisioned it on her first glimpse of the old house; black smoke and flame pouring from every window, many people toiling madly to prevent more tragedy, and others lying on the grass, victims of smoke and burns and exhaustion.

As they drew nearer, Josie said not a word, her eyes straining to pierce the drifting acrid smoke, seeking, seeking, for the beloved fair head, the limping gait, the slim energetic figure that must be—*must* be here, save that she could not see him.

Drummond shouted something and pulled up the scared team. Jumping down, he lifted the two girls out, yelled "Stay clear!" and ran across the chaotic lawn to vanish amid the smoke and confusion.

Faith realized then that only the central wing was burning. All efforts to save it had been abandoned, and the men who fought so desperately were striving now to preserve the rest of the house. Everywhere she looked were people passing buckets slopping with water. She was surprised to see her brother and his bailiff and several of their servants climbing one of the ladders. She turned to Josie, but the girl was running after Drummond. Faith picked up her skirts and followed.

Josie searched through the crowd, her eyes beginning already to burn from the smoke and heat, her ears deafened by the shouts, the screams of frightened horses, the terrible crackling roar of the flames. A grimy Pandora Grenfell knelt beside a prostrate man. Sick with fear Josie ran to them. For an instant she did not recognize the blackened face, the singed dark hair, the torn and scorched clothing, save that she knew it was not Dev. Then, long grey eyes were blinking up at her, and a cracked voice said, "Never look so scared, Elf. We might save it—yet."

"Mitch! Oh, Mitch, are you much hurt? Is—is Dev—"

And then, over the uproar, a shout rose. A tattered scarecrow came reeling through the front doors as though borne on a billow of smoke, waving his arms madly.

Josie's heart was choking her. She thought in a dizzying flood of relief, 'Dev . . . ! Thank God!'

Everyone near the house turned and ran away, the men sliding down the ladders with frantic haste. Dismayed, Josie started up, only to be dragged down as Mitchell grabbed her skirts unceremoniously. She was deafened by an explosion, and screamed as Devenish was hurled forward and down. The old wing seemed to leap into the air, then with a mighty roar it crumpled in upon itself, sending up a great gout of fire and smoke and sparks.

Not even aware that she was running, Josie flew to throw herself on her knees beside Devenish. He was already sitting up and gazing at the blazing mound that was all that was left of the old wing. Sensing that she was near, he swung around. She saw a scorched, grimy, blistered face, all but devoid of eyebrows, the hair singed and blackened, the blue eyes bloodshot.

A great light dawned in those red-rimmed eyes, and a sudden glitter brightened them. He threw his arms wide, and she flung herself into them. "Oh . . . Dev," she sobbed. "Oh—I am so sorry!"

Crushing her to him, he buried his face in her hair. His throat closed. All he could say was, "My . . . Elf . . . !"

The fact that a keg of black powder was in the barn, intended to be used in the construction of a better road, had saved the mansion. By blowing up the old wing, the fire was localized, and although there was great damage to the rooms directly adjoining on both the east and west sides, most of the newer wings was spared. Even so, the struggle to contain the fire went on far into the evening. The smoke had been seen for miles around, and carriages, curricles, gigs, wagons, carts, and groups of riders poured in from surrounding estates, farms, and cottages, to do whatever could be done to help. Fire was of all things the most dreaded in these times of open flame lighting and little if any organized fire protection, and not a man in the county could be free of the fear that at some time he, too, might be obliged to rely on the help of neighbours and friends to save his home and family.

While the men battled to keep steaming walls and roofs wet

down, and shovelled dirt and sand and upended countless water buckets on the great glowing pile, the women tended burns and blisters and abrasions, provided ale and fruit and sandwiches, and did all they might to sustain the workers. Redmond, still not fully recovered from his head injury, collapsed from exhaustion and was borne off to a bed, willy-nilly, but Devenish kept fighting until dawn, at which time it began to drizzle. Soon, rain was coming down in torrents. The weary firefighters packed up and went home, carrying with them the heartfelt thanks of the man they had assisted so unstintingly.

As always, the aftermath was crushing. Josie slept until late afternoon and awoke to a pervading smell of smoke. Maisie Fletcher was carrying in a tray of hot chocolate and biscuits. Before Josie could voice her immediate question, the gaunt abigail's features were illumined by a beaming grin.

"He's up already, miss. Proper wrung out, but won't own it."

Sipping her chocolate, Josie sighed, "Thank God no one was badly hurt. But—I dread to leave this room, Maisie."

Her dread was well founded. She stepped into a reeking hall, and although the suite she had moved into was on the northeast corner of the house, water had been bucketed along the halls, leaving the once gleaming floors thick with mud. Her eyes blurred. She thought, 'Poor old house!' but already the work of recovery had begun. Maids were scrubbing, rugs were being rolled up and carried away to be cleaned, smashed windows were being boarded up. A great sheet of tarpaulin billowed forlornly across the blackened end of the hall that had once turned into the old wing, but a footman told her that the side stairs were quite undamaged and that the master and Lord Redmond were in the bookroom. She hurried downstairs, her heart wrung by the chaos at the end of the inner court between the wings, and acknowledging to herself that the smoke and water seemed to have resulted in almost as much damage as the flames, and that the entire mansion would have to be redecorated, most of the draperies scrapped, furnishings reupholstered or recovered, and all the carpets and paintings cleaned.

Mitchell and Devenish were alone in the bookroom. They were talking in a rather subdued fashion when she went in, but at once both young men brightened and stood to greet her. She went to the peer first, and he kissed her hand and then her cheek with his customary courtly manners, and made light of her anxiety because his throat was bandaged, his dark hair had been roughly trimmed, and he looked, despite his cheerful grin, tired and drawn. "Whatever will Charity have to say to us?" she said worriedly.

"Not as much as we have to say to her," said Devenish, giving her a quick hug and a kiss on the forehead.

Scanning his face, she tried to hide her consternation. It was not the ugly graze above one eye that dismayed her, nor his bandaged hands or the fact that Hutchinson had been obliged to shear off all his thick curls, leaving him looking oddly juvenile with the fair hair sticking up at uneven angles all over his head. His smile was dazzling and his manner charmingly optimistic, but his eyes looked sunken into dark wells, and most alarming of all held the bright emptiness that had been so marked seven years ago, when he thought he had lost everything that made life worth living.

"What do you mean, dear?" she asked, longing to take him into her arms and comfort him.

"Why, this woodenhead has contrived to put me under obligation to him. Saved my life."

Josie felt cold and her hand flew to her throat as she turned to Redmond. He said indignantly, "Never believe it! *You* pulled *me* out of your little bonfire, Dev, and do not be saying otherwise!"

Devenish ushered Josie to a chair, protesting, "Fact remains, Mitch, that had you not come in after me, I'd have gone on up and been on the landing just when the third floor decided to join us!"

Clutching his hand, her own very cold, Josie whispered, "Oh—God! What are you saying? Dev, there is no possession worth risking your life to—"

"He thought you were up there," Redmond intervened quietly.

Her face crumpled, and she hid it against her guardian's sleeve, then said, "Dearest—you knew I had gone out driving."

224

He went over to straddle a chair and smile at her over the back. "Earlier, yes. But I was out riding all afternoon, and by the time we— I got back, the poor old place was . . ." His expression became sombre briefly, then he finished, "A trifle warm."

"But—did you not ask for me? Surely they would have told you—"

"Seems to have been a difference of opinion," Mitchell put in again, his gaze steady on Devenish. "One of the chaps who came to help thought he saw you upstairs at the window. Dev didn't wait to hear more."

She gave a gasp, chilled by the what-might-have-been. "*Was* there anyone in the house at that time?"

"Yes," said Devenish with a twinkle. "Thank heaven! Had she not been, I doubt you'd be chatting with either of us now, m'dear."

Curious, Mitchell said, "You didn't tell me a lady was with us."

"Don't tell you all my secrets, m'lud."

Mitchell did not return the smile, and Devenish went on. "She gave me a smacking great kiss—hot-blooded wench!" They both stared at him, and he laughed, "No, really! Have you ever had your face licked by a pig? I tell you, Lady Godiva's tongue is like coarse sandpaper! I wonder I've *any* skin left on my poor phiz!"

Awed, Josie said, "You never mean it? Lady Godiva went in there after you?"

"Not exactly. She was already inside when I got there. I'd pointed her in the right direction, but she hasn't the brains of a swine. When Mitch and I came rolling down the stairs, we were both rather knocked out of time, and I fancy the poor gal was anxious to get out, so she revived the nearest guide. You'll never know what a shock it was to come back from the land of dreams and find myself surrounded by smoke and flame and with a blasted porker slobbering all over my face! For a moment, I really thought my sins had caught up—" He checked, seeing that Redmond's amusement had been cut off and that he was coming to his feet. As he glanced to the door, his heart sank.

He thought, 'Gad—I'd forgot this business!' and he called, "Welcome, Monsieur le Chevalier! I trust you'll forgive our *désordre temporaire.*"

Coming forward to gingerly clasp Devenish's hand, the Chevalier Émile de Galin threw a shocked look from his insouciant host, to the amused and battered Baron Redmond, to the polite smile of the girl. *"Désordre?"* he gasped. *"Mon Dieu!"*

Walking carefully through the debris, Josie said, "It has been a great shock to him, you know, Mitch. However he tries to hide it."

Redmond glanced back at the house that looked rather wrenchingly forlorn. "Of course it has. Dev will have his hands full, restoring the place. Which may be as well." He slanted a glance at her. "He tells me you mean to marry soon."

After a pause during which they both halted and stood looking at the many figures toiling amid the rubble, she answered, "It is not official yet. In fact, I'm rather surprised he would mention it."

"Probably wouldn't have, but"—he turned to face her squarely—"he was a touch overwhelmed when we crawled out of the house yesterday and Cornish told him you'd not been trapped inside."

"Oh," said Josie huskily and, not daring to dwell on it, asked, "Mitch, do you know why the Chevalier is here today?"

"No. I've heard only good of him, though. Fine old family. Fought gallantly in the war—against us, regrettably. Got himself stove in at—Salamanca, I believe. St. Clair thinks the world of him. Interesting chap."

"Colley certainly thought so."

They both laughed.

"D'you remember," said Mitchell, "how Colley badgered poor Dev to sit for him, and—" He broke off, his fine eyes widening. "By Jupiter! Perhaps de Galin is come to ask permission to pay his addresses! I noticed how he stared at you the night of the ball. Though, of course," he added staunchly, "any fellow who did not do so would have to be blind."

She stood on tiptoe to kiss his chin. "Thank you, my lord,

but I rather doubt it is a case of *l'amour*. Now, tell me, dear peer, do you go back to Town?"

"Er," he said vaguely, "I may stop first and— Oh, your pardon, Josie, but I want a word with Cornish. He came into that furnace to help Dev drag me out yesterday. From the bottom of my heart I must thank him!"

He kissed her and went off, and he certainly did thank the footman until that brash individual was red to the ears.

Having safely pocketed a magnificent douceur, Cornish protested, " 'Adn't oughter done that, yer baronish. I'll tell yer straight, I went in there 'cause me little rocket got 'isself into a spota trouble."

"And would have left me to fry, had I not been with him, I suppose," said Mitchell, indignant.

Cornish pursed up his lips. "Dunno, mate. Lord mate. Mighta. I don't risk me littel silk socks fer many blokes, and that's truth."

"Why, you damned hedgebird! Give me back my gold!"

Cornish looked at him askance but, reassured by the twinkle in the grey eyes, gave his broad, gappy grin.

Mitchell laughed, his amusement heightened when Cornish's screaming mirth augmented his own. He drew the footman on with him towards the stables.

"I am already deeply indebted to you," he said, his manner sobering. "But I want more of you."

Cornish regarded him curiously.

Mitchell went on, "I must warn you, it is something that Mr. Devenish would not at all like . . ."

"I *wondered* why you insisted we come here!" Rushing into the low-ceilinged private parlour that separated their rooms, Lady Isabella tossed her sables onto the practical leather-cushioned sofa, and advanced upon her indolently sprawled brother, her dark eyes flashing fury.

Fontaine, who had just composed himself for a pleasant nap, opened one eye, but made no attempt to rise from the armchair before the fire. "You know, Bella," he murmured, "if you keep going into the treetops every time some little circumstance annoys you—"

"Some little circumstance?" she hissed, halting before him, livid with fury. "You have been skinning cats, Elliot! And—damn you! I'll not have it!"

Sighing, he sat up. "You know it offends me to hear a lady swear."

"And it offends me that you would try to kill the man I love! Oh, never deny it! I saw one of your sneaking spies downstairs! I might have known you stayed here because—"

"Because it gets the sea breezes, m'dear. Very bracing."

"Much you care for bracing! You are intent on destruction—not restoration!" She leaned closer. "Had you killed him, Taine, I would—"

"Do nothing." His voice was soft still, but deadly, the light in the cold blue eyes so menacing that Isabella paled and stood motionless.

Fontaine rose and stretched lazily, then wandered to the window. "You could see the smoke from here, they tell me. I wonder you did not." He chuckled. "So near. And yet—so far."

She sat on the arm of the chair he had vacated, looking at him resentfully. "And that is why we stay in this revolting inn, when we might be enjoying the comforts of Oak Manor, where—"

"There are too many eyes, m'dear. Too much interference."

"It is only sheer luck you are not a murderer today, *dear* brother."

"Nonsense," he retorted, perching on the deep window ledge and looking out at the lush sweep of meadow and hill. "I did nothing. Finlayson—"

"Set your miserable blaze, I've no doubt."

He bowed slightly, mockingly. "You are all intelligence, Bella. And another of my lads encouraged your cavalier to trot back into the blaze. From whence he duly trotted out—alas."

Her hands gripped passionately at the back of the chair. "Knowing his death would break my heart! My God! Much love you have for me!"

He shrugged and inspected a fingernail. "He—annoyed me."

"And because a man—*annoys* you, you have him murdered?"

"Upon occasion." Without raising his head, he glanced at her slyly. "I have suspected for some time that he has the unmitigated gall to judge me! I had hoped to cause him—shall we say, embarrassment?—in a pair of neat little schemes at the ball. The damnable clod would seem to bear a charmed life, for neither materialized. But . . . you know how that old saying goes, third time lucky . . . or something of the sort."

Isabella caught her breath. Magnificent in her rage, she leaned forward, her eyes blazing, her voice as low as his had been. "What is in us that makes us so intense in our loves and hates, I do not know. But my blood carries the same thirst for vengeance as does yours, Taine, and I tell you now, as God be my judge, if you hurt him again—"

"Oh, please! Do not bring your God into our quarrel! It will avail you nothing. And besides, I must reluctantly confess I was unwise. I should have denied myself such jolly but impractical ventures. I lost my temper, merely. And so—I have decided, lovely one, to help you."

Watching him uneasily, she asked, "How?"

"Trust me. I deplore your taste, but—you have my word on it. Before the week is out, you will be betrothed to your crippled cavalier."

∽ *Chapter 16* ∽

Devenish frowned a little, the apprehension that had seized him when first he took up the Chevalier's calling card returning full measure. "As much as I know of my ward . . ." he repeated slowly. "Hum. Well, to start with, sir, I have long suspected she is French born."

The Chevalier's brilliant eyes widened. *"Pourquoi?"*

"Because—when I found her—"

"And when precisely *was* that, *Monsieur, s'il vous plaît*?"

"In May, 1816." Devenish's thoughts turned back, his eyes becoming remote. "I'd been robbed and left afoot in the country, late at night and miles from anywhere. I met this poor little waif. I thought she was a boy at first."

"How old was she then?"

"Who knows? I thought perhaps seven, no older than nine."

"Not if my hopes, they are justified. But—pardon—from where had this waif come? There was no home? Parents?"

"She had nothing, God bless her!" Devenish's jaw hardened. "She'd been beaten and starved and worked half to death for all her young life by a set of the most rascally gypsies you ever saw. The damned rogues were getting ready to sell her to a Flash House! You wouldn't know what that is, but—"

De Galin swore and said in a near snarl, "Of a certainty I know it! So you rescued this waif, *n'est-ce pas*? But what have cause you to suppose she is French?"

"She spoke a few words of your language next day. Properly

230

conflummerated me, I can tell you! Here the little sparrow could scarce speak decent English and out she pops with *"Très bien, Monsieur,"* with an accent as perfect as—as your own."

De Galin gave a slow smile. "You recall the exact words, *mon ami*? After these many years?"

A little red in the face, Devenish said that it had been such a shock, he was not likely to forget. "Even," he added defiantly, "after a century!"

"Je comprends. And—this waif, what could she tell you? Did she remember anything? Anything of the smallest?"

"Very little, I'm afraid. A beautiful lady who once sang to her; a few words of French—then. She's very proficient now, as I fancy you've discovered. And the fact that she was stolen as a small child."

The Chevalier gripped his hands, obviously in a state of strongly repressed excitement. "And—was she called Josie Storm when you found her?"

"No, no. We arrived at that between the pair of us. Her abductors had nicknamed her Tabby, because she scratched them when they—abused her. I couldn't stand that, of course."

"Mais non! But—why, *Monsieur*, is it that you choose *these* names?"

"Well, I had, I thought, seen her safely home that night, and I went on alone. As it turned out, she'd gulled me and she followed and crept into a barn where I was sleeping. There was a tearing great storm when I discovered her, so we chose that for her surname."

"Ah—and, the other?"

"Josie? Not my choice. She said she seemed to remember it, and wanted me to—" He paused as the handsome face was lit by a beaming smile.

"Voilà! It is as I have think, then!" The dark eyes were suddenly full of tears, and de Galin bowed his head, muttering brokenly, *"Merci beaucoup! Merci beaucoup, mon Dieu!"* He groped for a handkerchief, and blew his nose, saying unevenly, "A thousand apologies! You—you will think me the silly emotional Frenchman."

"No such thing," said Devenish very gently. "To find your child after all these years, must be—"

"No, no, *Monsieur*! Would that it were so, but—she is not mine."

Devenish crossed to refill their glasses, taking his time so that the Chevalier might have time to compose himself before he returned.

"You are most kind," said de Galin gratefully. "And now, if you permit, I will tell you my short tale. You must know that I have a twin brother who was"—he shrugged sadly—"everything I am not."

Devenish stared at him, wondering if the brother had been a human being.

Interpreting that look correctly, the Frenchman smiled. "*Monsieur*, you are what the ladies would call a very handsome gentleman. Ah—you scowl. Why? Is it that your looks they have not been the boon?"

"A damned curse, more like. You also, eh?"

"*Oui*. Tragically so. We both, my brother and I, fall in love with the same lady. The most beautiful, sweetly natured, angelic of creatures. But, despite the fact that my features they have happen to come together so as to be pleasing to the gentle sex, Michelle, she love my Charles. I tell you before, *Monsieur*, that he have everything I have not. This it is very truth. Charles, he have charm, wit, and an intelligence that is near genius. All my life, he have make me feel—inadequate. Only in looks, over which I have no control, and for which I may take no credits, do I excel. Pah! What folly!"

Intrigued, Devenish asked, "And your brother's wife was, er, attracted to you after all?"

"No. She love Charles. Only he had—before they married, you comprehend—a mistress. And the mistress she was very jealous, so she begin to tease Charles that Michelle she spend a great deal of the time with me. And this is true, but only because Charles, he is a diplomatist and many times away from home, and I am bored also, and they have by this time the sweet babe of whom I am most fond. Charles, he love us both, Michelle and me, and he grieve that this lie it might be truth. Even my

Charles have the faults, and his fault is that he begins to suspect. He has seen many ladies become—silly because of my—my appearance, and he start to think Michelle also may— Well, the end of it is that we are in England for a month, and Charles he come one day when we do not expect him home. Michelle and the babe and I are in the garden—my niece had then four of the years—and it is—ah! the word, it eludes . . . *d'une chaleur étouffante* . . . ?''

Devenish frowned, then supplied, ''Sultry.''

''Oui—merci. Sool-tree. Michelle, she say she is so very warm, and I take my handkerchief and dry her little face and say I will fetch some lemonade. I go to the house and there is Charles. Watching. And enraged. He accuse. I defend. We quarrel very fiercely, so that Michelle she hear and come running. And we all three begin to quarrel even more. Perhaps—ah, *mon Dieu*—perhaps because it is hot and everyone sticky and cross. And then, when we stop to recollect ourselves, Michelle scream, 'My baby!' and she rush outside.'' He shook his head, anguished by the memory. ''The babe, she is gone.''

''Oh, Lord! How perfectly rotten for you. And you never saw her again?''

''Never again, *Monsieur.* Michelle, she blame herself. Charles, he blame himself. Me, I blame myself, *naturellement.* Charles spend the next five years searching from one end of England to the other. In 1813, he hear of a soldier who have steal a child and sell her to gypsies. A British soldier who is serving with his regiment in Spain. Charles go at once to Madrid to try and trace this man, but—'' He paused, a stark desolation coming into his face. ''He is caught by guerrillas who hate the French, and he is—robbed and . . . and murdered.''

''Oh—Lord! And the lady?''

''I was so blessed as to make her my wife a year later, *Monsieur.*'' The Chevalier smiled sadly. ''It was a brief happiness. Two years only we have together. She become ill with a fever then. The rheumatic fever it is called here. For some months afterwards she is the invalid, and then . . . I am alone again.''

''My poor fellow! I am so sorry. But now, you think my ward is . . .''

"Is the child of Michelle and my dear brother. *Oui, Monsieur.*"

"I see. But—it is a sad truth, de Galin, that hundreds of children are stolen each year, to be sold for climbing boys, prostitutes, or factory workers, or pressed at sea."

"This I know. But not every child so stolen is named—Josie. *Oui, Monsieur.* My niece was Josephine Claire de Galin. And will be today a very considerable heiress. More than this—" He drew a miniature from his pocket and handed it over. "I let you be the judge."

The likeness was of a young woman. Her features were of a more ethereal beauty than those of Josie, and there was a wistful quality to the smile rather than the buoyant mischief so evident in his ward's face, but Devenish noted the same rather fly-away hair, the same colouring and big dark eyes, the same rather pointed little chin. For a long moment he was silent. Then, he returned the painting to the Frenchman. "There is a resemblance, certainly. Well, *Monsieur*, what do you wish? Are we to tell her?"

"Not yet, I beg. I must return to Paris. When I come back, with your permission I will call again. Oh, it is not that in my mind there are doubts. It is only—to make a mistake would be a very bad thing for the young lady. Therefore, we must be very sure."

Devenish nodded. "*Monsieur*, you said that after the child was abducted your brother spent the five years until his death searching for her. That would mean, I believe, that Josie was nine years old in 1813?"

"*Oui.* She will be twenty in January, Monsieur Devenish."

"Then she was right—the little rascal!"

The rather wistful smile awoke the Chevalier's curiosity. He asked, "This, it is of *grande importance*?"

"It is of no importance whatsoever. Merely a joke between us. You must be very excited, Chevalier."

"I am—ah, beside myself with joy! You will not understand, I expect, but—but I have been a man very lonely since my dear wife died. To find her child, to perhaps watch her marry and have children of her own—a family circle into which I may be permitted to enter . . . There are no words, sir!"

"No," said Devenish quietly. "There are no words."

The fire had come and gone, and despite that terrible event, it could have been worse. By some miracle, Devenish had not been seriously burned. There had been no further sign of the threat that was Elliot Fontaine, nor had Dev made any reference of late to his alleged *penchant* for the beautiful Isabella. Josie should have been happy and carefree again, but she was neither.

In the days that followed the disaster, the old house was a beehive of activity. A small army was imported to haul away the rubble between the two wings and repair the havoc created on the once green lawns by horses, wheels, and the great depressions from which dirt had been dug to be dumped on the pyre. Wolfe and Mrs. Robinson worked feverishly to itemize all that had been lost and restore what was left. Carpenters replaced window glass and patched up blackened walls. Fires were lighted on every hearth in an attempt to dry out drenched floors and woodwork, no easy task with the cold outer air and a persistent drizzle falling. Neighbours came and went in steady streams to gawk at the stricken old house and commiserate with its owner.

Josie, trying amidst the uproar to replenish her wardrobe, since most of her possessions had been lost, and also to prepare for the fast approaching Christmas season, seemed to run from dawn to dusk, and the time whipped past at such a rate that she told Mrs. Bliss one cloudy afternoon that there was no least chance she ever could be ready in time. "For we are to go to Cloudhills this year, you know, to spend the holidays with the Leiths."

"How lovely," said Faith, putting down her teacup.

Josie glanced at her. "And—you, dear? Do you and Guy make plans to be— Oh, my! Never say you have quarrelled?"

Blinking rapidly, Faith concentrated on collecting some crumbs that had fallen onto her napkin, and said they had not quarrelled. "One cannot easily quarrel"—she smiled too brightly—"with a gentleman who never calls."

"Sir William?" asked Josie, dismayed.

"Oh, no! They have decided it between them. I must—must

look elsewhere for my future husband.'' She bunched up the napkin savagely, thus scattering all her carefully gathered crumbs. ''I wish I might knock their wooden heads together,'' she said, her teeth bared.

''But—I thought, now that the King has cleared Guy from suspicion, he would be accepted, and your brother no longer object. Whatever happened?''

''It seems,'' said Faith, her colour deepening, ''Guy is afraid that—that if we marry, I . . . might have children.'' She looked away, her lips trembling.

Josie slipped an arm about her. ''Oh, but that is so like him! Truly, he is the most caring of men. But—you are healthy, and—''

Faith was shaking her head so vehemently that tears scattered. ''It is not that. I think if it were, I could—could have convinced him. It is something I—cannot fight, do you see? Guy said the world could not endure another Claude or—or Parnell. And—and William says there is bad blood there, and he'll not have it introduced into our family!''

Josie wondered sadly if Devenish feared that she, too, had bad blood. She said, ''What nonsense! You're of age, Faith! You love Guy, and—''

''And he loves me! But foolish creature, he is fairly eaten up with pride!'' Her face crumpled and, bowing it between her hands, she sobbed out, ''I even said we need not . . . that is to say—we could lead separate lives at night, if it would ease his mind.'' She tensed and blinked through her tears at the troubled young face beside her. ''Oh, my apologies.'' She wiped impatiently at her eyes with the napkin, and sniffed. ''I should not speak so to a sweet innocent.''

''Pooh! You forget, I think, that I spent my early years in a gypsy encampment! I knew more when I was six, Faith Bliss, than you did when you were wed, I fancy!'' She sighed, and went on in a defeated way, ''Enough to understand Guy's reaction to your offer. He loves you so much, and likely knows he would not be able to abide by such an unnatural bargain. No more would you, I think.''

''No,'' whispered Faith helplessly. ''So—it is ended for me. And—enough of my problems. Now, dearest, I've scarce seen

236

you this past week. I saw Dev outside just now. His eyebrows are already beginning to grow back, but I'll admit he looks different without his curls.''

Josie smiled. ''Like a hedgehog, I tell him.''

''You scamp! He never does.'' Faith blew her nose daintily, and said in a casual way, ''He—*was* unhurt in the fire?''

''A few burns, but nothing— Faith! My heavens—you're not at your premonitioning again?''

''No, no, dear. Only . . . it's probably just my silly worrying nature, but—I know Dev has had—er, reservations about this old place, but—it *is* his ancestral home, and to suffer so terrible a loss, one might think . . .''

''I know.'' Josie's dark eyes were troubled. ''It has worried me, I own. He is almost—*too* cheerful. But—that is his way, you know. I think the fire brought home to him just how much he loves Devencourt, and when he is very much hurt, he would die sooner than allow anyone to see it.''

Faith squeezed her hand impulsively. ''How well you know him. Now, tell me—what have you bought him for Christmas?''

Devenish reined up and pulled the inordinately long and rather garish scarf a little more closely about his throat. Josie had knitted it for him, and for a moment he continued to hold the tasselled end, a faint smile softening his expression as he recalled the many winter evenings they had sat by the fire together while he read (or tried to) and she knitted and chattered at him like a bright little magpie . . .

Santana danced, impatient with the pause, and Devenish shrank to the touch of the icy wind, and started him off at an easy canter. They'd have snow before Christmas, at this rate. Josie would like that. He wouldn't mind either, so long as they could get to Cloudhills before it came down in earnest. If they went to Cloudhills. If the Chevalier returned with his confirmation, for it would be a confirmation, he knew—before the holidays, it could spoil their last Christmas together. Irritable, because he was selfish enough to wish a delay for such happiness for Josie, he moved in the saddle, his spurs touching against the stallion's sides. Santana needed no more. With a bound, he was away, his hoofs spurning the muddy ground, his powerful strides eating up the distance. Eyes narrowing, Devenish leaned forward, exhilarated by the speed, defying common sense. Within two minutes, he was obliged to rein the big horse in again. He bowed lower, waiting it out with eyes closed and breath held in check. By the time it eased, he was panting and wet with sweat, his right hand gripping his knee, his left clamped so tightly on the pommel he could scarcely relax his fingers. Straightening cautiously, he knew he had brought it on himself, but he knew also that it was worse than ever before, and the attacks much more frequent. It was madness to put things off any longer. Sooner or later it would happen in front of Josie, and if she once suspected . . . He swore, and headed Santana across the fields toward the smoke that drifted from the chimneys of a neat little hedge tavern he patronized from time to time on his way to or from Stroud.

The tavern keeper met him at the door. A warm breath of air on which hung the scents of woodsmoke and ale and a baking pie wafted to his nostrils.

"Ye look half froze, zur," said the stocky host, beaming at him. "Coom ye in by the fire, here. Ye'll likely be company for the gent as is biding wi' us a while."

The "gent" was John Drummond, seated at a hearthside table and staring gloomily at the leaping flames. He stood, flushing as Devenish came in, and asked if his cousin would care to join him.

Devenish had not wanted to meet anyone he knew, least of all one of Josie's suitors, but he lied courteously and limped over to occupy a facing chair while the tavern keeper hurried to pour a mug of scalding coffee and call to his wife to warm a piece of the apple pie.

"Back again, eh?" said Devenish heartily.

Drummond sighed. "Never left. I fancy you must think me a sorry fool to hang about here. Knowing it's all hopeless. But . . ."

"Not at all. Save that I do not see why you couldn't have stayed at Devencourt instead of here."

"You had your hands full, without me moping about the place.

238

Besides, I got off a letter to my sire. Just had his reply." He gave a wry shrug. "He's quite adamant. He's very fond of Josie, but . . . Well, if anything should happen to Arthur, I'd be the heir."

His quick temper flaring, Devenish said an acid "One wonders whether my ward would disgrace his line, or if the dowry I've settled on her is inadequate!"

Drummond stiffened, paling. Fortunately, the host returned at this moment with a fragrant slice of apple pie which he set with a flourish in front of Devenish. As soon as the rotund little man had gone, Drummond said with fierce resentment, "Your remark was completely uncalled for, and—"

"I know." Devenish gave a weary gesture. "You've my apologies, John. It's only . . . she's such a rare little creature."

For a moment John continued to glare at him. Then, relaxing, he sighed. "Aye, she is. And I had to tell her—poor sweet girl."

Devenish hacked out a piece of pie with rather extreme ferocity. "Upset, was she?"

"Yes. But you know how she is, Dev. So high in her moral values. She says she don't want to bolt to Gretna, which I wouldn't dream of suggesting, of course. And that she don't want to marry me in a clandestine way, because she would feel ashamed. God bless her! Dashitall, when two people care for each other, it's the very devil! I promised her I'd find some way out. I told her not to grieve too much, but—honestly, I don't know what to do."

The pie was tasteless and dry in Devenish's mouth. He slammed down the fork and thrust the plate away. So she really did care for Drummond. She must. Certainly, she'd not have told him so if she didn't mean it; she was no coquette. And what in hell was he resenting? John was a good, clean chap. Just the kind he'd always prayed for . . .

"Coz . . . ?" repeated Drummond, peering at him.

"Your pardon. You were saying . . . ?"

"I said—don't you want that pie?"

"Pie? Oh. No—damnable stuff. Dry as dust."

Drummond stared at rich, flaking pastry, juicy slices of apple, and the steam that drifted so fragrantly above the generous portion.

A reluctant gleam of amusement dawned in Devenish's eyes. Heartbroken this suitor might be, but he was not too far gone to covet another man's pie! He shoved the plate over. "Help yourself. I'm just not hungry."

Drummond gave the pie his enthusiastic attention. "I told Josie," he said rather thickly, "that we'd be wed, no matter what my father says. M'mother might be able to win him around. Knows how to handle him. It's the only hope we've got, as I see it."

"And—what if Lady Louisa cannot win your father over?"

The busy fork stilled. Staring at it broodingly, Drummond said, "Elope."

"Oh, very good. And what would you live on, pray?"

"No difficulty there. I've been administering Tyndale's Canadian properties these past months, and found I was quite able to do so, although his holdings are enormous. Craig would like nothing better than for me to take over on a permanent basis. There's a dashed fine house, and it's beautiful country."

Devenish sat very still. He'd thought *France* would be far away. Canada was halfway around the world! He asked, "You have mentioned this . . . to Josie?"

"Lord, no. But—it's a solution, if all else fails."

It was a solution. Two young people venturing upon a new life in a new land. Stunned, Devenish thought, 'Would she really have gone so far away? Would she really have left me?' And how wrong to think so. He must let her go. The time had come, very *well* timed, for him to step back. He nerved himself, and said, "John . . . I will tell you something—in confidence."

Five minutes later, Drummond drew the cork, poured the champagne, and swung his glass high. "A toast!" he cried, flushed with joy.

With a fixed smile, Devenish stood, glass in hand.

"To Josephine de Galin," said John. "The future Mrs. John Drummond!"

Devenish raised his glass, but the most he could make his lips utter was, "To Josephine de Galin!"

The ardent swain was full of plans and hopes, yet it was obvious he could scarcely wait to retire to his room, array himself in the best clothes he had with him, and proceed to Devencourt to woo his beloved. Having no least doubts of the rate at which Drummond meant to ride, Devenish said that he had other business to attend to before returning home. They soon parted, therefore, Devenish embarking upon a wide easterly loop before at long last turning west towards Devencourt. The gloomy afternoon did nothing to brighten his mood, and he scarcely felt the snow flurries. Everything, he decided, was falling neatly into place—provided Josie would believe him. That was going to be the most difficult part; to get her to believe what he would tell her.

A shout, distant and indistinct, cut off his introspection. He looked up. A rider was coming at the gallop. A man, wearing a heavy coat and a low-crowned hat, and who waved with frantic urgency. Devenish applied his spurs and Santana bounded forward. As they drew closer, Devenish recognized the new footman and fear of some further disaster clutched him. "What is it?" he shouted, reining Santana to a halt.

"Bad news, I fear, sir," gasped Finlayson breathlessly. "Word came from Cirencester. Lord Redmond has been shot!"

"Oh, God!" groaned Devenish. "They've not *killed* him?"

"It sounds bad, sir. His lordship lies at the Boar's Head—it's just beyond the town on the Cricklade Road. The valet said—if you *could* come, sir—to please come at the gallop!"

All thought of his own troubles disappeared. His heart twisting painfully, Devenish said, "I'll go at once. Does Miss Storm know?"

"She rode part way to Oak Manor with Mrs. Bliss, sir. Mr. Wolfe sent Klaus after her."

"Good. Pray tell her— No, wait." He took a pencil and a small notepad from his pocket, and scribbled, "Little one—I'll send word as soon as I learn something. Dev." He formed the paper into a twist and handed it to the footman. "Give this to Miss Storm directly she comes home. Ask Mr. Hutchinson to come to the Boar's Head with a change of clothes and my overnight necessities."

241

The footman inclined his head.

"Did Mr. John Drummond pass you, by any chance?" asked Devenish.

"I saw a rider, sir, but I had cut across country and was riding very fast, so I did not see who he might be."

"Never mind. You're a good man. My thanks."

The man bowed again. Devenish turned Santana and touched the sleek sides with his spurs. The big black snorted in surprise and leapt joyously into a gallop, Devenish leaning forward in the saddle, and horse and man like one being.

The young nob, thought Finlayson (which was not his real name), had a damn fine seat. He smiled unpleasantly. Much good might it do him! Still smiling, he read Devenish's note, then tore it into small pieces and let the wind carry it away before he commenced a leisurely return to Devencourt.

❧ *Chapter 17* ❧

"Oh my, but it has turned cold," said Josie, peeling off her gloves and handing her whip to Cornish as he opened the terrace door for her.

"Didya ride all the way to Oak Manor, miss?"

"No. It came on to sleet, so I decided to come back. Is the master home yet?"

"Not yet, mate. But young—er, I mean Mr. Drummond's waitin' in the bookroom." He accompanied her as she started to the hall, and said rather reluctantly, "Wouldn't 'ave a minute first, wouldya, miss?"

She liked the big man, and she smiled and asked if he would wish to speak to her in here.

"Ain't me. It's that there littel—" His jaw set, he said primly, "Mr. Finlayson. Arst ter see yer immedjit when yer come in."

Finlayson. Her brow wrinkled. That would be the cold fish. "I'll see him in the drawing room if there's a fire in there."

Cornish went off, saying he'd fetch "the slippery cove" there, and, stifling a smile, Josie left the study and turned into the drawing room. Before she had time to sit down, Finlayson was pulling the doors closed. Immediately, she felt the rush of dislike. He was never anything but polite, yet there was something . . . Impatient with herself, she said, "You wished to see me?"

"I have no right, miss." For the first time he appeared agitated, and went on hurriedly, "I may be making much out of

243

nothing, but—I know that Lord Redmond is most anxious about the master, and—''

Her heart gave a scared jolt. About to sit down, she stared at him. ''In what way?''

''I do not know, miss. I happened to overhear something he said before he left. I'd not meant to eavesdrop, I do assure you, but I came around the side of the house just as his lordship grasped the master's arm. He swore at him, and said, 'Dev—it would be suicide! By God, if I thought you really meant to do so crack-brained a thing—!' And then he saw me, and he stopped speaking.''

Inwardly frightened, Josie said, ''Well, you may be sure I shall— Oh, dear—is there more?''

His pale hands gripped and wrung. He said, ''If I alarm you for nothing, Mr. Devenish will be most provoked, I know, but— I was sent into Cirencester early this afternoon, to get the report from the Constable there.''

Surprised, she asked, ''About the fire?''

''Why, no, miss. About the champagne.''

''Good gracious! I did not know Mr. Devenish meant to bring an action because the wine was spoiled.''

''But it was not spoiled, miss. It was poisoned.''

Her heart seemed to stop. One hand lifted involuntarily to her throat in the gesture that always betrayed shock. For anyone to have done such a dreadful thing must point to a deepseated hatred for either herself or Dev. She certainly had not won the heart of everyone she'd ever met, but neither had she, to the best of her knowledge, aroused so deep a dislike as to result in this horrid business. Dev, with his hasty temper, his unyielding loyalties, his attraction for women, had made many enemies, but— who hated him? Claude Sanguinet had, but Claude was dead. There was Gerard, of course, Claude's deadly lieutenant who had disappeared after the abortive attempt to seize power in England, and had never been heard of again. And—Lyon . . . She was ashamed of the thought even as it dawned. Hot-tempered Lyon might be, but he was an honourable young man, and he would never do anything to hurt her, for she was very sure that he loved her devotedly.

Watching her paling face from under his meekly lowered lashes, Finlayson smiled to himself. "It was on account of that nasty business that what happened today has me a—a bit worried, miss. I didn't say anything to Mr. Wolfe, lest he think me stepping above my station, but I thought you might want me to . . . er . . ."

"Yes, yes," she said, trying not to panic. "Do please tell me what it is that concerns you."

"Well, it was whilst I was in Cirencester, miss. I chanced to stop at a little tavern while I waited for the Constable. I'd just gone out to the yard to get my horse, when the master rode in like the devil was at his heels. I went over to him, of course, but he—oh, miss, he behaved in so strange a way. Pushed past me, as if he didn't even know me, and muttered something about—nothing wouldn't stop him settling accounts this time."

Josie's tongue seemed to cleave to the roof of her mouth. That fierce pride of his again! She asked, "Did you see anyone else at the tavern with whom you were acquainted?"

"No, miss. Well—not to say 'acquainted.' I did see a carriage in the yard with the crest of Lord Fontaine on the panel."

Very pale, Josie started to the door. "You were quite right to come to me about this. I must go there at once. Be so good as to have the horses put to my new barouche and send Klaus to me."

The footman ran to swing the door open for her, and she saw John Drummond striding along the hall, his fine face aglow with an excitement that faded into alarm as he saw her expression. She stretched out both hands. "Oh, John! Thank heaven you are here!"

The elegant barouche proceeded at a spanking pace along the Cirencester Road, Alfred Coachman driving, and Klaus sitting beside him, arms folded and eyes worried. Inside, John Drummond held Josie's cold little hand and tried to ease her fears. Despite his calm words, he was much disturbed. There were rumours Devenish and Fontaine had come to blows at Josie's ball. If that was so, most certainly a duel was planned. And if

245

Fontaine had also been at that blasted inn, it might already have been conducted!

He patted Josie's hand and told her again that it was likely a lot of fuss about nothing, but he thought of how quiet Dev had seemed when he'd drunk the toast, and come to think of it, he hadn't been able to eat the pie, either. Naturally not, knowing he was likely going to his death! Gad, but it was a fine mess. And to think he'd come here hoping to clear the way for his nuptials! There could be no thought of a proposal now. Josie adored her tempestuous guardian, and if Dev had gone off and let Fontaine blow a hole through him . . . He thought, 'Poor old Dev' and stared glumly out of the window.

For Josie, the miles seemed to creep past. No less than Drummond did she dread the outcome of their desperate journey. Her fears were so magnified by the time they reached Cirencester that she could not stop shivering.

The coachman knew the Boar's Head, and a few minutes later they turned off the main road into a winding lane, and thence to the yard of a small, nicely maintained inn. Ostlers came running to hold the team. Klaus jumped down to open the door and let down the steps, and Drummond alighted and handed Josie into what was again a steady sleet.

The host, a spry little man, obviously pleased by the arrival of so luxurious a vehicle, hurried out with an umbrella. Cutting through his babble of welcome, Drummond said urgently, "Is Mr. Alain Devenish here?"

The man's jaw dropped, and he stared from one to the other like a bewildered owl. Another individual ran up, collar turned high against the freezing rain. Lifting his hat respectfully, he said, "Are you friends of Mr. Devenish? He is upstairs. This way!"

"Hold hard," the host objected, shaking out his umbrella as the little party hurried into the warm vestibule, "The young lady shouldn't go up there!"

He had as well speak to the wind. With a little sob of apprehension, Josie followed the other man to the stairs. Drummond hesitated, calling to Klaus to "wait with the luggage until we know what Miss Storm wishes to do."

The stranger had paused at the foot of the stairs, staring after Josie with a puzzled frown. Drummond strode to his side. "Is it very bad?"

The man turned to him. "Bad? Lord—perhaps it is! I wish I'd not been so helpful!" And with the words he all but ran for the door and was gone.

Josie had already reached the upstairs hall. There were three doors on each side of a narrow corridor. She knocked softly at the first door on the right and, receiving no response, ran to the door on the left. She thought she heard a woman laugh, low and throatily, but decided it must have come from the next room. She scratched softly at the panel, thought to hear a response, and opened the door. She stepped inside, only to halt, frozen with shock.

Devenish lay on the bed. He wore neither boots nor coat, and his shirt was unbuttoned to the waist, but there were no blood-stained bandages, no doctor hovering in attendance. The person hovering over him was a woman—a beautiful woman who lay beside him in her petticoats, struggling to remove his hand from her bodice: Lady Isabella was in a state of considerable dishevellment, her hair tousled and awry, one strap hanging from her bare shoulder to reveal the soft swell of an ample breast. Squealing, she glanced up and with a gasp of horror sprang from the bed.

Drummond, who had raced up after Josie, looked past the motionless girl and gasped, "By . . . God . . . !"

Through numbed lips, Josie whispered, "Dev . . . ?"

"How . . . how *dare* you!" cried my lady, striving with belated propriety to restore her bodice.

Hideously embarrassed, Drummond gulped, "We made—we made a mistake! We thought—er," He grasped Josie's elbow. "I apologize! Most dreadfully sorry. Good—er, good day!"

Josie pulled free. Her face very white, she demanded, "Dev, are you mad? To be here with this lady is—"

"La!" interrupted Isabella. "I suppose I may be alone with my affianced husband!"

The room seemed to rock. Dimly, Josie knew that Drummond

had muttered something and that another man had come in and stood beside her.

Devenish struggled to one elbow and peered at the new arrivals. "Jo . . . shie?" he uttered. "Whachou . . . doin' wi' *him*?"

Viscount Fontaine said a savage, "Your pardon, Drummond," and slammed the door closed. "Bella," he grated, "I fancy you do not have to be told that this behaviour is beyond the pale! As for you, Devenish—Gad, but your love-nest fairly reeks of brandy! Damme, sir! *Attend* me! My seconds will—"

With a shriek, Isabella threw herself between her justifiably incensed brother and the sagging Devenish. "We are betrothed, Taine! He offered, and I accepted!"

"And came at once to bed to seal the bargain?" The Viscount's lip curled. "Pretty behaviour, upon my word! If *you* want your name bandied about in every coffee house and tavern from here to Land's End, I may tell you that *I* do not! Get your things, ma'am!" She glared at him rebelliously, and he snapped, "At once!"

With a toss of her curls and a defiant glance at the girl who stood in stunned silence, Isabella snatched up her gown and flounced into the adjoining room, slamming the door behind her.

Fontaine strode to the bed and frowned down at Devenish, who was still propped on one elbow and peering blearily about. "Well, sir?" demanded his lordship. "Has my sister the straight of it? Or are you too far in your cups to know whether you offered or not?"

With difficulty, Devenish managed a slurred, "Wouldn' dream 'f . . . contra—dict'n . . . lady."

The appalled Drummond plucked at Josie's pelisse. "Come, m'dear ma'am. No business here. Best get out of this." He took her resistless hand and led her to the door, where he paused to direct an aghast look at the Viscount. "Very sorry, Fontaine."

Fontaine came to drop a gentle hand on Josie's shoulder. "I am sorry, too," he said, and opened the door.

Speechless, grief-stricken, Josie allowed John Drummond to lead her down the stairs, and away.

Fontaine closed the door, and paced to stare down at the man now lying motionless on the bed. "Sot," he muttered, and then, touching his jaw and the bruises that cosmetics barely managed to cover, he chuckled. "Let that be a lesson to you, future brother-in-law. Never twist the tail of a tiger until you're sure the tiger is dead! And this tiger, my fool, is—"

"Have they gone?"

He glanced to the connecting door. "All gone, Madame Siddons."

His sister laughed delightedly. "Was I not superb?" She danced over to the bed and scanned Devenish's unconscious figure with some anxiety. "My poor love! He *is* all right, Taine?"

"I'll not say he will awaken feeling full of *joie de vivre*, but—he will awaken. Now"—he perched on the side of the bed—"tell your dear brother all about it. You were in the parlour when the man I had waiting outside brought him up to Redmond's supposed death bed, correct?"

Isabella did a pirouette, holding out her skirts and looking very lovely. "Yes," she trilled. "And I said just as you instructed, dearest and best of brothers."

"That you had been passing through Cirencester, heard of the attack on Redmond, and came here at once. That they had said the doctor was still working on him, but that you could wait in the parlour."

"Yes. Oh, but he was suspicious at first, love, I could tell. Only, your man was superb and by the time he left—to call in more constables, he said!—I almost believed it myself. I played my part so well! You would have been proud of me."

He grinned and said not without some truth, "I am usually proud of you, Bella. Now—*you* did not suggest the wine, I hope."

"No. I merely sat and shivered and said I was feeling so nervous I was quite faint, and then I fell back and closed my eyes, and he fairly ran to bring me a glass of sherry. He was so white!"

"And so he decided to join you in a restoring glass! *Naturellement!* Well done, Bellissima!"

She curtseyed, but then ran to bend over Devenish again. "You are quite sure I didn't use too much of that dreadful stuff? He became helpless so soon, your man could scarce get him in here, and I was afraid he would be unconscious by the time they arrived."

He shrugged. "Even had he been, you would have contrived, I make no doubt." He eyed her musingly. "He'll not love you for this, you realize?"

"What matter?" she said airily. "Once I have him, I shall make him love me, sooner or later." And then, with swift anxiety, "He cannot escape, can he?"

"You know better. A gentleman does not draw back from a betrothal—especially so notoriously conducted a betrothal as this. Devenish is a pest, but as I said before, he is a gentleman. Oh, no, he is properly trapped." He grinned up at her. "I trust you are sufficiently grateful. I kept my promise."

"You did, you did! Dearest Taine." She swooped to kiss him on both cheeks and, drawing back, said curiously, "Why? Not just because you hate him, I think. Is it because it will give you a logical closeness to the girl?"

"Shrewd, aren't you? I mean to have the chit. Though not in the manner I had originally thought."

Isabella gasped and sat beside him. "Marriage? My heavens, can I believe my ears? Have you come to care for her, then?"

"I have come," he said with a slow smile, "into the possession of a secret. But you must keep a still tongue in your head, for I am not supposed to know." She swore to be discreet, and he went on, "Mistress Josie Storm is, it seems, actually Mademoiselle Josephine de Galin, niece to the Chevalier Émile de Galin, and a . . . considerable heiress. So you see, Bella, in wedding her I kill two birds with one stone. I get the girl I want, and I gain access to her fortune." He turned, to shake Devenish's arm roughly. "Do you hear, Sir Arrogance? You'll not dare name me an unfit suitor when I am the brother of your wife. Your ward will amuse me for a while, and long before I grow bored with her, I'll have control of her fortune! Sleep well, dear Dev!"

He looked at Isabella, grinning his triumph. She smiled also, but at the back of her smile dwelt a shadow of unease.

* * *

She had been so sure, thought Josie dully, that he would come home and tell them it had all been a trap. That the wretched Isabella had made him drunk and had then sent word to the house about the duel, knowing she would come and that Dev would be unable to escape the betrothal. But here he was, smiling at her across the fireplace, and telling her in that easy, pleasant way of his, that he apologized for his conduct, but that he was sure she would not have intruded had she realized he and Bella were betrothed.

The clock struck three, and she stared at it blankly. It had been three this morning when they had brought him home. Uproarious. Cornish and Hutchinson had had to carry him up the stairs. The intervening period was a blank. She could not remember what she had done, save to wander about and try to understand it all and keep praying it was some horrible mistake.

He was watching her. She thought, 'He looks so ill!' and she said, "Dev—are you sure you are all right? You look—"

He snatched out his handkerchief in time to muffle an explosive sneeze, then groaned, and clutched his head. With a wan smile, he replied, "Too much riotous living, I fear."

"We were told," said Pandora Grenfell austerely, "that you were gone to fight Elliot Fontaine. We would not term that— riotous living."

"Lord, no. Some idiot playing a practical joke on that fool Finlayson."

"We see no humour in the—joke," said Mrs. Grenfell, eyeing him with a cold, dispassionate stare.

"No," said Devenish, lifting a trembling hand to his head. "Well, there you are. Thing is—I was—er, celebrating on two counts, y'see." He took a sheet of paper from the table beside him. "I've some very wonderful news for you, little one."

Josie stared at him blankly. What could be wonderful now?

"There's nothing to stop your marriage to young Drummond," he said heartily. "This letter is from the Chevalier de Galin." He put it down again and looked fixedly at the toe of her slipper. "I did not tell you, for fear of—of a later disappointment. When the Chevalier collapsed on the night of your

251

ball, it was because he had seen *you*, Josie, and you—reminded him of someone he had loved very dearly.''

Intrigued, despite her unhappiness, she leaned forward. "Is that why he came back that day?''

"Yes, dear. He told me a very sad tale, but briefly, he believes you are his long-lost niece, the child of his dead brother.''

Her heart began to pound madly. The Chevalier? Her *uncle*? Was it possible? She put a hand to her throat, scarcely able to breathe.

Mrs. Grenfell, shocked out of her imperturbability, cried, "Why—this is stupendous news! Are you *sure*? Is there any proof?''

His eyes fixed on Josie's flushed, incredulous little face, he said, "The Chevalier writes that there is no longer any room for doubt. He says he must go to his mama's chateau at Orleans and will then come here. He is—quite overjoyed, I need not tell you.''

Josie was on her feet, her hands clasped, her eyes like stars. "Is it true? Oh, is it really true? I *belong* somewhere? I have a *family*?''

Pandora slanted a quick look at Devenish, but his face still bore that fond smile. She stood and embraced the ecstatic girl. "If it is true, my dear child, you have a very proud old family, a great name, and—''

"And are a considerable heiress,'' Devenish put in, coming to his feet but keeping a steadying hand on the back of his chair.

Josie stilled, the joy fading from her eyes. She watched him for a moment, a little frown coming to pull at her brows. "I see,'' she said thoughtfully. But joy would not be banished. She danced over to him and gripped his arm. "Dev, dearest Dev! Are you not happy for my sake? Say you are happy!''

"Of course, my Elf,'' he said, and swept her into a hug.

"And—say my name,'' she demanded, as he groped rather blindly for his chair again.

"You are Mademoiselle Josephine de Galin,'' he said, bowing unsteadily.

She gave a scream of excitement.

Devenish groaned, and clutched his head.

"It is a calamity!" Mrs. Grenfell leaned back in the chair to which Guy had ushered her. She accepted the glass of sherry he brought her, and waited while he supplied himself with some Madeira and made his slow way across the quiet drawing room of his charming house to settle himself on an adjacent sofa. Sipping her wine, she regarded him solemnly. "You know of the betrothal?"

"*Oui, Madame.* My valet—how is this saying?—the servants' semaphore? I confess myself *étonné!*"

"We *all* are amazed," she agreed dryly. "Firstly, that Devenish—who was always wild, you understand, but who my brother Alastair Tyndale made sure was properly bred up—would be so—crudely vulgar. Secondly, that he has confirmed his depravity and appears well satisfied with his choice."

Guy frowned at the amber glow projected through his wine by a ray of sunlight. "Josie—she was present to hear this announcement?"

She inclined her head regally. "And quite obviously shattered."

"And Alain? He have seem—er, quite himself?"

Her lip curled. She said with distaste, "He was suffering the effects of over-indulgence. Besides which he has managed to catch a bad cold and looked quite ill, in point of fact. But he was—jubilant is the word that comes to mind."

"Because of this so unexpected betrothal?"

"Unexpected? Hmmnn. Perhaps not that, my dear Guy. The creature has pursued him with singleminded determination this year and more. However—I have not told you the second development. When Devenish at last was sufficiently recovered to make an appearance, he read us a letter from Monsieur le Chevalier de Galin. It appears that the Chevalier believes Josie to be the long-lost daughter of his late brother."

"*Tiens!*" he gasped, jerking upright. "And Mitchell, he think de Galin came to ask for her hand! He is her—*uncle*? This, it is proven of the certain?"

"So we are told. Also, that she is a considerable heiress."

"What a thing *merveilleux*! She is much excited?"

"Very much. Devenish feels she will wed our nephew Drummond."

His heart sank. So poor Lyon still was not the favoured one. But that, it would not have been the case in any event. "Things they have happen very fast, *Madame*. Sir Martin will approve the match now that Josie is the heiress."

She said with some hauteur, "We cannot think Sir Martin would be influenced by such a vulgar consideration."

"Mais non! Forgive this clumsy fellow—I should not have speak these things!"

She relented, smiling into his flushed face. "The situation has changed admittedly, in that her birth is now impeccable, and her lineage such as to make her an eligible wife for any—" It was her turn to redden as Guy looked fixedly at the fireplace. "Ah . . . ! But how thoughtless! We crave your pardon. In view of your own situation . . . !" She took up her reticule. "We should not have come."

He leaned forward. "Please, *Madame*, do not go. There is not the need. I have accept that my own—situation, as you call it, is quite hopeless."

"We do not see that." She put down her reticule and took up her empty glass with a faint glinting smile.

Returning the smile, Guy hobbled over to refill her glass and his own. "Do you say you see some hope for us, *Madame*?" he asked ruefully, replacing the decanter. "I wish I might do so."

"You will excuse if we are gauche. This is a modern age, *Monsieur*. Does a gentleman know his way about, there is not the need for a continuance of the Sanguinet name."

Despite himself, his jaw dropped. Mrs. Grenfell regarded him calmly, and as he eased himself onto the sofa once more, she said, for once dropping the royal "we," "I am a large and intimidating old woman. When I was a large young woman I was also considered a beauty. But I think I have never been held to be a widgeon." She gave him a slow and deliberate wink, and beamed as he was briefly convulsed with laughter. "Well?" she said.

He recovered himself somewhat, and said unsteadily, "I think that you are a rascal, *Madame.*" He reached across to take her hand and added gravely, "But the rascal *très déliceux.*"

She smiled at him, her eyes very fond. He clung very tightly to the arm of the sofa and contrived to press a kiss on her fingers, then leaned back. "You will think me also gauche, I fear, for this aspect of—er, *l'amour*, we have discuss, my sweet Faith and me. And it will not do." Her brows twitched together, as he continued, "I will say to you, my dear friend, what I have say to no other lady, save one. I have not the happy childhood. I am not the—the dashing man about the town. I have a few ladyfriends." He gave a small and very French gesture. "I am a man, you comprehend. But always I dream of the one lady. The one . . ." he flushed shyly, "love. After my brother shoot me and I can no more walk, I know this dream it never will be. Now"—again, his hand went out in that so expressive gesture—"when I have give up hope, my dream it come within the reach. Almost. And still I think it cannot be, for so beautiful a lady will not want—should not be bound to . . . the cripple."

He stared at his glass, his eyes very sad and, watching him, Mrs. Grenfell blinked rather rapidly and found herself unable to say a word.

"And then," Guy murmured, half to himself, "the miracle, she happen. My so beautiful lady she give her heart to this—this unworthy fellow. And so, after the King have be so kind, I dare to hope there may be for us happiness after all. But . . . always there is one thing to make it not possible." His hand on the sofa tightened into a fist. His voice lowered. He said bitterly, "My so *accursed* name. The dark and evil heritage that is in my blood. The—the foulness that was my grandpapa, my papa, my brothers! Ah, *Madame*—you do not know . . . you *could* not know!" He closed his eyes for an instant, but Mrs. Grenfell had seen despair, and the warm heart that lurked behind her formidable exterior was wrung.

"My dear," she said gently. "Oh, my *dear*—I am so sorry."

He sat straighter and said with a quivering smile, "You are most kind. But you see, it would not do. I—I care for the lady most . . . greatly. If I should cause her to—to give birth to such as Parnell . . . Or *Claude*!" He put a hand over his eyes and

255

turned away. And in a moment, very pale, and his voice thready, he went on. "Besides this, my dear F-Faith, she was made for—for motherhood. And she so love the little children. It would be—wickedly wrong. Unfair. Someday—she will meet the man who—" His brave words failed. He struggled from the sofa, took his crutch, and hobbled to the window.

Mrs. Grenfell made a snatch for her handkerchief and wiped furiously at her eyes, then she took a large gulp of sherry and gasped. But after a second, she said in her customarily dignified tones, "What are we to do, Guy? Josie must not wed John Drummond."

He pulled himself together and returned to stand looking down at her, pale but composed. "You think she does not love him?"

"Do you?"

A faint twinkle brightened the wistful eyes. "I have, I admit, an admiration for the fine young fellow, but—"

She laughed. "Wretch! You know what we mean."

"*Oui*. But—*Madame*, the announcement it is in *The Gazette*." He shook his head. "*C'est tragique*, but—alas, the die it is cast."

Mrs. Grenfell glared at him. "Men!" she snarled. "What a mess you make of things!"

Watching Devenish saunter along the hall, humming blithely, if not very tunefully, Mrs. Robinson paused en route to the stairs, wherefore her two neat and pretty maids, laden with newly washed and ironed linens, paused also. "How happy he seems," said the housekeeper.

"What gentleman wouldn't be happy with that beautiful Lady Isabella going to marry him?" said the taller of the maids, with a yearning glance after Devenish's slim figure.

Mrs. Robinson pursed her lips and looked worried.

"Proper beauty *she* is," said the other maid, sniffing in a derogatory fashion. "Me cousin useter be a kitchen maid in their London house. Cor! Wot she said about—" She interrupted herself with a sudden squeal, then exclaimed with outrage and a dimple, "Oh, you *wicked* man, you!"

Cornish grinned at the housekeeper and went on past.

Mrs. Robinson would never forget that this was the man who had run up the steps into that inferno when Mr. Dev had been glimpsed staggering through the Great Hall, supporting Lord Redmond. Thus, it was less a reprimand than a reminder when she said, "We don't permit no carryings-on in this house, Cornish. In future, keep your hands to yourself."

"Wotever you say, missus," he said.

"Mrs. Robinson!" She shepherded her maids up the stairs.

Devenish, meanwhile, had entered the haven of his study. He closed the door and leaned back against it, breathing hard. 'One more day,' he thought. 'Only one more day . . .' The walk from the stables had been interminable. Even now, the desk looked miles away. He couldn't take another step. But he must. He thought, 'Don't mess up the damn thing now, old sport . . .' And started off. Reaching the chair at last, he half-fell into it, then sagged forward across the desk, his hands clawing at the papers that littered it. "Oh, Lord!" he whispered. "Oh, my Lord . . . !"

A hand was on his shoulder. Horrified, he tried to straighten up, and could not. Dimly, he knew he had let it go too long, after all . . .

A glass was at his lips. He had no recollection of having leaned back in the chair, but he gulped the brandy gratefully, and lay still, fighting to regain his breath and see who had rescued him.

A familiar voice came through the mists. "Feelin' top 'ole this mornin', are yer, mate?"

Cornish. He thought a relieved, 'Thank God!' and after another minute the footman's features swam into focus. He sat perched on the edge of the desk, his expression bland.

Devenish said feebly, "You damned impertinent clod crusher. If you breathe . . . a word . . ."

"Didn't last time, did I, sir guv?"

Devenish took the glass the footman offered, and was irked because his hand shook. Still, the pain was easing into the endurable, and he asked, "Last time?"

"Yus, mate. Bein' a footman gets proper boring sometimes, and when it does, I 'ops orf. I was 'aving a bit of a kip up in

257

the loft last week when you come in. Alf went orf with yer 'orse, but I was lookin' right dahn atcher. I says ter meself, 'Charles,' I says, 'the littel—er, the master's got somethin' givin' 'im pepper.' "

"Oh." Devenish looked at him wearily. "I don't mind if you share these pearls of wisdom with yourself. Just see you don't tell no one else." And after a pause, curious, he murmured, "Charles . . . ?"

"Yus, mate. Yer gimpy leg, is it? You'd oughter—"

"I am aware. Very well—Charles." Cornish beamed at him. "Get on with you. And—again, my thanks."

Cornish stood, but lingered. "Guv—'as this been goin' on ever since you was skewered?"

"Lord, no! Now, be a good chap and send in Finlayson. I want a word with him."

"As well y'might. 'E's gone. 'Opped the twig, as they say."

"Gone? Damn! Did Wolfe turn him off?"

"No, mate. Went creepin' orf arter dinner the night you went and got yerself 'alfway shackled, like. A good creeper is Finlayson. Wot 'e does best."

"Hum. Likely you're right. Thank you. That will be all." Cornish shook his head, but departed.

Watching the door close, Devenish thought with amusement, 'Halfway shackled, indeed!' He wondered then if the extraordinary footman could be relied on to keep a still tongue in his head. His was just the type of misguided loyalty that would impel him to go running to Guy or, God forbid!—to Josie! He sighed. Tomorrow, it would seem, was now too late. It must all be tidied up today. Just as well. And thank the Lord, he'd been able to ensure that the little Elf would be in reliable hands. The Chevalier seemed a good sort of man, even if she didn't wind up with—

The door opened. He glanced up, preparing himself, but saw no one. A snort brought his gaze down. Lady Godiva grinned at him. He grinned back and fondled her ear. "I wonder," he muttered, "who will take care of you, old lady."

From the open door, Josie asked, "Why, Dev? Do you mean to go away?"

His hand jolted. Then he stood, directing his pleasant smile at her. "Good morning, Milady Elf. I suppose I should really say, Mademoiselle de Galin."

She wandered over to occupy the fireside chair. "And soon, my name will change yet again, to Mrs. Drummond."

"Yes. You won't have long to enjoy your new status, little one. Shall you mind?"

Her eyes scanned him. "Dev—are you all right? You look—"

He coughed. "Blasted cold. Of all times to be so unromantical, just as I should be at my best."

"I am very sure Lady Isabella understands. After all, when one is in love . . ."

"Speaking of which." He took a small jewel case from the drawer and opened it. "D'you think she will like it?"

Josie took the case and gazed down at three fine diamonds mounted in an intricately filigreed setting wherein was the deeper gleam of small rubies. It seemed almost too cruel that he would show her the betrothal ring. And despite the fact that he was obviously proud of it, she was rather surprised, for his taste was usually good, and this was quite ostentatious. Somehow, she swallowed the lump in her throat and said, "It's lovely."

He took it back. "Thank you. I thought it just right for Bella. She's so vivacious."

"Yes. And seems very happy."

"Naturally," he said with a broad grin.

Why must she still think he was miserable? Why must she refuse to believe that his passion for the dark beauty was genuine? She thought, 'Because I want so to believe it is all a misunderstanding. And because Isabella Scott-Matthias is a shrewish, selfish witch!' But you could not tell a gentleman who fancied himself deep in love that his lady was a shrewish, selfish witch, and so, she asked instead, "Have you decided which architect you will commission?"

He stared at her.

"For the reconstruction," she said, puzzled by his apparent lack of comprehension. "Did you not say you consulted some architects whilst you were in Bristol?"

259

"Oh. Er, yes. Well, I want Bella to see the plans, first. After all, the decision is one that will mean a deal to her."

"I doubt Lady Isabella will wish to spend much time here," she remarked dryly. "She is more the Town type."

"Right! And, do you know, Josie, these past seven years have been jolly good, but—I'll not be sad to see the last of the old place." He saw his error even as her head jerked around to him, and added heartily, "Now, little Elf, you'll be wishing to run off to Sussex today, I do not doubt. John said he would arrive to carry you forth, as it were."

For a bewildering moment she wondered if it was really Dev speaking. The rapid words, the excessively bluff manner, the fact that he had scarce bothered to enquire as to her feelings, or given a thought to the wishes of the uncle she had so suddenly acquired and had scarcely even met, were all so foreign to her knowledge of this man. She thought, 'He is so dazzled by his Isabella, he can no longer think of any other!' And she said, "But you surely would not expect John to leave on the same day he arrives? He will want to rest, and to spend some time with you, discussing—"

He said airily, "You don't know how a man feels when he's smitten, my Elf. Mark my words, your John will be afire to rush you to Park Parapine. Not one to let any grass grow under his feet, is John. Were I you, I'd instruct Fletcher to pack your trunk at once." He stood, before Josie could comment, his blue eyes alight and a fond smile curving his mouth. "Bella!"

Josie stood, but did not turn to the door. After he passed her, she summoned a smile and prepared to greet the beauty. She was taken aback to see them locked in a passionate embrace, and all but gawked her astonishment at such behaviour.

Leaning back in his arms, Isabella murmured softly, "Hot-blooded devil. What will your ward think of us?"

"Oh, Josie don't mind," he said carelessly. "She's a good chit. Always has been."

Isabella turned, smiling, to the pale and silent girl. "Good morning," she purred, extending a beautifully gloved hand. "And pray accept my congratulations. I hear you are a considerable heiress."

"Thank you, ma'am," said Josie, miserably aware that she must look very drab by comparison with Isabella, radiant in a revealing blush-pink gown, with pink velvet ribbons wound through her curls. "I wonder you knew about it."

Isabella realized with a shock that Taine had expressly charged her not to mention the matter. She lied, "Why, Dev told me, of course, didn't you, love?"

He also had been watching his betrothed narrowly, but murmured politely that he probably had done so.

"It is certainly a fortunate circumstance," said Josie, who longed to meet her elegant new uncle and discuss with him certain tentative plans she had formed during the past few sleepless nights. "The Drummonds must be pleased, I think."

Isabella's brows arched enquiringly. "The—Drummonds . . . ?"

Devenish said, "Oh, I'd forgot to tell you, Bella. Josie is in the way of becoming betrothed to John Drummond."

'Oh, Lord!' thought Isabella, and said, "Why, my dear girl, what a lovely match! I am *delighted*! You must let me help choose your bride clothes." She took a fold of Devenish's neckcloth between her long fingers and murmured archly, "Speaking of which, darling . . ."

He smiled down at her, his expression so besotted that Josie yearned to kick him. She did not indulge herself, but instead slipped away. She had not intended to go into Sussex with John, thinking to plead that she must await her new uncle's arrival, but it was becoming more and more clear that she was in the way at Devencourt . . .

✑ Chapter 18 ✑

Lying back on the sofa, enfolded in the arms of her fiancé, Isabella opened languorous eyes and whispered, "Oh, Dev . . . I never dreamed you could be so . . ."

He chuckled. "Did you think I'd have gone along with this little plot if I did not care for you?"

She stiffened. "It was a horrid practical joke!"

He nibbled at the lobe of her ear, and felt her shiver convulsively. "Which had a most delectable conclusion. Though I'll be damned if I can remember much until I woke up in that bed with you beside me." He began to take the liberties he knew she wanted, and she raised no objection. Her senses were swimming, and she relaxed, thinking that he had evidently believed the tale she'd told him, and that perhaps it *was* truth that he'd not realized how much he desired her until he found her sharing a bed with him. Lord, but he was a skilled lover! "Dev," she moaned. "Oh . . . my beloved . . ."

"Jupiter," he exclaimed, ceasing his depredations and sitting straighter. "Whatever would my people think did they chance to wander in here?"

Faintly irritated, she protested, "We are, after all, betrothed."

"Yes, but not wed, dear lady. Speaking of which, give me your pretty hand."

Watching him slip the ring on her finger, she gave a gasp. "Oh! It is superb!"

He said with an odd little smile, "I was sure you would like it. And I especially wanted it to be something you would enjoy. You're quite a woman, Bella."

It seemed an odd remark, but he was leaning to her again, and with that glorious ring on her finger she capitulated so willingly that her submission was almost an attack.

An hour later, Isabella watched the wintry countryside slide past the windows of her luxurious carriage and wondered whatever she was to tell Taine. She had come to Devencourt armed with strict instructions to beguile her love into issuing an invitation for both her brother and herself to stay at her future home. Not that she intended to make many visits to the horrid old pile, once she was wed. Dev had seemed agreeable, but had been obliged to put them off for a week while he went over the marriage settlements with his man of business. A nuisance, but as he'd pointed out, he also wanted to get Josie packed off to Sussex, besides which the guestrooms were sadly damaged by smoke and water, and he must be sure his adored Bella would experience only the height of elegance when she came to him. It was as well he understood the standards to which she was accustomed. He would have more to learn when she got him to Town and showed him the house she wanted.

She frowned. There was the business of that revolting girl. If she told her brother of the unexpected and apparently certain betrothal, Lord only knew what he would do! She had the frightening suspicion that the only thing that kept him from calling Devenish out and killing him was his determination to wed the chit. She drew off her glove thoughtfully. She'd not tell him. Perhaps, by the time the betrothal was published, he would have found another interest. And after all, the Chevalier was very likely to request that any announcement be delayed until he'd had time to get to know his long-lost niece. That would be logical enough. A devastatingly handsome man, the French fellow . . . And unmarried. Very rich, too . . . It might be worthwhile to take him for her lover once she was wed . . .

She turned the ring in the ray of a sunbeam, and gloried in the resultant rainbow of sparkles that lit the carriage. What a lovely thing. And only the beginning.

It was silly to feel that Devenish was not as devoted as he seemed. She had him, as so many women had longed to do, and he in turn had won a beautiful and much-courted lady. Yet, how odd that she could not escape the feeling that although they had trapped Dev, they had played right into his hands.

John Drummond found Devenish in his study with Josie. John was elated. His parents, he told them, had been delighted by the news of Josie's good fortune. Always they had loved her. Now they were eager to welcome her into the family as their daughter. All his father asked was that any announcement be deferred until the Chevalier could be properly approached.

His eyes devouring his beloved, whom he thought adorable in the gown of pale orange wool trimmed with cream fur, John confessed, "I'd forgot he is the head of your house now, m'dear."

"Very true," Devenish agreed. "In which case, this would be the very best of times for you to visit Park Parapine, little Elf, and renew acquaintance with your prospective in-laws." He slanted a grin at Drummond. "Best not lose precious time, John. Josie has other admirers who are fairly yearning to steal her away from you."

Drummond gave him a rather startled smile.

Her heart contracting painfully, Josie laughed. "Dev is trying to hurry us off, John. He wants to be alone here with his lady."

Drummond had some reservations about his cousin's sudden betrothal, but said he was only too willing to set forth. "Now, if you wish," he said eagerly. His enthusiasm diminished a little when Mrs. Grenfell returned from Gloucester and announced that she would go along so as to visit her sister, Mrs. Alastair Tyndale. By far too well mannered to betray disappointment, John agreed with apparent pleasure, and went off to the stables to arrange for a fresh team to be put to his mother's travelling coach, which he had borrowed, thinking it would ensure a comfortable journey for his love. Josie went upstairs to prepare for the journey, and Mrs. Grenfell and Devenish were left alone.

He expected her to also go and make her preparations to depart, but she had waited for just such a moment and lost no time in bringing all her guns to bear. She refused his polite attempt to seat her, and folded her arms as she pierced him with a steady stare.

"You do not deceive us, Alain," she announced.

He had developed a healthy respect for her perception, and said uneasily, "I had no intention—"

"We do not know why you have embarked on this foolish and ill-judged course." She flung up one hand as he attempted to speak. "We are not just come from the schoolroom," she observed with a good deal of justification, "and it has been, for some years, very clear which way the wind blew. Your reasons for denying your own heart were admirable. To offer for the child to whom you stood guardian was not to be thought of. No! Do not attempt to flim-flam me, Alain!" He quailed into silence, and she boomed on. "We are out of all patience with you! You have learned beyond disputation that Josie is *not* half your age, as you had supposed, but is instead only about thirteen years younger than yourself, which cannot be held objectionable. Further, since she has her own family, she will be removed from your guardianship. That you reject her, just as the barriers have been swept away, allows but one conclusion. Your fortune is no more than adequate, whereas hers will be very considerable. Your pride will not allow you to offer. Nobility, Alain, has its place. But to pack the child off, breaking her heart for you—to form an alliance with that—that *deplorable* Scott-Matthias"— her eyes flashed fire—"is carrying martyrdom too far!"

"Martyrdom!" gasped Devenish, stung. "No, really, ma'am! You cannot think so!"

She advanced until she stood directly in front of him. She was taller than he, and, with the feathers of her turban waving above her high-held head, was so formidable that he recoiled until he was leaning against the desk. "What else may we think?" she demanded. "Josie is lovely in a way that far transcends mere beauty. We doubt she will wed Drummond, for she don't love the boy. More likely she will devote herself to her lonely and most endearing new uncle. Certainly, the Chevalier will delight in lavishing gifts upon her; on making her into the darling of all Europe. In time, she will love again, for she is too warm-natured a creature to waste her years in useless yearnings."

Devenish jerked away and wandered to stand at the end of the desk, turned from her, head down and silent.

She went on remorselessly. "You have broke her heart, but it is a young heart and will mend. It is for you that we fear, Alain. That beautiful bird of prey you have won is the evil product of an evil line. She will destroy you within a year of your marriage, for she loves only herself." He returned no answer, continuing to stand very still, one slim hand lightly resting on the desk top. In a last desperate effort, she stepped closer. "Why?" she pleaded in a very different tone. "Dear lad—*why*?"

His shoulders pulled back. He faced her, smiling, but with his eyes perfectly blank. "Sweet soul, I beg you will not grieve for me. I promise you I am not so big a fool as you suppose. I shall not wed Lady Isabella."

She gave a gasp. "Not—not *wed* her? But—dearest boy, how can you possibly escape it?"

Emboldened to take the hand she stretched out, he pressed it to his lips. "All arranged," he said lightly. "Take my word for it."

By four o'clock the great house was silent. Working at his desk with deep concentration, Devenish was surrounded. Scorning the rug before the dying fire that was customarily her favourite spot, Lady Godiva sat leaning against him so that he was twice obliged to move his foot before it was too numbed for him to do so. The white cat lay on the desk, his tail frequently draping itself across the sheet of closely written lines so that Devenish had to as often lift it out of the way. The ginger cat had taken up residence in a half-open desk drawer and lay with front paws hanging over the edge, kneading at the empty air, while she watched the master and purred grittily. Bits and Pieces had curled up on Devenish's lap and constituted a hazard, for each time he moved, the kitten almost was precipitated to the floor, so that he had to make a grab to catch it in time.

Completing his epistle at last, he read it over, absently placing the sliding kitten in the tray on the side of the desk, where he deposited any finished correspondence destined for the Post Office.

It seemed all right. He put the page aside and took up another, much less involved, sheet. Having scanned that also, he folded and sealed both, and impressed his monogram into the hot wax. He then enclosed both letters in a larger sheet, which he had already directed in his somewhat less than neat hand to a learned gentleman of the law who maintained chambers in Bristol. This last cover having been duly and repeatedly sealed, Devenish laid it in the centre of his surprisingly tidy desk top and sat staring at it.

It was done. He pushed back his chair, and at once the members of his group were wide awake. The ginger cat leapt from the drawer to wind in and out around his ankles; the white cat stood and sprang up to rest his front paws against Devenish's waistcoat and butt his head against the hand that came to caress him; Lady Godiva scrambled up and wandered about the room for a minute in a confused way, until she made a sudden dart back to lean against the master's left calf, thus earning an indignant hiss from the ginger cat who met her nose to nose.

"Peace, my children," said Devenish. He had guessed they would know, and had planned accordingly. He caressed each one individually, almost forgetting Bits and Pieces until she suddenly leapt from the tray and attacked his letter ferociously. He smiled and reached for her, but she chose to be terrified and shot straight up in the air, succeeding, as she landed, in knocking over the vase of flowers.

Devenish made a grab for it, and gazed down at the bright blooms Josie had found for him from among the few remaining in the greenhouses. He put the vase down hurriedly, and told Bits and Pieces that she was a bad cat. She paid no attention to this mild scold, as she was frenziedly attending to the tip of her tail which she had accidentally deposited in the puddle the toppling vase had left.

Devenish allowed his gaze to drift around the room in which he had spent so many happy hours these past years. There was where she had so often sat, pestering him with her studies and her chatter; there was the scratch on the wall made by the andirons that had toppled when she threw the cushion at him last summer, and missed, catching the heavy brass set instead. He would not let himself look at her portrait.

He took the several pieces of cheese from his pocket, wafted them under the noses of his interested and addicted companions, and limped across the room. At the door he scattered his largesse and they all scrambled in pursuit. His eyes fell on the vase again. He swore, but made a lunge for the desk, grabbed a handful of flowers, and ran for the door. He got out and slammed the door in the nick of time.

Ignoring the uproar, he limped as rapidly as possible along the hall. Wolfe stood waiting at the side door. The old man looked at him anxiously, and Hutchinson started down the stairs, carrying a valise and Devenish's new Garrick travelling coat. The valet assisted him to put it on, the blue tweed and long length making him look taller, and the three capes across the shoulders bestowing the appearance of a gentleman of fashion on this man who had never given a hoot for such matters, and would have been astonished if told he looked very dashing.

Patting the shoulder of the coat, which had dared to settle with a slight fold, Wolfe pretended not to notice the flowers the master thrust into a buttonhole, and asked, "When may we expect you, sir?"

"Haven't decided," said Devenish breezily. "A week, perhaps longer."

Taken aback, Hutchinson exclaimed, "But—sir, you said two days, so I only packed—"

"Never mind, never mind. If I decide to stay longer, I'll send a note and you can bring whatever I need."

"As you wish, sir," said Hutchinson, smarting both because of the brusque tone and the fact that he was not to accompany his employer.

"You will likely overnight in Swindon, sir," murmured Wolfe, handing Devenish his gloves. "In view of the fact you're getting such a late start."

"Probably," said Devenish, who had no intention of taking the Swindon road. "Now, Wolfe, I've left a very important letter on my desk. It has to do with the fire, and I want it hand-delivered to Bristol first thing in the morning."

Mr. Wolfe murmured his understanding and glanced to the right. "Good gracious! Only listen to those cats!"

"I shall rely on you to take care of them."

He looked unusually stern, and both men were shocked. The master knew perfectly well that they all were fond of his creatures. Wolfe said stiffly, "Naturally, Mr. Devenish."

Devenish recognized the affronted tone, and his mouth twitched. "Good man," he said, and let his hand rest for an instant on the butler's shoulder. They were both staring at him. He said hurriedly, "Put my valise in the carriage, Hutch, if you please," and wandered off as jauntily as possible.

He was almost undone at the door, for Mrs. Robinson came bustling in, carrying her shopping basket, and her cheeks rosy from the cold. They collided, and Devenish staggered. She caught his arm. "Oh! 'Scuse me, sir."

He did not move, looking down at her in a way that caused her to grip his arm more tightly, and say with the swift surge of woman's intuition, "Mr. Dev? Is anything wrong?"

He smiled and said slowly, "No, m'dear. Nothing's wrong." His gloved hand touched her cheek very gently. He murmured, "Bless you," and walked quickly into the blustery afternoon, leaving her staring after him.

She watched the groom close the door of the carriage and swing up beside Alfred. The whip cracked, the team leaned into their collars, and the luxurious coach jolted off down the rutted drivepath. For no reason she could have identified, Mrs. Robinson went out into the biting wind and watched the vehicle until it was lost to view. She turned back into the house and found Wolfe standing behind her. They went inside together and stood chatting about the weather and Miss Josie's new prospects, and neither of them referring to the matter that was on both their minds.

An icy blast announced the return of Hutchinson, who had gone into the stables to check on his hack, which had thrown a shoe the previous afternoon. He came in grumbling to himself, then jumped aside as two cats, a pig, and a small black and white ball of fluff darted for the outer door.

Mrs. Robinson muttered, "My, ain't they in a state . . ."

Wolfe commenced his slow journey to the master's study and, oddly troubled, she went with him. Opening the door, the old man checked and positively reeled. "What the— My heavens! How *dare* you tamper with the master's letters? You've lost your situation for this, I tell—"

"Glad you come in, mate," interrupted Cornish, looking up unrepentantly from the papers he held. "Wot's this 'ere jaw-breaker?"

"Well! If I ever heard of such impudence," gasped the house-keeper.

Scarlet with indignation, Wolfe trotted to snatch for the letter.

Cornish held it high in the air. "Cool down, old cove," he adjured. "You like the guv or don'tcha?"

Something in his manner was adding to Mrs. Robinson's unease. Overcoming her initial horror, she asked, "Whatever is it, Charlie?"

"If it's wot I think, missus," he said grimly, "you better tell them lazy grooms ter slap a saddle on that there big bay 'orse fer me."

"You're mad," Wolfe told him. "Stark, raving mad! Let me see that!"

Cornish handed him the paper. "You *read* it then," he demanded.

Wolfe read rapidly and turned white. Sinking into the chair, he gasped, "Oh . . . my Lord God!"

John Drummond edged the steaming plate of buttered scones closer to Josie, and she looked up at him, her eyes empty. He thought, 'It's this damnable place! Why that idiot of a groom would turn in *here* of all places!' But it had been cold and coming on to rain, and he'd thought Josie so pale that a hot drink and something to eat might restore her. He said with a hopeful smile, "Try some strawberry jam with those, won't you?"

She started as if suddenly becoming aware of her surroundings. "Oh! This is the Boar's Head, no? Where is Pan?"

He jerked his head and said a reluctant "Over there. One of her good friends came in, en route to Cheltenham Spa. My dear, do let me empty out that tea, it must be stone—" Her hand came to meet his and stay it. He knew suddenly, and his heart became heavy as lead.

"I am—so very sorry, John," she said softly.

His other hand came to cover hers, and he stared hard at their intertwined fingers. "I think . . . I always knew, really." And looking sadly at her, "You wish to go back."

"Yes. I know it is useless. But—it would be very bad of me to let you go on thinking—"

"Josie," he interpolated desperately, "if you cannot love me now, perhaps in the future . . . At least come to Park Parapine with me. I swear I won't pester you. I won't even ask you again, unless you tell me I may."

She turned her hand to clasp his strongly. "You are all that is good and kind and dear. But—I must go back, John."

"But—what will you do? When they are wed, Lady Isabella won't—"

"Let me stay? No. Nor should I wish to. But my uncle will come soon. If Dev prefers that—that I leave before he arrives, I shall go to stay with Guy, or with Mitch and Charity, or the Leiths. But—but not Park Parapine, John."

He thought, 'It is too close to Aspenhill, of course. And everyone would be speaking of Dev.' And, his heart aching, he said bravely, "Yes. I quite understand. We'll go back, of course."

"You will recollect Lady Hersh," said Pandora, returning to take the chair Drummond sprang up to pull out for her. "She was on her way to Bath. Dreadful gossip, but we had a nice cose. She tells me she saw Fontaine and his sister leaving Swindon on the London Road. We are not surprised. Isabella Scott-Matthias will stay in the country not one moment longer than is necessary."

Josie managed to speak steadily. "She is likely going to buy her bride clothes. Pan—I am sincerely sorry to be such a silly, but I want to go ho— I mean, I want to go back to Devencourt."

Mrs. Grenfell threw a keen glance at Drummond's set smile and desolate eyes. 'Poor lad,' she thought. 'But better now than later.' She said without equivocation, "We shall accompany you. No, there is not the need for you to turn about, Drummond. Do you arrange for a postchaise to convey us home. We shall be quite safe with Klaus to escort us. Be so good as to convey our affection to your parents and my sister Constance Tyndale. Goodbye, dear boy. Now—eat up, Mademoiselle de Galin, for it will avail us nothing to droop like wet lettuce leaves, and we mean to enjoy our tea.''

Between Mrs. Grenfell's hearty appetite and a further chat with her friend, Lady Anne Hersh, whose sharp eyes made Josie uneasy, the afternoon was far spent by the time they again approached Devencourt. Expecting to find the stableyard quiet and peaceful, Josie stared in astonishment at a scene of frenzied activity. Devenish's prize matched greys were being poled up to a dashing chaise with wheels picked out in bright blue; saddle horses were being led out of the stables, and grooms and stable-boys darted frantically about. ''Good heavens!'' she gasped. ''That is Mitchell Redmond's new chaise! Whatever can have happened?''

When they entered the east wing, Redmond hurried to meet them. He answered their anxious questions by saying cravenly that Guy could explain. ''Gad, but it's cold. I fancy we shall have snow soon, don't you?'' He led them back towards the study, making no attempt to take their wraps, nor did any servant appear to perform that service.

A maid let out a shriek. ''Miss Josie's come back!'' and from some unseen male came a hollow-voiced, ''Oh, my Gawd!'' Mrs. Robinson, clad in bonnet and cloak, ran to meet them, looking very agitated, and Lady Godiva darted along the hall, squealing.

''What is it? Oh, what is wrong?'' quavered Josie, suddenly much colder than she had been outside.

Struggling along the hall, Guy Sanguinet said, ''Ah, *ma belle*, and my good friend, you have come.'' He took Josie's hand and held it firmly. ''It is something we all should have guess long since, *ma chérie*. You must be brave now.''

Thomas Corwen Ruthwell, Lord Belmont, scion of a prominent Scottish Border family, had been a fighter all his days. As a boy he had fought because he was too tall and lanky for his years and thus became the butt of crude schoolboy jokes. As a young man he fought against entering the priesthood, the Army or the Navy, and was all but cast off by his outraged family when he declared he meant to become a doctor. Ten years after that, he was fighting colleagues affronted by his brusque manners and revolutionary methods. Now a leading light in his profession, long since elevated to the peerage, sought after by the finest families in the land and admired throughout Europe, he was as blunt and abrasive as ever. When he disagreed with hospital procedures, he bought a large house in Harley Street, and turned it into a private hospital he ran his own way. Implored to teach, he did so, but he brought his best students to work with him and drove them mercilessly. Among the survivors were some of the finest physicians in the land. In appearance, he was tall, thin, and erect, his iron-grey hair a shaggy mop. His lantern jaw reflected his implacable nature, his black eyes were fierce, and his bedside manner uncompromisingly blunt—a necessary defence against a very soft heart.

Knowing much of this, it was a dreary confirmation of his darkest fears when Alain Devenish opened dazed eyes to find the great man bending over the bed, compassion softening his gaunt features.

"Got here . . . did I?" said Devenish foolishly.

"My poor lunatic," said Belmont, his touch gentle as a woman's as he touched a cold, wet cloth to the waxy face against the pillows. "Why in the name of Mephisto did you not tell me? I'd never have let you go prancing off last month had I known it was this acute."

"Wasn't," said Devenish, clinging to the coverlet. "Fell downstairs. Made it—much worse. Been curst nuisance . . . ever since. So I came."

"You most assuredly did. When my porter opened the door of your carriage just now, you came down like a dead man. Not surprising, since they tell me you drove all night. I've some laudanum here, but if you can hang on until I've made a quick examination, it will help."

Devenish "hung on." Afterwards, the laudanum didn't help

much, and the cough didn't help either. The surgeon patted his shoulder and walked to a far corner of the quiet room.

Lyon Cahill, his face very grim, said, "It's the leg, of course, sir."

"Yes. Damned young fool. I warned him three years ago, it should come off."

"Did you, by Jove! He never told me that."

"Didn't tell anyone, I doubt. Thought if he ignored it, it would go away." Belmont swore softly. "I hope it may not take him with it!"

Despite himself, Cahill winced. "You think—it's the bone?"

" 'Fraid so. Oh, I'm sorry. I forget, you know him. Splendid madman. Dammit, but I wish he were in better condition. From what he says—and doesn't say, I gather it's been very bad for some time. He's worn to a shade, his nerves as steady as any weaver's shuttle, and that cough shaking him from hell to breakfast!"

"Bit of a fever too, sir. You shall have to delay."

"Is that a fact," sneered Belmont. Cahill flushed, and the older man said irritably, "If I delay, he—"

"No!" Devenish, propped on one elbow, watched them in white-faced desperation. "No more waiting! Get it done!"

"Ears like a hawk," muttered Cahill, and went over to the bed. "Dev," he said, attempting to lie him back down, "his lordship cannot—"

Devenish thrust him away. "Now!" he cried frantically. "For God's sake, now!" He threw back the coverlet and started up. "If . . . if you won't—I'll find some—some blasted apothecary who—"

"All right, all right." Belmont moved swiftly. "Here—take some of this, it will—"

"Make me sleep, you think! No!" Devenish gasped and lay back, flinging one arm across his face. After a moment, he panted feebly, "Lyon, if Belmont won't—*you* do it. *Please!* If—if only for old times' sake."

"Easy, easy." The surgeon met Cahill's eyes and shrugged resignedly. "He'll only work himself into a worse state, I suppose. You're a stubborn ass, Devenish!" Smiling, despite the harsh words, he wiped the strained face again and said in his kindest voice, "You do understand, my dear fellow—we have to amputate."

"Yes, yes. 'Course I understand. You warned me—often enough."

For Cahill, many things were falling into place. He muttered repentantly, "Dev—if I'd known— You lamebrain, if you'd had it done three years back—"

"I know, I know. But . . . I had three more years with—with her."

Belmont said sharply, "So there's a lady involved? Married?"

"Not to me," Devenish muttered with sudden ineffable sadness. "She's young, lovely . . . admired. Deserves—the best . . ."

Cahill's lips tightened and he turned away in silence. Cautiously, the surgeon sat on the side of the bed. "If she's as lovely as you say, and she cares for you—"

The fair head tossed fretfully. "Wasting time. Get it over, will you?"

Belmont persisted. "I know what you're going through, lad. But you must face the possibility that there may be legal matters you'll want to—"

"All done. Everything . . . tidy." Devenish's voice faded. "She'll be well provided for. And she's going to marry . . . dashed good boy . . ."

Belmont watched the drawn face and frowned unhappily.

Devenish opened his eyes and a singularly sweet and very weary smile pierced the surgeon's armoured heart. "So you see," he sighed, "it don't matter anymore. Just—get it over, sir. I'm—so damnably tired of it."

∽ Chapter 19 ∽

The three mud-spattered carriages and the six outriders set heads turning as they raced at reckless speed along The-New-Road-From-Paddington-to-Islington, and turned right onto Harley Street.

Lord Jeremy Bolster, who had been exercising his fine young dapple grey stallion amid the delights of the newly laid out Regent's Park, glanced idly towards the commotion as an indignant pedestrian shouted imprecations at the fast-moving cavalcade.

"By J-J-J—by thunder, that looked like M-Mitchell's new chaise, Harry," he exclaimed.

Sir Harry Redmond turned his green eyes to the south. "Not possible, Jerry. My brother went up to see Sanguinet."

"Did?" Bolster, unconvinced, battled his mettlesome and half-broken steed around again. "Why? Thought he just c-c—got back."

"Said he was uneasy about Dev. Something about the look of him after that damnable fire. We must go down, Jerry, no matter what Dev says."

"We sh-should've gone at once, my Tulip," his lordship muttered. "Y'know once or tw-twice I've had the notion old D-Dev ain't been quite— By God, Harry! They've pulled up in front of Belmont's n-new place!"

The two elegant young men eyed each other, then two more horses were racing along the sedate street. They drew rein in time to see Mitchell Redmond hand a strained-looking Josie from the leading vehicle and run up the steps of Lord Belmont's establishment to ring the bell.

Guy Sanguinet's pleasant face appeared at the window of the chaise, and he called to his friends as they dismounted, handing their reins to outriders.

The porter having opened the door, Josie ran precipitately inside. Two men who had been sitting in the luxurious waiting room sprang up as she entered. The Reverend Mordecai Langridge watched sympathetically as she ran into Leith's outstretched arms. "Oh, Tris," she gulped, blinking away tears. "How is he? Have they—have they—"

The tall Colonel bent to kiss her cheek. "They started to operate an hour ago, love."

Langridge, patting her shoulder kindly, added, "Lyon's in there, child. Never look so fearful. Alain is in God's hands."

Trembling uncontrollably, she sat beside Leith while the clergyman went to shake hands with his nephew.

Tristam said, "You got here very fast, dear. Did you drive all night?"

"Yes. I was able to sleep a little, but the servants were so good. Wolfe, and Hutchinson, and Mrs. Robinson are with us—they were all so grieved. And—and Cornish rode off ahead."

"I know. He found Langridge and me at Watier's. We've sent word to the others."

She whispered, her lips so stiff she could hardly make them obey her, "Is it—his leg?"

Leith squeezed her hand. "Yes. I'm afraid it is."

"Oh . . . God!" She closed her eyes and shrank against him, and he slipped his arm around her. "They—they're never going to . . . oh, Tris! Lyon told us only a little while ago he had amputated a poor man's leg—"

"W-well, then, there you go," said Lord Jeremy, hurrying into the room and taking off his hat as he dropped to one knee beside her. "Not a th-thing to fret about. Old D-Dev—game as they come."

She stretched forth her icy little hand, and he bowed his yellow head to kiss it. "But—the p-poor man—died," she finished.

"Lyon said—if it had been a little lower, there—there would have been more chance, but—"

"Tush, Milady Elf," put in Harry Redmond, coming in with Guy. He crossed to lean over Josie and plant a kiss on her ear. "Dev's only three and thirty. Got a long way to go yet. He'll likely be up and—and prancing around in no—" He broke off as a rear door opened, and Lyon Cahill, wearing a long white robe and looking unwontedly stern, started into the room, only to check, aghast, as he saw Josie surrounded by the staunch group.

Clinging to Leith, she stood, her eyes enormous in her pale face. "Is it over?" she whispered.

He nodded and came forward to take the hand she held out.

She gulped. "He is—not . . ."

"No, no. He came through it very well and without a whimper."

She collapsed against him, and he held her close.

" 'Course not," said Sir Harry, indignant. "Old Dev's not—" He met Lyon's eyes over Josie's shoulder, and blanched and was still.

Dashing away tears with an impatient hand, she said, "I want to see him, Lyon."

"He's unconscious, dear," he said kindly. "Just at the end, he drifted off. We don't mean to do anything to bring him round, but you can—"

Again, the outer door was flung open. With a swirl of ermine, a breath of perfume, and a cry of agitation, Lady Isabella swept into the rapidly filling room. "Is it truth?" she demanded shrilly, gazing wide-eyed at these men who shared a comradeship that was already a legend in this old city of legends. "I could not credit it, when my maid had it from the greengrocer's boy! Good God! What happened? Did that silly cold turn into . . ." She paused, noting their solemn faces, and because she loved Devenish, insofar as she was capable of loving any man, she whitened. "He's not . . . dead?"

Taking pity on her, Josie went to hold her hand. "No, dear ma'am. And it is so fortunate you are come." She managed to smile, though tears were blinding her. "I wish I did not have to break it to you, but—but they have had to—to take poor Dev's leg off.''

Isabella's lower jaw dropped and her glorious eyes fairly goggled with shock.

Josie went on gently, "He will want to see you. Why do you not go in.''

Mitchell Redmond exchanged a sardonic glance with his brother.

Isabella, paler than ever, sat down suddenly. "The . . . shock . . .'' she muttered.

Misunderstanding, Lyon said, "Yes, that's our greatest threat, but I must tell you—''

"If—I could have a . . . glass of water,'' whispered Isabella.

"At once.'' Lyon turned to the inner door, but glanced back. "It will be quite all right for you to come now, ma'am. Under the circumstances. In fact, it might give Devenish an incentive to—''

Isabella swayed, and her eyes closed. Leith leapt to support her.

"I'll come,'' said Josie, and followed Lyon.

He led her along an immaculate hall that smelled of soap and medicines and tar. She could hear the murmur of voices from two rooms as they passed, and then Lyon opened the door to a large, darkened room, where a tall man stood at the foot of a narrow bed. Blinking to adjust her eyes to the dim light, Josie saw first that the bedclothes were fashioned into a sort of tent, extending from about hip level to the end of the bed. Then her eyes found Devenish and everything else faded. She did not hear the great surgeon speak, nor Lyon's quiet response. She was beside the bed, bending over the still figure, the sight of the worn, ashen-pale face and darkly hollowed eyes wringing her heart. Dimly, she saw a vase on a small table beside the bed, and the handful of wilted flowers it held so wrought on her that her vision blurred and a muffled sob escaped her. With a hand that shook, she touched the short damp hair, and tears splashed onto the small curls that had plastered themselves across his brow.

The cold feel of those tears troubled Devenish, and drew him

279

back from the void where he had escaped pain at last. He thought for a minute that he was still alive, but then he saw the adored face bending above him. He smiled, but registered a faint complaint. "Didn't think it would . . . hurt so much, after I was dead."

Josie threw a hand to her mouth and battled for self-control.

Lord Belmont paced forward. "I'm afraid you will be rather uncomfortable for a little while, my dear fellow," he said softly, "but—"

"Eh?" Devenish's eyelids, which had started to drift down again, jerked open. "The devil!" he gasped. "I *am* still alive!"

Josie sat on the bedside chair, took up his limp hand, and kissed it repeatedly. "If you had—died," she gulped. "I'd never—*never* have forgiven you, Dev."

He smiled, and his hand turned to caress her cheek. "My little . . . Elf. You should not be here, but—I'm deuced glad you—" He coughed, and turned his head away, his lips gripping together.

To see him so weakened and in such pain was tearing her to shreds, but she fought for calm and, stroking his hair, said with loving reproach, "Dev, my darling Dev, how *could* you? How could you shut me out? Don't you know how—how I worship you?" He turned a blurred gaze back to her and she added, "Admit, wretched, *wretched* creature, that you do know it. And—and that you love me, too."

He was exhausted and pain-racked, and convinced there was very little time, his defences crumbled at last. A look of such tender adoration lit his ravaged face that Lyon, seeing it, held his breath, and Belmont frowned and stepped back to allow them this moment together.

His voice barely audible, Devenish murmured, "I have loved you for . . . so long, my little one. So very long. But—it was quite useless. No hope. On top of—everything else, there was this . . . stupid leg. I knew if I told you, and if I lived, you'd . . . devote your lovely life to a—sick half man, rather than following . . . your own heart."

'He came here, all alone, to die,' she thought, anguished. 'He'd never say these things unless he thought he *was* dying!'

And, terrified, she sobbed, "My darling! My idiot! *You* are my heart!"

He stared at her, coughed, and grabbed at the coverlet. Josie bent to press her cool cheek against his, and say achingly, "My dearest—is it very terrible?"

Terrible, perhaps, he thought. But how wonderful to feel her nearness just once more. To smell the sweet fragrance of her— to see the love in the piquant little face he had thought never to glimpse again. He frowned suddenly and answered in some confusion, "Not nearly so bad as I'd expected. I thought, after they sawed through a bone, y'know, it would be pretty—hideous." He peered downwards and, seeing more clearly now, discerned the tented bedclothes, the two physicians standing watching with sombre faces, and on a side table, a long, narrow box.

Lyon said, "Well, we didn't use a saw, Dev."

"Good Lord!" gasped Devenish, wrenching his eyes from that sinister box and looking about for the axe. "Shortcut, eh? I—I never . . . dreamed . . ." He was very tired now, and he closed his eyes and lay still.

Trembling, Josie allowed Belmont to move her gently aside.

A soft-footed nurse materialized from somewhere to draw the curtains, and pale winter sunshine flooded in. Lyon led Josie to a far corner of the room and began to speak very softly. Belmont turned from his patient to find the girl weeping in the young doctor's arms.

Cahill asked, "How does he go on, sir?"

Belmont scowled at the bed. "Not as well as I'd wish. I take it you are fond of him, my dear lady. You must—"

Josie gave a gasp. "Oh! My heavens! Lyon—Dev is betrothed to Isabella Scott-Matthias!"

"I saw the announcement. Why in God's name did he do so stupid a thing?"

She dried her tears and went to stand looking down at this man she had loved most of her life and without whom there would be no life. "Because he thought he was going to die," she said quietly. "Or be a one-legged burden. For which I could scratch him very hard. He wanted me to be free of him. He

281

knew I loved him and that I wouldn't leave him unless he managed to convince me he—cared for someone else."

"He chose a fine barracuda," growled his lordship, secretly enormously impressed by all this.

"He used her, you mean," said Lyon. "The lady is waiting outside. I'd best go and tell her—"

"Wait!" Josie spun around. From the corner of her eye she saw Devenish move his head restlessly. She lowered her voice and spoke urgently. Lyon said nothing, watching his patron with marked unease.

Belmont gave a snort of indignation. "Madam, I think you do not quite appreciate the situation. Devenish hides it well, but it was a most difficult and lengthy operation. He endured gallantly, but he has been through a harrowing ordeal, he is weakened, worn to a thread, and unless I mistake it, has no will to live. Every moment counts and—I'll own I don't like his colour! It is his life you play with. If you persist, I accept no responsibility."

Josie quailed before this terrible warning. Closing her eyes, she clasped her hands and prayed . . .

Some minutes later, Lyon ushered a white-faced Isabella into the sickroom. Josie hurried to take her hand, and at that instant, his mind wandering, Devenish coughed again and moaned faintly.

Cold with fear, Josie said, "Thank heaven you are here, ma'am. He will need you so. Perhaps, were you to speak to him . . ."

Lyon took up a tray at the rear of the room, started out, then checked. "My lady," he said gravely, "I cannot tell you how I admire you. Poor old Dev will need constant care for a long time to come. I can well imagine how much it will mean to him to have you for his comfort and support."

Turning glassy eyes, my lady saw the pile of crimson-soaked swabs and lint, and with a little yelp, she recoiled.

The sound restored Devenish's awareness. Blinking at her, his dry and cracked lips smiled and he said weakly, "Hello . . . Bella. Did they send for you, then? Very good've you . . . to come." His hand went out to her, but drooped as she edged back.

"I cannot stand—sight of blood," she quavered.

"Your pardon." Lyon set down his tray hurriedly and took up the long box. "Shall I take this, sir? You mean to donate it to—er, the hospital, I presume?"

Belmont, beginning to thaw, said, "Never donate what you can sell, my boy. It's a fine specimen. We should be able to get five pounds, at least."

His brows drawing together, Devenish managed to raise his head. "Hey!" he croaked, indignant. "That's my leg! Devil take it, you've no right to sell me off like dog's meat! Bella—don't let 'em!"

"I assure you it is quite the accepted thing, old chap," said Lyon, walking to Isabella with the box. "As you can see, ma'am—"

She shrieked as he started to lift the lid, and flung up a shielding hand. "My God! How can you be so callous?" Retreating, thoroughly panicked, she wailed, "I—I cannot stay here . . . !"

Devenish's head turned on the pillow. "Bella—don't go. I am so sorry I didn't tell you, but—"

"Well—you should have," she gulped. "It was monstrous unfair!"

"Lady Isabella is coming down to Devencourt to nurse you, dearest." Josie took a rag from a bowl on the table, wrung it out, and bathed his face very gently. "I would stay, but my uncle has sent word he wishes me to join him in Paris."

Because he was very weak, he could not keep the desolation from his eyes, and his valiant smile quivered in a way that almost overset Josie, but he said staunchly, "Of course. You run along, little one. No need for you—to stay." But as she turned away, his smile faded into a sigh and his eyes closed.

Very grim, Belmont stepped forward.

A swirl of ermine; a breath of *Toujours l'amour*, and the unkind slam of the door. Josie flew to ease it open again. Rapid footsteps echoed along the hall. She heard Leith's voice, anxious. "Is he—?"

"Very bad," said Isabella. "I was never more shocked! He

lied to me throughout. He knew he would shortly be—incapac-itated! I feel no obligation! None! Oh! What an ordeal! I am—quite unnerved . . ."

Another door slammed.

Devenish muttered dully, "Has my little Elf . . . gone, Lyon?"

Josie flew back to the bed and bent low. "Never, beloved. Oh, Dev! The most wonderful news!" She clasped his weak hand again. "Darling mine—Lyon—show him!"

Lyon carried the box nearer. Devenish became even paler, but watched unflinchingly as Lyon took the lid off. Frowning, bewildered, he mumbled, "Nothing *in* there . . ."

Lyon put the box aside. "Dev—prepare yourself. We didn't have to take your leg off, after all!"

"Didn't . . . have . . ." Devenish gasped. "But—I *felt* you—" His eyes beginning to gleam with a touch of his old fire, he turned to Belmont. "You said—the bone was diseased!"

Josie bowed her head, thinking that he had kept that terrible diagnosis to himself all these weeks, throughout the preparations for her ball, throughout his pseudo-betrothal. Her clasp on his hand tightened and tears slipped down her cheeks.

Belmont replied with dignity that he had believed that to be the case. "Lyon was about to start the incision, two inches above the original injury, when I suddenly recalled your having men-tioned that the only way they could remove the crossbow bolt was to saw through the steel shaft with a hacksaw. Did you hear me tell Cahill I meant to take over and cut directly over the old wound?"

Devenish said tautly, "I wish I could say I did not, sir!"

"Yes. Beastly for you, I know. But I was taking a desperate gamble."

"His lordship's gamble was well justified," Lyon put in ex-uberantly. "It was an incredible piece of skill and took a long time, which is why it was so very hard on you, Dev. But he found—this." He held out his hand, on the palm of which lay a discoloured, twisted thing, like a tiny, rusted fish hook.

Devenish stared at it, scarcely comprehending.

"It is, as you can see, a filing from the bolt," said Belmont.

284

"When I examined you three years ago and told you the leg should be removed, you will recollect I warned you of the possibility of bone disease. When you came to see me last month and the leg was still causing you so much discomfort, I was strengthened in my belief that the bone had been damaged by the bolt and had indeed become diseased."

Glaring at him, Devenish said accusingly, "Do you say now that it is *not*?"

"Healthy as the rest of you, I'd say." Belmont grinned, cheered by this display of spirit.

For a moment longer, Devenish gazed at him. Josie was holding his right hand. He raised the other and it shook visibly as he clamped it over his eyes. A deep groan escaped him. Josie's grip tightened, her heart leaping with terror.

Only once or twice during his long ordeal had such a sound escaped him, and then he had been half conscious. Alarmed, the physicians hurried forward.

Lowering his hand, Devenish said in an emotional snarl, "Damn you! *Damn* you! Of all the *filthy* tricks! You—you told me I would wake up dead!"

Stifling a sigh of relief, Belmont protested, "We said no such thing!"

"Lyon said . . . that his first patient died because—because the amputation was so high on the leg that— And I knew— Oh, Lord! How *could* you manoeuvre me into such a pickle? I have got myself betrothed to *Bella*!"

With a ripple of laughter, Josie bent to kiss as much of him as she could reach. "I very much doubt she will have you, dearest. I rather fancy you have been abandoned to my care. And . . . ." Her eyes soft with tenderness, she murmured, "Oh, my darling, I *do* care—so *very* much."

The room seemed to be closing in before Devenish's eyes, and it was becoming so fuzzy he could only see the Elf's radiant face. His wound was hurting savagely, but it was not the agony he had endured on the long drive here, nor the unspeakable torment of the knife. He knew he was very weak, and yet, a soaring exhilaration was beginning to overwhelm him. It seemed, wonder of wonders, that he was not going to die, after all! It

285

seemed—even more wondrous—that life might, just *might* offer more than he had dared to hope.

How dim the beloved features were growing . . . Lord, how he loved her! Probably, he should keep on protecting her from him. She was, after all, a great heiress . . . there was still the threat of what the world would say. He was still too old for her. Only, he didn't feel old. He felt giddy and rapturous with optimism, and so happy he could laugh aloud and dance and kick up his heels. Except . . . he was so very tired.

Still, peering, he could discern the glow in the dear eyes, the sweetness of the adored mouth.

"To hell . . . with the lot of it . . ." he whispered. And happily abandoning his principles, he lifted a trembling but determined hand to her cheek. He had meant to draw down her head, but couldn't seem to manage it, and his hand, very heavy now, fell again. He frowned a little, fretfully.

Josie gave a sob and bent to him, and with her lips on his, he fell into a deep, contented sleep.

White's was crowded on this dark, snowy afternoon. Christmas was only a week away, and the mysterious good fellowship that is always so much more evident at that season of the year than at any other pervaded the warm, brightly lit apartments so that the air rang with talk and laughter, and even in the card rooms the tension was less than usual.

In a corner of the main lounge, seven men had gathered their chairs into a circle so they might chat with the easy familiarity that speaks of long-established friendship. They were an attractive group, three very dark, one having fair hair, one—the quietest of the exuberant group—with straight hair of a deep gold, a Frenchman, with brown hair and hazel eyes and a countenance not at all in keeping with the reputation of his notorious house, and one, the only older man, with thinning grey hair and wearing a clerical collar.

Tales of the Nine Knights had spread, and many admiring glances came their way, and many were those who dropped over for a brief word of cheer with this indomitable band who had, or so it was whispered, saved England from some demoniacal plot—a plot so deadly that even now the details could not be released.

It was Guy who was speaking, his quiet voice not travelling farther than their circle. "Mitch, you see, have come straight to me after the fire, because he think all it is not well with Alain. I also suspect there is the deep trouble, and thought it wise that Mitchell have bribe Alain's footman to spy on him."

"And from Guy's house I went to you, Leith," Redmond put in, "and to my brother."

"And then, back to Gloucester again," said Harry, curious. "Why, exactly, Mitch?"

Mitchell shrugged. "Don't know, really. Just a feeling . . . Anyway, I'd no sooner arrived than Dev's footman *extraordinaire* came galloping in with our idiot's Last Will and Testament."

"And also," Guy said gravely, "a farewell to Josie of such tenderness it would, I think, have quite break her gentle heart if after his death she read it."

"We drove hell for leather to Devencourt," Mitchell inserted, "but we'd missed Dev, and were about to leave for Town when Josie came in. The rest you know."

Justin Strand asked, "How did you and Leith get the word, Mordecai?"

"Dev's—er, footman *extraordinaire*," said the reverend gentleman, his cherubic countenance a little flushed from the warmth of the noisy room. "Tris and I were at Watier's for breakfast, and Cornish saw us coming down the steps. He'd rid all night, the good fellow, but he was willing to go on after you, Justin. Leith wouldn't let him, of course, and sent some of his own fellows off after you and Craig."

"I'm only thankful," said the young baron, "that our block did not succeed in his ridiculous martyrdom!"

Lord Bolster said in his shy fashion, "Hope you m-m-may be right about that, Mitch."

They all glanced at him curiously and found his gaze locked on a small but raucous group standing near the fire.

Sir Harry's vivid green eyes darkened. He said, "Fontaine! That dirty bastard! If all I hear of him is truth . . ."

"Well, well, our prominent sawbones has arrived," said Leith. "Over here, Cahill! Now—tell us—how your foolish patient goes on."

Dragging a chair into that privileged circle, Lyon reported that Devenish was doing splendidly. "He means, in fact, to come to Cloudhills, though in my opinion, such a journey would be ill advised." He paused, to accept the tankard of ale a waiter hurried to offer.

Sanguinet asked, "Is this more progress than you have the hope for?"

"I'll tell you what I'd never tell him, sir. I was very sure we'd be burying him. If Josie had not come . . ." He hesitated, and the other men looked at each other soberly. "I'd never dreamed," Lyon went on, "that such complete devotion . . ."

"You may be very sure I shall attend to him," proclaimed Elliot Fontaine loudly. "A cunning ploy, arranged so as to allow the slippery rogue to get his hands on the poor chit's fortune." He added something in a lower tone, and there was a burst of ribald laughter.

Scowling, Mitchell started up.

His brother put a detaining hand on his arm. "He hasn't named names, Mitch. You'd but add fuel to his fire, which is what he wants."

Justin Strand's thin, intense face was flushed with an equal resentment. "I wonder how many others will think the same of Dev. I don't see how Fontaine can claim his sister was wronged. If anything, she's the one at fault. She must have fairly shot her notice to the papers that the betrothal between herself and Devenish was at an end—by *mutual* consent! Hah!"

"Her passion for him cooled the instant she thought she'd be saddled with a cripple," said Lyon scornfully. "I wish you may have seen it! If she truly had been Dev's light o' love, her conduct might well have killed the poor fellow."

Leith said, "There are rumours she's already agreed to wed Cromford."

"A merry dance she'll lead him!" Mitchell gave a derisive laugh.

"But finish a rich widow," said Lyon.

The reverend shook his head. "We should not speak ill of the lady, my friends. For it is—" He paused as a waiter came to murmur something in Mitchell's ear, and was sent hurrying off again.

"Our footman *extraordinaire* requests a word," muttered Mitchell.

"Now what?" said Leith uneasily.

Astonishingly neat, Cornish followed the waiter over to the expectant group and looked mournfully at Mitchell. "Wotcher mate," he said and, with a twinkle added, "I mean—me lord."

"You astonish me, you varmint," Mitchell told him. "What's to do?"

" 'E's poppin' orf again," said Cornish with a sigh. "Me littel rocket."

Lyon leaned forward and set down his glass. "Do you mean Mr. Devenish has taken a turn for the worse?"

" 'Pends 'ow you looks at it, mate. 'E didn't say nothin' to the young lady, y'understand, but when I come in 'e was splutterin' like one o' them there rockets o' Major Whinyates. Some good soul 'ad sent 'im a 'nonymuss note, sayin' as a certain gent"—his eyes turned to where Fontaine held forth—" 'ad 'ranged fer the wine ter be mucked up. And the same party's man 'ad set the fire wot about writ finish to the guv."

"And off we go," sighed Strand. "Someone don't like Fontaine, it would seem."

Leith frowned and said slowly, "Unless it was Fontaine sent the note. I've no doubt nothing can be proved against him, and he hates Dev with a passion."

Guy shook his head. "I cannot follow you, my Tristram. If Lord Elliot he wish to write the *fin* to Alain, why not simply call him out? He surely could delay until Dev properly is recovered?"

"I agree with Tris," said Sir Harry. "Fontaine wants Dev to challenge, do you see? Then *he'd* have choice of weapons."

"*Mon Dieu!* But what can he choose? The pistol, it is a pistol!"

Strand muttered, "And Fontaine is a master swordsman."

289

Startled, Langridge exclaimed, "Oh, come now! Surely not Swords are no longer—" He checked.

Sir Harry nodded. "That's right, sir. Fontaine has chosen swords before, as a result of which poor young Saticoy will never walk again. Where are you off to, Jerry?"

Bolster, who had come to his feet and stretched sleepily drawled, "Want a word with C-C-C—Dev's man," and wandered to Cornish, who had stepped a few paces distant, waiting for Mitchell's instructions.

Sanguinet muttered, "Poor Alain—all these years he—"

"All aboard fer the Nancy Lee," interrupted Cornish inexplicably.

Following his amused gaze, Sir Harry sprang to his feet. "The devil!"

They all turned in alarm.

His lordship had not been entirely truthful. Instead of chatting with Cornish, he had bestowed a kindly nod on the footman and walked past. Before his startled friends could intervene, he had stumbled into Lord Fontaine, sending the Viscount's brandy splashing down his white and silver waistcoat.

"What the hell!" snorted Fontaine, inflamed.

"Just an accident, Taine," soothed a friend, looking anxiously at Bolster's innocent countenance. "Jerry didn't mean it, did you, old chap?"

"Oh, yes," said Bolster. The would-be peacemaker gawked his incredulity, and his lordship continued, "Terribly sorry, but I cannot like you, Fontaine. N-never have. It's your—your feet, I think," he explained apologetically. "Too big, by half."

His incendiary temper flaring, Fontaine lashed out. His lordship reeled, and mopped a handkerchief at his lip. "Have to ch-challenge," he said mildly.

All conversation in the crowded room had come to a halt. Jeremy Bolster was very well-liked, his diffident manner and warm good nature having won him a wide circle of friends, and that so amiable a man should have deliberately provoked a quarrel with the deadly Viscount brought dismay into the hearts of many who watched.

Bolster said, "My s-s—my—"

290

"Your seconds will call on me," Fontaine snarled furiously. "Is that what you're bumbling at?"

Bolster flushed a little, but bowed and offered his card.

As he turned away, Harry Redmond was at his elbow.

"Dolt!" he gritted, and went over to Fontaine. "One thing I cannot abide," he declared fastidiously, "is to see a fellow come into White's wearing a filthy waistcoat! Offends my sensibilities, be damned if it don't." He raised his own glass and with slow deliberation poured the contents across the offending garment.

Watching, his eyes glazed, Fontaine gasped, "You're . . . ripe for Bedlam!"

Sir Harry smiled beatifically, and proffered his card.

"Personally," said Leith, politely removing Sir Harry from his path, "it's your mouth disgusts me, Fontaine. Every time I see the pretty thing, I feel sick!" It was necessary that he, too, wipe his lips, for he had hit a very sore spot, and Fontaine fairly sprang at him.

A small line had formed behind Leith. Someone at the back of the room, recovering from his stupefaction, gave a nervous giggle. Justin and Mitchell became involved in a slight argument regarding whose turn it was, whereupon Lyon slipped past and objected loudly to the mole on the Viscount's neck. His medical explanation for the presence of the mark reduced several present to barely contained hilarity, but did nothing to soothe Fontaine, who was by this time practically apoplectic.

"Have done with your nonsense," he raged, livid. "Give your stupid cards to O'Brien, and since you are all challenging, I reserve the right to choice of weapons. I'll oblige the lot of you—much good it may do the coward you shield. You may tell that conniving fortune hunter he'll not entrap his poor little ward whilst I—"

Strand had a famous right. He used it.

Looking down at the Viscount, Mitchell protested, "Now see what you've done, Justin. I wanted to tell him about that revolting hangnail on his thumb!"

Strand gave his card to a dazed Sir Martin O'Brien. "Now, be sure you don't get mine mixed up with Redmond's," he exhorted. "I'm *before* him!"

Major Marcus Clay, sharing a sofa with Sir Freddy Foster, bowed his head into his hands and howled with laughter. Sir Freddy, recovering from his own amazement, joined in. Within seconds the room was pandemonium.

And thus it was that my lord Fontaine, recovering to find dismayed friends bending over him, found also that he was engulfed in a sea of mirth.

For his part, he was not amused.

Seated beside Leith in the hackney coach that conveyed them to the Pulteney, Harry Redmond was silent. Leith glanced at him and saw the lean features rather grim. He said, "A bit slow, weren't we, Harry."

Perhaps closest of them all to Bolster, the baronet gave a grunt of irritation. "My fault. I know the block. It's just the sort of damnfool thing he'd do."

Leith's mouth twitched. "You weren't far behind him."

"I wish to heaven I'd been before him! He's the worst shot of all of us. And his *fencing*! Tris—what in the world are we to do?"

After a moment's thought, Leith said, "It's a dashed bad time to rope him in—just before Christmas—but I fancy Lucian will oblige."

"St. Clair?" Harry brightened. "Jove, but you're right! He's as good, if not better, than Fontaine! If he can get away. I fancy he and Deirdre and the children are down at Hollow Hill."

"He'll come. He'd move St. Paul's for Jerry."

Harry chuckled. "He'll have more students than Bolster. He'll likely have to work with the lot of us. Think of Lyon! Gad!"

Through the following silence, they avoided each other's eyes.

If Elliot Fontaine worked his way down to Cahill, they would both already have fallen.

↷ Chapter 20 ↶

ce again, snow was falling over old London Town, drifting
wn onto grim tower and graceful steeple, whitely etching
mes and statues and bridges, settling on the tall crowns of
ntlemen's hats, frosting horses' eyelashes, clinging like an er-
ne trim to fur-edged hoods and woollen bonnets, and turning
slush under countless wheels and hurrying feet. Yet every-
here was cheer and bustle. People tucked chins into warm
arves and ventured forth to shops and bazaars and emporiums;
eet vendors hawked warm gingerbread men, roasted chest-
ts, and toffeed apples; and carollers stood on cold windy cor-
rs and sang lustily. For it was just six more days to Christmas
e!

Alone in the pleasant room in Grillon's Hotel, comfortably
ttled on a chaise longue by the window so that he could look
wn into Albemarle Street, Devenish was deep in thought. Jo-
e and Mrs. Grenfell were out at the moment at his insistence,
r since his operation his love had scarcely left his side and she
eded some fresh air. His rather stern expression softened. He'd
ver suspected when he set off on that never-to-be-forgotten
ternoon eight days ago, that instead of having reached the end
his life, he had come to the real beginning of it. How unbe-
evably dear she was. How she delighted in fussing over and
mpering him. Those first few days he had done little more
an sleep, but always when he'd awoken, she had been there,
r soft eyes full of loving concern, her every touch a caress,

filling his heart and his mind with the joy of knowing she w
his; that she would very soon be twenty, and yet still she lov
him and *wanted* to become his wife.

Tomorrow, they were to set out on the first stage of th
journey to Cloudhills. He was to be carried downstairs, wh
was ridiculous, for he could already walk. Not with ease,
actly, but he could negotiate those stairs. If Josie would all
it, which, of course, she would not.

Truly, the future looked bright. He had the love of his l
securely promised. They would be married as soon as the Che
alier came and could be formally petitioned for the right to
licit his niece's hand. A hint of worry there—a jolly fi
gentleman was the Chevalier, but he had every right to cut
stiff. Still, it didn't really seem likely he'd refuse. And if
should, there were friends who would come forward to vou
for him. The rest of the Nine would, certainly . . . ?

The trouble in his blue eyes deepened. His friends had be
superb. Visiting constantly—until yesterday, when no one h
come. Bringing their gaiety and nonsense and the deep and tr
affection that bound them all. And yet . . . sometimes he h
thought to catch Justin's eyes blazing at him, or Leith's dark ga
would seem oddly cold, or Mitch would glance at him and
would sense that all was not well. Almost—as if they were a
gered. Could it be that they, too, believed he had kept Jos
hidden away, to hoard her to himself? Surely these fine m
could not harbour the horrid worm of suspicion that he real
did covet her fortune?

He jerked his head around eagerly as the door opened, b
instead of his love came the tall figure of Leith, Mitchell Re
mond's cool elegance, and a rather troubled looking Bolster.

"Well, it's about time," he said, grinning as he took up t
bell on the table near his hand. "I thought you'd deserted me

"Did you?" said Leith expressionlessly.

Devenish looked from one to the other, put the bell dow
and said quietly, "Will you sit down—or can you not stay?"

None of them made a move to take the chairs he indicate
They smiled, but the smiles were a formality. Devenish nerve
himself.

"We just came to say goodbye," said Leith.

"G-going up t-t-to Cl-Cloudhills," Bolster imparted.

"It wouldn't be wise for you to undertake the journey," said Mitchell, his grey eyes stern.

It was like a blow to the heart. They didn't want him. For the first time he was to be excluded from the close-knit group. And that meant Josie also was to be shut out. The memory of past joyous Christmases rose to haunt him. The warmth and laughter and teasing. The lovely women chattering together, the shared reminiscences of old times, old perils, old triumphs. The innocent excitement of the children when the great tree's candles were lit on Christmas Eve. The gifts and good food and singing, and above all, the comradeship, swelled by the presence of parents and loved ones drawn into their circle.

Stunned, he heard himself say politely, "No. Of course. Well, then—Merry Christmas!"

He could not know how white he had become, nor of the stricken expression that had crept into his betraying eyes. But Jeremy saw, and his soft heart was wrung. He moaned, "Oh—Lord!"

Devenish stared at him, then turned to look squarely at Leith. "I know it's bad form to ask, but—is it . . . because of Josie? I mean—do you think I've not the right to offer? Truly, I have not done so because she's an—an heiress."

"Be damned!" exclaimed Redmond, jolted out of his icy remoteness.

"Well, if that don't cap the lot," growled Leith.

Suddenly all judicial hauteur, Bolster said, "That was not called for, Devenish."

Unknowingly, Devenish quailed against the cushions. "M-my apologies, but—"

"We—*were*—friends," said Leith.

"W-well, yes—I had thought w-we still are. But if you do not—"

"A friend," said Redmond, throwing hat and gloves onto the sideboard, "don't turn his back on people when he gets in a fix."

"B-but—I—"

"One might have thought," said Leith, advancing to direct steely stare at his victim, "we were merest acquaintances."

"Going off like that," Bolster said severely, running a han through his bright hair. "D-dashed un-unpleasant, to p-put it r nicely."

"If that is all you think of us," said Leith, "you doubtles do not care to any longer associate with us."

"Suppose we *did* think you was after Josie's fortune," Red mond began.

"Would you g-g-give her up?" finished Bolster, selecting a apple from the bowl.

Devenish blinked rapidly and managed to croak an affronte "You could go to hell, Jerry! And keep your greedy hands from my fruit!"

Leith's voice made him jump. "Bolster! This is serious busi ness!"

Instinctively having sprung to attention, poor Bolster gasped "Oh—Gad! Forgot. S-sorry, Tris. We'd best be off then."

"Good day to you, sir," said Leith with a frigid bow.

"Cheerio," offered Mitchell, picking up his hat and glove again.

"M-m-m—happy holidays," said Bolster, starting off with th apple, and replacing it with a guilty flush.

Devenish said stiffly, "Goodbye, gentlemen." And watched desolate, as they strolled to the door.

With his hand on the knob, Leith turned back. "Of course if you care to apologize."

"Apologize . . . ?" echoed Devenish feebly.

"Abjectly," said Mitchell, trying to be grave, but with a sus picious twinkle in his eyes.

"Oh, God! What did you expect me to do? Come whining to you with my troubles? Don't you think I'd have screamed for help—if anything could have been done? I thought my damned bones were rotting! Could—could you have made them well?"

Bolster whitened and stared in sympathetic horror.

Made of sterner stuff, Redmond looked at Leith and shook his head. "Not very abject."

"Not at all abject."

"N-not . . ." mumbled Bolster.

"You didn't have to *whine*," said Leith. "You could have *told* us, Dev. So we'd have been prepared."

"So we could have helped Josie," said Mitchell.

"Awful sh-shock for *us*," Bolster pointed out, recovering himself.

"I—I had writ to all of you," Devenish pleaded humbly.

"Didn't get any letter," said Redmond.

"No. Well, I didn't—exactly . . . send them off. It seemed so—weak-kneed."

Mitchell looked at Bolster. "Weak-kneed, he says."

"But—he d-did write," said Bolster hopefully.

"Almost," said Leith, very much the Colonel. "Let's be off." He opened the door.

Mitchell put on his hat. Bolster sighed and walked out.

Devenish started up and threw pride away. "Tris! Jerry! Mitch! I'm sorry!"

They looked at each other. Redmond bowed low, and waved Bolster in again.

Turning back, Leith said with a slow smile, "Let that be a lesson to you, Dev."

Considerably shaken, Devenish leaned back against his cushions. Mitchell carried over the bowl of fruit, and they all gathered round and attacked it.

When he trusted himself to speak, Devenish said with gathering choler, "Damn you, Tris! What about when Rachel wouldn't marry you, and you went slinking back to Cloudhills and hid yourself for a month and more, and damn near went into a decline, so that we all had to come and seek you out? What about you, Mitch, when you pretended not to give a button for England and the Regent, and went off and took on our Claude all by yourself? And as for you, Jerry—well, I can't think of anything just now, but—by God, if I ever find *you've* been up to anything underhanded . . . !"

He had turned the tables with a vengeance, and his three inquisitors exchanged a glance that was very guilty indeed.

* * *

"Nothing sudden about it," said Craig Tyndale, guiding Devenish carefully over the threshold as Josie and Yolande embraced in the oval entry hall. "We wanted you to see our new Town house, at all events, and thought you'd not mind coming before the others."

"Besides, dearest Dev," said the beauteous Yolande, hurrying to take this loved cousin's pale face between her hands, scan it anxiously, and then bestow a very gentle kiss on his cheek, "it will allow you time to settle in and be nicely rested by the time everyone arrives."

Already rather tired, and leaning heavily on Craig's supporting arm, Devenish allowed himself to be shepherded along to a large room at the rear of the house, obviously hurriedly converted into a bedchamber. "Oh, Gad, Yolande," he exclaimed ruefully. "What a fellow I am to be causing you such an uproar. And everyone's plans blown to Jericho! Say what you will, I know very well all this fuss is to spare me the journey to Cloudhills, where Tris and Rachel have been preparing this age for all of us."

"Yes, indeed. You are a great nuisance, Dev," she agreed humorously. "Indeed, I cannot but wish Lyon had amputated your foolish head, so we might not hear all this farradiddle!" And stooping to ruffle up the curls of that same foolish head as he sank gratefully into a leather armchair before the fire, she added, "Silly boy, as if you would not do as much for any one of us, were we in trouble. Now here comes Mitch, so we shall leave you men to chat, while I show Josie my lovely new house and the nice bedchamber we have waiting for her."

"And gossip about all your dearest friends," said Mitchell, blowing Josie a kiss.

When Josie had been led up the graceful staircase, and had exclaimed over the beauties of the charming new house on Portland Place, the two girls waited only until they were alone in the dainty yellow and cream bedchamber before they held hands and sat in the window seat, looking at each other with anxious eyes.

Yolande said, "He does not suspect?"

"No. But—oh, if anything dreadful should happen, he will

never forgive himself—or me, for not telling him! But—never mind that. How is Jeremy? Does Mandy know?''

"He has gone down to Three Fields to see her, but he'll not tell her, I am very sure. Not with—with the new babe only a month from coming!''

"I know! Oh, I know! When I think how hopeful she is of giving Jeremy an heir at last, and he, bless him, saying he would as soon have a fourth daughter, when everyone knows how he longs for a boy . . .'' Her voice failed.

Yolande hugged her. "We can only pray. And we *must* not let dear Dev know any of it whilst he is still convalescing. He would be out there in a flash, likely jumping between the swords!'' Her own voice quavered, but she said bravely, "After all, dear, were it any one of them, Dev would have done the same with not an instant's hesitation.''

They stared miserably at each other. Josie said, "If *only* it was not Elliot Fontaine! And to think that wicked creature dares pretend it is all to protect *me*! Lord, but Dev would—'' She bit her lip. "When is it to be?''

Yolande's pretty mouth hardened. "When that horrid man thought it would be most wounding. The day after tomorrow.''

Lifting a trembling hand to her throat, Josie said brokenly, "Oh, my dear God! Only two days before Christmas Eve!''

Jeremy Bolster came back to Town the following afternoon, and was soon ensconced in the Tyndales' drawing room, full of news about his Mandy and the three little girls, and the state of the roads which were, he said, not too bad as yet. He appeared quite relaxed and at ease, and gave not the slightest indication that he had occupied himself during the long drive by composing a farewell letter to the wife he adored. Or that he was achingly aware he'd quite possibly never see the face of his eagerly awaited child.

The short winter afternoon was drawing to a close, and a footman was lighting the lamps and candles, when Guy Sanguinet was assisted up the steps. Hurrying into the hall to greet him, Craig's welcome was cut short. "I have bring another guest," said the Frenchman diffidently, "if it is permitted. A countryman of mine."

Thus it was that Josie, admiring the gown her hostess meant to wear on Christmas Day, was summoned to attend her guardian. At once anxious, she hurried down the stairs to check and stand on the third step, breathlessly still.

The Chevalier de Galin, slender and distinguished in evening dress, stood all alone in that gracious hall, the candlelight gleaming on his silver hair, the dark eyes so shadowed with past sorrows fixed upon her. He bowed in his elegant way and, straightening, said in French, "Permit that I introduce myself, Mademoiselle de Galin. I am your uncle Émile." And, as she did not respond, but stood staring at him as though rooted to the spot, he added, "I bring the very great joy from many members of your family who long to welcome you, most beloved lost one. And to beg you may, to a very small degree, allow me to be a part of your future."

She went quickly to stand before him. And looking into those wistful eyes, gave a sudden happy cry and threw herself into two very eager arms.

Later, when they all were gathered in the drawing room before dinner, the Chevalier, glowing with happiness, and with Josie very close beside him, explained how it had come about. "It was the two gypsies of whom you spoke, Alain," he said in his soft, courtly voice. "I have the friend high up in *la Sûreté*, who it transpires have a good friend among your Bow Street people. And this Bow Street gentleman, he have an assistant—oh, of the perception most acute, but cannot speak. And—"

"Daniel, by Jupiter!" exclaimed Harry Redmond.

"Then you're speaking of Diccon!" cried his brother, no less excited. "How is the old fraud?"

Bewildered, the Chevalier said, "You have know Colonel Paisley, *mes amis*?"

There was a brief silence as five pairs of eyes exchanged laughing glances.

"Yes," smiled Leith. "We know him. I didn't know he'd been elevated to the rank of Colonel." He wondered if the laconic and dedicated man who had paid so high a price for his years of service to his country was still with the Intelligence Branch. But one could not ask such things, so he requested merely that the Chevalier continue his tale.

"While I am in London," de Galin went on, "Colonel Paisley hear my story and at once call in Daniel. I leave to return to Paris and confer with my man of affairs, also my dear mama, who is"—he turned to smile fondly at Josie—"so very eager to greet her granddaughter; and also I have to see the family of my late wife. So many things to be done, you comprehend. And— *voilà!*—to me have come this Daniel to say they have found Akim and your—alas, the other name leave my brain."

"Benjo," supplied Devenish, scowling.

"Ah *oui. Merci.* Benjo. They find, Daniel and his fine people, these two rogues, and from them they learn of a little girl in 1807 won over the dice from a soldier who steal her, thinking to ask for ransom, or sell her for—" He caught Devenish's eye, glanced at Josie, and saw that she had become pale. He reached out to take her hand and hold it. "Suffice it to say, my friends, we have proven, beyond the shadow of doubt, that this lovely child belong to my family. Praise God! At last!"

He pressed her hand to his lips, then turned to Devenish. "To you, *Monsieur*," he said earnestly, "there are no words. You save this so precious little lady from—the unthinkable. You give her the care, the kindness, the good life. How may I thank you?"

Devenish longed to tell him, but this was not the time, so he said instead how very much pleasure Josie had brought him in return, how much her bright presence had meant to him, down through the years. And continuing with much inner reluctance, he said, "It is beyond words wonderful that she has found her people. I—er, expect you will wish to take her to France, Monsieur le Chevalier."

"You must call me Émile," the Frenchman replied. "Since we are almost, you know, the relations." He turned to Josie. "*Ma fille*, will you entrust yourself to me? You shall have the chaperon, *certainement,* but—will you allow me to take you to your family? They all wait with—oh, such an eagerness!"

It was so marvellous to have a name, a family; to have this gentle, kind, handsome gentleman wanting only to bring her

301

happiness. But . . . in anguished indecision, she turned to Devenish.

His face expressionless, he said, "Of course she will go, Émile. I can imagine the anticipation your mama must feel, waiting to meet her."

In a troubled little voice, Josie said, "But—Uncle Émile, could Dev come too? I would not—"

"No, no," Devenish interpolated. "This is your time to be with your family my Elf. It belongs to you and the—and to Émile. I would not dream of intruding."

"Ah," the Chevalier said gratefully, "how generous you are, *mon ami*. But I shall not steal her for so long. And, perhaps— if it meet with your approval also, she can be married to her fine John in the Spring, eh?"

Several muffled exclamations were heard. Devenish gasped, and stared at the Frenchman. Josie gripped her hands and searched her uncle's face.

"Ma foi!" exclaimed the Chevalier. "I am misinformed, perhaps? The rumour it reach my ears that you are all but betrothed to a fine young fellow by the name of John Drummond . . . ?"

Devenish, who had occupied a chair opposite his love, now stood and, leaning on his cane, limped to stand directly before the Chevalier. "Sir, I had not intended to speak of this, but—"

"I comprehend. You prefer to be private. *Très bien.* Later, we may—"

"No, no, *Monsieur.* You have come to restore Josie to her family. These people are—*my* family. I have no secrets from them, and so I will tell you now, that—er . . ." He summoned his courage, clenched his fist, and blurted out, "It has been for some years my impudent presumption to—to love your niece."

"This is very obvious, *Monsieur.* No man could have been a better father. Is it that this boy, you do not judge him suitable?"

Very red in the face, Devenish stammered, "It is that—I do not . . . love Miss—Mademoiselle de Galin as—as a father, *Monsieur.* But—"

Taken aback, the Chevalier gasped, *"You*—wish to . . . to marry her?"

"Yes, Monsieur le Chevalier. I love her with all my heart. I have loved her these—these four years and more."

The Frenchman's eyes shot to Josie. There was no need to ask her feelings in the matter; her whole attention was on Devenish, her face reflecting a mixture of pride and tenderness. His glance shifted to the other occupants of the room. Instead of politely engaging in low-voiced side conversations, or at least making an appearance of not noticing what transpired, they all were watching with deep concern, even as a true family might be concerned for one of their own. Beginning to comprehend something of what he had heard of these men, a twinkle crept into his dark eyes. Returning his attention to the man who stood before him, waiting so tensely, he said, "I think I do not escape this room alive if I fail to give my consent! And certainly, I can think of no man, my dear Devenish, upon whom I would more gladly bestow—"

Devenish lifted one hand. His head well up, his heart hammering, he said clearly, "You must know, sir, there are those who will believe—"

"No, Dev!" cried Josie, springing up to catch his arm.

"Who will believe," he went on, his hand closing over hers, but his eyes meeting the Chevalier's unwaveringly, "that I have kept Josie hidden away in the country so that she would not be—be courted by other men. That I now, having discovered she is a considerable heiress, seek to acquire control of her fortune, by marriage."

"Ah . . ." said the Chevalier very softly. He came to his feet. A small frown appeared on his forehead, and suddenly he looked dauntingly autocratic. "And is it not possible, *Monsieur*, that having, as you say, kept my niece—er, secluded on your isolated estate these many years, and now declaring your wish to make her your wife, people may think you also have perhaps taken advantage of this helpless girl?"

"It would be a filthy damned lie!" flashed Devenish.

Up went the Chevalier's graceful hand, and the angry outburst from those gathered in the room quieted.

Leith, tall and impressive himself, was also on his feet, as were Bolster and Mitchell. "Monsieur le Chevalier," Leith said

303

in a voice of ice, "there was no need for Devenish to point out the possibility. He is one of the most honourable men I—"

"Pardon—I did not say it was what *I* believe, *mon Colonel*. But is it not what may be said by others? I will be very vulgar and go farther. If you have enemies, Alain, and alas I fear you have enemies of the most *implacable*, they will not stop at this suggestion. They will instead circulate the gossip that you offer for this sweet girl because it is most—ah, necessary, for the sake of her reputation!"

Josie's voice rang out over the angry chorus. "It is not true! Uncle Émile, Dev has been so honest with you." She laid a pleading hand upon the Chevalier's immaculate sleeve. "I will be as honest, and admit I fell in love with him almost as soon as we met. Ever since he brought me here—a gawky, uneducated, plain"—she reached up to remove the hand Devenish had put across her lips—"and unwanted foundling, I prayed the same prayer—each night upon my knees. 'Kind Jesus—make him love me, even if it is only a little bit. Make him want me for his mistress'—no, darling Dev, you must let me finish! 'For his mistress, if he cannot want me for his wife.' These last few years I have seen love for me peeping from his dear eyes. I have seen his yearning for me reflected in the window, or a mirror, when my back was turned and he thought I could not see. And I have teased, and flirted, and done all in my power to make this—this very gallant gentleman admit he loved me. Not until he thought he was dying would he tell me of that love. He had sent me off, breaking his heart for me, thinking he would never see me again. I only thank God I caught up with—with the wretched creature . . ." Her voice was shredding now, tears gemming her lashes, but she went on unsteadily, "If I must give up the—the name, and the family I have longed for all my life— so be it. But—dear sir, I would die sooner than give up this— this dearest and best of . . . men."

She wept openly, and Devenish, his own eyes blurred, swept her to him and held her close, kissing her hair, his heart so full he could find no words.

"I perceive," said Émile de Galin with a slow smile, "that

my little niece, she have found the very finest kind of gentleman. The very greatest gift of love.''

Josie rummaged in Devenish's pocket, dragged out his handkerchief, and dried her eyes. ''Uncle Émile . . . ? You mean. . . ?''

''That you have my blessings, my dears.'' But he shook his head to quiet Devenish's ecstatic thanks, and halt Josie's impetuous dart at him. ''Provided,'' he said gravely, ''you agree to abide by my terms.''

''Of course, sir,'' said Devenish. ''Whatever you ask.''

''After my dearest love sits down, if you please, Uncle Émile,'' interposed Josie determinedly.

And when they all were seated once more, and Devenish quite boldly holding his lady's hand before all their fond and amused eyes, the Chevalier outlined his plans.

''I am very sure,'' he began, ''that Devenish, loving you so much, *ma chérie*, will not wish any breath of ugliness, any soupçon of scandal, to touch you. Monsieur Guy has told me of the burning of your home, Alain. You have, I imagine, put in train the plans to rebuild—no?''

''Er—well,'' said Devenish haltingly.

Surprised, Bolster put in, ''You have not, Dev? I'd thought—'' He checked. ''Oh. Didn't think you'd be n-needing it, eh?''

''But I will certainly do so now,'' said Devenish, scarcely able to tear his gaze from Josie's face.

''*Bon*,'' said the Chevalier. ''It is good that you should be busy, *mon cher*, for I am going to take your sweet lady away. She will be feted and adored, I do not in the least doubt it. Ah—that frightens you, Alain? It is perhaps that you fear she will be snatched from you?''

Terror had indeed seized Devenish at his words. Émile meant to take her to Paris, of course. Natural enough. But these blasted Frenchmen were so skilled in the art of love, and he so dashed awkward. What if she found someone ardent and closer to her own age? What if—

''It will be the fine test of love and constancy, for both of you,'' de Galin went on softly. ''Besides which, it will silence all tongues, *assurément*. In May I will bring your lady to London, and your marriage announcement, it can be made, if your minds are the same then." He paused, eyes twinkling as he saw the adoring exchange of glances; the tightened clasp of hands. "And in June, when all the world it sings and your house it will be ready to receive her, you can be wed with no smallest fear of scandal. This—I think it will serve, *mes amis*?"

"It seems . . ." Josie said in a very small voice, "a terribly long time. Over four months. Could not Dev come to France in—in March, Uncle Émile?"

"No, dearest," said Devenish. "The Chevalier is right. We will do the thing properly. Besides, I must not be selfish. Your uncle Émile and your family have been denied the joy of watching you grow up—the happiness I have known these seven years. Now—it's their turn."

Her heart full of terror at the thought of parting, Josie sensed the grief behind his lightly uttered words, and in an effort to match his courage said, "Yes, of course. I must be grateful to have found my own family, and"—she touched his chin very gently—"to have you safe and well . . . Speaking of which, my love, you are looking very tired." She glanced at Yolande, and caught that tender-hearted lady covertly wiping away a tear.

"Very true," said Yolande, blinking, and turning to her husband. "Craig, will you do the honours?"

Tyndale had already come to his feet and offered a helping hand to his cousin. "Bed for you, old lad. We'll have a tray of hot chocolate brought to your room. Help you sleep." And he thought of the dawn, and wondered whether any of the rest of them would get one wink of sleep this night.

Sanguinet struggled up, and went out with them. "I have forget that I fetch correspondence for you, my dear Alain. Your people, you know, have all go home for their holidays, but Wolfe and the faithful Mrs. Robinson, now are back in Devencourt, and remain."

Devenish thanked him, and at the door turned for one last look. Josie smiled, her heart in her eyes. He thought, 'Nigh five months . . . my God!'

He was still shrinking from the prospect of that terrible separation after Hutchinson had settled him into bed and, with the

306

firm reminder that his hot chocolate was on the table within easy reach, made his stately way from the room. Devencourt—without that bright presence, that merry laugh, the twinkling mischief in her eyes that always warned she was contemplating something outrageous. Five months almost, without her . . .

He caught himself up in disgust. He had been approved by her noble uncle, when, for a short while it had seemed he was to be sternly rejected. Besides, it would be good for Josie to see something of the world. De Galin, elegant, sophisticated, would show her Paris at its most enchanting. Likely he'd take her to Vienna also. Perhaps even to Italy, that warm land of warmhearted people that had always so lured the English from their cold little island. She would be loved and made much of by her family, and wherever she went, for with that glowing personality, that lovely, always cheerful face, how could they help but worship her? God bless her, she would have a lovely time.

But—suppose when she came home, she found Devencourt, however he tried to beautify it for her, dull and lonely after her glittering time with—

"Oh, for heaven's sake!" he muttered, irritated with himself, and reached for the pile of correspondence Guy had brought to Town for him.

He flicked through it idly. A bill from Rundell and Bridge—that would be for Josie's Christmas present—or one of 'em, though he might never summon the nerve to hand her the other. A letter for Josie from Faith Bliss, that he would give her in the morning. Another, directed in the fine flowing hand that indelibly marked it as coming from Val Montclair, and that he would read first unless anything of prime impor— With a sudden tightening of the nerves, he took up the next neatly inscribed letter and peered at the seal. It was not a crest he knew, nor could he decipher the frank, but the sense of peril was strong, and he knew it too well to dismiss it lightly. He spread the page, and read:

> Your cronies guard you well, Devenish, and I cannot break through the barriers they erect to keep me from naming you the lying, dishonourable thing you are. A

thing that hides and shivers and lets his friends fight for him. Six of the fools—willing to die for you! Bolster is to be first. I doubt that will disturb you, and I do not mean to kill the dolt. I'll teach him a lesson he will never forget, however.

As you enjoy your wassail, I wonder if the idiots who so stoically protect you will even tell you that I blinded him at sunrise on the 22nd, in Laburnum Field above Kensington Village.

Fontaine

"Now . . . by God!" whispered Alain Jonas Devenish.

✧ *Chapter 21* ✧

Monday, December 22, dawned bright and cold. The snow had stopped during the night, and the countryside was a fairytale place, blanketed in white, the rising sun drawing sparkles from the pristine purity of the meadows, and gleaming on mantled tree and hedgerow.

The carriage that moved swiftly through the hush of the early morning was occupied by five men with weary, sober faces, each occupied with his own thoughts so that silence prevailed until Guy Sanguinet murmured, "*Tiens*, but I wish our Jeremy he have not drive off by himself!"

"Caught it from Dev," said Lyon, and after a minute, "You ever think Fontaine would dare to—to—"

"Kill him?" Leith smiled ironically. "Even Elliot Fontaine would not dare deplete the population by putting a period to all six of us, I think."

Mitchell said, frowning, "No. But the fella's got such an ugly temper. Only look at how he served poor young Saticoy."

"My fear exactly," said his brother. "Since old Jerry is first, Elliot may do something really dreadful, just to try and put the fear of God into the rest of us."

Leith, who harboured the same fear, said brightly, "He'll catch cold at that!"

"The one for whom I feel," murmured Guy after another lull, "is poor Craig. When Devenish, he wake up . . ."

"The rocket will 'pop orf,' " said Lyon, faithfully imitating Cornish, and drawing a laugh from his friends.

The carriage jolted to a halt. Leith said, "We're here. Don't see anyone yet."

They alighted, the snow crunching beneath their boots. "There he is!" Sir Harry pointed to a coach drawn up near some skeletal birches some distance away. "Borrowed Dev's carriage."

They started off, each heart as heavy as their steps were light.

Mitchell kicked at a clump of snow. "We'll have to clear some of this stuff."

"It's a helluva surface for a sword fight," Harry agreed. "They'll likely be sliding all over the shop."

"Good," said Leith. "Might lessen Fontaine's advantage, and Lucian said Jeremy's done quite well this week." He unbuttoned his redingote and took out his watch. "Quarter to eight. You'd think the varmint would be here—he certainly must be aware there's work to be done."

Mitchell gave a derogatory snort. "*That* arrogant bastard? You jest! Poor old Jerry—he don't seem glad to see us." And, in sudden vexation, "How in the devil I came to be the *last* I cannot comprehend! I'm the best swordsman of the lot of us!"

He was of course promptly put in his place with much good humoured mockery, and it was a laughing group who came up to the quiet carriage.

"Hi, Jerry, old sportsman," called Harry, and swung open the door.

Bolster sat huddled in the far corner, collar up, and hat brim pulled low over his face. He lifted a gloved hand, but said nothing.

His friends eyed one another askance. There could be no question of Jeremy losing his nerve, but . . .

Leith jerked his head and closed the door, and they withdrew a few steps. "Let him be," said the Colonel understandingly. "He's likely thinking of little Mandy."

Gloom fell upon them like a pall, and they stood in silence until a postchaise dashed up.

Harry opened the carriage door again. "He's here, old felow," he said quietly. "Lyon's with us, so perhaps you'd—*Yi!*" He sprang back.

Alain Devenish clambered down the steps and clung for a moment to the door, glaring at them one by one. "You *miserable*, conniving—"

"No—now, Dev," stammered Sir Harry, lifting a restraining hand.

"When I *think*," snarled Devenish, outraged, "of what you dared—you *dared* run me through because I went to Belmont in secret! And *you*—"

"You'll be run through with a vengeance do you mean to face Fontaine in a sword fight," Leith interrupted dryly. "You can almost walk."

"I can stand. And I can shoot!" Devenish reached into the carriage and lifted the long box that contained his deadly Boutet duelling pistols. "Fontaine has been fairly slathering to get at me ever since I popped him on the beak. He'll have to settle for pistols, is all."

"Which will be no great disadvantage," said Mitchell, frowning worriedly. "He's a crack shot, Dev. And you—"

"May surprise you, my encouraging friend," interrupted Devenish. "No! Stay back, Tris! Damned if I'm not so curst disgusted with the lot of you, I'd as lief put a ball in your foot as not!"

Knowing his man, Leith halted, but said coolly, "Use your head for once, you crazy fire-eater. You were barely recovered from trying to box yourself in pine when our dear Fontaine started making ugly noises. You were in no case to—"

"So you generously sacrificed Jeremy in my stead? And just how, gentlemen, just *how* did you think I'd have felt, watching one after another of my former friends cut down by that slimy wart? Do you suppose I could have faced Mandy again? Ever? Why you blasted set of pinheads, Fontaine would have worked through the lot of you and *still* got to me, don't you realize?"

"My thanks for the vote of confidence," said Mitchell, stung.

Devenish threw him a blistering glance, but accepted his arm and leaned on it as they all made their way in silence towards the Viscount and his seconds, Sir Martin O'Brien and a heavyset

311

middle-aged gentleman named Benjamin Blanchard. Sir Harry Guy, and Lyon paused some distance from the other group and each man shook Devenish by the hand, their teasing words and bright smiles failing to conceal the anxiety and the deep affection that their eyes could not hide. Mitchell Redmond and Leith were to second Devenish and they walked on with him.

Fontaine, elegant in a leather riding coat and buckskins, but with light pumps on his feet, put up his brows when he saw Devenish approaching. "Well, well," he purred. "So the daring one has crept from his hole."

Devenish felt Mitchell tense and answered affably, "I was quite unable to keep away, Fontaine. The last time you wound up inelegantly on your arse, you were propelled by my fist, as I recall."

Sir Martin and Blanchard glanced at each other uneasily.

Leith muttered, "Dev. If you think—"

"The lady was fairly in stitches looking down on you," grinned Devenish.

Fontaine, who had become very white, flushed darkly and said in a quivering voice, "I shall get to you, *canaille*, in good time, but—"

"I beg to differ," said Devenish. "My friends are vexed, and I don't blame 'em, but the right to cleanse the world of your pollution, is mine and—"

He reeled back as Fontaine leapt and his open hand struck like a pistol shot.

"Elliot!" exclaimed Sir Martin, shocked. "The fella's just out of a sickbed! He can scarce challenge—"

"No . . . need, Marty," interposed Devenish rather unevenly. "Fontaine challenged me some time back."

"Devil I did," snarled Fontaine. "You—"

"Have I mistook it?" said Devenish with a puzzled look. "I was sure that after I knocked you down that day, you'd felt obliged to call me out. Didn't you think so, Leith?"

"I did. One might suppose any—gentleman—would have defended his honour after being struck. But if the Viscount drew back from—"

Aware that many pairs of eyes scrutinized him curiously, Fontaine bit his lip, cursed audibly, and grated, "Very well! Have it your way. The end will not be changed, save that I'll put some of your friends out of their misery before—"

"No, no," smiled Devenish. "Mine is the prior claim. You must face me first, my dear Viscount. If you can command your nerves."

Sir Martin grasped his principal's arm and held him back. "Really, Dev, this is most irregular. Fontaine is to fight Bolster, and—"

"The hell with Bolster," snarled the Viscount, livid. "This bastard is the one I want first! I fancy you've not the guts to fight with swords, Devenish?"

"I wonder you would ask, my lord," Leith put in grittily. "You must be aware that Devenish just underwent surgery—"

"Ah yes," sneered the Viscount. "The clever amputation . . . whereof it was thought he would politely die. A vainly awaited result that I shall expedite today. I presume, Leith, you are to act for the poor fool . . . ?"

Watching in helpless misery, Guy put a hand over his eyes. "Poor little Josie!" he said brokenly. "How shall we tell her of *quelle grande catastrophe? Mon Dieu*, but she will die of grief!"

Harry muttered, "It ain't a tragedy yet, for Lord's sake."

"Much chance Dev has of out-shooting Fontaine." Lyon shook his head unhappily and picked up his bag. "I'd best get over there. Looks as if they're ready. *Damn* that miserable Fontaine! Only see how he struts!"

The Viscount having selected his pistol meanwhile, Devenish took up the remaining weapon. With a confident smirk, Fontaine said, "Nice pistol. Very nice. Distance, Leith?"

Heavy-hearted, Tristram asked, "Fifteen paces, Dev?"

Fontaine shrugged. "Give the clod whatever he wishes." He grinned. "I can kill him as easily at twelve paces, or twenty . . ."

"Thank you," said Devenish politely. "Four."

There was a concerted gasp. Every face jerked to him.

"Wh-what . . . ?" gasped Mitchell, whitening.

"My God!" exclaimed Blanchard. "You jest, man!"

"Four . . . paces," repeated Devenish, calmly deliberate.

313

"You're out of your senses," said Fontaine, staring wide-eyed. "You'd as well shoot yourself now!"

"Devenish, be reasonable," urged Sir Martin. "It's suicide!"

Leith, aghast, said, "Dev—my dear fellow, you'd—you'd both be killed."

"Which is, after all, only fair." Devenish turned a faintly rueful smile on this faithful friend. "Fontaine runs no risk. He is by far the better shot. This merely evens the odds."

"Like hell!" exclaimed the Viscount. "I came here to fight a duel, not to commit suicide at the whim of a lunatic!"

Devenish glanced at him. "Whatever else, I'd not expected you'd show yellow, Fontaine."

"No such thing." The Viscount looked at his seconds. "Well, tell him you fellows. I don't have to agree to such stuff."

Sir Martin and Mr. Blanchard exchanged troubled glances. "Er . . ." said the latter diffidently, "you—*did* say you had challenged, Elliot. And you told Devenish to name the distance. I do not see—"

"Then you're a damned fool," rasped Fontaine. "You've more sense, eh, O'Brien?"

"Well—I . . . The thing is, Taine—"

"That you have no choice," said Leith coldly. "Either you're a man of your word, Fontaine—"

"Or you're a cowardly, sneaking, worthless mongrel dog," Devenish put in with a curl of the lip.

Purpling, blinded by hatred, Fontaine shouted, "Very well, you damned insolent commoner! I call your bluff! Get on with it!"

Mitchell felt terribly cold. "Twelve . . . feet . . . !" he muttered numbly.

The seconds proceeded to a level spot in the snowy meadow, measured out the distance, then looked at each other across that horribly short space.

Redmond whispered, "My God! Tris, it's—it's murder!"

His palms wet, Leith said "We tried, Mitch. Nothing more we can do."

Amid a hushed silence each protagonist shook hands with his friends and was led to his place. Their pistols were raised to

314

point in the air; they turned slightly, each from the other so as to present as slim a target as possible. And those who watched, trembled, appalled by the inevitability of the impending tragedy.

Devenish was white, but had himself well in hand.

Fontaine's sneer was marked, but the side of his mouth quivered betrayingly. "Retract, idiot," he said. "Before it is too late."

"Would you wish to make your peace with your Maker, before we go?" asked Devenish coolly. "I realize 'twould take some time, but . . ."

Fontaine's snarled response was crude and not quite steady.

Sir Martin, his voice hoarse, said the familiar, "Gentlemen, I will count to three. I will then drop my handkerchief. When I do so, you will fire. Is that understood?"

The seconds stepped back.

Sir Martin hesitated, bit his lip and, struggling to command his voice, croaked, "One . . ."

There was a pause. Beads of sweat began to stand out on Fontaine's brow.

Sir Martin said, "My God! I *cannot!* It's murder! Leith . . . you must—must call."

"Then—damn you—do so!" raged Fontaine, a little rivulet creeping down his brow.

Leith frowned, then reluctantly moved forward to take Sir Martin's place.

Fontaine, watching Devenish narrowly, hissed, "Madman! You would have a slight chance at fifteen paces! You have none like this!"

"I know you, Fontaine," Devenish answered as softly. "I know you were the man in the Morrissey affair." He saw the Viscount's hand jerk, and added, "You enjoy hurting people. It would please you to maim my friends, one after another. I shall deny you that pleasure."

Fontaine read death in the coldly inexorable eyes of the younger man, and moistened his suddenly dry lips.

Suspecting what Devenish was about, Leith judged it a forlorn hope, but gave no sign of it. "I shall start again, gentlemen," he said coolly. "One!"

315

His gaze steady on his antagonist, Devenish thought that the Viscount looked sick. He was a bad man—a merciless rogue who must be stopped. Josie's loved face was before his mind's eye, and he prayed she would understand. This fight was of his making and he must deal with it as any honourable man would. Certainly, he could not stand back and let his friends do his fighting for him!

"Two!"

The meadow was so quiet that Leith's voice was like a thunder clap. Fontaine jumped visibly. Sweat was running down his face now, and his mouth was twitching uncontrollably.

Delaying as long as he dared, Leith took a breath.

"Call it! Damn your soul! CALL it!" screamed Fontaine. And his nerve broke. His pistol whipped down.

"No!" shouted Mitchell, frantically.

The shot was deafening.

Devenish, every nerve strung to breaking point, had been watching Fontaine's eyes. In that deadly split second as Fontaine's pistol flamed, he thought, 'Josie!' Something jerked at his coat and he staggered.

Anguished, Leith shouted, "You stinking apology for a man! Dev! Are you—"

"Very—fine . . ." gasped Devenish, his knees like water. "My shot, I believe . . ."

Grey faced, shaking visibly, Fontaine let the smoking pistol slip from his palsied hand.

Devenish lifted his weapon with slow deliberation and aimed, his hand steady as a rock, at his enemy.

"N-no . . ." whimpered Fontaine, dodging aside.

"Good God!" breathed Redmond.

"Taine!" cried Sir Martin, horrified.

"*Stand*, you damned cheating poltroon!" roared Leith.

Devenish lowered his pistol. "I believe I will reserve," he said. "Until another time."

They all stared at him.

Fontaine, looking barely able to stay on his feet, said chokingly, "En-enjoying yourself . . . ain't you?" His voice rose to an hysterical scream. *"Damn you!"*

"I shall finish," said Devenish, "whenever I so choose. However, you must not arrange another duel, Fontaine, without allowing me my shot at you. That *is*, I believe, my right—gentlemen?"

Sir Martin, flushed and mortified, said, "Indeed it is, Devenish. Dashed decent under . . . circumstances."

Mr. Blanchard, also red with embarrassment, muttered, "Most awfully sorry, Dev. Can't tell you—Terrible business."

Knowing he was ruined and disgraced, Fontaine said nothing, but flung around, and reeled like a drunken man to the waiting carriage.

Devenish took Leith's ready arm and they made their way back to their own vehicle.

"You stupid, blasted block," gritted Lyon. "What a frightful chance to take!"

"If you don't think—my knees are blancmange," gasped Devenish.

"I don't understand how the hell he came to miss you!" Leith glanced at the silent Redmond.

"He was shaking with fright," said Devenish. "I'll own I was."

"You didn't show it. And to fire before the word! God! If ever I heard of such a thing!"

Conscious of an icy silence, Devenish glanced at Redmond. "Mitch? Are you—"

"You will excuse my braggadocio if I say I prefer to fight my own duels," said Mitchell acidly. "Much as I appreciate your intercession in my behalf."

Devenish grasped his arm. "Mitch, for Lord's sake—"

Redmond tore free and held out the pistol box. "Yours, I believe, sir."

Leith said sharply, "Dev! Are you hurt? Your coat's torn!"

"No, Tris. He—took off my button, though. Blast him!"

Leith touched the rent. "Just over the heart, by Jove. An inch or so to the right, or had you been standing square . . . !" He and Redmond exchanged sober glances.

Devenish said apologetically, "Mitch—I know *you* could have

317

dealt with that ruffian. But—you see, you were not the next in line . . .''

"Jerry." Redmond scowled. "I suppose—Fontaine would have killed him, all right."

"No. He writ me a letter. He had no intention of killing Jeremy. He meant to blind him."

Leith swore under his breath.

Redmond gave a gasp. "Then why in hell didn't you shoot and be done with the filthy swine?" And then, seeing Leith's grin, his own mouth curved to a smile and then to a laugh. He clapped a hand on Devenish's shoulder. "Damme if I ain't as big a fool as you are! You raving maniac! Of all the cork-brained starts! I about suffered a heart seizure!"

Whooping, Harry and Guy were hastening to meet them. The reaction set in then, and they were all laughing foolishly when they reached the coach.

On the box beside the coachman, Cornish, muffled to the ears and with a gigantic and lurid scarf wrapped several times about his throat, grinned at them. "Wot-cher, Sir Guv," he beamed. "Thought I'd 'aveter find meself a new gent, s'elp me!"

Devenish told him cheerfully that he was a blasted scoundrel and had no business to be here. Unrepentant, the atypical footman offered to guide them to a nearby tavern called The Country Gentleman. "If you lively gents is ready for a bit of a bite."

They were, they found, ravenous, and they piled into the coach. The coachman untied his reins and gave his horses a friendly curse and a light crack of the whip, and the carriage set off.

A shout of laughter came from inside, but Cornish glanced back at the Viscount's disappearing chaise and for once his unlovely face was set in sombre lines.

The Country Gentleman was a rather indifferent hedge tavern, and the food not exceptional, but the cheerful Corinthians were in no mood to find it anything but superb and their meal was consumed with all the joy and verve that could be expected of men who had started the day with the terrible anticipation of finishing it in mourning. They argued merrily about everything but the fiasco of the duel, discussed the forthcoming holiday

318

season, and generally behaved as if they'd not a care in the world until Lyon muttered, "D'you know, I still cannot believe our ignoble Viscount actually lost his nerve like that."

The grins faded; the eyes became sober, and there was silence.

Leith said thoughtfully, "Perhaps he'd never come face to face with certain death before. He's so accustomed to winning."

"That's what I counted on," said Devenish. "I hoped it might make him so offstride he'd fumble his shot."

"He fumbled all right, dirty bastard," gritted Harry Redmond. "When I saw him fire before time—by God, I couldn't believe you were not killed, Dev!"

Guy said in his quiet fashion, "He is a very bad man, that one. And ruined now." He shook his head. "He will find it a bitter road. Almost, I pity him."

"*Pity* the wicked devil?" exclaimed Mitchell, indignantly. "He deserves everything that may befall him! When I think he planned to blind old Jerry—"

"*Jerry!*" gasped Devenish, suddenly pale. "Oh, Lord! He'll kill me!"

Leith grinned. "I've meant to enquire how you persuaded him to stay in Town."

"I made no attempt to."

Awed, Lyon said, "You never—*hit* him?"

"Hard," nodded Devenish. "Then I tied and gagged him and rolled him under his bed." He contemplated his hysterical friends glumly.

"You're absolutely right," chortled Sir Harry. "He'll kill you.

An hour later, the three carriages had barely drawn to a stop on Portland Place, than the front door burst open and my lord Bolster, his long driving coat unbuttoned, a dark bruise on his jaw, and a wild look in his eyes, rushed down the steps.

Leith alighted quickly. "Now, Jeremy, dear old fellow, it—"

"Is he de-de-de—killed?" shouted Bolster.

Slinking down the steps after his tall friend, Devenish said, "Jerry, I'm dashed—"

Bolster sprang at him. Devenish shrank. Gripping him by the

319

shoulders, Bolster shook him as though expecting him to shatter to pieces. "Hurt?" he barked.

"No. But—"

"Hah!" said Bolster, and galloped into the house again.

"Good Lord," said Mitchell. "You'd best hide, Dev. Likely gone for his pistol."

Bolster's phaeton came racing along the street and stopped abreast of the other three.

"Ready for a getaway," said Sir Harry solemnly.

Bolster's valet sprinted from the house, clutching a valise, and made for the phaeton. An instant later, his many-caped coat still not buttoned and his hat tilting at a rakish angle, Bolster leapt down the steps and ran straight at Devenish.

His face one great beam, he cried, "M-m-m—" He slapped Harry on the arm, raced to the phaeton, flung himself inside, and let down the window. As the vehicle began to pick up speed, he leaned out and waved his hat, his yellow hair sticking up at all angles. "It's a b-b—it's a b-b-b—" His voice faded. "I've got a *son*!" he bellowed.

A cheer went up.

The phaeton turned and came charging back again. Half out of the window, Bolster shook his fist. "Dev, you madman," he shouted, "I'll d-d-deal w-w-w—" And the phaeton was gone again.

"No, really, Milady Elf," said Leith, smiling understandingly into Josie's reddened eyes, "I think you must forgive him, m'dear. He meant only the best. And it is, after all, Christmastime."

Clinging desperately to Devenish's hand, even as she refused to turn her head to look at him, Josie was still unnerved from the shock of awakening this morning to the terrible news that her love had rushed headlong into danger once again. "I do not blame him for trying to save dear Jeremy," she quavered. "But, to go without a word . . . Just as he did before!"

Upon his return, Devenish had cravenly, but not altogether untruthfully, pleaded exhaustion, and taken refuge in a long nap. They were gathered in the drawing room now, and he tried vainly to turn Josie's little chin with one finger and pleaded, "My heart, I am hopeless. I'll not blame you at all if you never come back to me."

Her head jerked to him at that. "Oh! How unfair to—"

"I hear a carriage!" Mitchell sprang up eagerly. "That will be Charity and the children!"

Just as eager, Justin, whose beauteous wife had presented him with triplets when he had begun to give up hope of ever becoming a father, cried that it might instead be Lisette and their little trio.

Watching Strand's hopeful face, Lyon said with a grin, "Only look at how brave he is—now!"

"And went down like a fallen tree when Dr. Bellows told him he had three babes, and Lisette was quite well," laughed Tristram.

"I can see I must find a wife, or I shall be the only bachelor among us," said Lyon, "and you will be casting me out for—" He broke off abruptly, slanting an embarrassed glance at his adoptive parent. His dark eyes narrowed. Guy was white as death, his eyes fixed in an unblinking stare at the doorway.

The butler announced austerely, "Monsieur Lavisse."

"Lavisse," breathed Lyon. He thought, Jupiter, it's the old fellow with the dog. What the deuce does he want?' and he stood, turning to the new arrival.

Devenish glanced over his shoulder and saw a thin, white-haired gentleman, dressed with quiet elegance, advancing to shake Lyon's hand. As he drew nearer, it could be seen that the narrow face was not elderly, and there was that about the carriage of the head, the thin lips, and cold, jet eyes, that brought a vague sense of familiarity.

Rachel Leith, looking from Guy to the newcomer, tensed, and stared.

"*Bonjour, Monsieur le docteur*," murmured the stranger.

Rachel whitened and shrank, a hand lifting to her mouth. Her tall husband, who had moved to stand behind her chair, dropped a hand onto her shoulder.

The sound of that voice brought Devenish to his feet, and he turned awkwardly to face Lavisse, his narrowed eyes deadly.

Leith said a soft "Dev—wait."

Lyon, sensing the sudden tension in the room, said uneasily, "If you wish to speak to me about your dog, *Monsieur*, we had better step into another room."

"But, no," said Lavisse, his rather nasal voice having little trace of an accent. "What I have to say concerns several of the people here this afternoon."

Tyndale said, "It's all right, Cahill. Do come in, Monsieur Lavisse."

Not quite understanding what was happening, Josie saw Rachel cringe away as Lavisse passed her chair. Guy looked ready to faint, and Dev's hands were tight-clenched. Praying he was not going to explode again, she watched the newcomer apprehensively.

"I said to you, when you helped my dog, that I would repay in a manner commensurate with your service," said Lavisse, taking the chair Lyon drew up, and accepting the glass of Madeira Tyndale handed him.

Devenish snatched up his cane and limped over to stand beside Leith, and Mitchell, who had stood as one stunned, made no attempt to sit down, but watched Lavisse with much the same savagely hungry expression as that of Devenish.

"I perceive," said Lavisse coolly, "that I am recognized." He leaned forward, having sampled the wine, and put the glass on the table before him. "However, first things first. Dr. Cahill, you relieved the suffering of the one creature in this world for whom I have affection. Tonight, I repay in kind." He shifted his gaze to Guy. "It surprised me to learn you had survived, *Monsieur*."

Puzzled, Lyon said, "You know my father, Monsieur Lavisse?"

"Quite well," Lavisse replied with a small, ironic smile. "Although, his brother I knew better."

Through his teeth, Devenish gritted, "I wonder you dare admit it, Gerard!"

"The devil!" Harry Redmond leapt to his feet, and Mitchell, his handsome face distorted with rage, started forward.

"If you throw me out, gentlemen," said Lavisse, his dark

322

brows lifting in a bored fashion, "you will, I do assure you, regret it greatly."

Mitchell threw a seething glare at Leith, who shook his head in an unmistakable veto of violent action.

Lavisse turned to Devenish. "So the leg it is still a problem."

"I collect," snarled Devenish, "you regret having lobbed that damned steel bolt through it!"

"Not in the least. You and Leith walked into Claude Sanguinet's stronghold with the full awareness of what you invited. I did as I was paid to do. No more. No less."

With a wary eye on Devenish's boiling wrath, Tyndale said, "I would suggest, Lavisse, that you say whatever you have come to say as quickly as possible. I cannot guarantee that either Devenish or the Redmonds will for very long respect your immunity as my guest."

"Oui. This I understand, so I will proceed." Contradictorily, Lavisse paused for a moment, staring rather blindly at the fire. Then he began. "By what paths I will not elaborate, but in my twenty-ninth year my uncle, who had worked when a youth for your papa, Monsieur Guy, contrived it that I enter the service of Monsieur—or Monseigneur, as it pleased him to be called—Claude Sanguinet. I served him in many roles. Again"—he shrugged—"I shall not elaborate. I am very sure you are aware that this man, he was, as were they all, insane." Guy winced, but he made no comment, and Lavisse continued. "Not in his own eyes, naturally. He was wont to assert in defence of some of his more savage deeds that he was a powerful and wealthy man, and that lesser people hate both these qualities. The truth was that he had no—soul. No conscience, if you will. In the course of my ten years under his heel, I suffered many indignities, countless humiliations. But I stayed. And the reason I did so was two-fold. Firstly, for the money he paid and the riches he promised. Secondly—but that is another tale."

The room was very still now. Lavisse took up his glass with perfect poise, and sipped the wine appreciatively. "My Uncle Armand told me much of the Sanguinets," he went on. "And he spoke often of the late Sanguinet Père. Henri. And of a certain very beautiful lady. Your Papa, Monsieur Guy, liked his

323

women beautiful, as you may recall. He owned this lady's father. Indeed, a word from Henri and the man would have been not only disgraced, but if he escaped the guillotine, it would have been remarkable. Need I detail the obvious? This lovely creature loved another gentleman. A young Englishman of fine birth and some fortune, but not sufficient, needless to say, to buy her freedom from Henri. The lady—her name was Lorraine—became Sanguinet's bride. She was unwise, for she allowed the old man to see her reluctance—her revulsion.'' He gave a small gesture. ''I will not have to tell you how she was treated. He was an animal. He behaved like an animal.''

Guy gave a small sound and bent his head, and Lyon, frowning darkly, rose and crossed to sit beside him.

Lavisse smiled faintly, and resumed. ''Henri was obliged to go to Switzerland, but whether he was there or not, always, there were guests at Chateau Sanguinet. While he was gone, Lorraine's former admirer slipped into the house with a group of Henri's friends. For a little while, my Uncle Armand did not guess what was going forward. Lorraine was at this time in the delicate condition. Her admirer worked desperately to get her away. Armand saw, but he said nothing, because it amused him to think that Henri Sanguinet, this great and terrible man, is being made a fool. Alas, Henri's eyes are everywhere. Young Cahill—''

Lyon started, his dark eyes widening.

Lavisse purred, ''Oh, yes, that was his name. Richard Cahill. And suddenly, he is no more seen. Poor Madame Lorraine, she is half crazed with fear. Then, Henri came home. He told her that her expected child will be illegitimate, because the ceremony they went through was a farce. And he told her also, that young Cahill had been found—floating in the sea, with a knife between his shoulders.''

Lyon felt Guy shake. He slid his arm across the back of the sofa, allowing his hand to grip Guy's shoulder. ''Easy, sir,'' he said gently. ''Shall I tell him to stop?''

Guy shook his head distractedly. ''My mama lost her mind—poor soul.''

''Not until after you were born, *Monsieur*,'' said Gerard,

much as though he discussed a shopping list. "And what you did perhaps not know was that the good Henri used to taunt the poor lady with promises of the life her child would have because she had displeased him. That, Monsieur Guy, was what drove her out of her mind, so that she killed herself."

"Ah, no!" cried Guy, starting up wildly. *"Mon Dieu! Mon Dieu!* Never say it is so!"

"Of course it's not!" Devenish limped forward. "You dirty, lying scum! You only came here to—"

"To tell Monsieur Guy," said Lavisse, his cruel eyes glinting, "that he is indeed a bastard. Just as Claude told him."

Tears filling her eyes, Josie pressed a hand to her mouth and watched Guy's white-faced anguish helplessly. Lyon gave a growl and sprang to his feet, his powerful hands clenching. Devenish, savage with rage, said, "This may amuse you, Leith. Be damned if I see why you allow it to continue!"

"But you see," Lavisse went on, impervious to the infuriated men who closed in around him, "it was as I said. Monsieur Guy, poor fellow, is far more of a bastard than his kindly brother told him. He cannot, in fact, claim the *slightest relationship* to the Sanguinets."

Through the following breathless hush, Guy uttered a strained, shaken, *"Gerard—je vous implore . . . qu'est-ce que c'est?"*

"My Uncle Armand, he also was a wicked man," said Gerard, cool as ever. "He did much that was bad—even as I. But— some things still disgusted him. He did what he might to help the poor Lorraine, and she was grateful. She thought of him, I think, as a friend. Just before she died, she told him that when she learned she was to be given as Henri's plaything—they were in England then, you understand—she went to her love, and they ran away to the Border together. Her papa found them, alas. The boy was beaten and left lying by the roadside. Lorraine was sent to Henri Sanguinet. But . . . she had spent four days—and nights—with Cahill."

Guy sat shivering, but said not a word.

Tightening his grip about the thin shoulders, Lyon asked intently. "Then Guy—is really . . . ?"

"His papa was Richard Cahill. And young Cahill, Monsieur

Guy, had every intent to make your mother his legal wife. Only through Henri's viciousness and his own murder was he prevented.''

Josie flew up to kneel before Guy and clasp one cold hand. "Guy—dear Guy, do you see? This means you can marry Faith!"

"By the Lord Harry, but it does!" exclaimed Leith.

His eyes still fixed on Lavisse, Devenish said contemptuously, "You've paid a debt. How does it feel to have done something decent for once in your life?"

Lavisse shrugged and bestowed a faint smile upon Leith, who came to refill his glass. "You are prejudiced because I put a crossbow bolt in you, Monsieur Devenish." He looked to the Redmond brothers, standing side by side. "Nor do I think you gentlemen have much admiration for me." He saw Mitchell's lip curl and laughed softly. "They very nearly hanged you for Parnell's murder, did they not, Sir Harry?" Mitchell whitened, and Harry cursed under his breath and took a pace forward. "Such a miscarriage of justice," Lavisse went on. "When a dear friend of yours once said that to whoever killed him should be awarded the highest honour this country could bestow . . ." He smiled, and drank his wine.

Harry whispered, "Diccon said that. My God, Gerard! Do you know who killed Parnell?"

Lavisse set down his glass and stood. "If you wish proof of what I have told you, Monsieur Guy, it is easy enough to find. There is in Somerset a manor house called Edleighdale, where dwells the father of Richard Cahill. He is a poor man, and his estate near poverty-stricken. His son, you see, told him of his liaison with Lorraine, but fearing lest his father also come under the vengeful gaze of Henri Sanguinet, he named no names. His father, Edwin Cahill, heartbroken when Richard was murdered, spent his entire fortune striving to bring the culprits to justice, and to discover the whereabouts of Lorraine and, he hoped, his grandson. He is a solitary old gentleman, but not an embittered one. He will, I think, be most pleased to see you, nor will you have to prove your identity, for you are very like the portrait of your papa that hangs in the entrance hall."

Still bemused, Guy stammered, "You—have been there?"

"I have. It is sad to see so fine an estate brought to such a condition. The old man tries, but—" he shrugged. "Had one a great fortune, of course . . ."

Lyon said eagerly, "Sir—you are very wealthy, perhaps—?"

"I have a little money left me by my—or as I thought—my aunt," said Guy. "I have never touched the Sanguinet fortune!"

Leith said, grinning, "Then now's as good a time as any!"

"Jove, yes!" exclaimed Devenish. "How furious old Claude would be to see it used in such a cause!"

A slow, joyous smile overspread Guy's pale face. *"Ca va! Ca va! Lyon! We will do this! I have mean to build you the hospital, also!"*

Lavisse started for the door.

"Wait!" cried Guy, struggling up. "I wish to thank—"

"Your thanks are not required, *Monsieur*. I merely repay. *Bonjour, Mesdames et Messieurs.*"

Harry cried, "Gerard—*please! Do* you know who killed Parnell?"

Gerard glanced to him, a queer little smile playing about his thin mouth. "As well, Sir Harry, as I know—myself."

"Good God! But—*you* were not at Moiré that night!"

Guy said sharply, "Yes, he was, Harry! I—" He broke off, torn by conflicting loyalties.

Harry and Mitchell stared at each other. Mitchell asked hoarsely, "But—*why*, Gerard?"

The dark eyes held upon him for an impenetrable moment. *"Monsieur*, I came here to repay Dr. Cahill—not to put my head into the noose for you. Your papa, young Frederick Carlson— many, many other innocents, are avenged. Be content. *Adieu.*"

Lyon ran to open the door, the Redmond brothers pounded each other on the back, and the others crowded, jubilant, around Guy.

Lyon said, "Monsieur Lavisse, from the bottom of my heart, I thank you! You have given him a chance for happiness, at last!"

Looking at that exuberant group, Lavisse said slowly, "He has known much of sorrow and pain. But I think he also knows a joy not given to many men." He smiled with faint warmth at

327

the earnest young face that watched him so gratefully. *"Joyeux Noel, Monsieur le docteur!"*

Lyon said fervently, "And a very Merry Christmas to you, sir!"

Their seventh Christmas together had faded into the past. The gaiety, the festivities, the gift exchanges, the merry, crowded hours, were over. The children, sighed exhausted parents, could start behaving like normal creatures again; the adults could take up the threads of everyday life.

Josie had been enchanted with a jewelled comb for her hair, in the shape of a butterfly. In turn, she had presented her beloved with a small portrait of herself. Lord Coleridge Bryce had painted it, at Mademoiselle de Galin's very precise direction. It depicted Josie, aged twelve, this made possible by some sketches Colley had made of her when Devenish first had brought her to Gloucestershire, and that he had developed into so faithful a reproduction of the bright little waif, that Devenish had gazed at the portrait, rendered momentarily speechless.

The friends had parted, vowing to meet again very soon, and supposing that occasion would be at the wedding of Guy Sanguinet (now Cahill) and Faith Bliss.

Josie and her love had returned to Devencourt on Boxing Day, the Chevalier tactfully refusing their requests that he join them, and saying instead that he would drive down on January 6th, to collect his new niece and bear her off to the land of her birth.

And today was Tuesday, January 6th, 1824.

For the past nine days, Devenish and Josie had striven to live each moment to the fullest, resolutely ignoring the fast-approaching moment of parting. But that moment had come. Even now the Chevalier, courtly as ever, waited in his luxurious carriage some distance from the old house. Looking out of the study windows to the rear drivepath, now become the main approach, Devenish stared at that carriage, willing it to disappear, but knowing that the sooner this was over, the better.

He let the curtain fall, and turned back into the room. On his desk was a vase full of branches of holly, beside it a small package. The latter contained the extra gift he had drawn back from presenting to his beloved at Christmastime, because it belonged only to them. And that, even now, he knew he should not give her.

He was staring at that small package, debating with himself, when he felt the draught of the door opening and knew she had come into the room. His heart seemed to stop, and suddenly he was icy cold. 'Dear God,' he prayed, 'let her want to come back to me. Please—let her still love me.'

And he turned to her. She stood in the doorway, wearing a pearl-grey woollen cloak, edged with paler grey fur, the hood thrown back so that he could see her rather frizzy hair and the ringlets that somehow never seemed as neat as those of the acknowledged Toasts of the day, and that were, to him, ineffably more dear. He had no idea what else she wore, for he saw only her white, anxious face and great terrified eyes. He held out his arms, and she flew into them and he hugged her crushingly close, bending his head so that he could breathe in the sweet scent of her . . . the fragrance that was hers alone.

"Dev," she said chokingly, "I cannot! Ah, my dearest love—I *cannot*!"

He closed his eyes and for one more priceless second felt the silk of her hair tickling his cheek. Then he put her from him. "Yes, you can, my Elf," he said gently. "You must—for my sake." Her eyes searched his face, and he touched the pert little nose with one fingertip and refused to notice how piteously her mouth trembled. "This is the only way to convince 'em all I have not seduced and lusted over you these seven years. No—don't defend me! In a way—they would have been right. I wasn't so lost to decency as to seduce a helpless girl, but—I was the very figure of selfishness, my darling one." He put one finger over her parting lips. "I think I knew, all the time, you were not as young as I pretended. Poor Lyon was right in his assessment of my character, you see. I—I could not bear to lose you—so soon. I wanted to keep you with me . . . just another year . . . or two." His smile went awry. "Very ignoble."

Josie buried her head under his chin, her arms tight around him.

He stroked her hair, knowing how easy it would be to stop

329

her from going. One word—and she'd never leave him. But he said, "You must seem bright and happy. You must flirt with all the fine young fellows who will fall in love with you, and sigh over you, and beg for a lock of your hair, or a discarded glove, or a worn little slipper. And—and if, when the time is up, you still should be—so very unwise as to choose the hot-headed idiot who was—so very gratefully—your guardian, and an isolated old house far from the lights and gaiety of London or Paris . . . why . . . then . . ."

Josie heard his voice scratch to silence and, knowing him as well as she knew her own heart, she lifted her face for his kiss.

Always, in these past few days, when they had kissed, it had seemed an eternity of delight. Now he put her from him quickly, and knew this must not go on too long, or his courage would quite fail him.

Josie saw his averted cheek, saw the little nerve that began to beat below his temple, and lifted his hand to her face. "Silly, silly creature," she murmured, her lips against that cold hand. "As if the man lives who could make me stop loving you. As if— Dev? What's this?" She pounced on the rather clumsily wrapped box and snatched it up. "For me?"

"Er—well. I mean . . ." And as she squeaked with excitement and tore at the wrappings, he said feebly, "I have no right. Yet. But I thought—it might remind you that . . . that I love you."

Josie removed the lid of the small box and uttered an exclamation of delight. It held a locket wrought in gold, with leaves surrounding it amid which were set seed pearls and small opals. The surface of the locket was chased and in the centre the initials "J" and "A." "Oh . . ." she breathed.

He said huskily, "Open it," and showed her the little twist that was the clasp.

She peeped inside and gave a gasp. A ring rested upon a sheet of very fine paper that had been folded into a tiny rectangle. Taking up the ring with fingers that trembled, she gazed down upon the dark fire of an oval emerald surrounded by small diamonds. "Dev," she whispered. "Oh . . . Dev!" And looking up at him, commanded, "Put it on for me, my dearest."

He shook his head. "It is not for now. I want you to give it to me when you come . . . home. If—you have not changed your mind. Then I will put it on for you. When I have the right."

"No," she argued imperiously. "Put it on now!" And as he frowned at the ring, she pleaded, "I shall wear it every night when I go to bed, and in the morning I shall kiss it, and put it away again in the locket until the day you once more put it on for me."

And so he did as she asked, slipping the ring onto her dainty finger, and bending, resistless, to press both hand and ring to his lips. When he trusted himself to look up, she had turned away, but in a moment she faced him, smiling brightly. "And— what's this?" she asked, taking the folded paper from the locket.

His hand closed over hers. "That is something for you to read tonight. When you are alone."

"Why not now?"

"Because it is—just some silly nonsense I wrote to you when I was . . . just before Christmas."

She frowned thoughtfully. "I remember that after your operation I would so often find you scribbling in a notebook. You said it was to do with the rebuilding of Devencourt. And the costs involved."

He flushed. "Well, it wasn't."

She held up the little folded paper and suddenly, with a squeal of mischief, she cried, "It is a love letter! My first love letter from you!"

"And your last," he said, very stern.

Her smile vanished. "What do you mean? Dev—you *will* write? Darling, you *must*! I shall die, else! I will write—every day!"

He said quietly, "Then I won't read your letters. No—do not argue, my Elf. This break must be complete. If I were to read words of love from you . . ." His gaze fell away. He clenched his hands and finished with a great effort, "I think I could not bear it, but would come and steal you away from your uncle and bring you home. And so—ruin everything."

For a long, silent moment she stared at him. Then she ran swiftly to the window. "Then I shall read this now, and—" She broke off, for her fingers had been busy even as she spoke, and the much-creased sheet was spread. Her dark eyes became very round. She whispered, "A . . . *poem*?"

Devenish thought, 'Oh, Lord!' and swung away to stare at the carpet and feel a complete fool.

Josie looked in awe at the bowed fair head. *Poetry?* Poetry from this reckless, kind-hearted, brave, but very unromantic young man, who had been heard to rate Lord Byron, the very figure of romance, as "a frippery fellow," and who she suspected had never read a poem from the day he had escaped University. Astonished, she lowered her eyes to the carefully printed words on the page she held, and read:

When life had lost all lustre and all meaning, you came.
You raised me up and taught my selfish self
That had no use for living,
To live for thee—all youth and joy
And giving

You poured warm sunlight on my soul, and laughter
Beguiled my heart to sing. Thus, ever after
It sang to thee, who banished sorrows,
Who brought your smile to brighten my
Tomorrows.

And yet, the right to thee could not be mine.
I must not claim thee for my own. And
Bowing to that truth, left thee
And went alone to meet whatever was
To be.

But wandering in the dark I found thee still.
In fact, as I lay sleeping that last
And deepest sleep, I knew
That you were near; and you
Were weeping.

Once more you rescued me, who'd thought to sever
All ties to life and love. Once more
You brought an end to tears, and gave
Instead, long years to worship thee through life
Into forever.

Waiting, dreading lest she giggle at his painful efforts, Devenish heard a muffled sob and spun around in time to see something glitter as it splashed onto the much-creased page. "Dearest heart," he cried, hurrying to her.

"Give me . . . your handkerchief—quickly," gulped Josie, who never seemed to have a handkerchief of her own. Taking it, she dabbed with great anxiety at the splash, then lifted brimming eyes to his anxious ones. Yolande Drummond, she realized at last, had been so right, and for the first time, knowing the deep sensitivity he hid beneath his blithe and careless exterior, Josie knew also how much she was loved, and that this time, Devenish offered his soul as well as his generous heart. "No wonder . . ." she said with a sniff, "you had to work so hard."

"It took forever," he groaned. "And—I kept meaning to just throw away the silly thing—"

She scowled at him and put her hand across his mouth. "It is the most beautiful gift you ever gave me."

Looking into her worshipful eyes, he mumbled hoarsely, "Josie . . . beloved . . ."

Her arms were about his neck, one hand closing in the thick hair. She yielded up her lips to a fiery embrace that left her limp and gasping. And that was, she knew, farewell.

Devenish thrust her from him and stalked to the window. As through a veil he saw Pandora Grenfell crossing to the carriage, Klaus and three manservants carrying luggage. His voice low and harsh, he said, "Go! For the love of heaven—go!"

For one last time she gazed at the dear curly head, the rigidly squared shoulders, the slim but beautifully proportioned shape of him. Then, blindly, she took up the priceless poem he had so laboriously written her, and fled.

Devenish heard the door close, and went and sat at his desk. In a few minutes he heard the carriage door slam, the sounds of hoofs and wheels receding, and he stared unmoving, at nothing, while the silence, the sense of irreparable loss, closed in and crushed him. His eyes focused eventually, on the vase of holly her loving hands had gathered, and a pang went through him that was sharper than the bolt Gerard Lavisse had sent tearing into him. He put up a hand to cover his eyes.

How long he sat there, lost in despair, he never afterwards could quite recall. A shove roused him. Startled, he blinked down at a pink grin. He lifted his head and discovered the white cat outstretched at his elbow; in the middle of the desk, the ginger cat, one leg thrown in the air as it industriously cleaned its nether areas; and curled up in the letter tray, a small black and white ball of fluff. The sense that he was not alone intensified. He looked up in time to see Cornish's anxious countenance whip back from the partly open door.

'Dear heaven' he thought. 'Shall I ever cease to be such a sorry fool?' And having caressed each of his friends, he called, "Come in here, you great galumph! We've a deal to get done before May!"

Brightening, Cornish went inside. "Right y'are, mate," he grinned. "Er—Sir Guv, I mean."

∽ Chapter 22 ∾

Breathtaking in his ball dress, Tristram Leith grinned and said to a solemn Jeremy Bolster, "Bet you a pony he faints before he says one word."

Scanning their pallid, shivering friend, Bolster shook his yellow head. "D-don't fancy the odds, Tris."

"Buck up, Dev." Mitchell Redmond fetched the coward a slap on the back that made him stagger. "This is your night, old lad!"

"She's *home*," said Justin Strand, his blue eyes full of sympathetic laughter.

"And is the Toast of Paris, the darling of Vienna, and they say will conquer London in one night," said Sir Harry, crossing to force up Devenish's chin and adjust his cravat.

"What . . ." croaked Devenish, "is she—wearing?"

They eyed one another. "Something . . . pink . . ." Mitchell said uncertainly.

"Pink!" Leith scoffed. "She has on a glorious gown of pale yellow, Dev."

"I mean—is she . . ." His throat seemed to close. "Is she wearing—a gold locket?"

Sir Harry tore his hair. "What in God's name does it—"

Bolster said, "I know! I know! A d-diamond pendant. B-beautiful thing!"

Devenish felt very cold.

With a slow grin, Craig Tyndale balanced his glass on the arm of his chair and crossed the elegant bedchamber of Lord Kingston Leith's great house on Grosvenor Square that his lordship had thrown open tonight for the ball that was to reintroduce the enchanting Mademoiselle de Galin to the *ton*. Taking Devenish by the shoulders, he looked into the white, sweating face. His cousin wore evening clothes so well that Craig wondered if the silly block could possibly be unaware of how dashing he was tonight. "You do not look too bad," he observed.

Mordecai Langridge came in, followed by a spectacular figure wearing black leather tunic and trousers, his pantherish grace and proud, dark countenance a startling contrast to the elegant Englishmen. Moving soundlessly to peer into Devenish's face in turn, Montelongo looked at his employer.

"You want me carry small white man?"

Craig Tyndale grinned.

Devenish managed, "You . . . damned fraud. Get away!"

The Iroquois permitted himself a faint smile. "As you wish, sir," he rumbled in faultless English.

Mordecai urged, "Dev, she is besieged!"

Lyon opened the door and joined them, laughing. "Lord, what a blancmanger! Come on, Dev. The reception line's been done this ten minutes and more. You have not a prayer of winning a dance with Josie, you looby."

"Unless she have save him one, *mon cher*," said Mr. Guy Cahill, limping in, leaning heavily on the elaborate cane his wife had had carved for him.

Leith flung up a hand. "Light Cavalry! By threes—*forward*!"

Montelongo swept the door open. Leith grabbed one arm and Mitchell the other, and the craven was propelled into the hall and to the stairs.

Somehow, Devenish was at the ground floor. Somehow, he was managing to walk steadily, longing to see her; dreading to see her; vaguely aware that friends called to him, and that he more or less responded. And then he was in the ballroom, and he did see her, and halted, stunned.

She was dancing with Ivor St. Alaban, the dashing young baronet laughing at some remark she had made. Josie—who had never been much of a hand at dancing—drifted, light as thistledown in Sir Ivor's arms. Her luxuriant hair was piled in glossy coils on her proud little head, and a jewelled comb fashioned in the shape of a butterfly sparkled among the dark tresses. She was clad in a décolleté gown of billowing gold-spangled gauze over a cream satin underdress cut in very sharply at the waist and extending into a great, swirling skirt. And she was radiant, so at ease and confident of her loveliness and her desirability. And as Bolster had said, around her white throat was a delicate and exquisite diamond necklace.

She glanced up and saw him, and smiled and waved her fan happily, as she might have done to any dear friend.

His hands were so cold. He waited, his friends hovering about him.

St. Alaban led Josie from the floor to where the Chevalier de Galin stood beside Mrs. Pandora Grenfell.

And whose eyes could hold more pride than those of the handsome Chevalier as his lovely niece was restored to him? Whose head could tilt more gracefully as he bent to murmur something in her ear than that of the beautiful Mademoiselle Josephine?

The gentlemen were crowding around her, clamouring for her dance card, and she was lost to sight.

Leith gave Devenish a little push. "Go *on*, you fiddlefoot!"

But Devenish, his jaw setting, did not move.

The music struck up, then faded. The crush around the Chevalier and his niece fell back.

Josie stepped onto the dance floor. The eager young gentlemen who rushed to solicit her hand, sighed and retreated. All alone, she walked with pretty grace across that wide, empty floor, her great skirts swaying provocatively, her fan gently fluttering, her eyes fixed upon the man who stood so straight, so still, at the edge of the dance floor, the rest of the Nine scattered about nearby.

A complete silence had fallen. Halting before him, Josie said softly, "Hello, Dev," and extended her gloved hand.

He bowed over it. "Mademoiselle," he said quietly, his heart thundering.

She was very aware of the emptiness in the eyes that were an even deeper blue than she had remembered. She said with a flicker of dimples, "And what do you think of your wandering ward?"

"That she is—the loveliest thing I ever saw."

The fan swept up to hide the dimples, but her eyes laughed at him, the flecks in them purest amber. "The other gentlemen seem to agree," she said.

A little pulse was beating below his temple. "Of course."

"And . . ." she pursued, "are you proud of me, Mr. Devenish?"

He searched her face. "Very, very proud. Only—"

Her brows lifted. He saw a poise that was new, and he thought, 'She is all grown-up.' "Only," he said, "I had hoped—you would wear a gold locket."

"Oh." She touched the sparkling diamonds that rested above the curve of her beautiful breasts. "But Uncle Émile gave me these, you see."

"Yes. I see."

She allowed the loop of the fan to slip down her wrist. Her face was grave suddenly as she held up that hand.

On the palm of the white glove lay a thing that glittered with the brilliance of diamonds and the deeper gleam of a fine emerald.

For an instant, Devenish felt dizzied, and afraid to look up at her.

She said, her voice very soft, "I have worn the locket every day, my dearest darling, but I didn't wear it tonight because—you would have known at once, and—I wanted to . . . to let you know that . . . I am not—quite on the shelf, or so . . . plain that no one else wants me."

He tried to speak, and his voice failed him. He reached out, and she loved him the more because when he took the ring and put it in the pocket of his elegant waistcoat, his hand trembled. His second effort was more successful, but scarcely profound. "Josie . . ." he croaked.

Blinking away tears, she murmured, "Oh, Dev. How terribly I have missed you. I have come home. If you—still want me . . ."

338

The music struck up. Somehow, he remembered to extend his arm, and she swayed to put her hand on it.

The crowd parted. Jeremy Bolster, his own eyes suspiciously bright, whispered, "Good show!"

With an ecstatic pride, Alain Devenish led his love away and, in a small, secluded alcove, proved how much he wanted her.

Charles Cornish leaned in the window of the bookroom and watched Mrs. Robinson adjust three volumes whose spines dared to project a fraction of an inch beyond those of their companions, run a finger along the gleaming shelf in search of non-existent dust, and peer suspiciously at the unmarred surface of a glass door. He sniffed disparagingly. "Cor, but you're in a proper state. Anyone'd think as the guv'nor and 'is missus was comin' up the drive this very minute."

"I hope not," she said with a glum shake of the head. "I want everything to be as nice as possible."

He stared at her, baffled, then glanced to the window and the light dawned. "Oh, y'mean on account o' the drizzle? Never fear, mate, that wouldn't bother Sir Guv, nor his lady." He winked, and grinned his broad, gappy grin.

"I'd hoped it would be a lovely summer's day," sighed the housekeeper, and added heavily, "But I wasn't thinking about the weather, so much as what . . . what might lie ahead."

Exasperated, he groaned, "If that ain't just like a woman! Arter all they been through, 'ere they is, comin' back ter wedded bliss at last, and wotcha go and do? Moan and groan and carry on like a perishin' funeral!"

"Don't say that! Oh, *never* say it!" Mrs. Robinson wrung at her apron and turned to face him.

There was real worry in her eyes, and he said curiously, "Something's addling yer brainbox, Mrs. R. Spit it out, mate. If you're frettin' bout Sir Guv's leg—"

She bit her lip. "I'm worrying about that evil, *evil* man. I know his kind and they don't never forget when they think they've been hardly done by. They brood, and plot, and—and, oh, Charlie, our dear Mr. Dev has had so much misery—I do so *pray*

339

they'll have a bit of happiness, poor things!" She pressed a hand to her mouth and regarded him tearfully.

"Wot—you mean that there nasty little Fontaine fella?" He gave a derisive snort. "He's took his nobby knees orf somewhere, ain't he? Fergit the perisher!"

"It don't do to forget a snake, Charlie. You can't never tell when they'll strike again. He's a murdering, cruel, vindictive man, and when he comes back, he's sure to—"

Cornish, who had turned and was directing a slyly amused gaze at the rainy gardens, murmured, "But s'posing 'e don't come back 'tall? Or 'e might come 'ome a reformed man. The sea air might've done 'im a bit o' good . . ."

Mrs. Robinson's eyes had grown very wide during this little speech. "Charles Cornish," she whispered with breathless incredulity, "what you been and gone and done?"

"Me?" he protested, injured. "Now, wot could the likes of a poor perishin' footman do agin the likes o' a rich lordship? Lookit all them animals out there. Where they orf to, I wonder?"

Not about to be diverted, the housekeeper crossed to peer up at him. "You said 'sea air,' " she pointed out. "How d'you know he went to sea? No one's seen the horrid gent since he dishonoured himself at that duel."

"Stands to reason," he replied with bland innocence. "Man with all that pride goes and disgraces hisself. Everybody sneerin'. 'E can't stand it. You mark me words, Mrs. R. 'E's em-barked, 'e 'as. On a long sea voyage." Mischief sparkled in his eyes. "With luck, he'll get right seasick." He chuckled softly. "Take 'im dahn a peg or two, I 'spect. Might even make a man of 'im. Perisher oughta thank me, if—Whoops!" He leered at her conspiratorially.

Mrs. Robinson took a deep breath. "You wicked devil," she accused with a brilliant smile. "Oh—you conniver, you!"

He winked. "Look 'ere, Mrs. R. I—"

"Not another word!" She threw up one hand. "I don't want to know nothing about the wicked business." But in an abrupt departure from so pious an attitude, she asked, "You're quite

340

sure, Charlie? The Viscount won't come back—not for a good long time, anyway?"

"A very good long time," declared Cornish, much amused. "You c'n take me perishin' word fer it, Mrs. R."

The two riders disdained the drivepath, and went side by side across the meadows. Devenish, eyeing his bride's bewitching profile and wishing the June afternoon had been a little more cooperative, sighed. Her bright gaze turned to him, and he said ruefully, "I'd so wanted you to see it at its best."

Josephine de Galin Devenish reached out, and he kissed the gloved fingers, damp or not.

"Just a little drizzle, my darling," she said. "And so very gently English."

They started up the last hill, the treetops blowing softly, the misted air lending a blurred mystery to the hills and the emerald valleys.

"Dev," Josie went on, her eyes dreaming, "it *was* a lovely wedding, wasn't it? And Uncle Émile and my grandmama so happy."

"And my bride the loveliest that ever was or ever will be," he declared.

"And my husband looking at me in such a naughty way at the altar that I fairly blushed," she scolded, the dimples peeping.

"Very fairly. And soon to be kissed by every rascally fellow in sight, and a few I'd not thought to see there, I can tell you! Gad, Elf, what a surprise to see old Diccon in all his regalia. I'll swear he looked positively handsome with all those medals, even with his left sleeve pinned up, poor fellow."

"Yes. And, bless him, so happy with his lady. And how very kind of the King to come!"

He chuckled. "And to leave *some* food for our other ravenous guests! Now, madam wife, enough of this chit-chat. You will please to keep your eyes on me."

Wondering, she watched as he swung lightly from the saddle and reached to lift her down.

341

"Look," he said, turning her about, but keeping his arms around her.

"Oh . . . Dev . . . !"

He had rebuilt Devencourt, but had moved the connecting wing to the rear, rather than the front of the mansion. The drive path now curved around the centre lawns between the east and west wings. A fine fountain lifted delicate sprays and was edged by bright flower beds. All signs of the fire were gone. Devencourt was bright with fresh paint, and shone like a new house. Astonished, Josie gasped, "How *very* lovely you have made it! But—surely, it must have been terribly costly?"

"Uncle Émile's wedding gift. And the fountain is from Guy and Faith, bless them. My Elf—are you *sure* you wish to honeymoon here?"

She leaned in his arms, smiling down at the great house. "Very sure."

"And," he said, kissing her ear, "now that you have seen so many glamorous places, you will not be bored to spend much of the year here? We will go to Paris once a year, and we can take a house in Town for the Season, but—"

"Not next Season, I think," she said demurely.

He turned perfectly white. "J-Josie . . . ? You cannot mean—"

"Of course not, foolish child," she said with her rippling laugh. "We were only married three days ago! But . . . in the natural order of—of things . . ."

He held her tighter and she drew back to look up at him wonderingly. "Dev? You *do* want children? I always thought—"

"I—I did. But . . . sweetheart, only to think that this precious woman's body—this miracle that can give me children . . ."

His voice failed. She pulled down his head and kissed his chin and the side of his mouth until he claimed a sweeter kiss. And sighfully, snuggling closer, she murmured, "Then why did you tremble so?"

"Because I have waited so very long, my lovely wife. And— I love and—and need you, so very much. If—if anything should happen . . ."

She pulled away, and seeing the fear in his eyes, touched his cheek and said, "My own, we live in a modern age. This is the

342

nineteenth century, and the days when every lady wrote her Last Will and Testament before going into confinement are done with, thank heaven! Besides, I am as strong as any horse, and you—"

"Have the Rat Paws," he inserted, grinning rather lopsidedly, "as witness—" he pointed.

The staff of Devencourt, eager to welcome the newlyweds, were as yet unaware of their imminent return. There were those, however, who knew of it, and accordingly, a small cavalcade had set out. Coming up the hill trotted a plump pink pig. Behind her was a white cat, his plume of a tail waving in the air, and, following, a ginger cat, with tail just as high, if not as bushy. Bringing up the rear, a black and white kitten—no longer a small round ball, but full of energy as it bounced along, very much a part of the committee to welcome the master and Milady Elf.

Josie laughed. "How very dear they are." She tucked her head under his chin, and he swiftly removed her dainty hat before the feather drove him berserk. "Oh, Dev, darling Dev, if only you knew how I have dreamed of giving you fine sons, and dainty, fair little girls, with your blue eyes. You will be so good with them—such a wonderful father. And I shall—"

"Shall be more loved than ever," he interrupted again, and kissed the top of her head. "However fat."

"Fat!" She leaned back in his arms to frown up at him.

"Well, after that lot, it would be quite understandable if—"

"Wretch!" she laughed, tugging his hair. "Come down here—and be still!"

And with the drizzle falling soft and all unheeded about them, and the horses starting to graze, Alain Jonas Devenish took his bride's advice and took also a firmer grip on the happiness that had come to him at last.